# *Katherine Hall Page*
## *Presents*

# MALICE DOMESTIC 11:
# MURDER MOST
# CONVENTIONAL

# MALICE DOMESTIC ANTHOLOGY SERIES

Elizabeth Peters Presents *Malice Domestic 1*

Mary Higgins Clark Presents *Malice Domestic 2*

Nancy Pickard Presents *Malice Domestic 3*

Carolyn G. Hart Presents *Malice Domestic 4*

Phyllis A. Whitney Presents *Malice Domestic 5*

Anne Perry Presents *Malice Domestic 6*

Sharyn McCrumb Presents *Malice Domestic 7*

Margaret Maron Presents *Malice Domestic 8*

Joan Hess Presents *Malice Domestic 9*

Nevada Barr Presents *Malice Domestic 10*

Katherine Hall Page Presents *Malice Domestic 11: Murder Most Conventional*

# Katherine Hall Page Presents

# MALICE DOMESTIC 11: MURDER MOST CONVENTIONAL

## An Anthology

Edited by
Verena Rose, Barb Goffman
and Rita Owen

Published by Wildside Press LLC
www.wildsidepress.com

# DEDICATION

As one of the editors of *Malice 11: Murder Most Conventional*, I take great pleasure in dedicating the first Malice Domestic Anthology in fifteen years to the following:

⇒ To Martin Greenberg – the original Malice Domestic anthologies were his brainchild and he was the editor of Malice Domestic 1 through 4.

⇒ To Beth Foxwell – who co-edited Malice 5 and 6 and edited Malice Domestic 7 through 10.

⇒ To the presenters – who were instrumental in making each of the original 10 anthologies a huge success. Over the course of 10 volumes, 29 stories were nominated for the Agatha award. Of those, four won the Agatha for Best Short Story.

⇒ To the Honorees of Malice Domestic 28 and invited contributors to this anthology –
  - Katherine Hall Page – Lifetime Achievement Honoree (Presenter)
  - Max M. Houck – (Contributor)
  - Hank Phillippi Ryan – Toastmaster (Contributor)
  - Victoria Thompson – Guest of Honor (Contributor)

⇒ To the selection committee –
  - Rhys Bowen – Agatha winner and former Honoree
  - Earlene Fowler – Agatha winner and former Honoree
  - Douglas Greene – former Poirot Honoree and Malice 28 Amelia Honoree

⇒ To the Malice Domestic Board of Directors – the greatest team I've ever played on.

⇒ And to my fellow editors, Barb Goffman and Rita Owen, without whose support and expertise the vision of reviving the Malice Anthologies could not have happened.

Finally, we dedicate this anthology to all readers of traditional mysteries whose love of the genre inspired these stories.

Verena Rose
April 2016

# ACKNOWLEDGEMENTS

The editors would like to thank John Betancourt and Carla Coupe at Wildside Press for their constant and unwavering support to Malice Domestic and these editors. We also thank Judy Barrett of Judy Barrett Graphics, Alexandria, VA, and illustrator Deane Nettles for their delightful graphics.

Nancy Gordon in New Jersey has been generous in her unfailing dedication to the excellence of proofreading of this Anthology and Malice Domestic's annual convention materials.

Barb Goffman did the developmental and line editing of this anthology, and she'd like to note that she learned a number of things while working on the book, including how many types of conventions there are in the world, and that *whisky* without the *e* means Scotch in the U.K., which is why you'll see the word spelled *whisky* in the stories set there. Barb has been proud to help the authors in this book make their stories shine.

# TABLE OF CONTENTS

*All stories are original to this Anthology except*
*"Conventional Wisdom" by Marcia Talley*

Dedication ................................................................. v
Acknowledgements ...................................................... vi

**KATHERINE HALL PAGE PRESENTS** ............................ ix

**MURDER MOST CONVENTIONAL**
Conventional Wisdom, *by Marcia Talley* ........................ 1
Djinn and Tonic, *by Neil Plakcy* ................................ 11
The Vanishing Wife, *by Victoria Thompson* ................... 23
The Right to Bare Arms, *by John Gregory Betancourt* ...... 35
Message in a Bottle, *by Su Kopil* ............................... 39
Anonymous, *by Kate Flora* ...................................... 49
What Goes Around, *by B.K. Stevens* ........................... 59
The Hair of the Dog, *by Charles Todd* ......................... 69
The Best-Laid Plans, *by Barb Goffman* ........................ 81
A Dark and Stormy Light, *by Gigi Pandian* ................... 93
The Clue in the Blue Booth, *by Hank Phillippi Ryan* ...... 105
Wicked Writers, *by Frances McNamara* ........................ 123
Coverture, *by KB Inglee* ......................................... 133
Dark Secrets, *by Kathryn Leigh Scott* ......................... 143
Tarnished Hope, *by KM Rockwood* ............................. 155
Not Forgotten, *by L.C. Tyler* .................................... 165
Boston Bouillabaisse, *by Nancy Brewka-Clark* .............. 175
Killing Kippers, *by Eleanor Cawood Jones* .................. 183
Elemental Chaos, *by M Evonne Dobson* ....................... 197
Outside the Box, *by Ruth Moose* ............................... 211
The Perfect Pitch, *by Marie Hannan-Mandel* ................ 219
Two Birds with One Stone, *by Rhys Bowen* .................. 233
A Gathering of Great Detectives, *by Shawn Reilly*
    Simmons ............................................................ 243

**AFTERWARD**
"Hello, My Name Is Plot," *by Max M. Houck* ................ 259

**AUTHOR BIOGRAPHIES** ....................................... 267

# PREFACE

## KATHERINE HALL PAGE PRESENTS

Just as there was a Christie for Christmas, there was a Malice Domestic Anthology of Traditional Mystery Stories for spring. From 1992 until 2001, the books with their distinctive covers—many of which featured teapots definitely not suitable for Earl Grey—arrived in time for the Malice Domestic convention. The editors of the award-winning collections comprise a star-studded crime writers' Who's Who: Martin Greenberg and Elizabeth Peters, *Malice Domestic 1*; Mary Higgins Clark, *Malice Domestic 2*; Nancy Pickard, *Malice Domestic 3*; Carolyn Hart, *Malice Domestic 4;* Phyllis Whitney, *Malice Domestic 5*; Martin Greenberg and Anne Perry, *Malice Domestic 6*; Sharyn McCrumb and Elizabeth Foxwell, *Malice Domestic 7*; Margaret Maron, *Malice Domestic 8*; Joan Hess, *Malice Domestic 9*; and Nevada Barr, *Malice Domestic 10*.

The list of anthology contributors adds further luster to the pantheon, among them: Robert Barnard, Stephanie Barron, Simon Brett, Jan Burke, Dorothy Cannell, P.M. Carlson, Kate Charles, Jill Churchill, Camilla Crespi, Amanda Cross (Carolyn Heilbrun), Barbara D'Amato, Mary Daheim, Diane Mott Davidson, Carole Nelson Douglas, Charlotte & Aaron Elkins, Frances Fyfield, Jonathan Gash, Ed Gorman, Jan Grape, Sue Henry, Edward Hoch, H.R.F. Keating, M.D. Lake (Allen Simpson), Janet Laurence, Peter Lovesey, Edward Marston, Marlys Millhiser, Gwen Moffatt, Miriam Grace Monfredo, Walter Satterthwait, Marcia Talley, Charles Todd, Carolyn Wheat, and Susan Wittig & Bill Albert. The editors also contributed stories to various volumes.

When word went round that there would no 2002 anthology, the mystery reading world wept—particularly readers of traditional mysteries, those books best represented by Agatha Christie and similar authors, celebrated by the Malice Domestic conventions.

And then in 2014, word went round that there *would* be a *Malice Domestic 11*, the volume you now hold in hand. Eyes were dried and readied to revel in what is a most fitting, though tardy, continuation of the anthologies. Here it is, in time for 2016's Malice Domestic 28 convention: *Malice Domestic 11: Murder Most Conventional*.

A word about the Malice Domestic convention. In 1988 a small group—Terry Adams, Gerry Letteney, Barbara Mertz, and Mary Morman—got together to plan a convention that would honor traditional mysteries, hitherto ignored or worse at other conventions, especially when it came to awards. They envisioned a gathering of like-minded folk interested in panels about Malice-type authors, both past and present. Rather than move the convention each year, they decided to root it in their own backyards, the D.C. region. They also wanted an inclusive gathering that welcomed writers, fans, editors, agents, and booksellers equally. No hierarchy. The only requirement for attendance was a love, dare one say passion, for the genre. Elizabeth Foxwell came on board to produce the program book and Dean James, the award process in which books are nominated and voted on by the convention's attendees only.

Selecting the name for the awards was easy—the Agathas were born. There were three types in 1989, that first year: Best Novel (now called Best Contemporary Novel), Best First Novel, and Best Short Story. Over time, the Agathas grew and there are now twice as many categories: the original ones, plus Best Historical Novel, Best Nonfiction, and Best Children's/Young Adult Novel.

The convention site has roamed the D.C. area and is now happily settled back in Bethesda, Maryland, the original location in many minds. Malice Domestic I in a Silver Spring, Maryland, venue was a test of loyalty! You may read all about it and much more in *Not Everyone's Cup of Tea: An Interesting and Entertaining History of Malice Domestic* (2013), edited by Verena Rose and Rita Owen, editors with Barb Goffman of this anthology as well.

The short story as such dates to the nineteenth century, but the form is as old as humankind—myths, sagas, tales told around a fire. "Not that the story need be long, but it will take a long while to make it short," Henry David Thoreau observed to a friend. Edgar Allan Poe, a master of the form, wrote, "A short story must have a single mood and every sentence must build toward it." Taken together, these are a fine summation of the challenge posed by short story writing: that paring-down process, the examination of each word essential for a satisfactory result. Rather than the longer pace of a novel, character is revealed through action and setting painted with scant brushstrokes.

There is a particular pleasure in reading short stories, similar to relishing small plates—tapas—or ordering several appetizers rather than a main course. Mystery fiction has always attracted writers wishing to provide this sort of experience, brief but lingering long. One has only to think of one's first Poe short story read—doubtless followed by a sleepless night. Or perhaps the first story to make an impact was an O. Henry with its surprise ending, or a Conan Doyle—"It was the band! The speckled band!" One may reread these for pleasure, but they are never forgotten.

The roster of traditional mystery short story writers must include Agatha Christie perhaps first and foremost, but she is joined by others, as prolific and proficient: Dorothy Sayers with the Peter Wimsey collection; Baroness Orczy's Old Man in the Corner; G. K. Chesterton's incomparable Father Brown; Mary Roberts Rinehart's Miss Pinkerton; Saki (H. H. Munro)—"The Open Window"!; Margery Allingham's quintessential gentleman, Albert Campion; and earlier, Anna Katharine Green's ground-breaking female detective, Violet Strange.

Yet, a bonanza of stories awaits more immediately. *Malice Domestic 11: Murder Most Conventional* is anything but a conventional undertaking. Unlike the other Malice Domestic anthologies, the project was open to all published and unpublished writers who met the cut-off date and wrote stories that matched the criterion: the story had to take place at or have some relationship to a convention. The convention could be of any sort, not limited to a mystery or writers' con. The selection committee read entries as blind submissions with the exception of Malice 28's Guest of Honor, Victoria Thompson; Toastmaster, Hank Phillippi Ryan; former Malice honoree Rhys Bowen, and Wildside Press's publisher, John Betancourt. The committee had a difficult, but delightful job narrowing their selections, and readers will appreciate their work in not only choosing the best, but selecting stories covering a broad range—first person, third person, historical, humorous, dark, and just plain outrageous. They all have a connection to a convention, yes, but the results suggest a title change: *Murder Most Unconventional*!

*Malice Domestic 11* contains four period pieces. "Coverture" by KB Inglee and "The Vanishing Wife" by Victoria Thompson invoke the early days of the women's suffrage movement in New York. They illustrate how authors can use the same setting to produce works that are unique in plot, character, and tone. Both stories are all too timely.

Agatha Christie wrote many short stories using her series sleuths, which add to our appreciation of their abilities—and personalities. Rhys Bowen and Charles Todd (Charles and Caroline Todd) have achieved the same thing here. In the Todds' "The Hair of the Dog," it's 1920 and Inspector Ian Rutledge is in London's Kensington, called out at dinner on a case. For fans, Hamish *does* make an "appearance"—and a member of the royal family is present, as well. Rhys Bowen's "Two Birds With One Stone" finds her Spyness, Lady Georgiana Rannoch, at Castle Rannoch and contains one of the most memorable opening lines in the anthology: "I have a confession to make. I'm actually not too fond of bagpipes, especially when played outside my window at dawn." The story contains a twist that's a throw.

Thirteen writers looked for inspiration from gatherings far afield from a mystery convention. Taking Strunk and White's timeless advice to omit needless words, John Betancourt delivers a wallop of a short story set at a state fair. This is indeed an ending that lingers. . . .

There's a wonderfully dark coda in KM Rockwood's "Tarnished Hope" with an ingenious use throughout of a narrator who appears at every convention of any nature, but is virtually invisible.

Librarians get their day in Ruth Moose's "Outside the Box" and it's one of three with supernatural overtones—watch for Moose's references to "lots of shiny silver pins."

Next, a magician pulls a rose petal, not a rabbit, from his hat, a bowler, at the start of "A Dark and Stormy Light" by Gigi Pandian. The sleight of hand continues. Be prepared. Time, place, and especially persons are not as they seem.

Unarguably the winner for best title, "Djinn and Tonic" by Neil Plakcy, is a magic carpet ride—truly—from start to finish and will leave the reader longing for Yegor's life-extending elixir. Plakcy's sensual descriptions should come as scratch–and-sniffs—"Biff smelled her perfume, a mix of salt water, coconut, and custardy ylang-ylang."

Kathryn Scott's haunted "Dark Secrets" lets us in on the ones behind a highly successful vampire soap opera whose child star is now grown up—long gone from Tinseltown. But the past is hard to escape and, with it, the darkest secret of all.

You may want to skip "Killing Kippers" by Eleanor Cawood Jones if you have a fear of clowns and your worst nightmare is being snowbound at one of their conventions. But you would be missing a macabrely humorous tale with a line that says it all: "Stranger things have happened."

One of the most fascinating conventions conjured up is the one in Su Kopil's "Message in a Bottle." Who has not picked up a bottle on a beach hoping for a scrolled piece of paper still intact inside? A treasure map? A love letter? A fifth-grade science project? The MIB hunters are a small group, but determined to uncover buried secrets. This is one of the most comic stories here, with unforgettable characters galore.

Think hard about taking a drink from a frenemy in "Anonymous." Kate Flora skillfully details the ramping up of competition in the fashion world where appearance is everything: "The eyebrows tried to rise but the frozen forehead wouldn't allow it." Watch out for a martini with three olives.

Jealousy also rears its ugly head at the booksellers' convention in "Boston Bouillabaisse." Nancy Brewka-Clark brings a deadly— and wickedly funny—perspective on the event.

"Elemental Chaos" by M Evonne Dobson is a short story for our time, and will force readers to take a close look at the science fair projects of those near and dear—especially the neighbors' kids. Think *Star Trek* and *Star Wars* meet *The Big Bang Theory*.

Inventiveness is at the fore in Marie Hannan-Mandel's "The Perfect Pitch," and there is no question that the narrator's product, the Lint-Locker, would make millions if only our protagonist could present it to the "megastar inventor" judge. This is another example of the blend of satire and good old whodunits represented in *Murder Most Conventional*.

Seven writers chose to set their stories in a mystery writers' convention with a plethora of fiendish results.

No, you are not trapped in a diabolical funhouse chamber of mirrors. All the Nancy Drew lookalikes are real attendees at a Nancy Drew convention in Hank Phillippi Ryan's "The Clue in the Blue Booth." It all comes down to "What would Nancy do?"

In B.K. Stevens' clever "What Goes Around," the amateur sleuths solving the crime perpetrated on one of them are mystery convention attendees. Who could be better equipped for this than devoted readers of traditional mystery fiction?

In similar fashion, Frances McNamara's "Wicked Writers" reminds us to never underestimate the power of women, especially well-read ones. Alfred Hitchcock would have loved this.

For past Malice attendees, "The Best-Laid Plans" by Barb Goffman is déjà vu all over again with its subtle referencing of the con. Others will find it equally delightful and an incentive to sign up. And think Angela Lansbury in the role of mystery writer Eloise Nickel.

"Not Forgotten" by L.C. Tyler is a devilishly conceived reminder of what goes around comes around, or as a mother would say, "It never hurts to be nice to someone. You don't know when your paths might cross again." It's also a paean to midlist authors everywhere!

Two stories in this category make perfect bookends for *Malice Domestic 11: Murder Most Conventional*. All the stories in the *Malice Domestic 9* anthology were an homage to Agatha Christie and included her own previously unpublished story, "The Case of the Discontented Soldier." Where better to start this volume than with "Conventional Wisdom" by Marcia Talley as she imagines what Tommy and Tuppence Beresford's grandchildren, Caroline and Stephen, might be doing? The apple has indeed not fallen far from the family tree.

Shawn Reilly Simmons' "A Gathering of Great Detectives" is a lagniappe, that thirteenth donut when you buy a dozen or other extra tidbits. It's the perfect ending to this anthology with its depiction of an annual convening of fans in character as their favorite detectives, no deviation permitted from the role for the duration. They're there to solve a fictitious crime, but reality intrudes. . . .

Now, pour yourself a favorite libation, sit back, and prepare to be entertained.

*Katherine Hall Page*

# MURDER MOST CONVENTIONAL

# CONVENTIONAL WISDOM

## by Marcia Talley

*Agatha Christie dedicated* By the Pricking of My Thumbs
*to the "many readers . . . who write to me asking: 'What has
happened to Tommy and Tuppence? What are they doing
now?'" By the time of her last novel,* Postern of Fate, *Tommy
and Tuppence Beresford have three children. Their adopted
daughter, Betty, is working in Africa, and the twins, Deborah
and Derek, are married. At the end of the novel, Deborah
makes a brief appearance at the Beresfords with her children.
Now, years later, I couldn't help but wonder what the
Beresford grandchildren might be doing today.*

It was after eight, yet the day was still dark, the sky a uniform gray
that shrouded the earth like a wet sweatshirt. It wouldn't be correct
to say the rain fell; rather it hurled itself against the plane's
window, beading along the glass in plump droplets. Caroline
watched one skitter down the oval pane, swallowing the smaller
drops in its path.

As her eyes gradually refocused further away, she observed the
airport routine going on outside her window. It reminded her of a
silent movie, and she amused herself by providing dialogue for a
workman wearing ear protectors like bulky headphones as he
waved the plane forward to the gate with laser wands. Lights
reflecting from the terminal building shimmered in an immense
puddle then shattered as a luggage train splashed through it. So
much for sunny California, Caroline thought. *I might as well have
left my swimming costume back in London.* She tried to remember
whether she had packed an umbrella. She'd set a brolly aside in her
flat, ready to stuff into her book bag. She recalled putting it in, then
taking it out again in order to make room for a last-minute
paperback. In her mind's eye Caroline saw the brolly, still sitting
on the hall table right where she left it. "Damn!" she whispered,
turning her head deliberately away from the gloom outside the
window. "Stephen had better be here to meet me."

"I beg your pardon?" Her seatmate, a scrawny woman
clutching a Marks & Spencer carrier bag on her lap like a precious

object, turned dark, serious eyes on Caroline.

Caroline flushed. "Oh, nothing. I was just hoping my brother wouldn't be late picking me up. He's flying in from New York." She sighed. "You can never tell with Stephen. He might be sitting in a coffee shop reading a book and have forgotten all about me."

"Don't worry, dear. I'm sure he wouldn't let his little sister down." She removed her reading glasses and dropped them into her bag.

"We're twins, actually," Caroline explained. "I'm slightly older, by a few minutes."

"Twins?"

"But we're not all that much alike." Caroline fumbled in her purse. "Would you like to see?"

Her companion made encouraging noises so Caroline opened her wallet and flipped through the plastic sleeves containing her credit cards. She turned to a snapshot of Stephen with his determined chin, squinting into the sun, his rather ordinary face split by an engaging grin. A shock of red hair was combed straight back over his scalp; an errant strand hovered over his left eyebrow. The woman's eyes moved from the photo to Caroline's face and back again. "I see what you mean, although there's a certain resemblance around the mouth."

"That was taken eight years ago when Stephen was on holiday in Florida." Caroline closed the wallet and stuffed it back into her book bag. "Stephen takes after our grandfather Beresford—they used to call him Carrot Top—while I," Caroline tugged at a ringlet of her own dark brown hair, "am supposed to look like my grandmother."

Caroline settled back into her seat and waited for the captain to turn off the seatbelt sign. In spite of the disappointing weather, she was eager to get on with her journey. Anything was better than sitting around in her flat feeling sorry for herself, hoping that something interesting might happen. Six months before, after the accounting firm she worked for had declared her redundant, Caroline had retreated to Swallow's Nest to be comforted by home cooking and buoyed by her mother's supportive and upbeat attitude. She'd thought about visiting Rosalie in New Zealand, but a visit to her sister was a nonstarter unless one of the jobs she'd applied for there actually came through.

"Are you going to MysteryCon?" the woman asked.

"Hmmm?" Caroline glanced up.

The woman pointed. "I couldn't help noticing your bag."

"Oh." Caroline guessed her book bag was, so to speak, a dead giveaway. Against the black silhouette of a revolver, last year's

MysteryCon logo was printed in stark white letters. She smiled. "Yes, I am, actually. My brother and I are presenting the Blenkinsop Partners in Crime Award." Noticing the woman's puzzled expression she quickly explained, "It goes to the best crime novel featuring a detecting duo."

"You mean like Holmes and Watson? Or Cagney and Lacey?"

Caroline nodded. "Exactly."

"I never read mysteries myself," her seatmate stated. "But I watch that Jessica Fletcher on TV." She bit her lower lip thoughtfully. "Blenkinsop. What a funny name for an award."

Caroline smiled. "Isn't it? It's related to a practical joke my grandmother once pulled on my grandfather. My uncle Derek established the award in their honor."

Caroline heard the ding of the seatbelt signal and the clicking of hundreds of buckles as passengers leaped up and scrambled for their bags in the overhead compartments. Caroline waited for her seatmate to step out, then snaked down the aisle behind her, through the business and first-class sections, past the flight crew muttering their buh-byes, and along the passageway to baggage claim. She watched a bag of golf clubs go three times around on the carousel before her own flowered suitcase eventually appeared. She set it on its wheels, jerked out the handle, and dragged it and herself into the gloom of the San Diego morning.

As she had feared, Stephen was nowhere in sight. Caroline loitered for ten minutes at the passenger pick-up area shifting from foot to foot, searching up and down the busy transportation plaza for the red Toyota Yaris Stephen had told her he'd rented. After a call to his cell phone went straight to voice mail, she gave up and followed the signs to the Shuttle for Hire island.

***

Caroline's usually cheerful face was still set in a scowl when the blue and yellow SuperShuttle deposited her in front of the Puesta del Sol on Mission Bay. She made her way to the reception desk and checked in. "Are there any messages for me?"

The desk clerk tapped at his keyboard, studied the screen for a few seconds, then shook his head. "Sorry, Ms. Greene."

Caroline shouldered her book bag and leaned once more against the counter. "Has Stephen Greene checked in yet?"

The clerk executed a few additional keystrokes, then, obviously happy to please her at last, exclaimed, "Oh yes." He pointed toward the restaurant. "You can use the house phone over there to call his room, or if you prefer, I could take a message for you."

"No, thanks," Caroline grumbled. In the past hour she had dredged up hundreds of four-letter words with which to blister

Stephen's ears, but this relentlessly perky fellow seemed only a decade on this side of *Sesame Street*. Certain words beginning with the letter F might not be in his vocabulary yet.

Caroline headed toward the elevators, weaving through the lobby crowded with name-tagged conventioneers who sat on every chair and sprawled on every sofa, purses, briefcases, and book bags heaped at their feet. Caroline noticed that the lobby was decorated with dozens of Halloween pumpkins, their elaborately carved faces leering at her from the planters that divided the lobby into more intimate conversational areas. She smiled in spite of herself, feeling immensely cheered. As she passed the last alcove, one pumpkin head stood up.

"Stephen!" Caroline dropped her book bag, controlling the urge to clobber him with it. "Where on earth have you been?"

"Waiting for you, ducks."

"You were supposed to meet me at the airport, you dunce."

"I thought we agreed to meet at the hotel."

"Airport, Stephen. We said the airport. Honestly, you do try my patience." She pushed her suitcase toward him. Stephen grabbed the handle, then kissed his sister on the cheek. "Sorry for the confusion, love, but all's well that ends well. Have you had anything to eat?"

"Nothing to speak of, except for the pretzels they gave me on the plane."

The elevator arrived and carried them to the tenth floor. "I'll make it up to you," Stephen promised. "Freshen up and meet me in the lobby and I'll feed you a proper meal." He checked his watch. "In thirty minutes."

The elevator doors closed, leaving Caroline alone in the hallway a good two hundred feet from the door with her room number on it.

Once inside her room, she pressed a hot washcloth over her face, then leaned close to the mirror and examined her gray eyes for puffiness. Satisfied to see little sign of jet lag, she fluffed up her flattened hair with her fingers, applied some lipstick, and returned to the lobby. Having ten minutes to kill before Stephen was scheduled to appear, she registered for the conference, pinned her name tag on her jacket, found a vacant table near the lobby coffee shop, and ordered some hot tea.

"Hello. Mind if I sit down?"

Caroline glanced up from the MysteryCon program booklet she was reading and shifted her chair a few inches to the right. "I'm saving a seat for my brother, but the others aren't taken." The man standing before her wore chinos and a striped shirt under a denim jacket. His lank, yellowish hair was caught back into a ponytail, and he carried a backpack. Caroline stole a peek at his name tag—Larry Townsend: Alexandria, VA.

Mr. Townsend settled himself into the chair and studied Caroline over the top of his round, steel-framed glasses. "You an author?"

Caroline smiled. "Not exactly. I'm one of the presenters."

Townsend patted his backpack, which now rested at his feet. "I'm here to meet my editor."

Caroline noticed no author ribbon attached to Townsend's name tag. "Really? Have I read anything you've written?" She smiled brightly.

Townsend gazed at her shyly from beneath long, pale lashes. "I'm not exactly published yet, but I hope to be soon." He leaned over and rummaged in his backpack. "This book, do you know it?"

Caroline groaned inwardly, recognizing a popular self-help book widely advertised on a home shopping channel by its author, the flamboyant king of infomercials, Jeremiah P. Jackson. *Write It! Sell It!* screamed at her in raised, red letters from a cover otherwise unadorned except for a head-to-toe shot of the author wearing an Armani suit, holding a copy of that same book and smiling toothily.

"I've read the reviews," she admitted at last.

"It's my bible." Townsend unzipped the breast pocket of his jacket and extracted a small, square notebook. He showed Caroline page after page of neat columns containing notations in infinitesimal print, the columns dotted with checkmarks. Caroline sipped her tea and nodded mechanically while Townsend rattled on about how he hoped to get published by following the author's advice. He'd attended conferences. *Check.* Networked with authors. *Check.* Schmoozed with publishers. *Check again.* Caroline found herself growing sleepy. If Stephen didn't appear within the next five minutes, she decided, she was going to ditch this bore and eat alone.

"I've written a mystery based on my experiences in Kandahar," Townsend told her.

"Hmmm." Caroline returned to studying her conference program, hoping, vainly, that he'd take the hint.

"Started writing in a foxhole in the desert. Wrote much of the rest on the Metro riding to my job at the Pentagon. But then I said, what the hey. Decided to take a leave of absence to finish up. Been living off my savings."

Caroline regarded Townsend with a sudden spark of interest. "Must have been hard on the wife and kids."

"Ex-wife," he said. "No kids." His face grew serious. "I have it all planned out." He turned the notebook in Caroline's direction. "See, here's where I've checked off all the steps in getting an agent."

"I hear it's hard to get an agent."

"Not really. Just followed what the man says in here." He fanned the pages of *Write It! Sell It!* with an ink-stained thumb, stopping about halfway through. "He suggests reading the acknowledgments in books written by authors you admire. They usually thank their agents. Then you come to conferences like this and contrive to meet them." Townsend's eyes swept the lobby. "There are lots of agents here right now."

"Clever," Caroline said.

Townsend shrugged. "It's all in the book. Got my agent at MysteryCon last year, and he sent my manuscript out to several editors. This particular editor's had my book for three months."

Caroline was searching for an appropriate reply when she saw, with relief, Stephen's tall figure approaching. She stood. "Well, good luck . . ." She looked pointedly at Townsend's name tag. "Larry."

Townsend smiled up at her. "Thanks, Caroline. But I have a feeling this one's practically a done deal."

Stephen hustled Caroline away from the coffee shop and into the restaurant. "Why were you talking to that kook?"

"He wasn't a kook. Just some guy desperately trying to sell his book."

"I don't know about that, Caroline. He looked rather shady to me. While I was waiting for you earlier, I overheard him talking to someone on the telephone. All very hush-hush and Tom Clancyish. 'Meet me in the terrace bar. I'll be wearing glasses and carrying a backpack' kind of stuff." Stephen studied the menu while they waited for the hostess to locate a table for two. "Wonder whatever happened to the good old days when you wore a red carnation in your lapel and carried a copy of *The New York Times* folded under one arm?"

Stephen carried on with his spy-among-the-fans-and-authors theory. Caroline half-listened until she felt the soft jab of his elbow in her ribs. "Hot-cha!" Stephen croaked. A certain well-endowed writer of American mystery cozies, clad in a low-cut blouse and a tea towel passing for a skirt, squeezed between them. She held a wine glass by the stem between her thumb and forefinger.

"Ha!" Caroline chided. "I'm surprised you notice anything going on around you."

"I'm a man of many talents, my dear. Why just now I've

noticed that our wait for a table is over. Mavis!" Stephen grabbed Caroline's hand and dragged her through the crowded restaurant to a table near the window, already occupied by a pair of diners. Caroline observed with pleasure that the table overlooked the bay. Outside the clouds had broken up and bright sunlight was transforming the flowering sage, lilac, and bougainvillea that bordered the patio into a Kodacolor postcard.

A middle-aged woman, attractive in spite of a thatch of too-black hair, beamed up at Stephen as he bent over the table and kissed the air next to her cheek. "Mavis! Good to see you. And George. How are you doing, old bean? I'd like you both to meet my sister, Caroline. Caroline, George writes those true crime novels our brother Andrew is so fond of reading. Mavis is his editor." Stephen snatched two vacant chairs from an adjoining table and Caroline soon found herself sandwiched between Stephen's friends. She hoped the waitress had noticed their arrival because the sight of the Belgian waffle sitting on the plate in front of George, decorated with fresh strawberries and dollops of whipped cream, was making her stomach rumble noisily.

"How's tricks, Mavis?" Stephen inquired while waving a hand in the direction of a passing waitress. Mavis slapped her forehead, a look of mock panic on her face. "Overworked, as per usual. Spending most of my time dealing with the merger and my conglomerate bottom-line bosses. Publishing's a crazy business now, not like the old days." She tapped the contents of a pink packet into her coffee, stirred, and tasted it. "Thank God I've got a capable assistant."

George raised his water glass and said, "To the indispensable Tiffany Carswell."

Mavis plucked a pair of reading glasses from where they rested on top of her head, settled them on her nose, and peered at her watch. "Can't imagine what's keeping her. She was almost dressed when I left the room." She scowled. "The bean counters strike again, Stephen. Never thought I'd be bunking with my assistant." Mavis relaxed into her chair, enjoying the last of her coffee. "But the girl's a jewel. Don't know what I'd do without her."

"Knows better than to call in sick every Monday like the last editorial assistant you had?" Stephen teased.

Mavis closed her eyes and shook her head. "Don't remind me."

A waitress had finally appeared to take their order when Mavis stood and laid her napkin on the table. "Well, it's been fun, folks, but I gotta go. My panel starts at noon." She patted her chest. "Left my damn name tag on the bedside table, but I don't suppose they'll turn me away at the door. Coming, George, or do you leave me to face the unpublished masses alone?" She departed in a cloud of White Diamonds with the faithful George trotting at her heels.

Stephen picked up the copy of *USA Today* that George had left behind and began reading aloud from the Money section. Caroline, who was used to having the news interpreted for her by her brother, munched happily on a piece of dry toast. She was halfway through her California fruit cup, considering which of the panels she'd attend, when a large black object hurtled past the window behind Stephen's head, glanced off the flowering shrubbery, and crashed to the terra-cotta paving. "My God!" a waitress screamed. "Somebody's fallen!"

Caroline, her stomach in turmoil and her brunch quite forgotten, surged outside with the other diners and hovered at the edge of the gathering crowd with Stephen's arm wrapped protectively around her. Paramedics arrived within a few minutes and were attempting to revive the victim. From the amount of blood pooling on the tiles beneath the woman's head and by the odd angle of her neck in relation to her shoulders, Caroline was skeptical. But then, she had never seen a dead person before.

Sirens screamed, followed in short order by the police. "She was pushed!" a man at the edge of the crowd shouted when the first officer appeared. "I saw a man. Up there!" The witness waved a wild finger in the direction of a terraced balcony. Caroline's eyes followed. The balcony stood empty, but hanging plants dangled in ragged tendrils from where they had been torn away when the woman went over.

Two uniformed officers held the crowds aside, making way for the EMTs carrying the victim away on a stretcher. Caroline swallowed a sob as they passed. An oxygen mask covered the woman's beautiful, surprisingly serene, and unmarked face. A sea breeze ruffled her dark brown hair and lifted the name tag clipped to her jacket.

Caroline shuddered, then clutched Stephen's arm so hard he winced. "Stephen! I've got to talk to the police. Now! I think I know who pushed that young woman and why."

*** 

"So that's how it happened." It was after dinner and Caroline sat with Stephen and George in the terrace bar where a jack-o'-lantern grinned mischievously from the planter behind her brother's head. Stephen stirred his martini. "Clever of you to notice the name tag, Caroline."

"Well, I knew the person on the stretcher wasn't the real Mavis Grant because we'd just had brunch with her. Tiffany must have thought she'd be doing her boss a favor by giving Townsend the bad news about his rejection. Mavis remembered that when she went to brunch she left her name tag sitting right next to the telephone. So when Townsend called the room —"

"Tiffany grabbed her boss's name tag . . ." Stephen cut in.

"And toddled up here to meet him in her stead." George finished the sentence for both of them. He shook his head. "Mavis told me she'd never met the bloke, just talked to him on the phone. She's despondent, poor old dear. Claims it will be impossible to replace the girl."

George stared into his lager, a look of profound sadness on his suntanned face. "Want to know the ironic thing? Mavis said that chap's book wasn't half-bad. Needed a bit of punching up is all. But he was such a colossal pain in the ass—calling her two or three times a week—she'd decided to give it a pass."

* * *

A few weeks later, in Stephen's New York apartment, Caroline took a brown envelope out of a desk and addressed it in a loopy, flowing hand. Stephen observed his sister in silence, watching over her shoulder as she affixed five forty-nine-cent stamps to the envelope. "San Diego Central Jail? Caroline, are you crazy?"

Caroline looked up, a half smile on her lips. "Paradoxical, really. When 'Mavis' rejected his novel, Townsend flew into a rage. It wasn't part of his plan, you see. But now, think of all the time he'll have to write." She picked up a copy of *Writer's Digest* and turned to a page she had marked with a yellow Post-it note. "Here, in the Markets column." She tapped a neatly manicured finger on the page. "It says prison fiction is big these days." She slipped the magazine into the envelope and smiled up at her brother. "I think it's a good idea to encourage aspiring writers, don't you?"

Stephen took the envelope from her outstretched hand, licked the flap, and sealed it securely. "I do. And I'm sure Grandma and Grandpa would thoroughly agree."

* * *

*A slightly different version of this story was originally published in* Malice Domestic 9 *(Avon, 2000).*

# DJINN AND TONIC

## by Neil Plakcy

There was real magic in the world, and false magic, and it took a genie to tell the difference. That was the basis of Biff Andromeda's private investigation business—using his skills to grant wishes and solve problems for customers.

The shrill ring of his cell phone woke him from a very pleasant dream involving his girlfriend, Farishta, and a Turkish carpet that flew in lazy circles around the dome of the Hagia Sophia mosque in Istanbul.

He grabbed the phone from the bedside table and groggily said, "Hello?"

"Biff? It's Yegor Kleyman. Sorry to call you so early but I'm in terrible trouble, and I need your help."

That was the problem with being a private eye, Biff thought, as he sat up in bed. People always needed something. If only he could use his magical powers on his own behalf, instead of having to grant wishes to clients in exchange for the money to support himself, he could be on that carpet in Istanbul with Farishta.

Though the body Biff inhabited was just a construct, it still required regular exercise, food, and other human maintenance. So he had opened a private investigation agency in the suburbs of Miami, Florida, where the climate and the cosmopolitan atmosphere reminded him of the good old days when Istanbul was called Constantinople, and he and Farishta had lived together in a gilded palace.

Now his palace was a townhouse, his magic carpet a Mini Cooper, and he needed a steady stream of clients to pay his bills. Yegor was one of those humans with a very slight degree of magic inside him—he could see people's auras, and he'd mentioned that Biff's was very unusual, a royal blue with white sparkles, indicative of a desire to help people coupled with a high level of spirituality.

"What's the problem, Yegor?" Biff asked.

"Remember I told you I was signed up for a booth at the Life Extension Conference at the Ambassador Hotel in Hollywood? I figured I could sell a ton of my bubbie's tonic to this crowd. But the conference is about to start, and I have no product to sell. All the packages I had shipped here have disappeared."

"Disappeared? How?"

"One of the valets signed for the delivery, but it's not in their storage room. Somebody must have stolen them. You've got to help me, Biff. This is going to bankrupt me."

"I can be there in fifteen minutes."

Biff rolled out of his ornately carved wooden bed, which had been built for the seraglio of a minor sultan a few hundred years before, then yawned and stretched. He pointed his index finger at the brass samovar across the room, and the flame beneath it ignited. There was already a clean glass in an enameled holder beneath the spout.

He pulled on a pair of khaki slacks and a bright blue polo shirt that highlighted his impressive upper body and ran a comb through his short dark hair. By the time he was dressed his tea had brewed, and the scent of oolong and coconut swirled around his bedroom. He grabbed the handle of the tea glass and drank it quickly, the hot liquid refreshing him.

It was dark and misty, about a half hour before dawn, and he shivered as he opened the door of his Mini Cooper. He wished he had one of Yegor's tonics himself. He'd sampled one a few weeks before and liked the taste, a mix of cranberry, chocolate, and chai tea. The herbs brewed into it provided a natural boost of energy.

He got into the car, but before he could close the door, a squirrel hopped inside, jumped across him, and settled on the seat beside him. "Watch the claws, Raki," Biff said.

One day outside his office, Biff had pointed his index finger at a bothersome squirrel on a tree branch, intending only to give it a minor electric shock. Instead, the squirrel fell to the ground, dead, and Biff felt bad, so he drew a burst of healing energy from the ground beneath his feet and brought the little rodent back to life. Since then, Raki wouldn't leave him alone.

There were only a few cars and delivery trucks on the road so early in the morning and he made good time, the squirrel dozing on the seat beside him, his front and back paws outstretched like a dog. The Ambassador Hotel was a forty-story glass tower that hugged the narrow strip of land between State Road A1A and the ocean a few miles from Biff's townhouse. He parked in the garage across the street from the hotel and hurried across the second-floor walkway, with the squirrel on his shoulder.

Before Biff walked through the sliding glass doors, Raki jumped off and scampered across the pavement to where a palm tree leaned close to the walkway. He leaped across the void, grabbing a frond that shook with his weight. "Yeah, have fun with your acrobatics while I work," Biff grumbled. "Maybe you can get a gig with the Cirque du Squirrel."

Though it was only six thirty in the morning, the two-story marble lobby was crowded. Biff hurried past a gaggle of young women in yoga pants, their hair pulled up in matching ponytails, and an elderly Indian man in a long, high-collared coat.

Yegor, an American-born son of Russian immigrants, tall and skinny with a hipster goatee, paced back and forth in front of the valet desk. "Thanks for coming. I'm going crazy."

Biff's clients were often drawn to him by the small bits of magic they themselves had, as in Yegor's case, or by some intuitive attraction to his aura. Most of the work he did could be handled by an ordinary PI, but occasionally he was pulled into cases where he had to use his special abilities. He never knew from case to case what would happen, but he was always interested to see the wackiness that had drawn him to South Florida play out in people's lives.

"No need to go crazy," Biff said. "Let's figure out what we can do."

Yegor introduced Biff to the head valet, a portly Hispanic whose name tag read Bernardo. "I don't know what happen," he said with a heavy accent. "See, I sign for boxes myself." He showed Biff a handwritten ledger that indicated a delivery the day before for Yegor, care of the conference organizers. "These my initials."

Biff nodded. "Where do you store packages?"

"A locker in the basement," Bernardo said. "I show you."

When the elevator door opened, Bernardo stepped in and slid his ID card into a reader, then hit the button marked SB. The door opened on the subbasement across from a locked wire cage, about twenty feet long and ten feet deep, filled with all manner of boxes, shipping tubes, and luggage.

"Packages stay here until the guest arrive," Bernardo said. "Everything locked up, and only valets have card key and know combination."

He slid his ID card into another reader, punched in a sequence of numbers on a keypad, and the electronic door lock opened. "How many valets do you have on staff?" Biff asked.

"Five, including me. I talk to all of them this morning. Nobody took Mr. Kleyman's package out."

Biff turned to Yegor. "How big a shipment are we talking about?"

"The manufacturer shrink-wraps a hundred spout packs together. I had ten packages shipped here." From his own purchases at the gym, Biff knew that a spout pack was simply a heavy-duty stand-up pouch with a pour spout at the top. They were easy to tuck into kids' lunch boxes or into the pocket of a pair of workout shorts.

Biff had seen one of the spout packs, with a photo of Yegor's grandmother who had come up with the recipe back in Russia. In the picture, she had a floral scarf wrapped around her head and tied under her neck. Her face was creased with wrinkles, her nose beaky, and her smile warm and inviting.

Biff noted the hand truck by the wall. "No security cameras down here?" he asked Bernardo.

"No need. Only staff have access."

"Can I have a minute, please?" Biff asked. He had an acute sense of smell, fifty times better than any bloodhound, and like a dog, he could hear up to one hundred thousand vibrations per second. He also could read a license plate on a moving car a quarter of a mile away.

He opened his third eye, the metaphysical gate to higher realms, and saw the shipment of Yegor's tonic packs in a corner of the room. But someone had placed an enchantment over them, so that they were invisible to the human eye.

Because of its cosmopolitan location, Miami attracted many with metaphysical powers, from fully magical beings like genies to humans with a touch of ESP. Only the most sophisticated had the talent to create an invisibility spell.

Each being, from the tiniest sylph to the most powerful genie, left traces behind, which a midlevel genie like Biff could recognize. But whoever had made the spout packs invisible had the ability to mask a signature, and all Biff could sense around him was the detritus that humans who had been in the area had left behind.

Biff opened his eyes and thanked Bernardo for the help. The valet apologized again, and promised to call Yegor if anything turned up.

"What am I going to do?" Yegor asked as he and Biff emerged from the elevator back into the lobby. "I'm going to lose my shirt if I can't sell product today."

"I have a couple of ideas." Biff couldn't tell Yegor that the spout packs were right there in the storage room, though enchanted. He nodded toward the coffee shop shoehorned into a corner of the lobby between a pair of tall Egyptian-style columns. "I don't know about you, but I could use a coffee." It was nearly seven o'clock, and there was already a line snaking away from the counter.

"Sure," Yegor said. "I could use a pick-me-up myself. I was going to drink one of my tonics while I set up the booth."

They stepped to the end of the line, behind a pair of young women in Roman-style white togas decorated with gold ankhs. The women were both blond and had their hair piled up on their heads. They carried tote bags that read, "Ask me about the ancient Roman secrets of eternal life." Biff shook his head at the colossal ignorance of most humans. Whoever designed the costumes hadn't realized that the ankh was an Egyptian symbol, not a Roman one.

He was willing to bet he knew a lot more about eternal life than any huckster, and that the people behind the product had never seen the Roman coliseum when it was still intact and hosting gladiator contests, as he had. "When does this show start?" he asked.

"The show floor opens at eight," Yegor said.

Once they had their drinks, Biff led Yegor toward the pool. The sun was rising above the ocean, and one of the pool boys was laying out mats on the wooden lounge chairs. "Let's start with the basics," Biff said as they sat at one of the round tables by the pool. "Who knew you were going to be exhibiting here?"

"Everybody. I put up big notices on Facebook, Instagram, Pinterest, every other social network. I took out an ad in the conference program, too."

"You have any rivals, Yegor? Anybody who would want to sabotage your business?"

"It's a competitive niche," Yegor said. "I'm a little fish in a big pond. I can't imagine somebody from Monster or Red Bull worrying about me."

"You have any other employees? Maybe one who's interested in competing with you?"

Yegor shook his head. "It's just me. I contract out manufacturing and packaging."

Biff sat back in his chair and sipped his coffee. Someone with magical powers had sabotaged Yegor's operation. Who? Why?

"Are there other companies selling similar products to yours at the show?" Biff asked.

"I haven't walked the floor yet," Yegor said.

"Then that's where we start," Biff said. "I've got a couple of things to check, and then I'll join you."

Yegor was energized for the first time that morning. "I'll look around." He left, and Biff pulled out his cell phone. He sent a quick message to Sylphanus18344857@gmail.com, an associate he'd used on other cases in the past. Syl was a kind of air spirit that often inhabited butterflies, and he and his cohorts could spread around the hotel more quickly than Biff could, checking every corner for magical beings.

When he finished, he rode the escalator down to the lower

level. He didn't have an ID, so he stood off to the side of the registration desk where a couple of harried women were taking credit cards and handing over badges. He focused his thoughts on a blank badge at the edge of the table, and moved it by tiny increments until it fell to the floor. Then he strolled over and picked it up. No one around him seemed to notice.

He used a pen on the table to write his name on the badge, then slung the attached cord around his neck and walked inside the huge ballroom. A dais at the far end had been set up for speakers, with rows of folding chairs facing it. Booths of different sizes and styles lined the walls and created two aisles as well. The noise was overwhelming to Biff's sensitive hearing, and he had to focus on shutting out most of it.

Displays of exercise equipment lined both sides of aisle one. He scanned the crowd and the vendors for magic and found no magic there, just hard work and sweat, until he entered the personal service zone. The air there twinkled with a low level of enchantment, though it took him a while to find the source. It wasn't coming from the reiki or yoga practitioners, but instead was focused around the booth with a sign that proclaimed, "Your Akashic records are the energetic records of your past, present, and possible future lives."

A very tall, very muscular African-American man in a tight-fitting T-shirt and compression shorts greeted him. "Good morning, sir," the man said in a lilting Jamaican accent. "Do you want to understand how your past can inform your future?"

Given that he had centuries of past to cover, Biff doubted that his Akashic record could be that complete. He realized that the man before him had only an ability to read auras and channel the occasional spirit. He wasn't nearly powerful enough to create an invisibility spell. "The unexamined life is a lot simpler to explain to strangers," Biff said and kept on walking.

A white butterfly landed on Biff's shoulder, and Biff left the show and rode the escalator up to the lobby level. With the butterfly flitting around him, he walked back out to the pool area, and found a secluded corner. Sheltered by a screen of bright red hibiscus, the butterfly's antennae lengthened into human arms and legs and his body blossomed into that of a tall, lanky young man dressed in a white Cuban-style guayabera shirt, white slacks, and white track shoes.

"Thanks for coming on such short notice, Syl," Biff said. He explained the situation. "I'm covering the show floor, but whoever enchanted the spout packs doesn't necessarily have to be there. Can you round up some of the other sylphs to help out? I'd like you to see if you can turn up any other practitioners of magic."

"Sounds like fun," Syl said. "You'll pay in nectar, right? The swarm will want to know."

"Absolutely," Biff said. Syl transformed back into a butterfly and took off, and Biff returned to the show floor.

At the food aisle, he spotted Yegor's booth. A big sign, in English and Russian, advertised *Bubbie's Tonic—Better Than Chicken Soup for Your Health!* A poster of Yegor's grandmother hung on the back wall of the booth, and the table in front of the empty chair contained stacks of brochures. No one passing by paid the empty booth any attention.

The booth beside Yegor's sold detox cocktails, colon cleanses, and something called "wellness in a bottle." The next several booths on both sides sold more vitamins and minerals than Biff thought possible to exist. Each one promised its own special function, from the formation of red blood cells and antibodies to promoting blood clotting, hair growth, or improved liver function. It was sad, Biff thought, that humans were so desperate not to eat as they should that they succumbed to these nostrums.

He stopped before a kind-faced older woman who sold crystals. Each stone was displayed with a list of its properties. The woman's aura was that of an earth spirit, a pale green with an inner glow that indicated an ability to imbue natural products with a low level of enchantment. She caught his eye and smiled. "Can I interest you in a crystal today?" she asked.

"Do you have any tiger iron?" he asked.

She nodded. "An interesting choice. Tiger iron is a combination of three minerals: golden brown tiger eye, hematite, and red jasper. It is full of grounding earth energy. It's the perfect companion for those who tend to take on the feelings and emotions of others," she said. "A piece of tiger iron will help you remain balanced and centered."

Biff didn't tell her that it could also be used to return a spell to its sender. Perhaps she already knew.

She reached for a smooth, faceted stone in the shape of a pencil, about six inches long. It was cocoa brown with light and dark streaks. She handed it to him, and he felt the warmth and power within it. "I'll take it," he said.

He paid the woman and took one of her cards, and then, with the crystal in his pocket, continued his stroll.

He sensed the magic around a Sri Lankan rice booth as he approached. It was a fairly sophisticated spell, one that activated the taste buds and sense of smell, drawing customers to the booth. The sign beside the booth promised that "this ancient variety of sacred rice is blessed by the work of small farmers who do not use chemicals, pesticides, or fertilizers."

The enchantment seemed to be working; there were customers lined up to buy, as if the magic was forcing their wallets out of their pockets and their purses. He was about to open his third eye and see if he could discover the source of the enchantment when he saw the Indian man he'd spotted earlier approaching.

He was almost assaulted by the reek of tainted magic rising from the man in his high-collared white coat and felt slippers. Tainted magic was the result of using spiritual blessings for material gain. It harmed the soul of the practitioner, and Biff didn't like to associate with it. But it was logical that such a man might have enchanted Yegor's tonic, so Biff forced himself to swallow his distaste and follow the man, who walked slowly, nodding beatifically at passersby.

The tainted magic surrounded him like a gelatinous mass in the air, visible only to those who had the sight. Biff wondered why he hadn't noticed that aura earlier, when he was with Yegor in the lobby, but he hadn't been looking for magic then.

The man stepped into a booth advertising a mystic Indian Vedic who provided palmistry, numerology, and psychic readings, and walked behind a curtain.

Biff followed him to the front table, where he surveyed a display of *rudraksha* beads, berries from a southeast Asian tree. The sign above them read, "These jewels of the gods are able to give you health, abundance, and happiness."

A young Indian woman in a saffron-yellow sari stood behind the display. "The ancient saints wore these beads for protection, tranquility, and concentration," she said to Biff.

While she spoke, he scanned her for traces of magic but found none. There was nothing special about the berries so he turned to the next display: metallic plates with Sanskrit lettering.

"These are yantras," she said. "They are inscribed with geometrical, mystical designs as prescribed by the sacred texts of India. Wearing one will allow you to tune into the universal cosmic energy."

There were traces of magic in some of the devices, though of a very weak sort. He also noticed a display of bottles of tonic that alleged mystical properties. Though the ingredients were similar to Yegor's, there were a lot more chemicals and nonorganic materials, and Biff doubted they would be as effective as Yegor's.

"Is your swami available for readings?" he asked. He needed to get close to the man to see if he had the power to create a sophisticated enchantment.

"Yes, he has an opening right now," she said. Biff paid her for a reading, and she led him behind the partition, where the swami sat at a small table.

"What kind of reading are you interested in?" the man asked in a lilting accent as Biff sat on a folding chair across from him.

It was hard for Biff to concentrate because he found the man's tainted magic so repellent. He opted for a psychic reading, because numerology would require him to provide his birthdate and his full name, and palmistry required the man to touch him. He didn't want to give this man any information or any power over him.

"Place your hands on the table, palms down," the man said. "Close your eyes and try to remove all distraction from your mind."

Biff did as instructed.

"You are a man who loves nature," the swami said. "I see you surrounded by animals. And there is a beautiful woman in your life as well."

The man did have some level of ability, Biff thought, but it was possible this was all guesswork, too.

"This woman holds a great deal of power," the swami continued. "Power over you, but also power in the world. Do not be afraid to call upon her for help."

He meditated quietly for a couple of moments. As he did, Biff opened his third eye and scanned the area around him. Up close, the swami's magic was not so badly tainted—but it was clearly not strong enough to have performed the enchantment spell.

The swami moved his chair back from the table with a loud creak. Biff sensed the fear emanating from him. It was clear he had recognized that he was in the presence of another's magic. "I am afraid that is all I can tell you," he said.

Biff stood and thanked him, then walked back out to the show floor. If the Indian mystic couldn't have spelled the spout packs, then who could have? He went back to Yegor's booth, where the young man sat dejectedly on a folding chair.

Yegor perked up as Biff arrived. "Have you found my tonic yet?"

Biff shook his head. "How about you? Any competitors who might have it in for you?"

Yegor slumped back. "Just one. A guy named Baba Rupasinghe sells a product similar to mine, which he calls Baba's Tonic. We were at another health fair together a couple of weeks ago, and he was angry that I was using Bubbie's Tonic as the name of my product. He accused me of trying to steal his customers."

"Where's his booth?" Biff asked.

Yegor pointed down the aisle. "See the rice booth? That's his. The tonic is an offshoot—it has some rice wine in it."

Biff remembered that he'd sensed some enchantment around that booth, but that he'd been distracted by the Indian mystic and his tainted magic. "I'll check it out," he said.

Biff was an *ifrit*; his strength came from the earth itself, and his magic was strongest when he was in physical contact with the ground. Being inside this hotel, with concrete below him, prevented him from accessing his full powers. But if he went outside, he'd be farther from the rice vendor and the distance would reduce the effectiveness of the earth beneath his feet.

He looked around the show and spotted a giant sandbox. It was called a "relaxation zone," and was sponsored by a company that sold small trays of sand with miniature rakes and an assortment of polished stones. People could sit on large stones in the sandbox and meditate or pick up a rake to do a little grooming. It was perfect for what Biff needed, because it gave him a clear line of sight to the rice booth as well as contact with the natural world.

He sat on one of the polished black rocks and his feet sunk into the sand. He opened his third eye and focused on the rice booth.

The enchantment that caused customers to salivate was still working, and a line of eager buyers snaked out into the aisle. Yegor's rival stood at the front talking to customers, and the magic was centered around him. In its signature, Biff recognized elements of the spell on the spout packs.

So Baba was the one who'd sabotaged Yegor. But how could Biff overcome him? Baba had cast a solid protective spell around himself that prevented any magical attacks.

Just as the Indian mystic had predicted, Biff needed help. On his way out of the ballroom he grabbed a hemp bag from one of the vendors, dropping a couple of dollars on the table. Out by the pool, he found a secluded corner and sent a summons to Syl, then another to Farishta, asking her to pick up Raki on her way.

While he waited, he faced the ocean, striated in shades of dark blue and green. Though he and Farishta were both genies, she was a *marid*, one who derives her power from the sea. Farishta was a troublemaker; she was the woman Biff couldn't live without, but living with her was full of drama and danger, things he instinctively fought against. She thought of human beings as her personal playthings, loving to create chaos wherever she went. He hoped she'd agree to help him make some trouble for Baba Rupasinghe.

Syl, Farishta, and Raki the squirrel arrived. Farishta wore a skimpy yellow bikini. Her voluptuous body was a flawless olive color, her long, dark hair pulled back into a ponytail. Raki jumped down from her shoulder as she kissed Biff's cheek, and Biff smelled a mix of salt water, coconut, and custardy ylang-ylang.

"Hello, my darling," she purred. "Thank you for summoning me to such a beautiful place. What brings us all here?"

Biff explained the situation. When he was finished, all four of them were in agreement.

Farishta reached into the air behind Biff's chair and magicked a low-cut dress, which she put on over her bikini. Biff noticed that she had also created a show badge for herself, and once more marveled at her powers.

She stepped into a pair of high-heeled sandals and then walked into the hotel. Raki jumped into the hemp bag on Biff's shoulder, and Biff and Syl followed Farishta inside. When they reached the rice booth, Farishta was already in conversation with Baba. Her long, slim fingers caressed his arm, and she laughed lightly. Biff opened his third eye and saw that the protective shell Baba kept around himself was floating freely. Time to act. He put the hemp bag on the floor, and Raki scrambled out.

Syl stepped behind one of the room dividers, and when he emerged again, he was back in his butterfly form, joined by the rest of his swarm. As people oohed and pointed, the swarm clustered around Baba. Biff hurried out to the service elevator, where he placed his fingertips on the control panel and the button for the subbasement lit up.

It was important to move quickly. By this time, Biff figured, Raki had begun climbing up Baba's leg, digging his tiny claws into the man's skin. Between the beautiful woman, the swarm of butterflies, the shocked crowd, and the crazy squirrel, Baba would be too distracted to maintain his protection.

Biff ran his fingers over the lock to the storage unit and the door opened. He pulled the tiger iron amulet from his pocket and wrapped his hand around it, pushing the crystal's power toward the invisible packets until, with a popping sound, he felt the spell evaporate.

When he opened his eyes, the packs were right in front of him. He grabbed the hand truck and loaded it, then maneuvered it back to the show floor. As he passed the rice booth, he laughed out loud at the chaos that had ensued. Baba was swatting at the butterflies and at the same time trying to fling Raki off his shoulder. Farishta stood to the side, a happy smile on her face.

Yegor was sitting behind his booth, and he jumped up as Biff approached. "Biff, you found them! Awesome!" They worked together to unload the hand truck, and by the time they were finished, the table was stocked with product.

The swarm of butterflies swept past, followed by Farishta, with Raki on her shoulder. "Thank you, my love," Biff said. He leaned forward and kissed her.

"It was my pleasure," she said, when the kiss was finished. Raki slipped off her shoulder and into the hemp bag, though he peered out the top.

Behind them, Yegor launched into a recitation of the ingredients and benefits of the tonic. "My grandmother was healthy as an ox until she died at ninety in Russia," he said to the crowd. "This tonic kept her strong."

People began to step up to buy.

"I am always amazed at your ability to make things happen," Biff said to Farishta.

She opened her hand to him. In it rested one of the hotel's key cards. "More things than you know," she said. "Will you join me in my room?"

Raki chittered, and on their way up to the room, they stopped outside and left the squirrel to play among the coconut palms. Then they went upstairs to play themselves.

# THE VANISHING WIFE

## by Victoria Thompson

*January 1899*

"My wife has vanished."

This was the last thing Frank Malloy had expected his well-dressed client to say. When rich men came to his Confidential Inquiries office in Greenwich Village, they were usually concerned with marital infidelities or dishonest employees.

"What do you mean, she vanished?"

Delwood Hooper rubbed a well-manicured hand over his pale face. "I came home last evening, as usual, but my wife wasn't there to greet me. I asked our butler where she was, and he informed me that she had left town."

"Then she didn't exactly vanish," Frank said, settling back in his chair. He was still breaking it in since it, like everything else in his office, was brand new. "Didn't he tell you where she went?"

"That's the problem, you see. Marjorie occasionally does go out of town to visit friends or relations, but she always leaves me a note telling me exactly where she went and when she will return. This time, she didn't."

"Maybe she forgot. She must've told her maid where she went, at least." Frank didn't have much personal experience with servants, but he'd learned a lot about life in the upper classes since he'd met Sarah Brandt a few years earlier.

"Her maid went with her. They took luggage, and our coachman told me he dropped them at the train station."

Because Frank really didn't need the business, being a newly minted millionaire himself, he had the luxury of being able to calm his clients down and send them home before they did anything too serious if he felt they didn't really need his services. "This sounds like a planned trip, Mr. Hooper. I'm sure if you just give her a day or two, she'll be back home like always."

But Hooper shook his head. "There's more. I . . . I didn't want to admit it, not even to myself, but now . . . I think she has a lover."

At least this made sense. Not that Frank would wish this on any man, but it did offer a reasonable explanation for the situation. "What makes you think so?"

"I have discovered that she goes out every Thursday afternoon, as regular as clockwork."

"She's probably visiting friends or maybe she belongs to some Ladies' Aid Society or something."

Hooper's eyes were bleak when he met Frank's gaze. "She goes to a hotel."

"A hotel?"

"Yes. Every Thursday at two o'clock. My driver told me he drops her off there every week. It's been going on for months."

"How long have you known this?"

"Only a few days now. I began to suspect something, so I questioned our driver. He didn't like gossiping about his mistress, but he knows I'm the one who pays his salary, so he told me."

"He doesn't know who she meets there, though?"

"He said he's never gone inside, and I'm sure he hasn't. He has the carriage and the horses to worry about, after all. He can't just leave them unattended in the street."

"And did you confront her about this?"

Hooper shifted uncomfortably in his chair. His chair was new, too. "I didn't want to accuse her of anything without more proof. I was going to follow her today. It being Thursday, I thought I could find out if she meets someone or what she does there. But now she's gone."

Frank considered the situation for a long moment, then chose his words with care. "If your wife has deserted you, then you don't need a private detective, Mr. Hooper. You can divorce her easily and quietly. No one will even criticize you since you're the injured party."

"But I don't want to divorce her, Malloy. I love my wife. You may think me a fool, but she means the world to me, and I can't imagine my life without her. I don't care what she's done or who she's done it with. I just want her back before anyone finds out she's gone."

***

Sarah had spent most of her morning answering letters at her desk when Malloy came home and found her. She jumped up and kissed him, but she was surprised at the expression on his face when she pulled away.

"What's wrong?"

He studied her face for a long moment. "I was just wondering what it would take to make me stop loving you."

"Oh my, I guess the honeymoon really is over," she said with a grin.

He shook his head. "I didn't really mean that the way it sounded."

"I hope not!"

"It's a case I just got this morning. The client, well, his wife has apparently left him for another man, but he wants her back."

He told her what he knew about the Hoopers.

"Not many men would be so forgiving," Sarah said when he'd finished.

"I can't imagine Hooper will be, either, if he can even get her back. She probably doesn't want to come home at all. But I told him I'd try to find her, in case she's in some kind of trouble."

"Of course. Whoever lured her away may not be the man she thinks he is."

"A man who'd steal another man's wife is *never* the man she thinks he is."

Sarah had to agree. "You need my help with this."

"Yes, I do. My fifteen years with the New York City Police taught me how to treat criminals, but not society ladies. I don't have any idea how a woman like this thinks or what she might do."

"How can I help?"

"We need to know where she went, of course, and I already sent Gino down to the station to see if anyone remembers selling her a ticket." Gino Donatelli had also been a police officer before coming to work for Malloy's agency.

"She probably had her maid buy the tickets, and no one will remember her. A porter might remember carrying their bags, but there's no reason for him to have made note of what train she got on."

"I know. I think our best bet is to find out why she went to the hotel in the first place."

"And he said she went there every Thursday at the same time?"

"Yes, at two o'clock. Sometimes she'd be home in a couple hours and sometimes she'd come back later. She usually took a cab home."

"I have to say that does sound suspicious, although there could be a completely innocent explanation for it."

"For a female going to a hotel alone?" he scoffed.

Sarah had no answer for that. "What are you planning to do while Gino is at the train station?"

"I thought I'd question Hooper's coachman and maybe some of the other servants."

"That's good. Servants always know everything that's going on in a household, even when we think they couldn't possibly."

"Which is why I didn't want to have any servants."

Sarah grinned at this. "Did you expect me and your mother to do all the housework in this monstrosity of a home?"

Malloy knew better than to answer that. "Do you think you should be the one to question the servants?"

"No, I'm sure you can handle that. I'm trying to figure out how I can help, and I think I know the perfect thing."

"What's that?"

"I'm going to this hotel at two o'clock today to see if I can find out what Mrs. Hooper was doing there."

* * *

Frank found the coachman in the mews behind Hooper's house, where he also had his living quarters. He was polishing the coach when Frank arrived, and he stiffened in alarm when Frank came striding toward him.

"What do you want?"

Frank introduced himself. "Mr. Hooper has hired me to locate his wife. It seems she neglected to let him know where she was going when she left town yesterday."

The coachman was a middle-aged man who apparently took great pride in his appearance. His thinning hair had been carefully combed and his uniform pants were spotless. He'd hung his jacket over a chair sitting by the door, and the brass buttons shone brightly in the early spring sunlight. The coach itself was also spotless, making Frank wonder why he was polishing it. The coachman glanced warily over Frank's shoulder as if to see if anyone had followed him in. Then he hurried to close the door to the carriage house. "I don't want anybody to get the idea that Mrs. Hooper has gone missing," he explained.

"But isn't that what happened?"

The coachman glared at him. "I won't hear a word against her. It must be some kind of mistake. I don't think she'd do anything bad."

"Well, then, tell me what you know about her trips to this hotel."

"I don't know anything at all," he insisted.

"Mr. Hooper said you take her there every Thursday at two o'clock."

"That part's true." He looked as if admitting even that annoyed him.

"Did you ever see her meet anyone?"

"No. She goes in alone, and no, I never followed her inside. It's not my place, is it?"

"What kind of a mood is she in when she goes there?"

"What do you mean?" he asked with a frown.

"You know what I mean. Is she nervous or frightened or—"

"Not nervous. Not frightened."

"What then?"

"I don't see what difference it makes," he tried.

Frank just waited, staring at him until he finally surrendered.

"She was . . . happy." Saying that made him unhappy.

*"Happy?"*

"Yeah, and kind of . . . excited."

"Excited?"

"A little bit. Sometimes. She . . . You won't say any of this to Mr. Hooper, will you?"

"Of course not." Frank didn't want to hurt the man more than necessary.

"She'd get out of the carriage and her face would be all . . . I don't know how to describe it. Glowing, I guess, and her eyes were real bright. I didn't tell Mr. Hooper that part."

The way a woman in love would look when she was meeting her lover, Frank thought, but he said, "I won't tell Mr. Hooper, either. I understand her maid went with her on the train."

"I suppose. They both had a suitcase. Not big ones. Looked like just enough for a day or two, but . . ."

"Mrs. Hooper was glowing again?"

"I never saw her look so happy. I asked her did she want me to meet her train when she come home, and she said, oh no, that wasn't necessary."

If she wasn't planning on returning, it wouldn't be necessary, Frank supposed. "I don't want to get the servants in an uproar over this, at least until we know for sure what's going on, but is there one who could answer some questions for me?" The one who was the biggest gossip, he wanted to say, but he figured the coachman would know what he meant.

He did. "That'd be Betty. She knows everything that goes on, but she loves Mrs. Hooper because she gave her a place when nobody else would. You'll see what I mean."

Before Frank could ask any questions, the coachman hurried out, leaving Frank to wait in the coach house. He didn't have to wait long. When the coachman returned, he brought what Frank at first thought was a child. A second look told him she wasn't a child at all but a dwarf. She probably stood only a few inches over four feet tall, but unlike other dwarfs he'd seen, she was perfectly proportioned, just smaller than average.

She scowled at him, just as suspicious as the coachman had been. "Rodney said you was helping the master find the missus."

"Yes, I am. He's very worried about her and wants to make sure she's safe."

"I knew it. I knew there'd be trouble when she didn't leave a note."

"You knew about the note?"

"Sure. She always leaves a note when she goes somewhere. She props it up against the clock on the mantle in the family parlor. That's because the master always goes in there as soon as he gets home. First thing he does is look at the clock, so that's where she leaves it, so he'll be sure to see it. But this time, there wasn't no note."

"You're sure about that?"

"I clean that room every day. I even aired it out yesterday because the weather was so nice. There wasn't no note there last night."

"Do you have any idea where Mrs. Hooper might've gone?"

She glanced at the coachman, but he gave her no encouragement that Frank could see. "Someplace fun."

"What makes you think that?"

"The way she was smiling when she left. I never saw her look so happy."

***

Sarah had the cab drop her in front of the hotel just as the clocks all over the city were chiming the hour of two. The large hotel was a perfectly respectable place. They probably had a ladies' parlor where female guests could sit without being bothered by cigar smoke or ill-mannered traveling salesmen. She didn't have any qualms about going in alone.

She'd dressed carefully, choosing a conservative but expensive outfit that would mark her as Mrs. Hooper's equal in social status. Hotels were careful about admitting females without luggage who might be prostitutes.

A uniformed doorman opened the door for her and wished her good afternoon. She stepped into the well-appointed lobby. As she'd expected, the room was filled with business men who sat in the armchairs scattered around the room, reading newspapers and smoking or chatting with each other. Hotel guests, mostly male, came and went, threading their way through the furnishings and potted plants between the elevators and the front door, followed by bellboys in snappy uniforms carrying suitcases or pushing carts laden with luggage. Several clerks worked at the front counter, accepting keys from departing guests or registering new ones.

A few of the loitering men glanced at her with interest, but she pointedly ignored them. Instead, she stopped and looked around, slowly and carefully, searching for anything that might tell her why a respectable matron would be here at this particular time on this particular day.

She'd been standing there a minute or two, discovering nothing of interest, when one of the bellboys came hurrying over. He looked about fifteen with peach fuzz on his cheeks and his hair slicked down beneath his perky cap. "Excuse me, ma'am. Are you here for the meeting?"

Sarah had no idea what he was talking about, but she said, "Yes, I am," just to see what he would say.

"I'm sorry to tell you, but they're not here today."

"But don't they always meet at two o'clock on Thursdays?" she tried.

"Yes, ma'am, they do, but not today for some reason."

Her mind raced, trying to put this new information together with what she already knew. "Are they meeting someplace else?"

He frowned. "I don't really know. I'm sorry."

"That's all right. Thank you for telling me."

He had melted back into the bustle of the lobby before she realized she should have asked him what kind of a meeting it was, although he would have thought that strange after she said she had planned to attend it. Who attends a meeting without knowing what it's for?

"Sarah?"

She turned to see her husband had arrived. They'd planned to meet there, but she'd wanted to go in alone to see if that would attract notice, which it had. "I think she came here for a meeting, Malloy."

"I know, but with who?"

"No, not a meeting with a lover. A meeting with other . . . people, I suppose. A bellboy asked me if I was here for the meeting. Obviously, he's used to seeing unescorted females come in to attend."

"Where is it then? Maybe she's here."

"He said they aren't meeting here today for some reason. Do you suppose they could be meeting out of town somewhere for some reason? That would explain why Mrs. Hooper left on the train."

"Yes, it would, but who are these people she meets with? And why would she keep it a secret from her husband?"

Sarah shook her head. "I didn't think to ask the bellboy what kind of meeting it was, and in any case, he didn't know where they are today."

"I'll ask at the desk. Surely they'll know," Malloy said and strode off, leaving her to her own thoughts. They weren't very pleasant. She could think of many organizations that met regularly and to which a respectable female might belong. She couldn't think of any that met in a hotel or which required its members to leave town secretly.

After a few minutes, Malloy returned to her.

"Let's get out of here," he said before she could ask him anything.

Outside, the doorman helped them into a waiting cab. Malloy gave the driver an address she didn't recognize. When they had pulled away from the curb, she said, "What did you find out?"

"It's the strangest thing. Nobody there seems to know what kind of an organization it is. It's mostly females, although a few men come to the meetings, too, but they don't allow any of the hotel staff into the room while they're meeting."

"Surely, the group must have a name."

"I told them that, even though nobody remembered hearing it. The manager finally looked it up in his book, and it was Suffering Saints or something like that."

"That sounds like a religious group."

"Which doesn't make any sense at all. When I talked to the coachman and one of the maids at the Hooper house, they both agreed that Mrs. Hooper always looked happy and excited when she attended these meetings."

"Maybe she had a religious experience of some kind."

"Maybe. Hooper might know. At least I found out that the group is meeting in Poughkeepsie today."

"That would explain why Mrs. Hooper took the train and stayed overnight. If that's even where she is."

"It's the best clue we have. I'm going to tell Hooper what we've learned and see what he wants to do."

"I know what I want to do," Sarah said. "I want to go to Poughkeepsie and see these Suffering Saints for myself."

"And I want to get Mrs. Hooper away from them if we can."

\*\*\*

Mr. Hooper also wanted to get his wife away from this mysterious organization, so without even bothering to pack a toothbrush, he and the Malloys set out for the train station. They were lucky enough to catch a train that would get them to Poughkeepsie around suppertime. The ride seemed long, and the three had little to discuss, not knowing what the situation would be when they reached their destination or even if they could locate Mrs. Hooper when they did.

When they arrived, bone weary and suddenly realizing they had no idea where in the town to look, they wandered through the station and out to the street. A few cabs waited to convey disembarking passengers to the hotel of their choice. One of them, spying Sarah, called, "Are you here for the convention, miss?"

"What convention is that?" Malloy called back.

"I don't rightly know, but I've carried about a hundred ladies out to it. I bet there's five hundred of 'em out there now."

Sarah exchanged a look with Malloy, who said, "Let's give it a try."

The three of them climbed into the cab, which carried them through the dusky evening out to the edge of town where they pulled up to one of the many doors of the largest building Sarah had ever seen. Sarah glimpsed a sign that said Vassar College. After instructing the driver to wait for them, they hurried inside.

For a convention, the lobby seemed surprisingly quiet. A pair of well-dressed ladies sat at a long table, prepared to greet people as they arrived, and a few others stood around chatting. They all seemed surprised to see the three of them, especially Mr. Hooper, who looked as if he were about to lose control of himself. Before Malloy could stop him, he marched up to the table and said, "I'm Delwood Hooper, and I'm here to find my wife."

To Sarah's amazement, the two ladies broke into delighted smiles. "We were so afraid you weren't going to make it, Mr. Hooper," one of them said. "The program will be starting in just a moment, but we've reserved a seat for you right in the front. If you'll come with me . . ."

Astonished, he looked at Malloy for guidance.

"Oh, are these your friends?" the other lady asked.

"Yes," Hooper said faintly.

"I'm afraid we only reserved one seat for Mr. Hooper, but we'll find you a place to sit, too, don't you worry."

The first woman was already leading Mr. Hooper toward the large doors located on the wall at the other end of the lobby. When she opened one of them, they could see an enormous auditorium that was filled to capacity.

"What's going on here?" Malloy murmured to Sarah.

Just then a band they could not see struck the first rousing notes of "The Battle Hymn of the Republic," and everyone in the auditorium, which was almost entirely female, rose to their feet and began to sing along.

Their guide took Sarah and Malloy to the far side of the auditorium and scurried up the aisle until she found two empty seats. They squeezed in, excusing themselves over and over, and when they were settled, Sarah finally had an opportunity to look around. Red, white, and blue bunting hung everywhere, and above the stage an enormous banner announced the name of the convention.

"It wasn't *Suffering* Saints," Sarah said into Malloy's ear. "It was *Suffrage.*"

The banner read, "Votes for Women," and the words they were singing to the "Battle Hymn" had been changed. It was now an anthem challenging men to support the cause. Sarah gave Malloy an amused glance, and he shrugged. There was no remedy for it. They were committed now.

The song ended and the program began. Several ladies got up and gave inspiring speeches on the topic of women's rights, interspersed with more suffrage songs set to familiar tunes. Finally, the mistress of ceremonies got up and said, "We have one last speaker before we hear from our featured speaker, Mrs. Catt. This is her first appearance with us, and this dear lady has never spoken in public before. Please help me welcome Mrs. Delwood Hooper!"

The crowd roared as a handsome matron made her way to the podium. Sarah craned her neck until she finally found Mr. Hooper sitting in the center of the front row. To his credit, he was on his feet, cheering along with everyone else, although he must have been mystified as to how he had ended up in this place to see his wife lauded by five hundred Suffragettes.

She began to speak, tentatively at first and barely audible in that crowded hall, but as she spoke of how she had become a champion for women's rights, her voice grew stronger and more confident. The audience stopped her several times with raucous applause that seemed to fluster her at first and then to inspire her, until her face glowed in just the way her servants had described. She closed by looking fondly down at her husband, who sat right below the podium.

"And I would like to thank my husband for coming this evening to support me."

As the audience cheered again, Sarah leaned over to Malloy. "Do you suppose he really does support her?"

"He'll have to now, won't he?" he replied with a grin.

Mrs. Carrie Chapman Catt was the final speaker, and when she had stirred the crowd to a fever pitch, they ended the evening with one more suffrage hymn. As the crowd began to break up, Sarah and Malloy made their way to the front of the room in search of Mr. Hooper. They found him just as he reached the circle of well-wishers surrounding his wife.

"Delwood!" she cried when she saw him and gave him her hand. "I was so afraid you wouldn't come, but I'm glad my note convinced you. I hope it wasn't too horrible of a shock."

"It *was* a shock," he said diplomatically, since they were not alone, "but not an unpleasant one. Can you come home with me tonight? We have a lot to discuss."

"The convention doesn't end until noon tomorrow. We ladies are staying here at the college, but I'm sure you can find a hotel if you'd like to stay over, too."

"No, I'll just go on home and see you tomorrow," he said.

She wished him good night and told him again how happy she was that he'd come, and then he turned and found the Malloys waiting for him. He looked a bit dazed, so they each took one of his arms and escorted him out of the hall, stopping occasionally for someone to welcome him into the movement or compliment him on his wife's speech.

Luckily, their cab driver really had waited for them, although they had to wake him from a sound sleep. He was very happy with his exorbitant fare and dropped them at the station in time for them to catch the last train of the night back to the city. Only when they were on the train did they feel free to talk.

"She didn't run off with a lover," Mr. Hooper marveled over and over.

"And did you hear what she said? She didn't run off without a word, either," Sarah said. "She did leave you a note."

"But what could've happened to it?" Hooper asked. "Why didn't I see it?"

The two men speculated for almost an hour, blaming careless servants and even ghosts at one weary moment, but they reached no suitable conclusion. Sarah kept her theories to herself.

Much later, in the wee hours of the night, they quietly entered Hooper's darkened house.

"It's this way," he told the Malloys, leading them down the hallway to the back parlor, where the family likely spent most of their time. He lit the gas jet on the wall, which bathed the room in a golden glow. The room was in perfect order.

Hooper pointed to the mantle where an ornate clock sat, ticking loudly in the nighttime stillness. "That's where she always leaves her notes, propped up in front of the clock."

Sarah walked over to the mantle, removing her glove as she went. Then she reached up with her bare hand and felt along the mantle, which was above her eye level. She almost missed it even then. It was almost entirely underneath the clock, in the shallow space created by the little feet it sat on. She pulled out a sealed envelope with Delwood Hooper's initials written on it in a feminine hand.

"I believe this is yours," she said, handing it to him.

"Dear Lord," he breathed, sinking down into the nearest chair. "Do you suppose it was there all the time?"

"Of course it was," Sarah said. "Your wife obviously expected you to read it and hoped whatever she wrote in there would convince you to go to Poughkeepsie and attend her speech. The question is, what happened?"

"It's obvious," Malloy said. "The note must've fallen over."

"But how could that happen?" Hooper asked.

"Your maid Betty said she aired this room out yesterday," Malloy said.

Hooper immediately perked up. "That's right, she did. All the windows were open when I arrived home. It was so breezy, the draperies were practically billowing. I had them closed at once."

"So the note must have blown over," Sarah said. "But it was almost completely underneath the clock, too, which is probably why you didn't see it." Sarah didn't add that the other reason he didn't see it was most likely because he was a man, and men could never find anything, especially things they were looking for.

"How could that have happened?" Hooper asked.

"If someone dusted the mantle, it might've gotten pushed under accidentally. It is a high mantle. I can't see over the edge."

"And your maid Betty wouldn't have been able to see over the edge at all. She's very small," Malloy said.

"She's a dwarf," Hooper added. "But a very hard worker. She carries a stool around with her so she can reach things."

"Then that explains it," Sarah said. "Your wife did leave a note, as always. You just didn't see it."

"I think you'd better read it before she comes home," Malloy said.

"I'm going to read it before I sleep tonight," Hooper said. "I can't tell you how much I appreciate your help, Malloy, and yours, too, Mrs. Malloy. If you hadn't figured out where she was, I might've . . . Well, I might've missed this evening, and I might've been less than kind to Amelia when she came home tomorrow. I would definitely have made a fool of myself at the very least."

"The only mystery now," Malloy said, "is whether you approve of having a wife who's a suffragette."

Hooper smiled crookedly. "I did say I didn't care what she'd done or who she'd done it with, didn't I? I think I can accept this."

# THE RIGHT TO BARE ARMS

## by John Gregory Betancourt

Behind the stage, Senator Bobby Bragg bounced lightly on the balls of his feet and surveyed the gathering crowd. County fairs always brought out the locals, and today's weather—dazzling blue sky, mid-70s temperature, a pleasant breeze—practically guaranteed a record turnout. Never mind that they came for the monster truck pulls, carny games, and deep-fried Oreos and turkey legs. A state senator—a *smart* state senator—knew where to find his constituency.

God, guns, and glory. That's what the people wanted. And he'd give it to them . . . and ride them all the way to the White House.

The mayor of Hicksville, or whatever this backwoods town was called, finished her official opening speech and turned to Bobby. She was pushing forty with a belly like a beach ball. Ready to drop a litter of babies any minute, from the looks of her.

"Please give a big hand to our man at the capitol, State Senator Bragg!"

As the yokels applauded, Bobby vaulted up the three wooden steps and onto the platform. His hair was perfect, his teeth gleamed unnaturally white, and with his high cheekbones and chiseled chin, he had the look of a Hollywood movie star. He knew; he'd paid enough for the plastic surgery.

"Thanks, sweetie." As he shook the mayor's hand, she leaned close.

"Make it quick, hon," she said in a low voice. "You may have pushed your way onto my program, but we still have a lot to get through. I don't want to be here till midnight."

Bobby forced a grin. "You got it, darlin'," he said. Mentally he added a *screw you.* She should be at home with her kids, not taking a man's job. But, of course, he could never say that to her face. She was probably one of those bleeding-heart feminazi troublemakers.

Taking a deep breath, he stepped to the microphone. This was the moment. The time he lived for. He'd have them eating out of his hand.

"Howdy!" he called, making eye contact with first one, then another, then another. "I want your vote. God. Guns. And glory. I'm Bobby Bragg, and that's what I'm all about!"

Motion caught his eye—someone pushing through the crowd.

A goddamn white-faced *mime*? Bobby glanced at the mayor, who was staring with interest at the carny performer.

The mime carried a giant satchel. He plopped it down in front of the stage, began rummaging through it, and pulled out a plate and a stick. When he set the plate spinning on top of the stick, the crowd hooted and clapped. Several pulled out cell phones and began recording.

"Hey, buddy," Bobby called down. "Can you wait till after my speech to do that?"

The mime cupped a hand to his ear, gave an exaggerated nod, and took the plate down. The crowd booed Bobby.

"There's a time and a plate for everything," he told them, grinning. His pun got a mix of groans and a few more boos. A few people wandered off toward the snack booths. "Like I was saying . . . God, guns, and glory. I'm Bobby Bragg, and that's what I'm about!"

The mime stretched out white-gloved hands and began feeling an invisible wall. Bobby felt the audience's attention slipping.

The mayor leaned over. "You done, hon?" she whispered.

"Back off, sweetheart," he growled. "I'm just gettin' warmed up."

Bobby gritted his teeth and stepped back to the microphone. He wasn't a preacher's son for nothing. He'd worked crowds since the age of three, everything from parks and storefronts to stadiums and conventions. He knew what to do.

"Hallelujah!" he cried. "There's a lesson from the Good Book here for all of us. We're here on this guh-*lor*ious day—"

The mime went back to his satchel.

"—under the eyes of God, to celebrate the freedoms of our great nation!" His heart pounded, the adrenaline rush that came when he worked himself to a fever pitch. "Your God-given right to bear arms is being taken away! I—"

The crowd hooted with laughter.

Bobby glanced down. The mime had rolled up his sleeves and was doing an exaggerated pantomime. *Bare* arms. Yeah, he got it.

*Find a common threat.* That always got them back.

"We *all* know there have been tragedies," he went on in solemn tones. His amplified voice boomed down the fairway. "Too many men, women, and children have died because guns got into the hands of a few crazies. But taking *your* guns away isn't the answer!"

Bobby tried to make eye contact with the crowd, but they had all focused on that stupid mime, who was rummaging through his satchel once more.

Beside him, the mayor said, "Wrap it up, hon. We have a busy program this morning."

Bobby cried, "There's a law pending that will stop you from buying guns at gun shows—"

The mime pulled a huge assault rifle from his satchel and swung it toward Bobby. That white face had the biggest, evilest grin Bobby had ever seen.

Yelping, Bobby dove for cover.

A loud *pop* sounded. The crowd screamed . . . with laughter?

Bobby peeked out from behind the mayor's skirt. That assault rifle . . . a prop? A wooden stick with a giant white flag stuck out from the barrel. "BANG!" it said. Then in smaller letters, "If this were a real rifle, you'd be dead, hon."

Bobby looked up at the mayor.

"Did you know," she asked, "that one of those crazies shot and killed my husband? *That's* why *I* ran for mayor, hon."

Two minutes later, cell phone videos of Senator Bobby Bragg diving for cover behind a visibly pregnant woman went viral.

# MESSAGE IN A BOTTLE

## by Su Kopil

Odie Dinkle found his first message in a bottle when he was ten years old. It never occurred to him back then that the bottle looked suspiciously similar to Grandpa Moonie's favorite brand of whiskey, or that the handwriting had the same weird slant as Great-Uncle Lemon's. All he cared about was that he held a real live pirate map in his hand. He combed the beach for hours searching for buried treasure, until Granny Lou finally confessed the map was a fake—a ruse to get him out from underfoot.

That was the same day the large safe appeared in the attic of their two-and-a-half-story house on Hook Island, and the same day Great-Uncle Lemon disappeared for good. Odie figured Grandpa Moonie and Great-Uncle Lemon's habitual fighting had finally come to a head with their last heist—robbing the Hook Bank & Trust. They'd considered themselves modern day pirates and were proud of it.

But when Great-Uncle Lemon disappeared, Grandpa Moonie changed. He hugged the bottle more and his family less. In fact, he and Granny Lou barely talked. He just roamed the beaches across the Outer Banks searching for washed-up bottles, and so Odie searched with him, until the day a hurricane hit and blew Grandpa Moonie out to sea.

Ten years later, Grandpa Moonie's obsession had become Odie's. The island's natural hook shape was a magnet for ocean trash. Odie found his share of messages in bottles or MIBs, as he liked to call them: one from a soldier off to war, one from a homesick girl on a cruise, and a few others that were illegible. He started an online forum where hunters could share their discoveries. He even organized the first-ever MIB Hunters Convention.

When he'd approached Granny Lou a few weeks earlier with the idea, he'd been shocked by her support.

"Odie Dinkle," she said, "that's the smartest idea you ever had. You get your hunter buddies to bring their bottles with them, like show and tell. Didn't one of them fellas just find a bottle clear down in Florida?"

"Yeah, Digger Tubbs. Wasn't a big find. Just numbers scribbled on the note." Odie squinted at her. "But how'd you know, Granny Lou? I thought you hated my—um, hobby."

"Wouldn't hurt you none to get a job. Too much like your grandpa, you are, but that's another story." She mashed the end of her cigarette in an empty flower pot. "I dip into your forum every little bit. Have to keep tabs on my only grandson, now don't I?"

"So you'll lend me money for the convention?" His excitement overrode the fact that Granny Lou had been checking up on him.

"Money?" She snorted. "You think I'd still be working as a maid—in them fancy hotels taking over the island, no less—if I had money?"

"You'd have money if you sold this rotten old house to one of them hotels," Odie said. "I seen them suits sniffing around here."

"Now you mind your business, Odie Dinkle. This old house is a piece of history. You know Blackbeard himself stayed here."

"That's just one of Grandpa Moonie's stories."

"Your grandpa had lots of stories. That's a fact. But some of them, dear boy, some of them are true. Now you forget about the money. You can have your convention right here. We got the room. I'll do the cooking."

Here? The house was falling down around them, and Granny Lou wasn't much of a cook.

"You tell them Blackbeard slept here, and they'll be begging to come," she said.

***

So Odie made the arrangements. He wrangled a handwriting expert, and an antique bottle collector, as speakers. He planted MIBs around the island for a scavenger hunt using Grandpa Moonie's old whiskey bottles. He sent out invitations to his forum members, playing up the Blackbeard angle. And most importantly, he got Digger Tubbs to agree to give the keynote address. That last was Granny Lou's idea. She said if they couldn't get Digger, they might as well scrap the whole thing.

Odie was starting to wonder if maybe Granny Lou had a crush on Digger. Maybe they'd hit it off on the forum. They were about the same age. Odie was proud that Granny Lou had held onto her looks. Except for the network of wrinkles around her mouth, she could pass for ten years younger than her sixty-odd years.

Now, all he had to worry about was whether the house would hold up as well as Granny Lou. Built by shipbuilders in the 1700s, it had seen its fair share of neglect, especially in the last ten years. The double front porch sagged in places. An upstairs bedroom had a crater in the floor, making it and the room below unusable.

But Granny Lou said by using the Blackbeard tales Grandpa Moonie used to tell, no one would pay attention to the warped heart-of-pine floors or the holes in the oyster-shell plaster. So Odie practiced the retellings in front of a mirror, adding a few embellishments here and there.

On the first day of the convention, Odie strung up a hand-painted banner—First Annual MIB Hunters Convention. Eight people showed up, plus the two speakers, and their keynote, Digger Tubbs. Odie had only expected five. So he had to scramble to work out sleeping arrangements—four each in the two front rooms on the second floor, three in the back room on the right, and one, Digger Tubbs, would bunk with him.

Once attendees were settled, he gathered everyone in the front room on the main floor and went over the schedule. After the initial meet and greet ended, Granny Lou would serve up fried cheese sandwiches. Then the handwriting expert would speak. Show and tell would follow with attendees showing off their collections. Then the scavenger hunt, back to the house for hot dogs and beans, Digger's keynote address, and finally, the night would end with Odie's Blackbeard tales.

The next morning, Granny Lou promised a continental breakfast like the big hotels offered with pastries she'd borrowed from work. Odie still wasn't clear on how pastries could be borrowed. Attendees could share their scavenger finds while they ate, and the convention would wind down with a lecture from the bottle expert.

"Any questions?" Odie asked. When no one raised their hand, he smiled. "Then let the First Annual MIB Hunters Convention begin."

Little groups formed, filling the room with the rise and fall of conversations. No one seemed to notice the lumpy furniture or faded curtains. Odie leaned against the brick fireplace and surveyed the scene with satisfaction and a generous helping of pride, until he saw Digger Tubbs striding toward him, scowling. Long gray sideburns bracketed Digger's pudgy face, matching the gray tufts of hair poking out of his ears. Odie had a moment to wonder what Granny Lou saw in the man before the tirade began.

"See here, Dinkle. You promised me my own accommodations. Bad enough the room is so small but to have to share with . . . with . . ."

"Me."

"You? Yes, well. I need my own room. If you can't provide that then I'm going to have to leave."

"Leave?" Granny Lou appeared, brandishing a rubber spatula, as though she'd been summoned by Blackbeard himself. "Why, of course, you should have your own room, Mr. Tubbs. It would mean disaster for our little convention if a man of your esteemed knowledge were to leave."

Digger's chest puffed so big, Odie braced himself to catch the man's buttons as they popped. Really, what did Granny Lou see in him?

"Odie?" Granny Lou and Digger stared at him.

"Huh?"

Granny Lou nudged him in the ribs. "I said that Mr. Tubbs—"

"Digger, please." Digger winked at Granny Lou.

"Then you should call me Louise." Granny Lou winked back.

Odie's stomach churned. He'd never heard anyone call Granny Lou, Louise. Not even Grandpa Moonie. Although, come to think of it, he did overhear Great-Uncle Lemon call her that once when they thought no one was listening.

Odie zoned back into the conversation in time to hear Granny Lou say, "Odie will make other sleeping arrangements. The room will be yours and yours alone, Mr.—Digger."

Odie sniffed. "Uh, Granny Lou, is something burning?"

"Horseflies on butter! My sandwiches."

***

Odie got the worst of the burnt sandwiches, though he noticed a few others surreptitiously scraping the crusts. Most, however, were too busy plying the handwriting expert with samples of their penmanship to be analyzed. The expert took it in good stride, adding their analysis to her talk after lunch.

Next up, show and tell. Four attendees brought their collections, the most notable of which was a postcard, in a corked, brown beer bottle, dated in the mid-1900s. The message was illegible, but everyone was suitably awed by the bottle itself.

Digger Tubbs brought four MIBs. He'd discussed them all before on the online forum, but everyone seemed to appreciate seeing them and hearing their stories in person. His first-ever find was a green bottle with a message from a man named Tom who thought highly of someone named Fanny. The second, his most recent find, was a whiskey bottle containing a slip of paper with a barely legible three-digit number. Next, he showed them a blue bottle with a swing-top cork. Inside was a letter from a boy on a trip to Norway asking for the finder to please write back.

"I wrote to the address given," Digger said, "and discovered the boy had died on the trip. The surviving family members claimed it was like their son was reaching out from the grave to them."

"Why didn't you return it?" an attendee asked.

"Finders keepers." Digger laughed. "I did, however, e-mail them a copy of the note, for which they were grateful. And last but not least"—he held aloft a champagne bottle—"I found this on the shores of Savannah, Georgia, last summer. Dropped into the ocean by a couple on their honeymoon. The year"—he paused for effect—"1913. The note says: John Beechum loves Harriet Beechum for all eternity."

A murmur rose. Everyone wanted to hold the bottle or at the very least touch it. Digger fended them off, placing the champagne bottle, along with the other three bottles, inside a special foam-filled suitcase. He carried the case to his room, returning in time to take one of the maps of Hook Island that were being passed around.

"Okay, everyone," Odie announced, "time for the scavenger hunt. There are ten bottles hidden on the eastern side of the island. The first one to return will win a MIB Hunter T-shirt." He held up the extra-large shirt he'd had made at a local store.

Odie shooed the last attendee out the door and turned to find Granny Lou puffing away on a cigarette. "Odie," she said. "We have a problem. Freezer's out. That'll be four gallons of ice cream down the drain. I told you not to spend money on ice cream."

"We have to give them something besides hot dogs and cheese sandwiches. What do we do now?" Odie slumped against the door. He'd spent his last dime on that ice cream.

Granny Lou puffed while she thought. "In the attic, get those buckets we use to catch the rain water. I'll pop down to the gas station and get a few bags of ice. That should keep things cold long enough."

***

Odie never liked the attic. It gave him the creeps with its spider-filled corners and broken remnants of years past. If Blackbeard really did haunt this place, this is where he'd be. Odie pulled the chain on the single bare bulb and shuddered as the room sprang to life in all its dusty glory. He found the first bucket under a poorly patched hole in the roof. The other was in the back corner on top of a cloth-draped box. The cloth slipped some when he grabbed the bucket. Fetid rain water splashed over the rim.

"Gross." Odie set the bucket on the floor to fix the cloth and realized it wasn't a box underneath. It was Grandpa Moonie's old safe.

Memories washed over Odie of himself and Grandpa Moonie walking the beach, searching for bottles. That was after Great-Uncle Lemon had disappeared, of course. Grandpa Moonie wasn't much for stories by then, except for one. "Odie," he'd say, "there's a bottle out there that holds the key to our future." He'd take a swig from his whiskey and Odie'd ask him what he meant. "A treasure chest, boy. All we need is the right numbers." The liquor would slur his words. "Damn bottle is a long shot from hell." Then he'd say something even stranger. "You're lucky you got no brothers, Odie. Don't you trust no one but yourself."

"Odie."

Odie nearly fell into the bucket, catching himself in the nick of time. "Granny Lou, what're you doing scaring me like that?"

Granny Lou stood beneath the naked bulb, the light haloing her silver hair. "I thought maybe the bogeyman got you, you was taking so long. Never mind about those buckets. The freezer's back to working."

"Look." Odie pulled the sheet away. "Grandpa Moonie's old safe."

"That's what it is all right," Granny Lou said. "Now let's get back downstairs."

Odie dropped the sheet on the bucket and followed her out of the attic. "Granny Lou?"

"Hmmm?"

"What's inside the safe?"

"Darned if I know." She kept walking. "That thing ain't been opened since the day it was drug here."

"You think maybe Grandpa Moonie hid the money from the bank robbery in it?"

Granny Lou stopped and pulled the cigarette from her mouth. "What are you on about? How many times I gotta tell you Grandpa Moonie's stories were just that—stories."

"I thought you said some of them was true?"

"Well, I suppose some are. But not that one. Now come help me get supper ready."

\*\*\*

Everyone was famished from the afternoon spent searching the beaches. It seemed all of Odie's planted bottles had been found, plus a surprise find from a newbie hunter. Everyone exclaimed over the new discovery—a beer bottle, sent four months ago, from a man in Atlantic City wishing for money.

The hot dogs, beans, and especially the ice cream were a hit, making everyone lazy enough so that the pompous start to Digger's keynote address didn't ruffle any feathers. Odie couldn't sit through it. His mind was too full of other thoughts. He carried dirty dishes back to the kitchen, expecting to find Granny Lou washing up, but she wasn't there. He couldn't blame her; it had been an exhausting day.

Digger's voice rambled on from the other room as he shared yet another story about himself. But Odie wasn't thinking about Digger. He was remembering Grandpa Moonie's stories, especially the one about the Hook Bank & Trust heist. How Grandpa Moonie and Great-Uncle Lemon were going to live the good life. They just had to wait awhile before they spent the money so the cops couldn't track it. That was the morning they sent Odie on his wild-goose chase.

Granny Lou's remark about the safe never being opened in all these years played on Odie's mind. Is that why she wouldn't sell the house? Because the bank money was locked in the safe in the attic?

He remembered how Great-Uncle Lemon disappeared right after the fight with Grandpa Moonie. What if Great-Uncle Lemon had tossed the combination to the safe into the ocean just to spite Grandpa Moonie? Was that why Grandpa Moonie started obsessively searching the beach? And what were the odds that that very same bottle, a whiskey bottle, had ended up in the hands of Digger Tubbs, who was right now pontificating in this very house?

Odie's legs had been moving as his mind made the connections. He was at the top of the winding staircase headed toward his bedroom, temporarily Digger's room. All he had to do was slip inside, find the bottle, and read the numbers on the note.

A round of applause sounded from below. For once, Digger hadn't been long-winded enough. Odie would have to hurry. He reached for the bedroom knob the same instant the door swung open, and nearly lost his supper.

"Granny Lou," he stammered out.

"Odie, why aren't you downstairs with the guests?" Granny Lou's lips looked naked without a cigarette.

"I . . . I needed something from my room. What are you doing here?"

"Making sure our guest of honor has fresh towels for the morning."

"Granny Lou? You and Digger, you're not . . ." He couldn't finish the sentence, could barely finish the thought in his head.

"I know you think I'm old, Odie, but I still got a right to my privacy. Now I need a cigarette." She swept past him. "And change your shirt. You stink. Nerves or not, you got a talk to give, so quit dawdling."

He entered his room or rather Digger's room. A pile of fresh towels sat on the corner of the dresser. Granny Lou hated doing laundry. She must have it bad for Digger. The thought made him gag. He found a clean shirt and quickly changed. Digger's suitcase sat on the end of the bed. He unzipped it and lifted the lid. Four bottles lay nestled inside. He lifted out the whiskey bottle. Sure enough it was Grandpa Moonie's favorite brand. But when Odie peered inside, it was empty. No slip of paper. He searched around the foam in case it had fallen out. Nothing.

"Odie." Granny Lou's voice called to him up the stairs like he was a little kid late for school.

He put the whiskey bottle back and zipped the case. He'd have to continue his search later. Maybe Digger forgot to put the note back and had it with him.

***

Everyone was waiting for Odie in the front room. Granny Lou sat with Digger in the back. A few people stifled yawns, but most looked eager to hear his talk.

Using the back of a chair for a podium, he told his heart to quit racing and began. "You've all heard of the legendary pirate Blackbeard—the fiercest pirate of them all?"

Everyone nodded.

"Did you know Blackbeard stayed here, in this very house, back when it was an inn? He and his crew had ambushed a ship in the dim light of dusk the previous night. Pirate ships are hardest to see in dawn and dusk."

There were murmurs of agreement.

Satisfied that he had their attention, Odie continued. "Legend has it that Blackbeard removed the gold from his ship while it was being repaired and brought it here with him, along with his wife. He drank hard, favoring whiskey, of course. Could be that whiskey bottle Digger found was from Blackbeard himself." All eyes turned to Digger who smiled and nodded.

That's when Odie noticed Granny Lou was gone.

"When Blackbeard was getting ready to leave, seems he had a falling out with his wife. Their fight could be heard clear across the ocean. Blackbeard got so angry, he up and hung her from an oak tree in the backyard. Sometimes, if you listen carefully, you can hear her screams in the night."

Odie paused for effect and everyone started talking at once. Some claimed they were going to stay awake all night to listen, others said they were going to search for the gold. Pleased by the reaction, he told a few more stories. When he finished, there was a general swapping of ghost tales.

Digger headed for the stairs. Odie escaped from the others to intercept him. He asked if he might have another look at Digger's collection. "Not tonight. Early bird catches the worm. Meaning I retire early so I can get up with the sun. That's why I'm so successful at finding bottles. Didn't you listen to my speech?" Digger brushed Odie aside, then paused and asked, "You haven't seen your Granny Lou, have you?"

Odie shrugged. "She's probably in bed so she can get up with the sun."

Digger, oblivious to the dig, nodded his approval. "See you in the morning," he said and climbed the stairs.

Odie waited until he heard the bedroom door shut, then made his way up. He knew dang well Granny Lou wasn't in bed yet. In fact, he was starting to have a darn good inkling of why she was so agreeable to this convention and where she was right now. He left the second floor behind and climbed the stairs to the attic.

He could hear her cursing even before he reached the top step. Dust motes danced in the light of the bare bulb. Granny Lou perched on a box in front of the safe, the slip of paper from Digger's bottle in her hand. She stared at him, her face streaked with dirt and frustration.

"I don't know what you think you figured out, Odie, but it doesn't matter. These aren't the numbers. The safe won't open. As your Grandpa Moonie would say, it was a long shot from hell."

"So I was right? The money from the bank is in there? That's why you never wanted to sell the house? Because you couldn't get the safe out and you didn't want to risk anyone discovering the money?"

Granny Lou stood, her shoulders hunched like she'd been beaten. "It doesn't matter." She walked past him, the slip of paper falling at his feet.

Odie picked it up and studied the numbers. Two were clearly legible in his Great-Uncle Lemon's peculiar slant. The ink had faded on the third number. Odie held it closer to the light. He could just make out the indentation in the paper. Could it be? Granny Lou's eyesight wasn't as good as his.

He went to the safe and spun the dial four times to the left, then stopped on the first number, three times to the right, then the second number, two times left, stopping on the third number, then he turned the dial to the right, until he heard a click.

He yanked the door open, but instead of the piles of cash he'd expected to see, there lay a single sheet of folded paper.

He picked it up, unfolded it, and read aloud, "I killed Lemon Dinkle."

The confession was dated August 13, 2003. Odie squinted at the signature, then looked at Granny Lou, who had come back to watch him work the safe.

"I don't understand," Odie said.

Granny Lou shook a cigarette from the pack in her sweater and lit it with trembling fingers. "Guess there's no sense keeping it from you now. Your Grandpa Moonie was a gambler, Odie. We never had money because as soon as he hit it big, he'd lose it all. It was a hard life, but he couldn't stop. He couldn't help himself. Lemon, he was a . . . a comfort." She exhaled sharply and blew the smoke toward the ceiling.

"When Moonie found out, he and Lemon went at it. I didn't realize, until I saw them struggling, how much I still loved Moonie. But your Great-Uncle Lemon, he was killing Moonie. I had to do something. So I shot him." She puffed hard, no doubt waiting for some kind of reaction.

Just to be sure he understood, Odie asked, "You killed Great-Uncle Lemon?"

"I didn't mean to. I never seen Moonie so angry, even though I chose him. He had me write that confession and locked it in the safe. Then he took the paper Lemon wrote the combination on, stuffed it in a bottle, and tossed it out to sea so I could never open it. He said if I ever tried to leave him again, he'd have the cops come in and bust open the safe."

Odie shook his head trying to make sense of it all. "So why did Grandpa Moonie spend all his time searching the beach after that?"

"He done what he did in the heat of the moment. We could never be a true married couple again with that damn confession hanging over our heads."

Odie thought about it. "So Grandpa Moonie never was a modern-day pirate."

Granny Lou gave him a sad smile. "Some stories, Odie dear, are just stories after all."

He handed Granny Lou the paper with her confession on it and watched her walk away. At least now they could sell the house. When he turned back to close the safe door, he noticed something else—a white sheet of paper laying so flat on the bottom he almost missed it.

He picked it up and turned it over to reveal a photocopied, hand-drawn map. The type someone might have made while sitting in a bar, downing a beer. Odie could see the ring stains from a long-ago drink in the right-hand corner. The handwriting was unfamiliar, almost elegant. Dotted lines and measurements crisscrossed the paper. And in the bottom left corner sat a dark X.

It took Odie a minute to understand what he was seeing. In his hands was a photocopy of Blackbeard's map to the hidden gold. Who had put it there? Great-Uncle Lemon? Grandpa Moonie? He blinked, then quickly folded the paper, shoved it into his back pocket, and closed the safe. Maybe they'd hold on to the old house just a little while longer after all.

# ANONYMOUS

## by Kate Flora

Conventions—strange cities, travelers' hotels—have a delightful anonymity ordinary life seldom affords. True, at this fashion writers convention, there would be people she knew, but they were all task driven, and even when they might chat over dinner or even for an hour in the bar, they didn't see each other. They were looking out. Looking for success. Contacts who could be used. However intimate the storytelling might get over a second or third drink, that would all be forgotten in the morning. No one who couldn't advance them mattered at all.

She was just like them: a predator. The difference was that at this particular convention, she wasn't after sales, contacts, new marketing ideas, or new people to connect with on LinkedIn. She was here because her annoyance with a business rival had reached the point where it had become a distraction from her forward momentum. In this phase of her five-year cycle, distractions were not a part of her business plan. She had always been ruthless about pursuing her goals. Right now, that meant eliminating the woman. She thought of it as a clearing of the air. Her air. Her airspace. Like finding a way to get rid of that annoying wisp of hair in the corner of her eye. Scratching an itch.

Her ex-husband had used the word *ruthless* as though it were a negative. Her "ruthless pursuit of success," he'd said, had caused the breakdown of their marriage. Unfortunate, since having a husband who took care of the house, the yard, and even the children had been liberating, freeing her to do what she needed to do. But his continual complaints about the ways she chose to go about things had undermined her. Drained the energy she needed to go out into the workplace every day and bring home the bacon.

Her ex had never been very honest about how much he enjoyed the bacon.

As she checked in, she surveyed the lobby. Bland wood, clusters of little chairs and sofas and tables, people, mostly women, with lanyards around their necks like lassoed cattle, and youngish men in tight pegged trousers, jackets over untucked shirts, and shoes without socks. In the far distance, the darker, more inviting bar, where she planned to spend most of her time. Some of the regulars were already there.

As if on cue, her victim, glamorous and rail thin, in a pencil skirt, silver leather jacket, and matching silver stilettos, strode through the room, beige stick legs working like chopsticks, oversized silver bag in the crook of one elbow. A veritable symphony in silver. The only big thing about her was her mass of curly black hair, styled a la Kardashian. Soon this symphony would crescendo, come to a smashing climax, and end on sad notes.

She was overcome by a sudden need for a martini. Up. Very dry. Three olives and a twist. Weren't olives a vegetable? One must eat vegetables, after all. Better get her suitcase into her room first. Hang up the fancy outfits that she would need to wear for the next few days. As she normally lived in a work uniform of designer jeans, crisp white shirts, and blazers, she jokingly called these fancier outfits her ball gowns. Everyone else would be wearing ball gowns, too. It frankly cost a fortune to attend one of these conventions just because of the clothes she had to buy. Never mind the good example set by the current FLOTUS of recycling outfits and buying at affordable stores. In this crowd, if your ass waggled by in something that wasn't designer, nostrils would rise and there would be faintly audible sniffs.

*They were all such liars*, she thought, heading toward the elevator. Dragging their little rolling suitcases to their identical, anonymous rooms, putting on their costumes and game faces, to emerge in the lobby, flashing their just-whitened teeth in red-lipsticked smiles and greeting each other like long-lost sorority sisters. She wasn't unique in her desire for revenge, or, as she liked to put it, reordering the world. A woman's talent for backstabbing was born and honed in middle school. It had always been more surprising to her that women could be friends than that they could be such good enemies.

She'd been at this hotel before and the design had always puzzled her. Despite attempts to make it seem stylish, with hanging plants and a tarted-up lobby, she figured the architect had developed his (definitely his, no woman would design a building with so much useless space) skills designing prisons. That's what the open atrium style and the rising tiers of rooms suggested. The way that doors banged and their closings echoed around the open center, all that was missing, really, was to replace wood with metal, put a guard tower in that odd space above the lobby, and you'd have the "big house."

She smiled to think that, if all went well, there would definitely be a crime here, and she, innocent-looking, blond, and sweetness itself, would be the criminal. People were so easily fooled by appearances. Writers might write about cold blue eyes or the eerie blue of a husky, but hers were the blue of summer skies and light. Cornflower blue, nice-girl blue, wide-eyed blue. She had pink and porcelain skin. Full pink lips that she left natural, just a touch of gloss in contrast to all that predatory red. Her fingernails and toes a demure rose in a room full of toes and fingers that looked like they'd been dipped in dried blood.

She hung her ball gowns in the closet and swapped her black leather blazer and pencil jeans for Louboutins, a Lacroix silk pencil skirt, and a cropped Armani jacket over a cream cami that only hinted at the black lace bra underneath. Swapped plain gold studs for chandeliers. Freshened her makeup. Then she tucked three small bottles and a small plastic baggie—two liquid doses of poison in case the first attempt failed, herbs in powdered form in the baggie in case she couldn't access her victim's glass, and a quick pick-me-up of gin—into her Cavalli bag next to the stupid cheaters she needed to read small print, and headed down to the bar.

During her unpacking and dolling up, the siren cry of that martini had been getting louder. She could almost taste the icy, astringent gin and hear the olives—always three, please—whispering "eat me" in a seductive, Mediterranean way. She drank at home, of course, but could never entirely get beyond her mother's admonition that a nice woman never drank alone; it was the first step down a slippery slope. Besides, she liked being alone in company better, surrounded by chatter and low light, and that almost religious moment when the glass, brimming with the slightly oily gin, was set before her.

When she sat at the bar, in a good bar, there was something like foreplay in watching the bartender stir that gin against the ice cubes. The tinkle of ice, the way the bar's pendant lights fragmented as they played on the silver of the stirrer and the shine of the cubes. The ceremony of the lemon twist—yes, olives *and* a twist, please—being swiped across the glass. A holy ritual. A pagan incantation. The prelude to a drink.

Across the bar, she saw her rival—Nemesis? Victim?—enter. Silver had become something else now. Something better with the raven hair. Bronze, maybe? Or was it just the light? She played with words, all those lovely words to describe the current trend toward metallics. She liked the phrase "shot with silver" or perhaps "shot with bronze." Of course, if she were to use a handgun in this crime, it would be "shot with brass," but brass led the mind automatically to "brassy," and that was a word never used—aloud at least—in this company.

Anyway, that was not how her victim would be departing this

life. She would shuffle off her mortal coil in a slower and rather nasty way. A shuffling that wouldn't even take place here, among these dear friends and colleagues. The plan was so natural, so organic. A simple plant, a plain item easily acquired from the natural world, would set the death in motion. Timing mattered, of course. The essential ingredient couldn't be given too soon. There would be a closing luncheon. They would be at the same table. It would take only a simple sleight of hand to introduce the chosen herb into her victim's lunch. Perhaps twelve hours later, when all traces had vanished from her victim's body, a slow paralysis would begin at the feet.

She stared into the oily swirls and imagined it. First those pretty little feet would wobble in their stilettos, going numb as the paralysis began. The woman might sit, rub her feet, wondering if maybe she'd finally damaged the nerves by forcing her entire body weight down on them. Then that numbness would spread to her knees, her thighs, gradually creeping up her body until it reached her lungs. Death would occur before paralysis reached the already Botoxed face. Stately, unstoppable death for which there was no remedy.

She especially liked this choice because her victim was such an advocate of all things natural. Mineral makeup. No animal testing. Yadda, yadda, yadda. Like having a face-lift and injections in her face were natural. Like converting frizz to elegant waves at a dry bar was natural? Or hair on a woman of fifty without a touch of gray?

What was natural was that a self-made woman like herself should resent a woman like that. A woman who'd invested vast amounts of her husband's money on becoming a presence in their field. Who'd risen not by her own smarts, but the smarts of a team of hired bloggers, PR folks, and stylists, her elegant slimness crafted by two hours a day with a devoted trainer.

A while ago, she had sat down and had a stern talk with herself about Nemesis and why the woman's purchased success bothered her so much. These days it was practically the norm. She could afford to do it herself. So what was there about this particular woman that made her a target?

She'd had the answer—because this woman pretended that it was all her. "Who me? A publicist? Never!" The list of those "who me? Nevers" was long, and they were all lies. She wasn't creative or insightful. She was just a good manager. Mother said that there was nothing on earth uglier than a woman liar. While there was much that she disagreed with her mother about, she agreed about this. She'd always been open about how hard she'd worked to get here, so when her victim, with a throwaway giggle, talked about her western country background—since when was Denver the country?—and her granny's egg remedy for shiny hair, she just wanted to gag. Granny's eggs had surely never been near that gleaming, exquisitely colored, and blow-dried head.

She set aside bad thoughts and gave herself over to pleasure, slipping on her cheaters for a moment to admire her drink. She approached a martini the way some people approached wine. First, she liked to inhale the aroma. Then take that first tiny sip. More and more, bars were ignoring traditional gins in favor of trendy, artisanal varieties. She lived and wrote in a world of trends, trends like sandals imbedded with copper disks to connect walkers with the earth because their actual feet never came in contact with actual earth. It was her job to have her finger on the pulse of trendiness. But when it came to gin, she was very traditional.

Ah. Nemesis was coming her way. Quickly tucking her cheaters away, she lifted her bag from the adjoining stool and swiveled with a warm greeting. Air kisses, the familiar "you're special to me" hand on a shoulder, and breathy compliments. She waved a hand at the seat. "Join me?"

"Love to, darling, but I have to run. TV interview you know. So tiresome." Shrug of the narrow shoulders. "But what can I do when they ask?" A beat and then the startling green eyes—colored contacts were a marvelous thing—swept the glass. "You're starting early."

"Am I?" She ran her blue eyes down the crowded bar. "I thought I was very much on trend here." A shrug of her own. "Oh well. I have that meeting with Anna later, and one must brace for her." Anna hadn't become editor of a major fashion magazine by being a pushover.

The eyebrows tried to rise but the frozen forehead wouldn't allow it. Nemesis settled for a slight pursing of the mouth. Something else to be avoided. One didn't want to get those little lines French women often had. Hateful the way lipstick would creep up them like blood up a pipette. "I'll see you at the cocktail party?" Nemesis said.

"Wouldn't miss it. Have a great interview. You look wonderful!"

Really it was true; Nemesis's stylist was excellent. Still, she thought her own printed silk pencil skirt was more interesting with its artsy, Parisian quality. Wasn't toning kind of yesterday?

A few lovely sips of her drink and she felt a warmth toward the world creeping through her. Martinis were like rose-colored glasses. They made the world look better. Even the small, flamboyant knot of boy bloggers at the far end of the bar, who usually annoyed her with their noise and gestures, seemed sweet, reminding her of her own son. She wished her son would turn off his video games, get out more, dress better. But that was her husband's influence. When she and her ex divorced, the children chose to go with him. A relief, really, but sometimes it depressed her to see them. Her daughter all Goth and pasty, acned skin, her son interested in nothing that didn't have to do with computers.

Nemesis gone and with no one looking her way, she slipped her cheaters back on and gazed into her glass, at the way the gin magnified the olives into plump green orbs. Just as well she didn't have the children live with her. They'd be a huge distraction. Children needed attention. So did building a career. At least she kept them in style. The ex might bitch, but he didn't have to work. If she'd been a man, nothing about who she was or how she approached earning a living would raise an eyebrow. Being hard charging and ambitious was unfeminine. Her mother again. But much of the world sent the same message.

So why was it that she begrudged her nemesis success? Did it really make such a difference how each of them went about it? Was she such a hateful person that someone else needed to fail so she could succeed?

No. It wasn't that. It was that her nemesis was just too damned nice. Or at least she pretended to be. Striving and fighting for position, and relentlessly connecting and networking and keeping her name out there, seemed to be something that Nemesis actually enjoyed. Nemesis also loved to flash pictures of her hunky spouse and children—all things she never enjoyed. She enjoyed her martini.

*** 

As she headed to the ballroom on Sunday morning, she reflected on the weekend. So tedious but rich in blog fodder. Plus Anna gave her peach assignments to do a couple of fascinating articles. And the workshops, for once, were content rich instead of boring or aimed at newbies who knew nothing. The boy blogger fashion parade was endlessly amusing, as was the way they jockeyed for attention with each other, instead of finding out who might advance their careers. Oh, Millennials. It was kind of like watching puppies at play.

At last it was almost over. Just the luncheon and a keynote address, and then she could strip off these Spanx and go back to her comfortable uniform again. She was at an A-list table, with some well-placed editors, fashion bloggers, and, of course, her nemesis.

Nemesis usually spent most of any meal table-hopping, which

she had counted on since she needed Nemesis away from her plate so certain ministrations could take place. But Nemesis didn't seem to be on her game today. Her makeup was too thick. Her hair too frizzy. She wasn't in her usual perky form. She wasn't leaving, and she wasn't eating.

"Are you all right?" she whispered.

Nemesis gave her a rigid smile. "I'm fine."

*Go visit other tables*, she thought. If wish were only father to the deed. But Nemesis remained glued to her chair. She didn't eat and she didn't converse and, dammit, she would not leave. Finally, it was coming down to a choice between trying to get the damned poison into her coffee or onto her dessert. Neither one was as easy as sprinkling the herbs on rubber banquet chicken while everyone was distracted, eating. She entertained the momentary thought that Nemesis was waiting to doctor *her* food, that this was a game that two could play.

Her agitation growing, she felt the call of a martini. But she couldn't publicly order a martini at the end of a luncheon. Luncheons suggested ladylike and genteel. She'd get labeled a lush. Not even a hard-charging businessman ordered a martini with coffee and dessert at a luncheon.

So no martini. And no poison either—when Nemesis finally excused herself to visit the ladies' room, it was too late. They were already clearing the plates.

As she left the room, the unused poison still in her purse, an old friend, and inveterate gossip, grabbed her arm and pulled her aside. "Did you hear? Did she tell you at lunch? It's just the saddest thing."

Was something wrong with Nemesis? "What's the saddest thing?"

"She's got one of those awful diseases."

Gossips just loved to string this stuff out, get the biggest bang for their stories. She put on her brightest and most curious smile. "What kind of a disease?"

"Oh. One of those ones where your body falls apart but your mind keeps working, so you kind of watch your body get more helpless and you can't walk or speak while your brain is still trapped in there. Honestly, if that happened to me, I'd want someone to kill me. Just put me out of my misery. And the poor thing. So lively and such a sweetheart. You know, she's never a snob, and she's so nice to everyone."

"She is nice. Nicest one of any of us."

"I guess she just got the news. Right while we were here. She was fine yesterday."

Gossip headed off to tell the gruesome tale to someone else.

She went into the ladies' room. Found it strangely deserted except for Nemesis, braced against the counter, staring unseeing into the mirror. Runnels of tears on her face and dripping off her chin. Still, her makeup was perfect, her mascara unsmudged, red lips still bright, shiny, and bold. Nemesis looked so brave.

She was swept by a wave of compassion. She rarely had time for it and rarely indulged it, but while she wanted Nemesis destroyed, she'd never wanted it to happen this way, via a slow and horrible death. And if she were honest with herself, she wanted to be the instrument. Not the devil or God or whoever sent these kinds of horrible things to torture people. She wanted Nemesis knocked off stage in her prime, not slowly fading with endless bouts of mourning.

"I just heard about your diagnosis," she said.

Nemesis nodded as she flicked a tissue from her purse and gently dabbed at the tears.

"Are they sure? Shouldn't you get a second opinion?"

"They're sure. They say it will happen very quickly. The losses, I mean."

She opened her purse, took out a little plastic vial, and handed it to Nemesis. "If you decide you want to be in charge, this will end things quickly and without a trace."

Nemesis tried to cock an eyebrow. It wouldn't move. She answered the unasked question. "For my mother-in-law. A nasty cancer. She asked if I would help. I'm seeing her tomorrow. I brought two, in case she fumbled it."

"Right. So kind," Nemesis murmured and tucked it in her purse.

***

Later, back in her own clothes and in the bar, she kept putting off the moment when she'd dive into that waiting martini. She decided to freshen her makeup, and came back from the ladies' room to find Nemesis on the stool next to hers with a martini of her own. Identical. Three olives and a twist. Nemesis seemed happier than she had at lunch. Even before tasting the drink, she was waving to someone across the room and sliding off the stool for a hug good-bye. Very much her old self again. It seemed the offer of an easy end had had a positive effect.

She slid onto the stool, set down her bag, then slipped out a vial and dumped the contents into Nemesis's drink.

Nemesis returned, sat on her stool, and lifted her glass. "To the future," Nemesis said.

And her suspicions were confirmed. Nemesis's fakey smile was so broad she knew the contents of the vial that she had given Nemesis now resided in her own glass. The hatred went both ways with them.

It didn't matter, though. She'd only given Nemesis her emergency stash of gin, carried in case a martini couldn't be had. The real stuff had been in the other vials. See, it was just like she'd thought all along. She'd made her way up by being smart and anticipating and planning, so she'd anticipated Nemesis's move, while Nemesis had staff to do her thinking. She was just a manager.

*** 

Before she left her minibar behind and headed for the airport, she grabbed a nip of gin to replace the vial she'd given to Nemesis. She opened her purse to set the gin beside her remaining vial of poison. But alas, when she slipped on her cheaters, she discovered it was gin, not poison, in that remaining vial.

Live by the sword, die by the sword. Or in this case, refuse to wear your glasses when you're traveling with a vain crowd, and suffer the consequences. She sighed for the columns she'd never write.

Twenty-four hours later, the poison had done its work—twelve hours to start and twelve more hours to do the job. Members of the fashion-writing community were grieved by the sad news of the deaths of two of their most beloved members.

# WHAT GOES AROUND

## by B.K. Stevens

The trick was not slowing down, not hesitating. Walk quickly, make his choice before taking the last step, grab, go, don't look back. He'd done it before, dozens of times, and it had always worked. He was that good. Still, though, he always felt the same excitement, the same small, sharp thrill of fear. Sometimes, he thought it was the fear he craved, more than whatever might be inside.

He chose it as soon as he saw it, seconds after it started going around on the carousel—that one, the large anonymous-looking brown one, slightly battered but good quality. The person who'd bought that suitcase might not be rich, but chances were he or she could afford to vacation in the D.C. area, or to go to one of the dopey weekend conventions held here. Or maybe he or she worked for a company successful enough to send employees on business trips to pricey cities. One way or another, the person who'd bought that suitcase had probably packed things worth stealing.

He walked up to the carousel, seized the handle, yanked it out, and strode away, pulling the suitcase behind him. Out of the corner of his eye, he saw two women walking toward the carousel, talking, laughing, nodding. Who knew? Maybe one of them owned the suitcase. If so, he was safe for sure, because they were too wrapped up in their conversation to notice him rolling their property away. They were casually dressed—slacks, sweaters, sensible shoes—and looked relaxed and happy. Probably not on a business trip, he decided. Tourists, then, or friends on their way to one of those dopey conventions.

Not that it mattered—not that he cared. Already, he'd reached the door. Another three seconds, and he was outside in the soft early-May heat. Safe, he exulted. He still had to walk to the hourly parking lot, but at this point it'd be silly to worry that some security guard would come running after him and tap him on the shoulder and—

Someone tapped him on the shoulder. "Excuse me, sir," the young woman said.

His spine snapped stiff, and he wheeled around to face her. No, not a security guard, just a pale, bony girl in her late teens, wearing threadbare jeans and a wrinkled orange T-shirt, her lank, dark blond hair falling halfway to her waist. His shoulders sagged in relief. "Who are you?" he demanded.

She shrugged. "I'm Maya. I noticed your suitcase looks really heavy, and I wondered if I could help out by pulling it to your car for you and—"

"Yeah, right," he cut in. "What do you think I am, some kind of idiot? I let you get your hands on my suitcase, and you'll run off with it and steal it."

She looked down at the pavement. "I couldn't do that, sir."

No, he realized, she probably couldn't. She looked too weak to run anywhere. Even rolling the suitcase behind her would probably take all the strength she had. "So you'll take it to my car and then hit me up for twenty bucks," he said. "Is that how it goes?"

"It wouldn't have to be twenty." Maya didn't look up, but he could tell she was blushing. "Five, maybe, or even one or two. I've made mistakes, and now I'm trying to put some money together so I can go home. I can't ask my mom. She's been pretty sick, and my stepfather stole her savings before he took off."

He chuckled. "Sure, sure. Everybody's got a sob story. You want that money for another fix, don't you? Or another bottle."

"No, sir." Finally, she looked up, her face bright pink now, but her eyes steady. "I swear. For a bus ticket. And maybe a sandwich."

That made him laugh out loud. "So now you're hungry, too. Great story, kid. I especially like the bit about the sick mother. Take an acting class, and maybe next time you can pull it off." He took a step closer. "Or maybe it's all true. You know what? I don't care. I work hard for my money, and I'm not gonna hand it out to losers whining about their tough breaks. Get a job. Another five seconds, and I call the cops and have you arrested for panhandling. Go on, now. Take off."

She took off. He walked the rest of the way to his car, dragging the suitcase behind him, shaking his head. Pathetic, he thought. The only way she can even try to support herself is by begging. She should come up with something better. Take me, for example. Sure, my business involves some risk. And it takes initiative, it takes creativity, it takes courage. But I do it. Day after day, I get up in the morning, I go to an airport or a mall or a Metro station, and I do it. If I see something I want, I take it. I don't beg for it. Begging? That'd be beneath me.

*** 

Delores looked up from her computer screen. "Another suitcase? Really, Eddie? That's all you brought home today?"

"Plus dinner." He set the still-warm brown paper bag on the

table, kissed her on the forehead, straightened up. "Chinese, I think. I'm pretty sure I smell ginger. I stopped off to pick up a six-pack, spotted this dumb broad fussing over belting her brat into a car seat. She'd left the bag sitting on the hood, never noticed when I snatched it and strolled away. So. You wanna eat first, or you wanna see what's in the suitcase?"

"You see what's in the suitcase. I'll eat." She reached into the bag, pulled out the first white cardboard carton, peered into it, made a face. "Oh, yuck. *Moo goo gai pan.* You know I hate mushrooms."

"So eat something else. It's a big bag. There's gotta be something you like in there." He heaved the suitcase onto the sofa, unzipped it, paused in anticipation. Maybe this time, he thought. Maybe, finally, this would be the payoff. He pulled the cover back. "Here goes nothing."

He started pawing through it. "Clothes, mostly," he announced, feeling the usual disappointment well up again. "Mostly nothing special."

Delores sniffed the carton of mongolian beef. "Men's or women's?"

"Women's. So you'll be the one hitting consignment shops this time." He held up a pale blue blazer. "Decent quality, but I don't see any designer labels or—wait a minute." He reached deeper into the suitcase, took out a silky silver-gray dress, and peered at it. "Nope. Not designer. It's classy, though. Maybe you'd like to keep this one for yourself."

She glanced at it. "Too small. Anything else besides clothes?"

"Lemme see. What's this?" He pulled out something long, fuzzy, and purple. "A feather boa? I had a great-aunt used to wear one of these, and even back then we all snickered at her. How come someone who picked out such a classy dress also picked out a ridiculous thing like that?" He lifted something else out of the suitcase. "Or a ridiculous thing like this?"

It was a hat, broad brimmed and high crowned, made of some stiff hot pink lacy stuff, decorated with large organza daisies and long, flowing green ribbons. He stared at it, then shrugged. "I don't get it."

"Maybe she's going to a costume party," Delores said, and chuckled. "Poor little thing. No costume now. Anything *good* in there? Jewelry, electronics, prescription drugs? *Anything?*"

He grabbed a small wooden box, glanced in it, tossed it aside. "Earrings and stuff, but all costume—nothing that'd interest my fence. I guess everybody knows not to pack good jewelry in checked luggage now. Toothpaste, deodorant, cosmetics, perfume.

Oh—here's something electronic. A travel alarm clock."

Delores snorted. "Great. We only got about twenty-eight of those. Maybe we should open up a travel alarm clock store. We already got the stock. How about shoes?"

He picked up a shoebox and pulled out a pair of silver-and-black flats. "These look nice. Not much of a heel, but they got buckles—crystal, I think. Manolo Blahnik, the label says. You ever heard of that?"

"Oh yeah." Delores tossed aside her eggroll and walked over to look at the shoes. "This is good, Eddie. I've seen these online. Upscale but comfortable, leather lining, made in Italy—new, these things sell for hundreds, sometimes over a thousand. You're holding half a month's rent in your hands."

"Fantastic," Eddie said. "So tomorrow you'll take these to a consignment shop and—"

"No. They're size six. That's awful small. Consignment shops might not want to take them. Even if they did, it might take them months to sell. We can't wait that long to make rent."

Eddie scratched his head. "So they're no use to us?"

"Sure they are." Delores grabbed the shoes, carried them back to the kitchen table, took out her cell phone, snapped a picture, turned to her computer, and started typing. "You gotta get with the program, Eddie. Technology's a wonderful thing. Somewhere in the D.C. area, there's a woman who wears size six shoes and owns a dress that'd go perfect with these. But consignment shops aren't the quickest way to reach her. Leave this to me. So. Anything else that looks like it's worth anything in that suitcase?"

"I don't know." Eddie raked through the suitcase again, lifted out a large fabric bag, and peered inside—something pink and soft, a ball of yarn, a pair of knitting needles. "Looks like about three-fourths of a sweater. Looks nice. Maybe, if you finished it, we could—"

Delores snorted again. "Me? Knit? Get serious. I got no time to waste on knitting. That goes in the garbage. What else?"

He held up something wrapped in tissue paper. "Maybe this is a present for somebody? Let's see." He unwrapped it and sighed. "Nope. Just a book. Looks like an old book. A used book. There's a name written on the inside front cover. Sorta scratchy, sorta hard to read. Dorothy Somebody." He started flipping pages. "Not a high-quality book, either. Full of misspellings—*rumour, centre, colour.* Guess it was put out by some fly-by-night publisher who couldn't afford to get it edited."

"Worthless." Delores scooped up some rice. "That goes in the garbage, too. Not much of a haul, but maybe you can get a pawn shop to give you a few bucks for the suitcase. You might as well come eat. Afterward, we'll go through everything more careful, pick out anything a consignment shop might take, stuff the rest in a trash bag so you can toss it in a dumpster. No sense hanging onto junk that'll clutter up the place and might get us in trouble with the cops if the owner files a complaint. I still got high hopes for those shoes, though. I bet I can make them pay off. And maybe you'll have better luck tomorrow. Maybe you should try a public library again. People get feeling too comfortable, leave their purses sitting on tables while they slobber over books. You did pretty good there last time. You should go back."

"Great idea, Delores." Eddie grabbed a spoon and lit into the now-tepid carton of *moo goo gai pan*. "First thing tomorrow, I head for a library."

***

"I feel awful about the sweater, Lisa," Sharon said. "You were so close to finishing it, and it was looking so beautiful."

"I should never have put it in the suitcase." Lisa clipped the tags off the pajamas she'd bought less than an hour ago. "But I couldn't fit everything in a carry-on, and I didn't want to take both. Anyway, the TSA people might've given me a hard time about the knitting needles, and—oh, I shouldn't have brought it at all. It's just that I enjoy knitting during the panels, and I wanted to get it finished before my aunt's birthday. I should've known better."

"You're being too rough on yourself," Sharon said. "Who could foresee something like this? I fly all the time, and I never think twice about whether the airline might lose my luggage."

"Or about whether someone might steal it." Lisa sorted through the shopping bag of toiletries—toothpaste, deodorant, cosmetics, perfume. "I bet that's what happened—I bet someone snatched it before we made it to baggage claim. That's why I filed a police report. The officer was sympathetic, but he didn't seem optimistic about my chances of ever seeing my stuff again. Honestly, I don't know why airlines still bother with claim checks and luggage tags. It's been years since I've seen anyone stationed at a baggage claim to make sure the checks and the tags match up."

"I read an article about that," Sharon said. "Apparently, before September eleventh, lots of airports hired private security guards to police the baggage claims. After September eleventh, the TSA took over airport security, and making sure people left the airport with the right luggage wasn't a priority. The TSA focuses on what people take *onto* planes. After you get off, you're on your own."

Lisa sighed. "I guess that makes sense. Anyway, it helps that everyone's being so nice. Wasn't it sweet of Barb to spend the dinner break driving us around to stores so I could buy toiletries and so on? And I'm so glad that Diane packed an extra outfit, and that she lent it to me for the banquet. It's adorable!"

"It is," Sharon agreed. "It's too bad you won't have a boa for the breakfast, though, or a hat for the tea."

"That's okay. Most people don't wear hats to the tea anymore, now that we've stopped having the contests. And it was time to retire the boa—it shed feathers every time I sneezed. I'll get a sturdier one for next year. But I dread telling Don about the shoes. He insisted I buy them. They were a once-in-a-lifetime indulgence, for our twenty-fifth anniversary. He'll be so sad to hear they're gone."

Sharon nodded slowly. "Those shoes are so valuable. If your suitcase *was* stolen, do you think the thief might fence them? Do you think the police might be able to trace them? Or wouldn't a fence be interested in size six designer shoes?"

"Probably not." Lisa walked over to the laptop set up on the desk. "But maybe the thief would be tempted to try a more direct approach. It'd be risky—it'd be stupid—but he or she might try anyway. We love reading mysteries about clever criminals, but in real life, most criminals aren't all that smart. I'll check Craigslist."

Sharon glanced at her watch and stood up. "Better check it later. We should go. It's almost seven thirty."

"You go. I can't stand to go to the auction this year. I'm too sick at heart about the book."

"I know." Sharon sat back down on the bed. "It's so terrible. A first edition *Murder on the Orient Express*—Dorothy Sayers's personal copy, with her name written on the inside front cover. I remember how touched you were when your mother left that to you, and I thought you were incredibly generous to donate it to the auction. I can't imagine how devastated you must feel about losing it. Look, I don't have to go to the auction, either. I'll stay here and keep you company."

"Thanks, but you should go. Maybe there will be something you want to bid on, and it's for a good cause. I'm going to play around on Craigslist for a while—not that I seriously expect to find anything, not that I seriously think even a thief could be stupid enough to advertise there. Then I'll join you at the welcome reception. Quarter of nine, right?"

"Right." Sharon looked at her doubtfully. "If you're sure."

"I'm sure. Honestly, I'll feel better if you go, if I can brood by myself for a while and work my way into a better mood. Then we'll eat all the chocolate in sight at the reception, and by tomorrow morning I'll be feeling great, ready to enjoy every minute of the conference."

Sharon smiled at her. "Okay. And who knows? Maybe you'll spot your shoes on Craigslist."

"Maybe," Lisa said, smiling back as Sharon left. But she didn't feel hopeful as she turned to the computer screen. Thieves couldn't really be foolish enough to advertise stolen goods on Craigslist, could they?

They could. A few clicks and she found it—an off-center, slightly fuzzy picture of her silver and black, size six Manolo Blahnik flats with square crystal buckles, sitting on a crumb-littered kitchen table, with something white and soggy-looking off to the side—a carton of Chinese food, maybe? The thief wanted six hundred dollars for the shoes, but they were worth so much more than that to Lisa and her husband, for sentimental reasons even more than financial ones.

She dug through her purse until she found the number of the police officer she'd spoken to when she reported the possible theft, now a definite theft. Maybe he could set up a sting right away. Chances were, she wouldn't get her shoes back in time for the banquet—they'd probably be held as evidence for the trial—but she'd get them back eventually. More important, the thief or thieves could be arrested before they had a chance to victimize someone else. That was what really mattered.

What about the book? That was the loss that hurt her most. She went back to Craigslist and clicked on "books." Textbooks, cookbooks, children's books, last month's bestsellers. No unspeakably precious classic mysteries written by Agatha Christie and signed by Dorothy Sayers. The thieves probably didn't realize how much it was worth, Lisa thought as she dialed the police officer's number. They probably tossed it into the fireplace or dumped it in the garbage. That's so sad. Maybe the officer can put these thieves out of business. Maybe he can eventually get my shoes back. But the book is gone forever. From the moment I first read my mother's will and saw she'd left it to me, I'd hoped I could use that book to do some good, to help somebody in some way. There's no chance of that now.

***

The night had turned cold. Maya wandered the streets, hugging her thin arms against her chest, longing for home.

Her stepfather had made life at home unbearable, and her mother had been oblivious to what was going on. Then Cal had come along, and he'd made escape seem possible, exciting, irresistible. But he'd proven to be as bad as her stepfather. She'd been on her own for five months, and then she'd found out her mother was on her own now, too, and sick, and broke. They needed to be together so they could help each other. Wisconsin was so far away, though. Maya didn't know how she could ever get back there.

She kept walking, hoping to find a safe place to sleep for a few hours, and spotted a dumpster down the block. Maya hated going through dumpsters. She'd done it many times, but it disgusted her. Always, there were roaches. Often, there were rats. But she was cold and hungry and desperate. She had no choice.

She walked over to it, gathered all her strength, forced up the lid, pulled out the top trash bag. Not too bad. It looked like a relatively fresh bag, like it hadn't spent much time here. Maybe she'd get a break tonight. Maybe it was finally time for things to come around for her.

She lugged the bag into an alley, sat on the ground, and gritted her teeth. Please, she thought, don't let there be anything too gross in here.

The first thing she found was a large brown paper bag—soggy, but it smelled pretty good. Ginger, she thought. Chinese. She opened up carton after carton, using her fingers to scrape up remnants—a little chicken and lots of mushrooms in some kind of white sauce, beef and vegetables in some kind of brown sauce, rice. And half an egg roll—clammy, but it made her stomach stop churning. Now. What else could she find?

She found a pajama top, pulled it on, and stopped shivering. And that fabric bag looked pretty. She looked inside—knitting needles, a ball of soft pink yarn, about three-fourths of a sweater. It's lovely, she thought, stroking it, pressing it to her face and savoring its warmth. I bet it'd fit Mom just right, and Grandma taught me how to knit. I could work on this on the bus, and if I kept at it steady, I could finish it in time for Mother's Day. It'd be a way of telling Mom I'm sorry I left, of saying from now on we're in this together.

She sighed. She could picture herself sitting on that bus, knitting this sweater for her mom. But it was a fantasy. How could she ever get on a bus when she had no money for a ticket?

She pushed the image away and kept going through the bag, stuffing everything she could use into her pockets or the fabric bag. Toothpaste, deodorant, cosmetics. And half a bottle of perfume—how long had it been since she'd worn perfume? She dabbed some on and instantly felt better. She found something purple and fuzzy and frowned at it in confusion; she found a pink hat decorated with daisies and smiled at it before putting it back in the trash bag. Then she spotted a book.

I know this book, she thought, staring at the cover. Agatha Christie, *Murder on the Orient Express*—Grandpa read this to me when I was a little girl. And this copy looks really, really old. It couldn't be a first edition, could it?

She checked the copyright page: 1934. That seemed about right. She flipped a few pages, scanning them quickly. Rumour, centre, colour—obviously, this hadn't been printed in the United States. England, maybe. As she turned back to the copyright page to make sure, she noticed the name scrawled on the inside front cover. Dorothy L. Sayers—wasn't that the woman who wrote *Gaudy Night*? Grandpa had given her a copy of that book for her thirteenth birthday. He'd loved golden-age mysteries, and his enthusiasm had made her love them, too.

She also knew someone else who loved them. That nice old lady—in January, she'd let Maya shovel her sidewalk, and had paid her more than Maya would have dared to ask for. Then the lady had invited her to come inside, and they'd sat in her elegantly furnished living room and shared a pot of tea. The walls were lined with books, more books than Maya had ever seen outside a library. Maya had mentioned them, and the lady had said she collected books and especially loved mysteries. She'd been delighted to learn that someone as young as Maya had read Agatha Christie and Dorothy Sayers. When Maya left, the lady tried to give her another twenty dollars, but Maya said no. She'd do odd jobs for people, and if they paid her too much, she took it, even though she knew they were giving it to her out of pity. But she wouldn't beg, and she wouldn't take outright charity.

This time, she wouldn't have to. She had something she could sell. She didn't know how much the book was worth, but the lady probably would. Maybe it'd be enough for a bus ticket.

Maya stood up. It'd be a long walk to the lady's house, but Maya could reach it by morning, especially since she felt so full of energy now. She'd tell the lady the truth about how she found the book, but she bet the lady wouldn't mind. Maybe she'd think the story about finding the book was interesting. Maya smiled. Maybe, while she was telling the story, the lady would give her a cup of tea.

But first she should clean up here. Maya put everything she wasn't keeping back in the bag and carried it to dumpster. The lid didn't feel nearly as heavy now. Then she hesitated. I'll keep one more thing, she decided, and opened the bag again. There it was. She grabbed it, tossed the bag into the dumpster, and walked away, a new bounce in her step.

As she walked, she inspected her just-claimed treasure and

smiled. This thing always made her smile. Really, she thought, it doesn't look silly. It looks pretty. And it's the perfect thing to wear while enjoying a cup of tea.

She put the hat on her head and quickened her pace.

# THE HAIR OF THE DOG

## by Charles Todd

*London, 1920*

The Royal Society of Geographers was having its annual conference in the Society's handsome red brick headquarters in Kensington. It was an important event, as they were expecting to publish a report on the frontier changes brought about by the Treaty of Versailles and its aftermath. New lines had been drawn, new countries had emerged, and mapping these was of paramount importance. Members as well as guests from the Empire and Colonies were expected to attend, as were geographers from other countries.

Friday evening was set aside for a dinner with a speaker who'd just returned from Tanganyika, where he'd been studying changes in the former German colonies after the Armistice.

The Honourable Henry Mellon Grayson had followed in the footsteps of his illustrious explorer father, Lord Grayson, who had devoted his life and his fortune to geography and had been instrumental in the mapping of Nepal and Tibet. His son had chosen tribal Africa for his life's work.

Dinner was served at eight sharp, with a brief welcome by the Prince of Wales, standing in for his father. Grayson's speech was scheduled for nine thirty.

The American delegation, led by Thomas Meadowes, was seated near the head table, and during the meal they struck up a conversation with their Canadian counterparts seated across from them.

It was a little before nine when Grayson excused himself, nervously adding that he needed a moment to prepare himself for his talk.

Half an hour later, as the last course dishes were being removed and the coffee service was wheeled in, Lord Willingham, the head of the Society, looked at the guest's still empty chair and quietly summoned a waiter.

"Will you look in the cloakroom, if you please, and inform Mr. Grayson that I am ready to present him?"

The waiter nodded and disappeared quietly in the direction of the antechamber where drinks had been served earlier. The cloakrooms were just off the passage beside it.

He returned very quickly, bent over Lord Willingham's shoulder, and said something in his ear. Willingham, his glass raised halfway to his lips, sat there without moving for a moment. Then he set his glass down carefully, excused himself to his neighbor, the Prince, and followed the waiter from the dining room.

Five minutes later, Willingham used the recently installed telephone in the lobby off the Society governor's office, and put in a call to Scotland Yard.

* * *

Chief Superintendent Markham had left for the evening. When the call came in, Sergeant Gibson studied the duty roster and then hurried down the passage to knock lightly on Inspector Ian Rutledge's door.

Rutledge called, "Come," and then, as he saw it was Gibson, he said, "No. I've finished for the day. It will have to wait."

"There's a call come in from Kensington, sir. The Royal Society of Geographers. An attendant will be at the door to meet you. There's a dead man in the cloakroom, and the Prince of Wales is a guest. Sir, it's you or Watkins."

Watkins? At the Royal Geographers? He shuddered at the thought. The man would make a muddle of it. Besides, the Society's proceedings were private, although the highly regarded journal it published was available for a subscription.

Rutledge was tired; it had been a long day. And yet the chance to step inside the well-guarded portals was tempting. "I'll need a team to cordon off the premises. See to it, will you? They haven't moved the body, have they?"

"No, sir. I was going off duty at twelve, myself, but I'll head up the constables, if you like."

Rutledge was surprised. The taciturn Gibson avoided large private gatherings of any sort. Why would a conference of the Geographers be any different? Was the sergeant human enough to be curious as well?

"Done." He set the report he'd just finished in his desk, locked the drawer, and with a nod to Gibson, left the Yard.

As he drove toward Kensington, Rutledge heard Hamish MacLeod's voice from the seat behind him, the voice that had given him no peace since the Somme Offensive of 1916, following him through the rest of the war and to the Yard when he returned to duty there. The young Scots corporal was dead. He'd seen him die, and Rutledge was no believer in ghosts. But he'd never had the courage to look over his shoulder to see if Hamish was there. Dr.

Fleming had called it survivor's guilt, and told him he must find a way to deal with it, but Dr. Fleming didn't have to live with Hamish sharing his head. The general public called it shell shock and considered anyone who suffered from it nothing less than a coward, lacking the moral fiber expected of an English soldier.

The general public had never been in the bloody trenches of Flanders.

"Ye'll be all the night questioning the lot of them," Hamish said. "Men who spend more time in the back of beyond than in England? Ye ken, they could kill a dozen men and who would know the difference?"

"I won't know if it's murder or natural causes until I get there," Rutledge replied, and caught himself speaking aloud. A habit he found it hard to break. "Either way, the Society did the right thing, summoning the Yard."

But when he got to Kensington and rang the bell at the Society's door, the man who opened it, his dress telling Rutledge that he was a waiter, looked shaken.

Rutledge identified himself and was led without a word to the passage outside the cloakroom, where Lord Willingham himself was standing guard. The head of the Society was easily recognized: his luxurious white moustache was famous.

Willingham nodded as Rutledge identified himself a second time, and said, "In there, Inspector." He indicated the cloakroom. "I don't think I can bear to see him again."

Rutledge opened the door and stepped inside the cloakroom. It was paneled like the antechamber, a rich dark wood, but the fixtures were porcelain and the tap handles were globes, the countries and the oceans detailed exquisitely. The floor was marble in the popular black and white diamond pattern.

The dead man lay just inside, his eyes wide and bulging. His face was nearly black, his tongue protruding. There were a number of daggers in his chest, each with a distinctive handle. Wood, steel, horn, inlaid with precious metals, or gold decorated with jewels. Rutledge counted eight.

Looking at them, his first thought was of Julius Caesar, waylaid in the Senate. One man stabbed by many so that no single person could be blamed for the killing. Standing together in murder, friend and enemy alike. But where was this man's Brutus?

He knelt by the corpse, trying to determine if one knife had done the deed, or if Grayson had bled to death internally from so many wounds. There was not a great deal of blood around the body. But only the postmortem could answer how Grayson died. What intrigued Rutledge was the man's face. Had there been some sort of poison on those daggers? He remembered what Hamish had said about geographers and exotic corners of the world. Anything was possible.

Not a tribal killing, he thought. Or a religious one. Not in London.

Were the daggers a warning? Or an explanation?

He rose to his feet and examined the windowless room. There was no sign of a struggle. And only one door led in and out of it. He rather thought no one had lain in wait—it would have been impossible to know when or if Grayson would come in here, or even if he would be alone. Who then had followed him? Surely the absence of eight men from the banquet tables would have been noticed?

Satisfied that he'd seen all he needed to see at the moment, he walked to the door. "Who found the body?" he asked Willingham.

"The waiter. The man who let you in. Coffee is still being served, they haven't really noticed his absence yet. Grayson's, I mean. The Prince is here, with small entourage. What shall I do about that? The King won't care to hear his heir has been questioned in a murder case."

"Is there a doctor among the attendees tonight?"

"Yes, Dr. Haldane. He's a medical missionary as well as a cartographer."

"Then find him. Announce to the diners that the speaker has been called away, but that he will be returning within the half hour. After you've done that, speak quietly to the Prince's equerry. Ask him to take the Prince to a private parlor and wait with him there. But casually. All of this should be done casually."

Willingham said, "And how am I to be casual, after seeing that?"

"Surely you've seen worse on your travels," Rutledge replied.

"Good God, man, he was a friend. And murder *here*? Not even when John Speke and Richard Burton fiercely contested the finding of the source of the Nile was there bloodshed. Although," he added, almost as an afterthought, "it was a close run thing."

With a nod Willingham walked through the anteroom and after the briefest pause, straightened his shoulders and opened the door into the dining room. Rutledge could hear voices, louder now as the meal and wines had relaxed the guests. He walked to the door and through a crack studied the conference attendees. At a guess, half a hundred well-dressed men sat at the long tables. The room itself was quite handsome, dark paneling lined with oil portraits of famous geographers, and he could just see the Prince of Wales seated beneath the likeness of the Society's founder. Quietly closing the door again, he turned to the waiter.

"Have you kept the outer door locked?"

"Yes, sir, I have. And the other doors as well."

"Have any of the guests left the room during the dinner, to your knowledge?"

"No, sir, every plate was accounted for. Nor are there any empty chairs."

"How did you come to find him?" Listening to the man's account, he added, "And no one followed him into the cloakroom?"

"Sir, no, not to my knowledge. It's usually not until coffee has been served that there is a general exodus. Before the speaker. Although I've never been fond of coffee myself. What is served here comes from the highlands of Ethiopia, I'm told." He reached into his coat pocket for a copy of the menu. "It's all foreign dishes, for that matter. The soup was an African bean dish, and in the main course, the potatoes were from Peru, the aubergine from France, and so on. The pudding has maple syrup in place of toffee sauce, as a nod to our North American guests."

"How many guests are there tonight?"

"Sixty, sir. And twenty-seven staff to prepare and serve the meal." As if anticipating his next question, the waiter added, "All of them have been with us for at least ten years, save for two who came after the war. Offering a soldier a job." That had been essential to help the severe unemployment that had followed the Armistice.

"Grayson is a member, I take it?"

"Yes, sir." The dining room doors opened and the Prince of Wales came out, an equerry at his shoulder. The waiter bowed, and Rutledge formally inclined his head. He had met the Prince once before during a royal visit to the battlefields.

"What's this about?" the Prince asked, looking from the waiter to Rutledge.

"There's been an accident in the cloakroom, Your Royal Highness," Rutledge said. "A rather unpleasant one. We thought it best for you to leave the dining room as inconspicuously as possible and wait in more comfortable surroundings."

"An accident. You're from the Yard, aren't you? Captain . . . Rutledge, is it? Yes, I thought so. Then it is a suspicious death."

"I'm afraid so, sir. The evening's speaker."

"Grayson?" the Prince asked in surprise. "Good God. Would you prefer that I leave? It will make your evening less—er—complicated."

"If I may ask, sir, if you've visited the cloakroom this evening?"

The Prince smothered a smile. "No, I have not. Nor has Mandville, here. You have my word."

"Then it might be more comfortable for everyone if you considered making this an early night, sir."

"Thank you, Inspector. Yes. I rather think I shall." With a nod to his equerry, who went to fetch their hats, the Prince said, "If you will convey my excuses to Lord Willingham?"

"I'll be happy to, sir."

The equerry returned, and the two men went toward the door, the waiter scurrying ahead to unlock it, then close and lock it behind them.

"I didn't know the Prince was such a short person," he said, coming back to stand by Rutledge. Just then the dining room doors opened again and a thin, sallow man stepped through them.

"Dr. Haldane. Willingham says there's a problem."

"In the cloakroom," Rutledge told him, and followed him, leaving the waiter to stand guard.

"My God," Haldane said, stepping back and nearly colliding with Rutledge as he saw the body for the first time. And then, after a moment, he said, "Dead, of course. But not for very long, I daresay." He went forward to stare down at the body. "My God," he said again, this time almost to himself. Kneeling, he examined Grayson. "I should think that one, with the horn handle, might have done the trick. He would be incapable of defending himself as the others struck. But alive." He gestured toward the handles. "I recognize these. They come from a display in the Members Room. Or there are others very like them on the walls there."

"Show me."

"You aren't a member, are you?"

"Nevertheless."

"Quite. Very well, this way." He rose and led the way back to the antechamber, taking another door, walking down a short passage, and then opening one more.

There was a lamp burning in the room, and Rutledge could see that it was cavernous, with a high vaulted ceiling, dark paneling, and an array of chairs that could be used to read or be set aside for more to brought in for other events. He stepped farther into the room. There were bookshelves containing an array of volumes, several globes and an astrolabe, chart tables with many drawers, and maps everywhere, in books, in portfolios, under glass. There was also a king's ransom of treasures in cases and mounted on the walls. He looked into several of the table cases and saw a shrunken head from Borneo, a shaman's pouch from the American Southwest, a variety of witch doctors' bags containing God knew what, and an assortment of arrows from the Amazon, with vials of the poison designed for the tips lying beside each. All neatly labeled.

He found himself thinking the Yard's Black Museum of crime weapons could hardly compare to this room. But it was the space above the doors to the room that interested Rutledge. An array of weapons of every imaginable variety and probably every era and continent were displayed in patterns.

Haldane turned up several lamps. Rutledge could see, above the door he'd just entered, an intricately patterned "rose" formed of daggers.

And eight empty spaces where there were none.

So much for the weapons. Now the question was, who had wielded them? And why had Grayson's face turned black? He went back to the glass cases for another look and noted that all of them were carefully locked.

With Sergeant Gibson's help, he spent the next two hours interviewing the dinner guests. They were—they claimed— appalled to a man to hear of Grayson's death. They appeared to be cooperative and helpful. Grayson had no enemies. They were sure of it. He was a fine man, a fine geographer, an ornament to the Society. He had had a glorious career mapping Africa, and everyone had looked forward to his speech with great anticipation. The subject, Rutledge learned, dealt with the relationship of African tribes to the land they occupy and the difficulty of drawing modern boundaries that didn't divide them into minorities in one nation and the majority in another. The title was "The Potential for Genocide Resulting from Improperly Drawn Frontiers."

Rutledge made a show of examining each man's hands, but he had no real interest in them. The killer, after all, could have washed them in the cloakroom. But the cuffs he found intriguing. Not a speck of blood on any of them. What had been used to protect the wearer as each hand thrust a dagger into the body? As Rutledge took statements and searched for answers, he saw small clusters of guests questioning Willingham and Haldane, but both men invariably shook their heads in answer.

It was well after midnight before Rutledge had questioned every man present, member or staff. Haldane had gone to oversee the removal of the body, and the guests were pressing to be allowed to leave. Willingham had been trying without success to set up a future dinner.

Gibson, coming to stand beside him, said under his breath, "You'd think, sir, that the killer was invisible. In and out without a soul seeing him. Now, I'd not be surprised if this had been a magician's convocation. But geographers?"

It was then that Hamish spoke for the first time: "Search the room."

Rutledge frowned. He thought Gibson and his men had done just that while he was questioning the guests. He walked toward the head table, which had been cordoned off just as the announcement of Grayson's death had been made. Two sturdy constables blocked access to it still.

He searched the chairs closest to the speakers, looking under them, then concentrated on the remnants of pudding congealing on the plates. It was there that he found a small folded square of paper, just under Grayson's dish. It read, simply, *Did you taste the difference in your soup? You are a dead man.*

He was considering it and the handwriting when Haldane came up to him.

"Strangest thing I ever saw, Rutledge. Dead man's face is perfectly normal now."

"Are you sure?" He looked up from the message in his hand.

"Damn it, man, I'm a doctor."

They went together to have a look. Grayson was lying on a stretcher in Reception, wrapped in a sheet, save for the head, and Rutledge could see that the doctor was absolutely right. Grayson's face, pale in death, was no longer black.

Africa. The soup. Rutledge turned to Haldane.

"Are you quite certain those daggers killed him? Or was he poisoned, and the daggers merely a trick to confound the Yard?"

"You can't be serious!"

"But I am. He must have realized he'd been poisoned and tried to rid himself of it. Poisoned with something for which there was no possible antidote. He must have seen it in his travels. He must have *known* what to expect. And on the menu, the soup was described as African." Rutledge held out the note, so that only Haldane could see it.

"But everyone drank the same soup."

"A good point. But he had only to *believe* he'd been poisoned for it to work."

Shocked, Dr. Haldane stared. Finally he said, "Of course, there's the castor bean. If one swallows it whole, the body's system destroys any harmful effect, but if bitten into, it causes a very painful death. We were served a bean soup, after all." He listed two or three other poisons, adding, "And that's merely what *I've* learned. There must be a dozen—two—more that I don't know. But dagger or poison, this man died by someone's hand."

"So he did. Do you have a magnifying glass in your case?

Good, give it to Sergeant Gibson. But before you do, see the stretcher out, and return to the dining room. Gibson, collect the guests there. The staff as well. Then guard the doors."

In five minutes' time, Rutledge had his audience, still impatient, still demanding release, or standing ill at ease amongst the men they'd served.

He regarded all of them for a moment, then reached into his pocket. He took out his handkerchief and made a show of carefully opening it up.

"Mr. Grayson died at the hands of a killer. He is in this room now. But Mr. Grayson didn't die quickly. He had time to leave us a clue to his murderer."

There was instant uproar. Rutledge waited until it had subsided.

"In my hand I have this clue. Will the staff please move to the right side of the room. Yes, thank you. And the guests to the opposite side of the room." There was grumbling, but it was done. "Thank you. Sergeant Gibson, will you please begin with the trouser legs of the staff, and examine them carefully, making note of what you may find there."

Gibson stared at him, then with two of his constables, he slowly walked down the line of nervous, frightened waiters, cooks, and other staff, writing in his book after each inspection. Finishing, he came forward to where Rutledge was standing. Leaning over he whispered, "What the hell was I looking for, sir? Sixteen have dogs, five own cats, and one keeps pigeons. Nine are gardeners, and one is very tidy."

Rutledge had been watching the room as a whole. "It doesn't matter, Sergeant. Just take note of anything you see there." And then for everyone to hear, "Now on the other side of the room, if you please."

Gibson went about his search with a poor grace, and was halfway down the line of watchful faces when the American, Thomas Meadowes, stepped forward.

"The police clearly have no evidence of any sort. This is a charade intended to impress us with their abilities. Hands first, and now trousers. I for one am going to my hotel. I'm tired. Lord Willingham, your servant, sir."

And with a nod, he walked toward the door and demanded that the constable there let him through.

A few others followed him, but the constable on duty never moved.

Rutledge said in the voice he'd used to command soldiers, "You are going nowhere. Now move back to your place or you will be taken into custody for refusal to obey a police order."

Meadowes glared at him. "I will not."

"Sergeant Gibson, will you take out your glass and examine this man's trouser legs, and tell me if you find the hair of a dog there." He held out his handkerchief. "And if you do, will you please bring it to me for comparison."

Meadowes said, "Examine as you please. Dogs cause me to itch. I stay away from them."

Gibson knelt to do a very thorough examination. Rising, he said, "There is no dog hair on this man's trousers."

Meadowes smiled coldly. "I have told you so. Now may I be allowed to leave? You will find your murderer elsewhere, I'm sure. He has nothing to do with me."

"Let him go, Constable," Rutledge ordered, and Meadowes put his hand on the door.

Before he could turn the knob, the waiter who had opened the Society's door to Rutledge leapt away from the wall and cried, "I will not hang for you! He was already dead. I had only to plunge the daggers into his body, as you asked. I did worse in the war, and was paid for it. But never as well as this."

Meadowes turned on him. "I know nothing about you. I have never been in this building before, nor have I ever seen you before tonight."

"Yes, that's the truth. So far as it goes." The waiter reached into his pocket, clearly intending to take out the money he'd been paid, the only way to prove his claim.

All other eyes were on him, while Rutledge was watching the room as a whole. And so he saw Meadowes bring out the small revolver, raise it, and fire.

He shouted a warning, but the waiter must have seen the movement, too, for he dropped like a stone before the bullet could hit him. The constables and several of the guests were already wrestling Meadowes to the ground, where he fought and swore.

The little revolver fired a second time, and one of the chandeliers made a tinkling sound. The struggling group of men, grunting and swearing, seesawed back and forth across the room. And then, without warning, it was over.

As soon as the American was subdued, Willingham leaned over him and asked, "In the name of God, Meadowes, why did you kill him? I don't understand."

"The book I'm writing. My observations in the field on the same subject. His paper would have put an end to it. My publisher was already asking questions about my work's value in light of that damned speech. A cable this morning warned me."

"And do you have a dog?" Willingham turned to ask the waiter as Gibson cuffed the American and hauled him to his feet.

"My sister has a little spaniel. I live with her. I have nowhere else to go."

A constable was preparing to put handcuffs on him.

Rutledge shook his head. "He's an ex-soldier. Treat him accordingly." He folded his empty handkerchief and put it in his pocket.

"The evening is not over, gentlemen. My sergeant and his men will be taking statements from each of you about what you just saw and heard. If you cooperate, it will go faster." The geographers complained, but they had little choice.

Willingham faced Rutledge. "How did you know?"

"The handwriting on the note. It was an American's. I didn't know which one." He showed it to him. The lettering was bolder, more open, than an Englishman's would be. "He didn't have time to retrieve it."

As the room settled into some sort of order, Rutledge walked away, into the meeting room. There he took a deep breath and listened to the silence.

And then he heard Hamish say, "Do ye believe it was fear that killed yon geographer?"

"The mind's a strange thing. It can believe anything, if persuaded by enough fear or need. Or even guilt."

"Who are you talking to, sir?" Gibson asked, opening the room's door.

"No one, Sergeant."

But even as he said the words, Rutledge knew them to be a lie.

# THE BEST-LAID PLANS

## by Barb Goffman

It's a good thing my fans couldn't see me. Between my narrowed eyes, pursed lips, and burning cheeks, I probably looked like the killers I wrote about.

My hands shook as I raised the newest copy of *Mystery Queen Magazine* back toward my face. I'd opened the glossy issue so happily just a few minutes ago. Sitting on my chintz loveseat, a cup of Darjeeling tea in hand, I'd eagerly begun reading the cover article about the future of the traditional mystery. I'm considered one of the grande dames of my profession, and I'd been thrilled when a *Mystery Queen* writer sought out my opinion a couple of months ago. I'd expected this resulting article to be the beginning of a wonderful month, culminating with the annual meeting of Malice International, one of the world's most prestigious mystery conventions. It celebrates the traditional mystery no matter where on earth it's set. And this year, they're honoring me for my lifetime achievement.

So imagine my surprise when I read this:

"The traditional mystery is at a crossroads, with Malice International clearly trying to straddle both routes. Stalwart Eloise Nickel"—Stalwart? They might as well have called me an elderly hag—"represents the old guard of lighthearted mysteries focused on the warm setting and eccentric characters, what many these days would call the cozy subset of the genre. Kimberly Siger, who will be Malice's guest of honor this year, represents what some call a more modern type of mystery, with a darker mood, deeper characters, and plots that are edgier and more complex."

Son of a ... . Sure, plotting hadn't ever been my strongest suit, but my readers were in it for the comforting small town, the characters who are like old friends, the clever puzzle. Who needs a complicated—or in Kimberly's books, convoluted—plot? Or violence on the page? And since when did Kimberly write deeper characters than me? Just because they're filled with angst they're deeper? The nerve of that magazine.

"'Eloise and I represent both ends of the mystery spectrum,'" the article quoted Kimberly as saying. "'She writes quiet mysteries. They're cute. *Cozy*. I grew up reading Eloise's soothing books, and I understand why her readers love them. But a growing number of readers, especially—to be honest—younger ones, often want to toss out their cup of tea and drink some high-octane java. That's where my books come in.'"

That bitch! My fingers curled into claws, eager to squeeze Kimberly's pasty neck. Until now, I'd been eagerly anticipating the convention, trying not to focus on the fact that Kimberly would be the guest of honor. She was a user—something I'd learned firsthand twenty-five years ago, when I was a rising star in the industry and she had her first book out. We met at the bar at Bouchercon Philadelphia. She was micropublished. Her contract was lousy, but her writing showed promise, so I gave her tips and introduced her to a lot of important people. Kimberly used every bit of my help, gaining an agent and a new publisher before leeching onto bigger authors and dropping me like a bloody knife.

Considering our past, I'd been less than delighted to learn we'd be sharing the limelight at Malice. But I'd been willing to do it because of the great honor the convention was bestowing upon me. But for Kimberly to effectively call me and my readers old and say my writing was out of date in *Mystery Queen* just weeks before the convention? This was war.

I leaned back on my loveseat and read the rest of the article. My quotes were on the next page. I'd emphasized that the traditional mystery was like a big tent, and many subgenres could fit in it. I'd been polite and inclusive, not passive-aggressive like Kimberly. I wish the reporter had told me what Kimberly had said so I could've stood up for "quieter" mysteries. My fans deserved nothing less.

I was about to hurl the magazine across the room when my phone rang. It was my agent, Janette Meade.

"How the hell did this happen?" I yelled when I picked up.

Janette sighed. "I see you've read the article."

"Article? That's no article. It's a hatchet job. Kimberly made me sound elderly, out of touch, and boring."

"It's not that bad."

"Are you kidding? And now I'm supposed to smile and play nice with her at the convention?"

"You know there's no such thing as bad publicity. I guarantee your interview and panels at Malice will be packed now with everyone waiting to see how you respond. It will be your opportunity to tell your side of it. Besides, the convention is filled with your people. Cozy readers who love tea. Kimberly has probably angered a lot of them. You go to the convention with your head held high, and you'll come out smelling like a rose."

I thanked her and disconnected. Janette was right, I realized as I sipped my tea and its fruity scent began soothing my nerves. A lot of people would be mad at Kimberly because of what she'd said. If I went to the convention taking the high road, pretending I wasn't bothered, I'd gain more respect and more readers. This could work out well for me in the end.

And if Kimberly were to have a little accident during the festivities—nothing fatal, just painful—well, those things do happen.

I laughed long and loud. Who said I wasn't good at plotting?

***

As expected, I wasn't the only person angered by the *Mystery Queen* article. Within hours, the normally collegial mystery community was in an uproar, with cozy fans expressing their outrage on social media. They weren't old (well, not all of them), they were tired of being condescended to, and there was nothing wrong with a light mystery, they said. One particular quote stayed with me: "Sleeping around doesn't make a character edgy, and liking tea doesn't make her boring. I'll take a smart heroine in a quiet book any day over a cynical one who pretends to be an action hero."

In other words, Kimberly, take your high-octane java and shove it!

I didn't comment publicly about the hullabaloo, and my fans' outrage was still boiling over three weeks later when I arrived at the convention. I couldn't have been more delighted as I pulled my suitcase into the lobby of the Hyatt Victorian early Thursday afternoon. A group of people sitting in the lobby bar under a white banner welcoming Malice International's guests rushed over to me.

"Eloise, welcome!" Convention Chairwoman Verbena Daffodil enveloped me in a hug. "We're so pleased you're here."

I received hellos and hugs from others on the Malice board, as well as some friends and fans. My old buddy Taffy Harig whispered to me, "Don't worry. *She's* not here yet. And no one will care when she arrives."

I doubted that, but I appreciated the sentiment.

"Can I get my picture with you?" superfan Lou-Anne Dove asked.

Moments later, that selfie was uploaded to Facebook for the world to see with the comment that "Eloise Nickel is in the house."

Indeed I was. And I couldn't have been more excited. I dropped my suitcase in my suite and returned to the lobby bar, where I spent a lovely few hours catching up with, well, it seemed like everyone in the world. I'd attended Malice regularly for years, and while my readers had always been happy to see me, I'd never experienced such adoration before. Over and over they told me how they loved my books and my main series character. They whispered how inappropriate they thought Kimberly had been. They asked for my autograph and to take photos with me. Of course, I obliged each time. I barely had a moment to breathe. Being the lifetime achievement honoree certainly had its benefits.

But so did being the guest of honor. I hadn't noticed when Kimberly walked into the lobby, but I figured it out pretty damn quick when the bar erupted in excitement and people ran toward the hotel's front doors. Not everyone, mind you, but a lot of people. It gave me the chance to reach into my purse for my lip balm. My aloe-vera lip balm. Kimberly was allergic to aloe. It's one of the things I remembered from being her friend so many years ago. Aloe made her skin itch and burn upon contact.

I slathered on the balm and watched Kimberly head to the bar. I planned to kiss her hello so everyone could see I was the bigger person. She looked better than I'd expected. Still thin from her love of exercise. No gray in her wavy, dark-brown hair. No lines by her eyes or mouth. Her skin was tight, her teeth, sparkling. Clearly she'd had work done.

"Kimberly." I rose and opened my arms in a welcoming gesture.

Her eyes narrowed for a second, seemingly confused. But she plastered on a smile and stepped toward me. *Revenge step one, here I come.*

"You're here," Malice board member Cherub Lapp shouted, jumping between us and hugging Kimberly. "I've been waiting for this moment all year. You are one of my absolute favorite authors. Can I buy you a drink?"

Kimberly grinned. "That would be a perfect way to start the weekend. Thank you."

And before I knew it, Kimberly had turned from me, and my chance was lost. Damn that Cherub.

Thankfully, I had additional plans.

***

Shortly before seven p.m., I returned to my room to change and throw some necessities into my purse. The Malice board was having dinner at Morton's with all the honorees. I planned to sit next to Kimberly to show everyone there were no hard feelings.

I also planned to wipe some aloe gel on the tines of Kimberly's fork when she wasn't looking. If aloe burned her skin on contact, it would be doubly agonizing inside her mouth. Maybe it would hurt so much she wouldn't be able to participate in any of her panels this weekend. Or her honoree interview. Maybe she'd even end up in the hospital.

Wouldn't that be nice?

So it was with a contented heart that I entered Morton's that evening. The restaurant smelled delicious, and the sharply dressed waiters and crisp white tablecloths throughout the dining room set the perfect mood. Malice had reserved a private room in the back. I walked into it eagerly—and my eyes bugged out. Before me stood one long table with place cards on it. Assigned seating? And Kimberly's chair was at the other end of the room from mine.

Gritting my teeth, I sat by my name. Verbena took the chair at the head of the table, beside me, and leaned toward my ear. "I'm so sorry about that unpleasantness in *Mystery Queen*. I took the liberty of assigning seats tonight so there would be no chance you'd end up sitting next to Kimberly. I hope that's all right."

"Of course it is." I squeezed her hand. "Thank you." Verbena was always so gracious. So thoughtful. It took all my willpower not to break her fingers.

But it was only Thursday night, I reminded myself as I reached for a crispy roll. The convention would run through Sunday afternoon, and I had more plans for Kimberly. I'd bide my time until tomorrow.

***

Friday came, and I went to the hotel restaurant for an early lunch with friends. I figured if we arrived around eleven o'clock, before the crowds, I'd be able to finish my meal in plenty of time to get to my one o'clock panel before anyone else did. Kimberly and I were both scheduled to be on that panel, and I had some plans for her water glass, plans that required privacy.

The restaurant wasn't crowded when we arrived, yet it took nearly ten minutes for our waiter to come and take our drinks order. By the time we ordered our food, another ten minutes had passed.

"Eloise, don't worry," my friend Taffy said upon catching me glance at my watch for probably the fifth time. "It's only eleven thirty. You'll get to your panel on time."

I nodded, livid inside. On time wouldn't be good enough. I needed to get to the panel room well before one.

Finally our meals came. As I speared my first forkful of ahi tuna salad, a woman stopped short while passing our table, her eyes wide. "Oh my God, you're Eloise Nickel," she cried. And suddenly a troop of women were fawning over me and my author friends. Normally I'd have been thrilled, but wow, this timing was bad.

I took photos with them all, trying repeatedly to eat some of my food. But the restaurant was growing more and more crowded—the morning's author/fan speed-dating event had just ended—and for every fan who had their fill of me and walked off, another two spotted me.

"I love your decorator series," superfan Lou-Anne gushed, towering over our round booth, her brown eyes twinkling in the light.

"Your *Mystery of the Empty Closet* was beyond wonderful," added her friend Jamie Bix about my newest book.

"And your titles are divine," Lou-Anne said. "They always remind me of Nancy Drew."

A grin stretched my cheeks. "That's on purpose," I said, delighted that she'd noticed. "Early in my career, my editor suggested coming up with Nancy Drew-type titles, hoping readers would have a good association with the books even before they read them."

"Well, it works," Jamie said.

Before I knew it, these two fans had squeezed into our booth and we all dived into a discussion about mystery titles. This was the beauty of conventions like Malice, having the opportunity to meet your readers and chat about books and—

Oh no! I checked my watch. We'd been talking for ages. The panel was scheduled to begin in twenty minutes. "I've got to go," I blurted, interrupting Taffy.

Her jaw dropped. "Wow, how'd it get so late? But don't worry. There's plenty of time before the panel. I'll pay for your meal, Eloise. You head over. We'll see you there."

Normally I'd never let Taffy pick up my lunch tab, but time was fleeting. I thanked her, grabbed my bookbag, and hurried off. Well, inched would be a better word for it. So many fans stopped me on the way, it took ten minutes to reach the panel room. I walked in and . . . damn. At least fifty people were already there.

But not Kimberly. In fact, the dais was empty. No other panelists had arrived. No moderator. I could still make this work.

I strode toward the front of the room, avoiding all eye contact, determined to forestall further interruption. When I stepped up on the riser, I sat behind the panel table by a pitcher of water with slices of lemon floating in it. I set my bookbag by my feet and reached inside. Aah. There it was—the small eyedropper full of aloe water that I'd brought from home. My fingers slid around it. Then with my other hand, I grabbed the water pitcher and—

"Ms. Nickel." A balding man with glasses and a mustache reached out from the floor and grasped hold of the pitcher. "Please, let me do that for you." Wrenching the pitcher from me, he introduced himself as the room monitor. "I'm sorry. I should have gotten here earlier to fill these glasses."

As should I.

He filled all five glasses, put out our name placards so the audience could tell who was who, and then returned to his seat in the audience. After checking that I was sitting beside Kimberly—Verbena wasn't here yet to mess that up again—I quickly revised my plan. I picked up my glass and pretended I needed something from my bookbag, glad that a large white cloth covered the table so my legs—and hands—couldn't be seen. With my glass in one hand, I leaned down behind the table to empty the eyedropper contents into the glass and—

"Eloise, did you lose something?" Verbena asked, taking a seat on my other side.

Blast! Verbena was the moderator, and damn if she didn't have the worst timing.

"I was checking that I turned off my phone." I glanced up over my shoulder while squeezing my palm closed. "I'd hate for it to go off in the middle of the panel. Talk about embarrassing."

Verbena laughed. "I think our audience would cut you a little slack."

Smiling, I once again reached down toward the floor, aimed the concealed eyedropper into the glass, and pinched it empty. Success. Finally. I straightened up and set the glass beside the one originally meant for Kimberly, unable to stop grinning. I waited a few seconds, then picked up Kimberly's undoctored glass and took a big gulp from it, leaving a lipstick stain behind. Her glass was now mine, and there was no chance our glasses would get mixed up. My lips were puckering from the sour-tasting water, but it was worth it. This hotel always put out flavored water for the panelists, and the lemon tang would mask the taste of the aloe in Kimberly's glass.

Moments later, she hustled up onto the platform and slid into the open seat beside me.

"Sorry for cutting it close, Verbena," she said. "I had to run back to the room. My hair was feeling ratty."

Typical. Kimberly had always been big on freshening up so she'd look just right. Too bad she didn't spend as much time working on her personality as she did on her appearance.

"No problem," Verbena said.

Kimberly nodded at her, then smiled so sweetly at me you'd think she mistook me for one of her fans. "Having a good time, Eloise?"

"I'm having a wonderful time," I said.

And soon, it would be even better. While most people used aloe water to treat constipation, too much of it could cause cramping, bloating, and severe diarrhea. Who knew what it would do to allergic Kimberly? I could hardly wait to find out. *C'mon, Kimberly, drink your water.*

The toastmaster and the international guest of honor joined us on the panel, and Verbena tested her microphone.

"I'd like to welcome everyone to You've Got Fan Mail," Verbena said to the packed room, "where we ask our honored guests to share fun letters they've received from fans over the years. So let's get right to it. Kimberly, I hear you've got a doozy to share."

"I do," she said, flinging her arms out. Her hand slammed against her glass, knocking it over. Oh no! All my precious aloe water began seeping into the tablecloth. Kimberly and I both grabbed for the glass at the same moment, causing it to roll away from us, off the table.

The room monitor jumped from his seat. "Don't worry. I'll get you a new glass," he said and hurried into the hall.

Kimberly turned to me and smiled again. "Isn't he helpful?"

I bit my tongue to keep from cursing.

***

By the time late Saturday morning rolled around, I was beyond frustrated. I'd planned multiple ways to screw with Kimberly, but I hadn't imagined I'd need to try so many of them. No matter. I knew her hour-long honoree interview had begun at ten thirty, and at noon we both were scheduled to sign books. Surely in the half hour between the interview and the signing, she would return to her room to freshen up. That's when she would clasp her doorknob, and all the beautiful pepper spray I'd just spritzed onto it would rub off onto her hand. Her skin would begin to sting, then burn. If she rubbed her hand against any other part of her body, the pepper spray would spread, as would its effects. Oh, the things you could learn on the Internet.

I headed down the hall to my room, grateful that the hotel's two nicest suites were on the same floor and that the convention had arranged for Kimberly and me to each have one. In about twenty minutes, right around when Kimberly would return to her room, I planned to prop my door open so I could hear her screams. It would be glorious. I could hardly—

"Aaaaah! *¡Dios mío!*"

I dropped my bookbag and turned. Sweet Jesus. One of the hotel maids was screaming outside Kimberly's room with her hand outstretched. She must have just tried to enter the room to clean it. I swallowed hard. It hadn't occurred to me that someone else might touch the knob. Why hadn't I anticipated that? Oh, that poor woman.

I nearly hurried to help her, but if I revealed what the substance on her hand was, I'd be discovered as the culprit. I couldn't let that happen. So with my stomach knotting from the terrible guilt settling in it, I walked to the elevator to go to the lobby bar. As the glass-walled elevator whisked me down several flights, I hoped that maid was assigned to clean my room, too. I intended to leave her a huge tip.

***

Nearly an hour later I entered the large atrium the convention used for its signing area. From the number of tables and placards set out, it appeared at least forty authors would be signing at the same time. Kimberly and I and a few other bigger-named authors were assigned to a table in the center of the room, where longer lines could be accommodated.

I settled into my seat, slid my hand into my bookbag, and clutched the container of aloe gel I'd brought from home. My next plan was to rub a thin coating of the gel all over a hotel pen. I'd then hand that pen to Kimberly, asking her to autograph one of her books for me. But now I didn't know if I could go through with it. I could still hear that maid screaming, and Kimberly's pain would be worse because of her allergy.

Maybe I should let my grudge go and be the bigger person. I'd been acting crazy.

Kimberly walked into the atrium and took her seat a few chairs down. Another author whose name escaped me scurried up to her.

"Your interview was fantastic, Kim. And you're right. The only way for the traditional mystery to succeed in this thriller-centered world is for it to become faster paced," she said leaning in, lowering her voice. "We need strong women characters who kick ass, not amateur sleuths who knit."

My mouth nearly hung open.

Kimberly laughed. "And not amateur sleuths who decorate houses and solve mysteries with the same poison over and over."

Oh my God. Did she think I couldn't hear her? That was a direct jab at me. That effing bitch. My revenge plans were back on.

I smeared the aloe gel on my pen, grabbed Kimberly's book, and hurried over to her. The other mean author smirked as she walked away. If it wouldn't have been obvious, I'd have tripped her.

"Eloise," Kimberly said. "You'd like me to sign your book?"

I set the book—her newest hardcover—down before her and held out my pen. "Yes, I wanted to get your signature before they let the fans in. I know both our lines will be long."

"You're right about that." Kimberly reached for my pen, then stopped and shook her head. "What am I doing?" She jerked her hand back and pulled an expensive-looking pen from her blazer pocket. "My lucky pen. I only sign with this one. Now, should I make this out to my dear old friend Eloise?"

I could swear she emphasized the word *old*. Seething, I nodded yes.

***

My honoree interview was that afternoon, and I was so enraged with Kimberly that when the interview ended, I had little recollection of what I'd said. Had I stuck up for quieter mysteries? Made all the points my agent had encouraged me to make? I had no idea.

I guessed it went well because a bunch of fans happily mobbed me right after. "Ladies," I said, "let's go to the bar and relax." I needed a drink. Badly.

Minutes later we settled at a table and ordered. I tried to focus on what these fans were saying to me, but I couldn't keep from scanning the room. Was Kimberly here? I had to find her. The convention was more than two-thirds over, and Kimberly hadn't suffered at all.

*She had to suffer.*

Suddenly, there she was, entering the bar with a group of friends. She dropped her bookbag onto a chair, laughed at something someone said, and headed toward the ladies room. This was my chance. I grabbed my bookbag, excused myself, and hurried after her.

I entered the restroom just as Kimberly closed the door to her stall. The lavatory was otherwise empty. Perfect. I reached into my bookbag, pulled out a large water bottle, and turned on a faucet. The running water would mask the sound of me pouring my bottle—filled with vegetable oil—all over the floor right outside Kimberly's stall. When she opened the door, she would slip and maybe break a hip. Oh, how I hoped so.

I unscrewed the top of my water bottle and—

"Eloise Nickel, it *is* you," a freckled woman said, entering the restroom. "I missed your signing. When I spotted you across the bar just now, I thought, perfect solution. Would you sign my book?"

She thrust one of my earliest books at me. I stood there, my mouth hung open. Had this woman actually followed me into the restroom and asked me to sign a book? Had she no propriety?

"Now?" I stammered.

She nodded like a bobblehead doll. "And Kimberly, Ms. Siger, I know you're in here, too," she said. "Could you also sign a book for me? I'll hand it to you under the stall door."

Kimberly flushed her toilet and stepped out of the stall. "Here would be easier." Her smile looked real, but her icy tone indicated she was as annoyed as I was.

We each signed the woman's books. She thanked us profusely before scurrying away. Kimberly rolled her eyes and walked to the sink. "Did you finish filling your water bottle, Eloise? Should I shut off the faucet for you?"

Dumbfounded, I nodded.

She washed and dried her hands while I stood there, trying to comprehend what had just happened, how my chance had slipped away. Again.

"You know," Kimberly said, her hand on the door, "if I were you, I'd spill that out and ask the bartender to fill it with bottled water. You're not really going to drink water from the bathroom sink, are you?"

She made a gagging noise as she left the room.

***

I hardly slept that night, tossing and turning, furious that Kimberly kept sticking it to me, while eluding my plans again and again. By morning I was bleary, but I knew one thing: I would not leave this convention without getting satisfaction.

All my aloe schemes were out. It was like they were cursed. So I had to improvise. I recalled that nasty author from the signing yesterday, the one I'd wanted to trip. And I remembered how Kimberly often took the stairs, despite that—or perhaps because—there were four exceedingly long flights between the main level of the hotel and the lower one.

I'd follow her discreetly. Eventually she'd take the stairs down, and I'd walk with her. And clumsy me would wobble, tripping Kimberly. She'd tumble down, spraining an ankle or wrenching her back. Anything painful would do.

Finally, in the late morning, I saw her enter the stairway door. I dashed after her. But when I pushed open the door, she wasn't there. Had she *run* down the stairs?

I hurried down the first flight to catch up with her, turned the corner, and suddenly I was flying. Tumbling over and over, my head banging against the cold steps, my right hip screaming in pain, my mind getting fuzzy.

When I reached the bottom, I knew something was drastically wrong. Blood was pouring from my temple. I became lightheaded and began to shiver. They say that people don't die from stairway falls in real life as often as it happens in fiction, but it was possible. And now I was living it. Or rather, I was dying from it.

I heard someone clomping down the stairs and blinked my eyes open. Kimberly.

"That was quite a fall." She smirked. "Did you think I wouldn't figure out you were up to something, Eloise? That business with my water glass. And that pen you wanted me to use so badly. And the sabotage to my hotel room doorknob?"

She squatted down so our faces nearly touched. "But you were only trying to injure me, right? Maybe if you'd tried to kill me you wouldn't be in this position." She laughed. "You were always way too cozy for your own good. Rest in peace, *old friend*."

With my last bit of strength, I reached up and raked my nails across her cheek. Kimberly screamed. She wouldn't be able to hide that injury. And I'd die with her skin under my fingernails and a smile on my face.

That's the beauty of being a cozy author. I could always plot a good twist in the end.

# A DARK AND STORMY LIGHT

## by Gigi Pandian

"Why are you looking at that old postcard from India instead of packing for your conference?" My best friend twirled his bowler hat in his hands. A mangled rose petal escaped from the interior of the hat and wafted down to my coffee table. "Damn. I thought I'd solved that problem."

"Did I ever tell you about the second history conference I ever attended?" I asked. "It was back when I was a grad student."

"I don't think so," Sanjay replied, but he was only half paying attention as he fiddled with the secret compartments in his magician's hat. "Boring? We all have to pay our dues, Jaya."

"That wasn't the problem."

"Traumatic?" He tossed the hat onto his head. With his signature hat, perfectly styled thick black hair, and impeccably pressed tuxedo, he looked far more mature than his twenty-eight years. The boyish grin that followed ruined the effect. "I didn't take you for someone who'd get stage fright from public speaking."

"I'm not. It was the most exciting conference imaginable. I'm procrastinating on my packing because I can't imagine any future gathering living up to it. All I have to remember it by is this postcard of Pulicat."

"The conference was in India?"

"No, it was here in the U.S. And I wish I'd known you then. I could have used your skills of misdirection to figure out what was going on before the situation got out of hand."

"*I'm* supposed to be the cryptic one, Jaya." Sanjay plucked the postcard deftly from my hand. He's a stage magician, so I couldn't have stopped him if I'd tried. His eyes widened as he looked over the text. "This postcard is signed by Ursula Light. I don't care if I'm late for my dress rehearsal. Now you've got to tell me how you crossed paths with the famous mystery writer. What does she have to do with an academic conference and a postcard from the east coast of India?"

***

A few years ago, while I was still a graduate student, I began attending Asian History conferences. At the fateful gathering I will always think of as *The Conference*, we didn't fill up the entire hotel. Instead, we found ourselves sharing the space with a mystery writers' convention.

If I'm being true to the story, I need to say that it began on a dark and stormy night. If it hadn't been for that storm, the whole fiasco would have been avoided.

I was drenched after my brief walk from the metro stop to the hotel. After changing into dry clothes, I was more than ready for a warming drink at the hotel bar. That night I learned that mystery writers are even bigger drinkers than historians. It was barely five o'clock and there wasn't a single free table. Two women invited me to join them. They moved two hulking bags of books to make room for me and my behemoth three-olive martini, even after I confessed I wasn't there for the mystery convention. These mystery folks were a friendly bunch. They introduced themselves as a mystery novelist and a children's librarian.

"What do you think?" The librarian tilted her head toward a gaudily dressed woman standing at the bar. "Is that Ursula Light?"

I'd heard of the famously reclusive mystery novelist, of course. Even though I prefer historical adventure novels, I don't live under a rock. The woman who might have been Ursula Light adjusted an oversized pair of dark sunglasses and the scarf tied around her head.

"Isn't Ursula Light younger?" I asked.

The librarian tried and failed to suppress a smile. "Her book jacket photos are a few years out of date."

"A few *decades* is more like it," the writer added, raising an eyebrow beyond the confines of her cat-eye glasses.

"Why don't you ask her?" I suggested.

"The convention hasn't officially begun. She's probably trying to get a drink in peace."

"She doesn't look very peaceful." I watched as the woman gripped the stem of a martini glass with a forcefulness usually reserved for killing a mortal enemy. She looked to be in her seventies, but I certainly wouldn't have wanted to tangle with her. She knocked back the drink and scanned the crowd. Was she looking for someone? I revised my opinion about mystery writers being a friendly bunch.

"She hates being in public," the librarian said. "She's only here because she's being honored."

"In that case I'm sure she'd be happy to be recognized. She probably feels bad that nobody is talking to her. Why don't we—"

"Jaya!" Stephano Gopal called to me from across the bar and waved for me to join him. He was impossible to miss. He stood over six feet tall, wore the thickest glasses I'd ever seen, and had a full head of white hair that framed his dark brown complexion.

I excused myself from my new friends and joined my professor. As he pulled me farther away from the crowds of the lobby bar, I caught a glimpse of the two women walking up to Ursula Light. A second later, all thoughts of mystery novelists disappeared from my mind.

"Milton York," Stephano said, "is missing."

"What do you mean, *he's missing?*"

"Exactly that. This is a disaster. He's supposed to give the keynote lecture, but he's gone."

"Do you mean he's late arriving? I heard that the storm is causing flight delays."

"No, it's not that. We had a preconference meeting today. He was there this morning but missed the afternoon half of the meeting."

"He's a grown man. Why are you so worried?"

"He was afraid," Stephano said, his dark eyes filled with intensity, "that something would happen to him."

"Because of that Dutch East India Company discovery he made on his last trip to India?"

"Of course. Milton was paranoid about another historian getting an advance look at his findings. He told me last night that he was certain *someone had searched his briefcase.* He was quite shaken. And now he's gone."

Milton York was a historian who focused his research on Indian colonialism, the same subject Stephano had spent his long career researching, and the research area I was focusing on at the start of my career. Milton claimed to have discovered a diary that would change some widely held assumptions about why the Dutch lost their stronghold in India. He found the diary in Pulicat, India, amongst the records of a Dutch East India Company cemetery. If his findings were accurate, the life's work of many historians would be called into question. Stephano and I were concerned most specifically with the British Empire's impact on India, so Milton's research didn't affect either of us as directly as it did others, but it was still a big deal.

"So you think someone killed him," I said slowly, "to steal his briefcase?"

"*Ada-kadavulae*, Jaya." Stephano gaped at me.

"What?" I left India at age seven and my Tamil is rusty, but I was fairly confident he hadn't said anything worse than *My God, Jaya.*

"I had no idea you had such a brutal imagination."

"You're the one who said—"

"I'm not afraid he's *dead*," Stephano said. "I'm afraid he got cold feet and left before presenting his controversial findings."

"Oh."

Stephano adjusted his horn-rimmed glasses and appraised me. "It all makes sense now."

"What does?" I looked down at my black slacks, black cashmere sweater, black heels, and pseudo-briefcase. Was I underdressed for a professional conference of historians?

"Your draft dissertation chapters are the least dry chapters I've read in decades. The way you get inside the minds of the figures in the British East India Company you write about, it's like you're writing narrative nonfiction that's being adapted as a screenplay for a big-budget movie."

"Um, is that a compliment?"

"I'm not sure. I—" He broke off and swore creatively in what I'm pretty sure was Italian; Stephano's father was from India, but his mother was Italian. "Reggie, you scared the life out of me. Don't sneak up on an old man like that."

I hadn't seen Reggie Warwick approaching either. Like Stephano, he was a professor of South Asian history, and I don't think he was attempting to be stealthy. He's simply a small man. And I don't say that lightly. He was only a few inches taller than my five feet.

"Sorry, old boy." Reggie slapped Stephano's shoulder, knocking him off balance. What Reggie Warwick lacked in height, he overcompensated for in other areas.

As a grad student, I probably should have thought of Stephano and Reggie as Dr. Stephano Gopal, Professor of Indian History, and Dr. Reginald Forsyth Warwick, Distinguished Herodotus Chair. But Stephano was a casual enough professor that he insisted we all call him by his first name, and Reggie was a snooty enough scholar that he *hated it* when people, even peers, failed to address him as Dr. Warwick—which, of course, caused everyone to jokingly refer to him not only as Reginald but Reggie.

"Milton still hasn't returned," Reggie said to Stephano. "Quite childish, if you ask me. All so he won't have to give his presentation."

"Reggie, you remember my student, Jaya Jones?" Stephano nodded in my direction.

"A pleasure," Reggie said, barely acknowledging my presence. "He's done a runner, Stephano. Damn shame. I was hoping to give a rebuttal to disprove this nonsense he's claiming. We're going to need a replacement speaker. Even though it's short notice, I might be able to—"

"You're thinking of nominating yourself?" I cut in.

Reggie looked at me directly for the first time. "It would not be the same presentation, of course, since Milton York's was rubbish."

"Nobody even knows the man is gone," I said. "Maybe he got food poisoning and isn't up for answering his phone. Maybe he's simply taking a nap."

"No," Reggie said. "We know. I saw him leave with my own eyes earlier this afternoon. When the rest of us were walking back into the afternoon meeting room, I saw him sneaking out of the lobby with that bedraggled briefcase of his."

"You did?" Stephano frowned. He was nearing retirement, and I knew he worried that he wasn't as sharp as he'd once been.

"Perhaps," a woman's voice said from behind me, "I could be of assistance."

Reggie gawked at the newcomer. It was the flamboyantly dressed woman from the bar.

"I couldn't help overhearing your conversation," she said. "I, Ursula Light, will solve the case!"

"Ursula Light?" Reggie sputtered.

"She's a mystery novelist," I volunteered.

"What business is it of yours?" Reggie asked. "*Ursula*, was it?" He squared his shoulders. Was he afraid of being upstaged?

Ursula grinned at us. "I've always wanted to solve a real-life mystery."

I was immediately taken with her. In person, she wasn't at all like the press reported. I'd expected her to be socially awkward, but her anxious display at the bar a few minutes before had vanished. A mischievous gleam in her eyes was visible through her sunglasses.

A woman in a purple jumpsuit ran up to our quickly growing circle. "Ms. Light, your assistant said your flight had been delayed and you wouldn't be arriving until tomorrow. I'm so sorry, if only I'd known you were here—"

"Not to worry." Ursula gave the woman a warm smile. "As you can tell, there's something more important than the convention. A man from our neighboring conference is missing."

"Couldn't someone simply see whether or not he's checked out of the hotel?" I suggested.

All eyes turned to me. For a moment, no one spoke. Then everyone began to speak at once. Ursula led the group to the front desk. Stephano and I lingered behind with our drinks—until raised voices carried across the lobby. We rushed over to see what was going on.

"How could his room have been *ransacked*?" Reggie huffed. "I don't understand how—"

"That's *not* what I said," the manager insisted. His shiny name tag, matched in brightness by his polished black shoes and glistening helmet of blond hair, identified him as Bertrand Burglund.

Reggie jabbed a thin finger at the bedraggled clerk standing next to the manager. "Your associate says otherwise."

If it had been possible for the manager to supply a more withering look than he was already giving Reggie, I'm sure he would have done so. "That particular maid who reported it has an overly active imagination. The room was *messy*."

The woman in purple from the mystery convention wrung her hands. The two women I'd met earlier tried to calm her. Stephano and Reggie stared at each other.

"There must be some mistake about the room you're looking up," Ursula snapped.

"*Muttal*," Stephano muttered under his breath. I hoped Ursula didn't speak Tamil and wouldn't realize he'd called her an idiot. "You're the one insisting there is something untoward to investigate."

"I simply meant," Ursula said, "that the man that these scholars were speaking of doesn't seem like a messy sort of fellow. I've done extensive research into the criminal mind. If I could gain access to the room and its safe, I could determine—"

"That's entirely impossible," the manager said.

"So he didn't check out," I said, "and his room was potentially ransacked, yet you're not concerned?"

"There was no ransacking!" A lock of the manager's hair escaped and fell onto his forehead.

"Could we talk to the maid?" I asked.

The manager tried to refuse, but between me and Ursula, he was defeated. Ten minutes later, the young maid joined us in a windowless meeting room that smelled of stale coffee. She'd changed into casual street clothes and had a backpack slung over her shoulder.

"No matter what Mr. Burglund says," she told us, "the room was ransacked."

"How could you tell?" Ursula asked. She scrutinized the maid with a troubled frown that caused deep lines across her forehead. Though it seemed like she'd begun this investigation as a game, she was now taking it seriously.

The maid met Ursula's intense gaze with confidence. "I'm working this job to put myself through night school, majoring in criminal justice."

"Why didn't you call the police?" I asked.

She shrugged. "I need this job. I didn't see blood or anything that suggested he was hurt. Just that someone had tossed his room. Instead of cleaning the room, I reported what I found to hotel security. They saw it, too. If we called the police every time I see something weird in a hotel room, they would be here constantly. I'm sorry your friend is missing, but I've gotta get to class. Is there anything else?"

"One last thing," I said. "What time did you go inside the room and see that it had been ransacked?"

"This morning," she said, "shortly before ten o'clock."

Stephano shook his head. "You must be mistaken. A group of us went back to our rooms together during a mid-morning break. One of our colleagues on a delayed flight had contacted us to say she'd arrived at the airport and would be here shortly, and we wanted her to be present for the next item on the agenda. Milton York went into his room at *ten thirty*, and aside from his minor worries about presenting his findings, he acted perfectly normally when we resumed our meeting at eleven. He didn't disappear until sometime after we broke up for lunch at one and when the two o'clock session began."

"That's impossible," I said. "Why wouldn't he say anything about a robbery in his room?"

"It simply means the maid got the time wrong," Reggie said. "I'm sure the tedious days blur together for someone in that line of work."

"I'm right here," the night-school student maid said, crossing her arms. "My name is Martha. And furthermore, *I didn't get the time wrong.*"

"You're sure?" I asked, surprised that Ursula wasn't taking the lead after her earlier declaration.

"I remember," Martha said, "because the guy in the room next to your friend's yelled obscenities at me when I knocked on his door, then gave me a lecture about how he was on vacation and it wasn't even ten o'clock. He swore he'd left the DO NOT DISTURB sign hanging on his doorknob. Those signs are a big headache. They're badly designed and often fall to the floor, so we can't tell if guests are requesting maid service or if they want to be left alone. So yeah, I remember the time. Look, I'm sorry, but I need to go. Best of luck finding your friend." She tightened the straps of her backpack, gave Reggie one last glare, and left.

"Blackmail," Stephano said. Thanks to Ursula's fame, our group had commandeered one of the high tables at the lobby bar. "Maybe the person who searched his room didn't find the Dutch East India Company diary, so they left him a note telling him not to say anything, and to bring the diary to them. They could have threatened him with bodily harm."

I dismissed the idea with a wave of my hand. "Even supposing he's a good enough actor to hide something like that, which I doubt, there's one big hole in that theory: Martha the maid would have seen the note first."

"But that diary *has to be* what the ransacker was after," Stephano said. "Milton was so worried about the repercussions. Do you think he's been kidnapped?"

"Let's not jump to conclusions," Ursula said. "I think we all need a break to think. I'm going to my room." She stood and swooped up an oversized purse.

The tables were packed closely together. A man and a woman at the table closest to me were watching our group with interest. "Aaron," the white-haired woman whispered to her friend, "something isn't right about Ursula." She spoke so quietly that I was surely the only person besides her friend who heard her.

"You've never met the woman, Barbara," her friend replied. "How many G&Ts have you had?"

She barked out a laugh, and they resumed their own conversation.

"Please sit down, *Ursula*," Reggie said. "I believe I know what happened."

"Do tell," Ursula said dryly. She left her purse on her shoulder but took her seat.

Reggie cleared his throat. "The old boy snapped. Milton realized his findings were bunk, so he ransacked his own room in a fit of insanity, then ran away without checking out. He couldn't face anyone. We should spare him a modicum of dignity and *let this go*. Thank you for your offer of assistance, Ursula, but there's no mystery to solve."

"Reggie," I said, "that's brilliant."

He beamed at me in spite of the fact that I hadn't called him Dr. Warwick.

"You're completely wrong," I continued, "but you and the woman at the next table have given me the answer."

Reggie frowned. So did Ursula. "I don't know about the rest of you," she said, "but I really do need a break for my mind to function properly. I'm sure better ideas will come to me in the tranquility of my room. Once we have better theories, that imbecile manager will have to let us examine the missing man's room for clues."

"I think you'll find everything you're after *right here*," I said. "The diary isn't in the safe in his room, Ursula."

Aside from a single flash of surprise that caused her nostrils to flare, Ursula's face retained its mask of mild curiosity. "Why would I care about this historical diary? I'm simply attempting to figure out what happened to your missing friend."

"You're good," I said, "but your motivations aren't exactly what you led us to believe."

Stephano gasped. Reggie choked. Ursula smiled enigmatically.

"The facts, as presented to us, were impossible," I said.

"Indeed?" Ursula said. "I'm intrigued."

"Let's go over what we know," I said. "Milton York discovered a diary on his last research trip to India. He planned on presenting his findings at this conference, and told his colleagues that he was worried his findings might meet with a hostile reception. Several people's flights were delayed due to this storm, but not Milton's. He arrived at the hotel last night, for a day of preconference meetings today. Milton noticed that his briefcase had been searched last night, but he didn't say the diary had been stolen. This morning, Milton attended the meeting— At what time did it start, Stephano?"

"Nine o'clock on the dot."

"At nine o'clock," I resumed, "Milton York, Reggie Warwick, Stephano Gopal, and several other scholars specializing in South Asian history began their meeting. Sometime before ten o'clock this morning, Milton's room was ransacked—presumably by someone searching for the Dutch East India Company diary. At ten thirty, Stephano, Milton, Reggie, and several others returned to their rooms while waiting for another historian to arrive. Once she did, the group reconvened their meeting at eleven o'clock. And now we come to the key piece of information: Milton acted the same as he had *before* seeing his ransacked room."

"I told you," Reggie said, "that damn maid must have gotten the time wrong."

"She reported it," I said. "I'm sure we can confirm the time. But I don't think that will be necessary. If we only accept the facts that multiple people can confirm, and dismiss everything only one person claims to have seen, an answer presents itself."

The din of the bar around us had quieted. All eyes were on me.

"She's an even better storyteller than Ursula," someone at a nearby table whispered. "Who is she?"

"Reggie was right about something important," I said. "Milton ransacked his own room. But not for the reason Reggie asserted. Milton didn't snap. He knew exactly what he was doing."

I paused and looked around at my wide-eyed audience, hoping I was right about what I was about to say. "Everyone thought it was odd that Milton was being secretive about the diary, but it's not unreasonable that he'd want to keep his findings close to his chest. But what if he found out his discovery didn't prove what he thought it did? Or even that it was a fake? Rather than admit his mistake, he would want to save face. What better way to do that than have the diary *disappear* before he could present his findings. Of course, it didn't need to be a *real* theft. All he had to do was leave the diary elsewhere, ransack his own hotel room, then call security and claim to have been robbed."

Stephano exclaimed a mix of Italian and Tamil curses, then shook his head. "But he didn't call security."

"Because," I said, "*he was waiting for the rest of the historians to arrive.* Too many people were delayed by the storm. If he waited, there would be more suspects, and a believable way for the diary to slip through the authorities' fingers and disappear forever."

Reggie groaned and rubbed his eyes.

"What Milton didn't count on," I said, "was that the DO NOT DISTURB sign on his door would fall to the floor. He didn't plan on the maid entering the room and seeing what he'd done before he was ready for it to be seen."

"Then where is he now?" the librarian asked, gripping her writer friend's arm. "Surely his own disappearance wasn't part of his plan."

"That's where things got muddled," I said. "Milton didn't realize that *someone really was trying to steal the diary*." I turned to face that person. "*Reggie* was the one who had everything to lose if the diary proved to be real. And Reggie was the only person who swore he saw Milton leaving the hotel of his own free will."

"Don't be ridiculous." Reggie glowered at me. "I'm not a common criminal. I'd never break into someone's room or kidnap them."

"I know," I agreed. "But you'd hire someone to act on your behalf. You'd pay someone to steal a document, although from what I've seen of your actions tonight, it looks like kidnapping is a bit much for you. That's why you've been trying so hard to mislead us into thinking Milton left on his own, and attempting to convince us we should be done with the matter. You never meant for there to be a kidnapping. You've been trying to let the thief know that you want no part of finding the diary if it includes kidnapping. But it's not working. I'm guessing the thief has a reputation to protect."

Reggie's face went pale.

"You're talking like the thief is here amongst us," Stephano said.

"She is," I said, locking my eyes on the thief's.

The circle of readers, writers, and historians followed my gaze.

"Ursula Light," I said. "Who isn't really Ursula Light. The *real* Ursula Light had her flight delayed due to the storm, as her assistant told the convention organizers, giving our fake Ursula this evening to pretend to be the mystery novelist. Nobody has seen what the reclusive author looks like in many years, so nobody really knows what she looks like up close." I paused as Ursula raised a martini glass and winked at me from across the table.

"When our Ursula was mistaken for the author," I continued, "she seized the unexpected opportunity. A guest of honor at the conference would surely be above suspicion, and as a famous author helping the authorities, she'd be granted greater access to the hotel. Remember, as soon as she began her 'investigation,' she asked the manager if she could see the safe in Milton's room. I suspect that when she searched his briefcase and room last night, she failed to find the diary she was hired to steal—*because the diary was never here at the hotel in the first place.* She confronted Milton when he was alone in between the meeting sessions today, in an attempt to get him to tell her where the diary was. Since he didn't have it, he couldn't give it to her. I'm betting she's got him held captive somewhere nearby, thinking about how she can get him to talk. That's why she looked so tense at the bar, right before she was mistakenly recognized as Ursula Light. She was trying to figure out how to gain access to the safe in his room, which was the only remaining place the diary could be, assuming it was here at the hotel. But . . ." I trailed off. "Hey, where did she go?"

The woman we knew as Ursula Light, whoever she was, had vanished.

***

"How does the story end?" Sanjay asked. He'd gotten so wrapped up in my story that he'd been unconsciously picking at his hat. Mangled rose petals surrounded us, filling my apartment with a calming aroma.

"When hotel security searched the room of the woman who fit the thief's description," I told Sanjay, "they found Milton York bound with comfortable silk ropes. There was no sign of the thief, but faced with evidence of a wire transfer and incriminating e-mails, Reggie Warwick confessed that he'd hired her to steal the diary. He insisted he had nothing to do with the kidnapping, and pointed out that he'd tried to get her to stop. He cut a deal to avoid jail time by giving the authorities all the information he had on the fake Ursula Light, but his academic career was over. Milton York, on the other hand, is still teaching. He convinced enough people that my theory about him ransacking his own room wasn't true, and to this day he swears Reggie managed to steal the diary. The *real* Ursula Light showed up the next day, after the storm ended."

"How long did it take to find fake Ursula?"

I held up the postcard of Pulicat, one of the Dutch East India Company's trading ports in India. "She sent me this postcard a few months after disappearing from the hotel. I have no idea if she's really in India or if she had someone send it for her."

"They never caught her?"

I shook my head. "But I found out some of the information the authorities have collected on her over the years. They're on to her, but she's never been caught. She really is in her seventies. That's her cover that makes her a great thief. Along with her quick thinking. The information they've pieced together on her suggests she only took up a life of crime in her sixties, and she turned out to be quite good. There are several thefts that have been attributed to her."

"I can see why this latest conference you're off to won't live up to that one."

"One never knows. The keynote speaker is Milton York."

# THE CLUE IN THE BLUE BOOTH

## by Hank Phillippi Ryan

I could be sitting right next to you on the subway or standing behind you in the grocery store line or waiting for my latte while you get your tea. You'd never notice me, and that's exactly how I like it.

My skill—for blending in and being ordinary—is the hallmark of my trade. The reason I get the big bucks. I'm so careful about my identity, I don't even meet my clients, but simply leave that to "Thomas," my colleague. That's not his real name, of course. I call my security company Griffin and Co., even though there's no one else, except for "Thomas," in the co. It would be nice to have someone else, but right now we're the tiniest bit strapped for cash. The "big bucks" I referred to earlier was the tiniest bit sarcastic. But we'll be fine, as long as nothing goes wrong.

I made a final adjustment to my black felt cloche as I walked toward the massive convention center. My unremarkableness, I supposed, was the reason I was assigned to this ridiculous job.

Well, maybe not "ridiculous" so much as "waste of time," I thought as I pushed through the heavy revolving doors. Nothing would go wrong, and it was my job to make sure that was true. If by some chance something *did* go wrong, it would be my job to assess, respond, subdue, and resolve. And then instantly, as always, blend back into the woodwork.

Pausing past the bank of revolving doors, I scanned the triple-tall skylighted entryway from left to right and then back again, calculating, knowing the first-response assessment often sets the stage for what's to come. And then I almost burst out laughing.

There were no men here. And every woman looked exactly like me.

I touched the flowered silk scarf tied around my neck, and the strand of pearls underneath. It's not usually necessary for me to go undercover to blend into a crowd, because my whole life is undercover. But coming here in costume had seemed prudent, and now, surveying the lobby, the line of registration desks, and the vast convention floor, it turned out my costume was not only prudent, but hilarious. It was like being in a massive hall of mirrors.

Blond wigs—or, on some, I supposed, real blond hair—scarves

and pearls and twin-set cashmere sweaters, stockings, and sensible shoes. Plaid skirts. Some women carried magnifying glasses, and some, like me, wore little vintage hats tilted rakishly over one eye.

A fluttering canvas banner suspended from the erector-set ceiling announced why we were all dressed that way, and why we were here—not exactly why *I'm* here, of course, but why the rest of them were here. NANCY DREW CONVENTION, it trumpeted. They'd included a huge graphic portrayal of the iconic silhouette of the 1930s girl sleuth, all waved hair and cloche hat and pearls and cardigan. Just like me.

Just like *all* the attendees, because all were requested to dress as Nancy Drew. Clearly, these women followed directions. The organizers had promised a big-time surprise guest speaker, and as of now, word hadn't leaked about who that would be. Not even to me, which was somewhat unnerving. I don't like surprises.

I touched a newly pink-polished finger to my Cutex Nearly Pink lips—might as well be era-authentic. My mission was first to find booth 2583, home base of the up-and-coming Costigan Publishing Company. And make sure its new up-and-coming CEO was not— Well, no one told me exactly what they were worried might happen to this woman. Complicating things, the CEO wasn't even supposed to know I was there. Apparently she'd laid down the law about security. "We're Nancy Drew aficionados," the file Thomas gave me quoted her as saying. "Nothing is going to happen at the Nancy Drew Convention."

Famous last words. In this case, I needed to make sure she was correct. And even though the guy who came to our office had insisted to Thomas that I didn't need to know anything, well, *that* truly *was* ridiculous. Go to an assignment without some reconnoitering? Or contingency planning?

What would Nancy do?

So, doing some sleuthing of my own, I'd discovered that the fifty-something Ms. S—you might recognize the name, but I'm not allowed to reveal it—was in possession of a new Nancy Drew manuscript. Old-new, I mean. Not one of those contemporary Nancys who uses a cell phone, drives an electric car, and listens to Pandora.

Try as I had, though—and I have pretty fabulous sources—I could not uncover the title of this purported new manuscript. Obviously the teams of original Drew authors had already used diaries, clocks, staircases, mansions, dude ranches, bungalows, hollow oaks, brass-bound trunks, hidden letters, and twisted candles; and when the local dangers ran out, they sent our girl to exotic locations like Hong Kong and India and Crocodile Island.

But no matter the title, scuttlebutt predicted Ms. S would lead her company (and stockholders) to glory because she'd unearthed this truly long-lost Nancy—"Book 61" by the real Carolyn Keene, who, like me, was invisible, but who everyone at least understood did not actually exist. Carolyn Keene was a pseudonym for all the writers-for-hire who'd banged out Nancy after Nancy for ten cents a word. Or however much. Rumor had it Ms. S planned to show this Book 61 to a few selected visitors at this convention. And then sell it to the highest bidder. That had to be why I was hired, not just to protect Ms. S, but also to make sure nobody swiped the new Nancy.

Why wasn't Costigan publishing the book itself? I wasn't too up on the publishing biz, but I figured maybe there was something more to the potential deal. Possibly it wasn't so much the story as the value of the actual manuscript. Perhaps they'd decided it'd be more lucrative to sell the precious pieces of paper—it had to be paper, I figured—than to publish a certainly outdated and possibly politically incorrect book, no matter how hot the buzz or how strong the market. Maybe they thought the original Nancy publishers would pay big time for it. Maybe.

Standing in the increasingly bustling registration area, watching the lines of arriving Nancys, I wondered if everyone's name tag said Nancy Drew. I tried not to laugh about that as I adjusted the little camera I had hidden in my handbag—very Nancy, right? I made sure the camera was recording and the lens was peeking through the hole I'd cut in the side of the leather. I fussed a minute with the silk scarf I'd tied over the bag's shoulder strap, its fluttering flowered ends covering the camera lens. When I moved the scarf away, the lens was unobstructed and I was rolling on reality. If I let the scarf cover the hole, I'd only have pictures of the scarf. I was pretty good at it, though. If something happened, I would get it on tape and cross fingers the pictures were in focus. I cleared my throat, ready for action.

I heard the nonstop whiffle of the three revolving doors behind me as the time drew near for the convention floor to open. Most attendees carried empty canvas bags over one shoulder, appropriate for conveying new Nancy-loot and convention treasures. I scanned for suspicious lumps and unlikely heaviness—not every empty-looking bag was actually empty, and if someone had a concealed weapon, I needed to know that. The real Nancy had carried a little pistol in the earliest version of her adventures, until the publisher decided gun-toting girl sleuths weren't appropriate for preteens. But a dressed-up Nancy-in-disguise might still have a gun. Part of the costume, she'd explain. Until it wasn't.

But so far, no revolver-shaped bulges.

Even in my I'm-a-team-player Nancy getup, not one person had met my eyes. To be fair, maybe they were too busy checking out everyone else. The registration line was a sight—a quickly lengthening cordon of plaid skirts and Mary Jane pumps and ladylike pocketbooks. Made me wonder, briefly, if anyone else here, like me, was using her disguise for more than harmless fun and conviviality.

Because underneath the banter and costumes, I knew this was a hard-core crowd. Nancy Drew-abilia could go for big bucks. With the baby-boomer women who'd read the books as little girls now scions of industry and law and medicine and publishing, there was lots of discretionary income left after college tuitions, Botox, and splurgy shoes. How many said to one another at Pilates or in the boardroom, "Oh, I started on Nancy Drew! I *love* Nancy Drew!" Apparently the passion of Nancy Nuts (don't blame me, that's what Thomas said the guy who hired us had called them) was relentless. And the competition for collectible good stuff was fierce. "Golly," as Nancy might say.

Nancy was cool and ahead of her time, of course, with her roadster and self-confidence and self-sufficient lawyer aunt and handsome father. And Hannah Gruen, her housekeeper. I'd devoured all the original Nancys when I was twelve. I'd even caught up a bit before today, rereading online. Okay, sure, all these years later, Nancy can be a little precious. The books are all about her, her, her. And how she always had to make everything perfect. (And didn't Nancy describe her pal Bess as "plump"? Some pal you were, Nanc.) Don't even get me started on Ned, who was henpecked from page one. Still, you've gotta love Nancy. She changed our lives, and we are grateful.

Anyway, point is, I'm Nancy-savvy. And kind of Nancy-ish myself. So, perfect for this job.

They'd already sent me my convention pass, which read simply "Guest." I slid the stiff white cardboard into the pink plastic name tag holder, draped the pink strap around my neck. Scarf, pearls, hat, name tag. And hidden camera. And my own gun, of course, which was hidden in an outside pocket of my patent leather handbag. Er, camera bag. The gun couldn't be packed inside with the camera, because it had to be more accessible. Even though nothing was going to happen.

Showtime. With camera rolling and my brain on high alert, I snapped up a glossy program from a stack in a metal wire container, stashed it in the other outside pocket of my bag, and began the long walk across the marble expanse of lobby toward the convention floor, ready to join the other Nancys.

It required all my willpower to resist the impulse to make sure my camera really was rolling. I'd checked it in the car, and out of the car, and before I arrived at the sidewalk outside. My batteries would last an hour or so, then I'd have to do a switcheroo in a bathroom stall. With all the technology we have today, we still rely on batteries. Did Nancy ever run out of batteries? Was there a *Clue in the Dimming Flashlight*? I prided myself on my hypervigilance, but it was time to let it be. The game was afoot.

I know, that's from another detective altogether.

\*\*\*

*The Clue in the Convention Center?* I contemplated title possibilities for the new Nancy as I strode along a strip of bright green industrial carpeting crisscrossed in a geometrically perfect grid. At the intersection of each green street and avenue—for want of a better description—a signpost displayed the booth numbers. Left, 1000 to 2000. Right, 2001 to 3000. *The Secret of the Old Signpost?* That could work. I turned right, heading to 2583 where the mysterious (of course) Ms. S was supposedly holding court.

I arrived at 2583, the Costigan Publishing Company cubicle, and saw it was different from the others. First, most of the booths were overflowing with stuff, tabled and chaired within an inch of fire safety, plastered with posters and graphics, stacked with pamphlets and catalogs, and crowded with clear acrylic cylinders of give-away merchandise. Nancy lapel pins enameled with her silhouette, and jewelry with rectangular charms depicting each book cover, and endless, *endless* T-shirts.

I will admit to being tempted by one of the tees. "Everything is Evidence," it said on the front. I loved that. But for me this was no time for shopping. For everyone else, though, it was. While organizers had scheduled seminars and panels, and announced a couple of new research papers being presented, "stuff" was what the Nancy Drew Convention was all about. Selling Nancy, the myth—and the merchandise.

And, of course, the long-lost manuscript. Maybe.

But the Costigan booth, 2583, didn't have any froofy decorations or commercialized Nancy-ness. Its blue drape only displayed the Costigan logo (a magnifying glass—*aha*), and the open space had a spotlessly clean (and empty) glass table and two curvy red leather chairs. No loot, no tchotchkes, no memorabilia. Costigan had snagged a high-visibility spot on the convention floor. It was at an intersection most conventioneers would have to pass to get to where they were going. Weird, considering there was nothing to see and no one in the booth.

Not now, at least.

But who knew what Costigan and Ms. S had planned for later? Standing to one side of the booth, like I wasn't really interested in it, I sighed, yet again, in frustration. Would have been so much simpler if they had filled me in on their plans, not to mention their concerns. But the customer is always right. (Although I must say, not in my business. It's one of those universal truths that's sometimes not true.)

The other thing that set 2583 apart—it was double wide and double deep. I'd scrutinized the convention floor map in my program as I made my way toward it, and saw from the blue-printy sketches that the Costigan booth took up twice as much space as most. You couldn't tell from the convention floor, but the curtain backing the Costigan seating area concealed another whole cubicle. What—or who—was behind that curtain?

Clearly it was the perfect spot for private showings of the million-dollar Nancy, Book 61.

I fake-sauntered around the corner, trying to assess whether there was an opening in the curtain somewhere. Hard to tell. I fake-paused along the side of the hidden booth—*The Clue in the Hidden Booth? The Secret of the Sapphire Curtain?*—and listened, hard as I could, for voices coming from behind the heavy blue fabric. My sixth sense told me the booth wasn't empty. The way you know a house isn't empty when you open the front door, it just *felt* occupied. In this case, there was no real way to confirm that, except to listen.

But every time I thought I heard something, the blaring voice of an announcer blasted over the convention's public address system. This time, her plummy voice was making sure conventioneers knew the Hannah Gruen cooking class was commencing on the pop-up stage, and the panel debating *Nancy—Role Model or Retro?* would begin in fifteen minutes. "And don't forget our surprise guest speaker," the voice boomed provocatively. "On the main stage at eleven!" I checked my watch. Ten a.m.

*Whoa.* I took a step forward, spooked. Someone behind me—behind the blue curtain—had coughed. I heard it, no question. And then something had moved inside that cubicle. Maybe backed up against the curtain, forgetting there was a corridor behind the cloth. So, I was right. Someone—or someones—was inside. What were they doing in there? Who was it? And how could I find out?

Had Ms. S even arrived? I'd checked her out on Google and the Costigan website and every other research resource on the Internet, but all the photos of her were blurry or bad or clearly outdated—and the Costigan site didn't have one at all. So I didn't know her, and she didn't know me, and I didn't know if anything was supposed to happen. Or was going to happen. But in the spirit of Nancy herself, I would be persistent. Determined. I would stake out this booth until the convention day was over. Just me and a thousand other Nancys, waiting to see what adventure lay ahead.

***

"Nice hat."

I turned, surprised. A man. That alone was remarkable. I hadn't seen another man since I pushed through the revolving doors. He wore an official pink-strapped name tag.

"Too funny," I said, after reading it. "Ned Nickerson."

He shrugged, actually quite un-Ned in a not-very-1930s Oxford shirt and expensive jeans. Dark sweater tied preppily around his shoulders. *Reporter*, was my first thought. Except for the sweater. And he didn't have a notebook. Maybe a spy from a rival publishing company? An emissary from a potential manuscript buyer? Probably not some attending-Nancy's husband because he wasn't wearing a ring.

"Ned." I pointed to the name tag. "Really?" I was thinking two things: one, he was kind of cute. And two, he'd noticed me. In a Nancy Drew novel, Ned was a good guy, and if this were a meet-cute moment that "Ned" and I would recall years from now for our children, it'd be nicely symmetrical. But I knew life wasn't often like that.

He pulled out a little spiral notebook. "You got me," he said. His eyes were chocolate brown behind tortoise-shell glasses. "Not really Ned. But I *am* really—"

He stopped. A woman and *another* man had approached the Costigan booth and paused just outside the blue curtain. Each carried a pink-printed foam cup of coffee. "Ned" and I took a step or two away from them on the green walkway, his expression as surprised as mine must have been, and then, instantly, his reaction turned to bland disinterest. That meant he was pretending not to notice the two people who had arrived, and that was interesting. Because a person who didn't care would at least be curious. And so would a reporter.

"So what brings you here?" Ned asked me. His voice seemed a little louder than necessary. Exactly what I'd do if I were feigning disinterest in the arriving couple. Which I was. And I bet he was, too. Why?

I claimed the facing-the-booth position in Ned's and my continuing phony conversation as I focused on the woman's name tag. Ms. S. And proving her exalted station, she was not dressed as Nancy Drew. Nor was the slim, youngish man in a navy blazer who accompanied her. He wore a name tag, too, but his I couldn't read. The two were now deep in conversation outside the booth, heads almost touching, and he seemed to be texting as they talked. Neither was holding a manuscript box or envelope or briefcase, nothing that might contain Book 61. Their postures didn't seem intimate, as much as . . . conspiratorial. But that may be just my suspicious nature.

"Oh, I adore Nancy Drew," I chirped in response to Ned's question. "Always have."

"Oh, my phone," Ned lied. He pulled a cell from his jeans pocket. Smiled, apologizing. "One moment."

Ms. S did not acknowledge me, or Ned, who was now fake-talking on his cell phone. Duh, because his phone had not rung. However, it *was* a good ploy, so I pulled out my cell, too, from where it was safely tucked in the pocket of my plaid skirt. I was proud of myself, how I'd casually managed to keep the hidden camera pointed right at my unknowing subject. Now, queen of multitasking, I kept an eye on Ned, pretended to talk on the phone, and kept my camera focused on Ms. S while I did my best detective body-recon scan, committing her face and figure to memory.

Fifty-something, gray hair bobbed in a sleek pageboy. Chunky gold earrings, chic and subtle makeup. Black dress, pearls. Name tag, not on a pink lanyard but a black one. I recognized the designer logo on her black pumps. That pair of shoes alone could pay my salary for the day. Clearly she'd ignored the dress-like-Nancy-Drew edict.

"Funny," I said into the phone. And I was thinking—*funny*. Because we don't actually know how Nancy Drew dresses. Sure, we have her style down pat for her teenage years. But Nancy Drew at fifty? Maybe Ms. S was going for that.

A few more packs of bag-toting Nancys bustled by. It was still pretty amusing to see them—*The Case of the Duplicate,* what, *Dames*? The opening panels were about to start, so any time now, the crowded convention corridors would clear. Would any Book 61 customers show up at the Costigan booth while the attention of most convention-goers was focused elsewhere?

Or maybe a customer was waiting inside. Right now. And maybe, instead of sending him—or her—away while they conferred, the CEO and her colleague had gone for coffee, and then were taking a moment in the corridor to decide whatever they were deciding.

It was all speculation, but that's my specialty, because speculation leads to problem-solving. Everyone is always trying to hide something from someone else, and everyone needs protection from those someones. And that was me, and the background was where I liked to be. It was my favorite setting, in fact. So here I was, hiding in plain sight. Just another Nancy.

*** 

Not a minute later, with a whoosh of fabric and a clatter of heels, a blonde in a black hat barreled through the blue curtains and out of the Costigan booth. She shouldered Ms. S and Not-Ned aside, shoving the elegant woman against a metal stanchion. Head down and arms clutched across her chest, the Nancy plowed through the battalion of similarly dressed women crowded in the corridor and disappeared into the throng, swallowed up in a sea of bobbing blond heads. She'd been carrying . . . *a book-sized box.* And my heart—and head—knew it held Book 61.

Why had they left her alone with it?

In the fraction of a second I used to take it all in, Not-Ned began helping Ms. S to her feet, Ned ran after the woman, and I stepped toward the back of the Costigan booth. As the curtains closed behind me, I knew my assumption had been wrong. Running Nancy hadn't been alone. Another Nancy Drew—this one wearing no name tag—was dead on the floor with a knife in her twin-setted chest.

I pivoted, ready for pursuit. We had to find the escaping Nancy, who not only was a thief but a murderer. Plan of action: get the convention put on lockdown, keeping every single Nancy inside until we could do a lineup for identification. I paused for an infinitesimal second, picturing the array of suspects. We had quite the ID job ahead of us.

The blue curtains were yanked open, letting in the lively hubbub of the convention. Ms. S, eyes blazing, pointed toward the body on the floor as the curtains closed behind her.

"Yes. That's her!"

"Who?" I asked, stepping toward her and gesturing to the victim. "You know her? Who is this person? Someone just stabbed her! And it's the same one who ran—"

"Get back. Get away from me! What have you done with our manuscript? It's worth *millions.*" Ms. S was stage-whispering now, voice straining, jabbing a finger at me, backing up, her pearls askew, name tag flapped backward and one earring gone. She turned, pulled someone else into the cubicle. Ned.

And she pointed again. At *me.*

"That's her." Her stress-twisted voice rose a full octave on the second word. "She's been *casing* our booth. You saw her, you talked to her. She's in on it. *Millions!* You have to—"

"No, no," I said. Wow, did she have it wrong. "Call 911!

Someone has to make sure no one leaves the—"

Ned was also now pointing at me. With a big black gun.

"I *am* 911," he said. "And you're under arrest for the murder of . . ." He paused. Glanced at the dead woman. "Nancy Drew."

"What are you *talking* about?" I couldn't believe this. "Nancy Drew is a *fictional character.*" More important, they should be focused on the other Nancy, the one who got away. The real murderer. I jabbed my finger toward the corridor, then looked at the CEO and at Ned. And at the gun. "You *saw* her, the woman who ran out of here just seconds ago. Didn't you run after her? She pushed you, ma'am, and then—"

"You have the right to remain silent," Ned was saying.

***

Somewhere in the convention center, readers were discussing how Nancy managed to cram a flashlight, magnifying glass, gun, notepad, compact, and lipstick in that little handbag. Somewhere else, Nancy Nuts were scarfing up T-shirts and lapel pins and scouting for the precious blue-jacketed, yellow-lettered volume that would complete their book collection. I, however, was a participant in the as-yet-unwritten *Case of the Dueling Security Guards.*

Sitting in the back room of the Costigan booth, parked on a metal folding chair and ordered not to move, I might as well have been in lockup. Turned out, Ned—Edward Elkens, he'd revealed— was, like me, a hired-gun security guard, called in by Ms. S to make sure nothing went wrong. Ned, snarking a bit, said the CEO's assistant had apparently been "trying to help" but "clearly blew it." Anyway, bottom line, they'd each, separately, hired a person to do the same thing. At least I now knew there *was* a new Nancy manuscript. Question was, where.

"You can't arrest me," I told Ned, eyeing that gun. "You're not a cop. And anyway, I wasn't *casing.* I'm here to do the same thing you are. I was *watching.* Just like you were. At which we have both failed because we're both sitting here, and the Nancy with the manuscript is probably halfway to China by now."

"So *you* say." He wasn't as cute as I'd first thought he was. "Why'd you let her get away? I figure you two gotta be in it together. You were the lookout."

"You kidding me?" Now he also wasn't as smart as I'd assumed he was. "*You're* letting her get away."

"Let's see your bag," he demanded. "And your cell phone. Hand 'em over."

"*Kidding* me?" I said again, trying to put every ounce of skepticism possible in my voice. I knew my stuff here. A warrantless search was illegal, and he knew it, too. Plus, no way he could get a warrant, because as he knew I knew, he wasn't even a cop. In fact, now that I was able to think a bit more clearly about it, I could just walk away. Except for Ned's—I couldn't think of him any other way—gun. Pointed right at me.

Why? They had to know I hadn't done it. My ace in the hole was that hidden-camera video I had of the fleeing thief. Ned—Elkens—had to be in league with this scam, whatever it was, since I had not *imagined* the woman in the black hat (like mine, I realized) running from the booth. The video would prove I wasn't the bad guy, but if I showed it, Ned might grab it and destroy it. I had to keep those images to myself until the real cops arrived. Sadly, the thief's image and description would be profoundly unhelpful. She'd looked just like me, as did just about everyone else in the place.

Including the corpse on the floor.

"You gonna call an ambulance?" I asked. "At least?"

"Who is she? Why'd you kill her?" Ned said. "And what did your pal do with the manuscript?"

The blue curtain parted, and the convention buzzed in again as Ms. S stepped inside with Not-Ned. And, hallelujah, they were accompanied by a real police officer. Man in blue, badge, gun, everything.

"*Millions*," Ms. S said again. Apparently they'd been discussing the missing manuscript.

"Oh, thank heaven," I said. "Officer, tell him to put the gun down, okay? Ma'am, I'm working for *you*. You just don't know it." I pointed to Not-Ned, trying not to roll my eyes too much. "Ask *him*. And anyway, I saw the murderer. And I saw who took the manuscript."

"Awesome," the cop said. "Got a description?"

***

"I'm afraid it's gone," Ms. S said two hours later. The CEO's icy elegance had softened and her shoulders had deflated as she sat, legs crossed and one patent toe tapping the floor, in one of the red leather chairs in the front of the Costigan booth. I stood next to her, quiet in the aftermath. The rear of the booth, with its now-stained green floor, had been sealed off with yellow crime-scene tape. Thankfully, at a convention like this, the tape was simply accepted as an appropriate and authentic decoration.

With the convention in a subtle and unannounced lockdown (conventioneers only being told there'd been a robbery), and my identity (and innocence) finally accepted, all the Nancys had been escorted to the front half of the Costigan booth one by one, in the apparently plausible prospect of being auditioned for the cover of a new Nancy novel. I wouldn't have bought that ploy for a second, and legally it was way beyond iffy, but hey, these supercompetitive Nancys believed the whole cover-girl proposition. And, unquestioningly, even happily, lined up to be scrutinized.

But, sadly, Ms. S hadn't recognized a one of them, nor had Not-Ned, and I was afraid I didn't either. Elkens was no help at all, and the two cops just stood there. Even when we watched my hidden-camera video of the escape, it was so shaky and out of focus all you could see was a blur of plaid and someone's black Mary Janes. Just like mine. So, not helpful to the cops at all. But since I was shooting the video, they knew it wasn't me who'd gone on the run.

It was clear whichever Nancy had taken the manuscript, she was—as I had predicted from moment one, thank you so much—long gone.

The convention had been allowed to open up again after the organizers (and fast-moving EMTs) had scuttled the dead Nancy out through a side entrance, unnoticed, behind a barricade of blue curtains. I decided to ignore the irony that there'd been a murder at the Nancy Drew Convention and not one of the Nancy wannabes had a clue about it.

Well, except for one. And she was, like I said, gone.

And whoever she killed couldn't reveal her murderer or even her own name. She had no identification, and her name tag said Guest. Just like mine. But guest of whom?

"I apologize, Miss . . ." Ms. S reached up, touched my arm. "We'll still pay you, of course. It all happened so fast and then—I suppose I just got it wrong. I feel so terrible, accusing you. And what makes it all the more tragic, and so silly of me, is that now the manuscript is gone."

"Yeah," I said.

"Luckily it's insured." She waved toward the now-deserted convention floor. "William's gone to call the insurance company. Of course, that's not . . . the same."

Not-Ned turned out to be William Something; I didn't quite hear his last name. The cops had questioned us all and seemed to be satisfied, but I wasn't. They'd decided someone could have gotten into the booth from the other side, which, okay, was possible. But I think I would have seen that. Still, Ms. S and her William insisted they didn't know the victim. They did not have a drop of blood on them, and the pink-cup coffee guy had given them an alibi for the time of the murder, so that was—according to the cops—enough. No one had called a lawyer.

"We'll be in touch," the police officer had said. And he left.

"Sorry for the confusion," Ned said. Mr. Understatement. And he left.

I hadn't had a bite of food in the last five million hours, so I knew I had low blood sugar, and that might account for my crankiness. But there was something big-time wrong here.

"Why'd you leave the manuscript in the booth?" I had to ask.

"We didn't *leave* it," William said. He rolled his eyes at me, like that was a dumb question. Which it was not.

Ms. S, the picture of gloom and regret, slowly shook her head. "We just went to get coffee."

***

The next morning, I screened my hidden-camera video again. And again. The running Nancy and the dead Nancy both looked exactly like me, which wasn't a surprise, but I mean, *exactly* like me. In fact, the dead Nancy had my exact same outfit. It crossed my mind they'd—whoever—killed her thinking they were killing me, which was scary, but didn't make any sense. But what did?

I needed to run through scenarios.

One, the two Nancys could have been in the booth together, doing whatever, and someone else came in, killed one and left. Before I got there. The second Nancy, who must have been in on it, waited for the killer to get away, then took the manuscript and ran. Dumb plan.

Okay. What if someone had killed the dead Nancy and run out, leaving her on the floor. Then the second Nancy came in, by chance, and found her. She grabbed the manuscript and was about to leave when she spotted Not-Ned and me outside, so she waited for the coast to clear. Eventually she realized we weren't leaving, so she ran out. Just as Ms. S and William arrived. Possible. But risky. And dumb.

So. What if the two Nancys were in the booth. Just the two of them. One killed the other, took the manuscript, and ran.

I sighed. Yeah. That sounded right.

And now whoever that was had a million-dollar manuscript. Still, what could she do with it? The minute it went on the market, the alarms would go out, she'd be caught, and the CEO would get her manuscript back. If that didn't happen, and some Dr. No-ish collector was hoarding it, the CEO could take solace in all that insurance money. Minus what she'd paid me and the other "security" guy. Even though we'd both blown it. *The Case of the Botched Security Job.*

I watched the video again, even though it wouldn't make a whit of difference. Neither would the convention center's in-house surveillance. All the comings and goings would be completely unremarkable.

We all looked so very much alike.

I fussed with the little label in my plaid skirt. The Dress-Up Center, it said. That's where I'd rented my whole outfit.

What would Nancy do?

*** 

It took me fifteen minutes to get there. I didn't even stop for coffee, which proves how much I thought this was a good idea.

A slouching clerk slacked behind the counter, a skinny-faced kid in a Minecraft T-shirt. Probably his first job. As I opened the door, metal bells jangled my entrance. He looked up, looked right at me, looked down again. Naturally.

I went right up to the counter, where he had to notice me.

"Returning my Nancy Drew costume." I handed it over. "It worked great," I said, all perky and appreciative.

"Cool," the kid said.

"Lot of people rent these from you?"

"Yeah," he said.

"Cool," I said. "You get them all back?"

"Huh? Yup, you're the last." He rolled my Nancy outfit into a ball and stuffed the clothing and hat into a black nylon bag.

My shoulders sagged. "Really?" So much for my brilliant idea. "Can you check again?"

"Lady. Like I said . . ." *Way too much trouble*, the kid clearly wanted to say. But he didn't. "Hang on." In passive-aggressive slo-mo, he dragged out a shoebox-sized file crammed with yellow slips of paper slotted between cardboard dividers. Fingered through the dividers. Pulled out a yellow slip. Squinted at it. "Huh. There's one still out. She only had a one-day, so she's gonna have to pay the overage if it's not in by noon."

"Bummer," I said. *Ah.* "Maybe you should call her? It'd be nice of you."

The door jangled, and a pack of T-shirted little boys, shepherded by a harried-looking mom, converged on the superhero suit display, grabbing colorful fabrics as they one-upped each other in volume and excitement.

"Dudes!" The clerk whirled, turned his back on me, and headed for the Spiderman rack. "Don't yank the latex!"

What would Nancy do? I spun the box of yellow tickets toward me, snatched the still-sticking-out one he'd pulled from the file. It was the same costume as mine, exactly. I saw the name. Saw her phone number. Memorized it. Put it back.

"Later!" I called out, though of course the clerk, now enswarmed by superhero wannabes, paid no attention. Like I said, I'm background.

I'd started dialing before I even got to my car. Voice mail:

"This is the Society of Professional Authenticators, the SPA. No one is here to take your call right now, but please leave . . ."

Which was all I needed to hear.

***

Yes, it was the same costume. So yes, it proved the victim was Aliana Kemper-Julian, a renowned local manuscript authenticator. And yes, when I arrived, the door of her tiny SPA office was locked and the minuscule front window was dark. And yes, it made sense this manuscript expert had been in the blue cubicle with the newfound Nancy novel. I'd left a voice-mail message for the cop on the case, mentally patting myself on the back for my prowess, knowing the police would be impressed with my detective methods.

Proud of my discovery, I went straight to the Costigan offices to tell Ms. S about it. Trying to make good, to some extent at least, on my failed mission. Even so, the CEO didn't invite me to sit down in her tastefully taupe office. Guess I was still in the doghouse.

"Did you hire her?" I asked, standing before Ms. S's desk. "To authenticate the manuscript?" Then I had another idea. "Oh. Was she the special speaker who was appearing at the convention? She was going to announce it with you, right? The new book?"

"I appreciate your time, Miss . . ."

She didn't even try to hide that she was checking her e-mail. What could she be reading? Oh. *Oh. Dumb me. Now I get it.*

"Have you heard from . . . whoever has it?" I asked. I'd kept wondering what could be the point of stealing this thing. And I'd just figured it out. What if someone was holding it for ransom? 'Whoever,' and I didn't know who yet, could threaten the CEO, saying *pay me to get it back, and never say a word about it, or I'll burn it.*

That's exactly what someone would do. And to prove it, that's why Ms. S was ignoring me. I was on to it. Definitely. Maybe that's even why she was focusing on her e-mail. Though no one would send a ransom note by e-mail.

"Ma'am?" I said. Very careful here, didn't want to spook her. "I understand what might have happened. I think you have an idea where the manuscript is."

She kept staring at her e-mail.

"If you're thinking of paying the . . . whatever you might call it. To get it back? Remember, I'm not the police."

The CEO tucked a strand of blonded gray hair behind one ear. "True," she said.

I waited. Her office door opened. A slim brunette in a leopard pencil skirt came partway in. "Your next appointment is here," she said.

"Thanks, Cora," Ms. S replied. She pointed to the open door. Smiled at me. "We'll be in touch," she said.

Dismissed.

***

"One more time," I said to Thomas as I curled up in the corner of our battered old office couch an hour later. "I'm looking at this video one more time."

"I'll go get lunch," he said. "You're too cranky when you have low blood sugar."

As the door to Griffin and Co. clicked closed, I rewound my hidden-camera video yet again. Farther back this time, to when I walked into the convention. And this time I watched Ned, on camera, coming toward me on the green-carpeted corridor. I'd been looking at the map in the program then, and hadn't noticed him. And, of course, he hadn't noticed me. I hit pause, thinking. And then I pushed rewind again. And play.

He'd come right out of the Costigan booth, clutching a Nancy tote bag to his chest. But in the video he was *wearing* a dark sweater. When we'd talked, he'd had a sweater tied around his shoulders, that's what made him seem so preppy. So he must have taken the sweater off after he passed me, which was after he came out of the booth.

*After he came out of the booth.*

*Because maybe the sweater had blood on it.*

The phone rang, the jingle of an outside call. Thomas would have answered it if he had been here.

"Griffin," I said.

"Love to chat with you about your . . . idea." Ms. S did not identify herself, apparently assuming I'd recognize her voice. "Let's meet somewhere private? It would have to be very secret, of course. Since what we're discussing—the, well, you were so right about what happened. Only you know about it, correct?"

"Oh, correct," I assured her. "I didn't breathe a word."

"Good." She named a little park north of town. "See you there in thirty minutes. And come alone."

"Of course," I said. And hung up.

And then I did what Nancy never does. I called the police.

## EPILOGUE

I probably wasn't cut out to be a security guard anyway. The failure at the Nancy Drew convention concerned me. I mean, it had resulted in a death. Not my fault, but it haunted me. And even more proof I wasn't right for the job: I'd been so blazingly wrong about what had happened.

Wrong because after I called the police, they surreptitiously accompanied me to the clandestine meeting. And who arrived at the park?

Not Ms. S herself, no surprise, but a slim brunette. Still in her leopard pencil skirt. Ned accompanied her. Again with his gun. Again, pointed at me.

In movies someone always explains the whole story right then, in the midst of the confrontation, but not this time. This time the cops leaped out, nabbed them both, and hauled them away. And—because as Nancy says, "Everything is evidence"—the district attorney is using my video in court.

But I didn't find out about the rest of the story. The police did. I mean, they're cops.

Anyway, my whole manuscript-for-ransom scheme, while a cool idea, was incredibly wrong. Aliana Kemper-Julian had not been about to reveal the new Nancy. She'd been about to debunk it. As phony.

When she'd threatened to reveal the Book 61 ruse to the convention, Ms. S and William regrouped, went for "coffee," and called in their muscle, Ned, and secretary Cora as their costumed Nancy. The two went into the curtained booth. Ned killed Debunker Nancy and ducked out. But I showed up before Cora could get away.

William (Not-Ned) was the first to rat. He admitted he and Ms. S had switched to Plan B when Debunker Nancy threatened to ruin their plans. Once she was dealt with, they'd report the manuscript as missing, figuring they'd make out like a bandit on the insurance money.

Win-win. Except for that dead person thing. I'd noticed Ms. S and William being "conspiratorial." At least I was right about that.

They'd used me as their credibility. If all had gone as planned, hiring me would be proof they'd been concerned about their valuable manuscript. When things went bad, they'd been clever enough to use me another way. As their ploy. All the while they were "interrogating" me, they were actually stalling. To let their Nancy escape with the now-burned phony manuscript.

Drives me crazy. I mean, I'd *asked* them: Why are you letting her get away? They never answered because, of course, the real reason was: we *want* her to get away.

Ms. S, sidekick William, Cora, and Ned are now behind bars, awaiting trial for conspiracy and murder and a whole bunch of other stuff.

But I was so bummed about my mistake and my inadvertent role in this thing that I decided to call it quits as a security guard and move on to my new life.

As a writer.

Now I can still get involved in murder cases, but the victim won't be real. And my invisible-me-ness is invaluable in my new career. Like I said at the beginning, I could be sitting right next to you on the subway or standing behind you in the grocery store line or waiting for my latte while you get your tea. You'd never notice me, and that's exactly how I like it.

# WICKED WRITERS

## by Frances McNamara

"I looked up the entrée, and it's six points if you skip the rolls and dessert."

More dieting advice. Lucy O'Donnell attempted to ignore the drone of her older sister Norah's voice as she entered the hotel ballroom. She was searching for her sister's good friend Catriona Cantwell, who was hosting the table they were assigned to. Some men and a lot of women were pouring in, swarming the round tables set for lunch. She assumed that most of them were the wicked writers mentioned in the name of the *Wicked Writers Conference* held annually in Warwick, Rhode Island. Apparently the one-day feast of blood and gore attracted like-minded ghouls from all over New England. She counted an awful lot of gray hairs on the sea of bobbing heads. It made her uneasy. They needed some new blood in this group.

Lucy herself had just retired after thirty-five years on the Boston police force. A final assignment that involved human trafficking of young women had convinced her it was time to go. There came a time when she had seen enough of man's inhumanity to man, or in that case woman, to give up trying to be the one to fix things. But ever since she woke up with no shift on the schedule, she felt like she had stepped off a cliff and was falling into a black gulf of emptiness. And she had been gaining weight. So her sister put her on a diet and arranged for her to speak on a panel about what it was really like to be in law enforcement. Not all of Norah's ideas were bad ones. The panel had been easy duty. It included a former DA and a current member of the sheriff's office. Each of them told a couple of colorful stories and, before you knew it, they adjourned for lunch. If only Norah would stop harping on the diet.

Lucy was sandwiched between her sister on her right and Catriona on her left. Cat was a local pharmacist who had made her name as the Poison Guru by lecturing at mystery conferences about how to use poisons to kill fictional victims. She was the one who got Norah involved in the conference. A great reader, Norah had never put pen to paper herself but she enjoyed hobnobbing with the authors and experts. As a well-known speaker, Cat had been asked to host a table that would include the authors nominated for best first mystery novel. She had asked Lucy and Norah to help fill out the table.

"Lucy, here's Molly Keane," Norah told her. Lucy nodded at the trim, gray-haired woman who waved while heading toward them. "Molly's got twenty books in her garden mystery series." The prolific author was surely not one of the nominees who would be seated with them. She was a good friend of Cat and Norah, who had been talking about the hellish divorce Molly was going through on the drive over that morning.

"I enjoyed your panel on the real challenges of law enforcement," Molly said. "Thank you so much for coming. It's so helpful to get the information so we don't make mistakes and embarrass ourselves."

"Glad to do it."

"Speaking of accuracy," Cat interrupted, "I looked it up for you, and I believe aconite will do what you need to do." Cat turned to me. "With so many books involving gardens, Molly is always searching for new ways to do someone in—ones that she hasn't already used."

"And Cat always comes through with good suggestions. That's why she's our resident expert. I don't know what we'd do without her." Molly suddenly stiffened. "If you'll excuse me, I think I need to go sit with my editor over there." The woman made a quick exit, and Lucy turned to see what had driven her away. Behind them, a short man with a beer belly under a sport coat and a felt fedora tilted over one eye toddled toward her with two bottles of Sam Adams in his hands.

"Captain O'Donnell, join me, won't you?" he said to Lucy. "I was glad to hear you'd be at our table, so I made a visit to the bar before coming in here to join the old biddies. You'll need it with this group. Take it from me, a little alcohol helps to make the rubber chicken go down." He was sneering. But he had extended a hand with one of the bottles. Apparently he considered Lucy some kind of kindred spirit.

Lucy sensed her sister and Cat bridle, and she understood why Molly had left so suddenly. This had to be Jake Keane, the husband Molly was divorcing. Unlike his wife, who wrote what were called "cozies," where there was as little blood and gore as possible, Jake wrote about a hard-core, tough-as-nails private investigator. Apparently he had started writing years after his wife's books became a financial success, and his work wasn't up to snuff as far as Cat and Norah were concerned. But then his book was up for best first novel this year, so that opinion clearly wasn't shared by everyone.

Since Molly had already left, and the beer was extended to her,

Lucy accepted it. Even if the guy was a louse, she liked the idea of a beer to go along with the meal. A beer at lunch was one of the perks of retirement as far as she was concerned. Jake Keane then promptly grabbed the seat beside an outraged Norah. He was trailed by a sassy blonde trying to stave off forty, who was introduced as Lorna Lisbon. Apparently she was trying to sell her first novel about a sassy blonde who kicked ass in an unlikely manner. While Jake began a monologue full of advice on getting published, another finalist for best first novel, a younger woman named Suzie Lu, sat at the table. She had stunning hair, straight, black as night, hanging down to the middle of her back. Her book was a police procedural about an Asian American detective. Two other first-time novelists were introduced, a long-haired young woman with thick glasses and a middle-aged man in a tweed jacket. Neither of them could get a word in edgewise once Jake started talking.

Lucy sipped her beer as she listened to Jake monopolize the conversation. He attempted to align himself with her as if they were the only ones who knew the reality of the "mean streets." She said nothing, but wondered why these sorry little men, who only ever took on someone weaker or who couldn't hit back, were the ones who always wanted so badly to appear tough. Tough, as if that consisted of four-letter words and heavy drinking. The toughest guys she knew were soft-spoken and had a sense of humor. A powderpuff like Jake would be subdued by the flick of a wrist of one of those really tough men. Yet it was the Jakes who talked big and even struck out at the helpless. Like his wife. Jake had abused Molly mentally for years, Cat had said that morning. It was only when he began hitting her that she finally left him a few months back. Norah and Cat were thrilled Molly was finally standing up for herself but also outraged because Jake was trying to take the house they shared as part of the divorce settlement, the house where Molly had invested years of work on the garden she loved so much.

Lucy had murmured sympathy at this story on the ride over. But she'd kept mum about the similarity between Molly's and Cat's marriages because Cat had never told Norah her sad secrets. Norah didn't know about the times Cat had called Lucy to come and intervene when her now late husband had attacked her in a drunken rage. She'd been too embarrassed to tell her old friend, and Lucy had always respected her privacy. At least that was over now. The previous year, Cat's husband had been stung to death by bees—he'd been extremely allergic. With her background in pharmaceuticals, Cat might have been suspected of having a hand in the death but, luckily, she was traveling with Norah and Norah's wonderfully gentlemanlike husband at the time. Lucy could certainly see why Cat was not happy about having Jake at her table. But since he was a nominee, she had no choice.

When Jake finally took a break to sip from his bottle, Norah took up the conversation. "So, congratulations to all of you for being nominated for best first novel this year." Lucy thought this was a subtle poke at Jake, reminding him that despite his pontifications he was only a first-time novelist. The other nominees smiled and nodded their thanks. Jake raised his beer bottle.

"Thank you, I am so honored to be named." Suzie displayed the mechanical smile and polite demeanor of a well brought up Chinese woman. Lucy was reminded of her favorite laboratory techie, another well-mannered Asian American with sharp, dark humor. Lucy had learned not to underestimate what could be going on beneath her smiling veneer.

"Yeah, good first effort, kid," Jake said, clearly resenting no longer being the center of the conversation. "There's something you need to do, though. Go out and really listen to what happens on the streets. Now, what I did to really get into it, was a ride-along. You need to do that. We had a great time. There were these two cops . . ." He hogged the conversation again with anecdotes about a couple of nights he spent in a squad car in Newton, a nice suburb of Boston. Lucy hid a smile thinking of the stories the cops probably told about the obnoxious would-be writer who rode along with them. Most cops were pretty skeptical about that sort of thing, even cops from Newton. Boston guys could be downright rude, she knew. When Jake advised Suzie to get Lucy to find her a ride-along, the retired policewoman nearly choked on her beer.

"Thank you, but I have a cousin who is on the Boston police force and I use him as a consultant." Suzie mentioned a name Lucy recognized. Her cousin was a homicide detective who specialized in human trafficking. With contacts like that, Suzie didn't need her help. She noticed that the young woman's face was unreadable as Jake continued to criticize her work and offer his profoundly ignorant advice. Lucy had not read the books by either author, but she hoped Suzie would be the one to win the award.

Meanwhile, the waitresses were starting to set plates of food in front of everyone. Earlier, Norah had grabbed the basket of rolls away from Lucy and passed it on to others whispering about how many points were involved. Now, Lucy looked at the plates of salmon, salad, and a few sliced potatoes with a sigh. Jake grinned at her, and he grabbed the arm of his waitress. He was ordering more beer for Lucy and himself.

Lorna, on his other side, attempted to get his attention while he did this. She was pointing at her empty glass that had held a martini or cosmopolitan or some such high-octane drink, but Jake ignored her, brushing off her hand. If she wanted a refill, it seemed she'd have to order it herself. The others were passing the salad dressing (Norah snatched it away from Lucy, too many calories) and making polite conversation.

"Where's the salt?" Jake demanded.

"Now, darlin', you know that's not good for your blood pressure," Lorna told him. He glared at her. Suzie reached for the salt and pepper shakers in front of her and handed them across to the little man without comment. "You'll be sorry, hon." Lorna turned to the rest of us, rolling her eyes. "Between the salt and the sweet tooth, you are heading for a coronary, Jake."

He ignored her, emptying half the salt shaker on his chicken breast entrée. When Lorna patted his arm in a proprietary manner, he flinched.

"What kind of mystery do you write?" Lucy asked her. The beer arrived and she accepted hers. She turned toward Lorna to avoid Norah's glare.

Lorna ordered another appletini and put down her fork after a desultory investigation of the food on her plate. Lucy guessed her trade-off for keeping a slim figure was alcohol instead of solid food. "I've written a modern thriller about a sexy young woman scientist who finds out about a global conspiracy during a field trip to the Amazon. She gets chased by thugs hired by a multinational conglomerate that wants to steal the formula she developed."

"Very interesting," Lucy replied. The others were diligently attacking their food. She assumed Lorna didn't need a ride-along with local cops to fill out her novel. It was unlikely any of them would have relevant experience. She pictured introducing Lorna in her three-inch heels to a squad assigned to Roxbury. The thought boggled her mind. She was grateful for the beer.

"Jakey thinks it's good, don't you, honey? He's going to give it to his editor at Black Door books for me." She beamed.

"I didn't say I'd do that," he objected.

"Why yes, you did. Don't you go tryin' to back out now," she scolded him. The rest of the table tried to ignore their bickering as they cleaned their plates.

After the plates were swept away, the conference chair went to the podium and began to make announcements in preparation for the award ceremony. Lucy saw Molly Keane, who was seated at another table, staring at her soon to be ex-husband and his blond companion with a look almost of sorrow. Having had enough experience with the man to consider him a complete loser, Lucy had to restrain herself from shaking her head. Like other women Lucy had heard of, Molly had stayed with her abuser for over twenty-five years without even having children. And even when she was finally free, she couldn't quite let go and stop caring.

As the waitress removed the dinner plates, Cat pulled out a plastic container of special desserts. In addition to being a pharmacist, she was a very accomplished baker, so she had prepared cupcakes for each of the nominees with initials of their main characters and a candle for the first birthday of each, wishing each of the authors many more years with novels about their characters. It was a typically thoughtful gesture.

Norah waved away the dessert of plainly frosted ones for herself and Lucy, only allowing coffee. Jake snorted at the good wishes, but he wolfed his cupcake down, then ate the one Lorna pushed away. They were getting ready to start the awards with the one for best first novel so the table came to attention. While the presenter was being introduced, Cat pushed away her own chocolate cupcake, offering it to anyone else at the table who might want it. Lucy was tempted. While it wasn't anything extraordinary, just a chocolate one with a pink frosting and white sprinkles, still it would go well with the black coffee. She could feel Norah staring at her, willing her not to reach for it, but, after all, what did it matter if she was a few points over the limit? It wasn't like she was going to need to chase down runaway suspects or anything. Not ever. Not anymore. But before she could give in, Jake Keane reached across and pulled the plate toward him. Saved by the glutton. Lucy sipped her coffee and heard the announcement.

"Suzie Lu for *Nightblind*." There was applause and glee from the rest of the table. Lucy figured Jake wasn't really surprised, as the Chinese woman rose and approached the podium to accept a plaque. He probably wanted his mouth full so he wouldn't have to comment. But just as Suzie was preparing to speak, he began to shake. His trembling moved the whole table so they all turned toward him. Covered with sweat, his face was convulsed as if he were about to heave, and he turned to get up but collapsed on the floor.

There was a moment of disgust as the women at the table didn't seem to believe what they were seeing. But Lucy did. There was something really wrong. Jake was moaning with pain and grasping his abdomen. Lorna jumped up with her hand over her mouth, staring down in horror. There were shouts to make room and call 911. As Lucy stood to help, a doctor who had been on another panel rushed over and beat her to it. He was assisted by the sheriff's deputy who knew first aid, but the little man kept writhing for several minutes, then all motion stopped. Lucy's tablemates were dumbfounded, and they looked on as Molly hovered helplessly over the doctor. When the EMTs hurried in, they consulted, checked Jake out, and declared him beyond help. At that, the woman who had spent so much of her life with the obnoxious little man broke into tears and several friends led her away.

Lorna was sitting alone by the door, white faced, as the EMTs put Jake's body on a stretcher and began to carry him out. She rose, demanding to accompany them, but the medics asked Molly to go instead, which angered Lorna. It made sense, though, Lucy thought. She was still his wife, and they probably needed the name of his physician and his medical history.

"That was pretty awful," Norah said as she, Lucy, and Cat sat back down at their table. "But when you consider the way he ate— all that salt, and then three desserts. He didn't take care of himself. Really, what can you expect?"

Not to mention the stress of not winning the award, going through a divorce, and arguing with his mistress, Lucy thought. Jake's death made Lucy realize she'd have to pay attention to Norah's eternal warnings about her health. What a way to go, and she wasn't ready to go yet, even if she was a little at sea in this retirement thing.

From the podium they announced an early adjournment of the conference, doing a hasty reading of the other award winners and promising that a newsletter would be published with details. No one questioned the need to put an end to the day after such drama. They didn't try to eulogize the man as it was too soon to digest it all.

When Norah and Cat went over to check with the organizers, Lucy lingered at the table. She'd been on the job too long to ignore her gut, and her gut had begun telling her something was off. Before the servers could sweep in, eager to finish their work, she grabbed a couple of napkins and quickly wrapped up the salt shaker, Jake's beer glass, and some large crumbs from his cupcake, and shoved them in her purse. On the way out, she nodded to Suzie Lu, who looked grim as she gathered up her award and her belongings.

*** 

Two weeks later, Lucy was invited to a memorial get-together for the deceased author. Norah and Cat were going, and she decided that, although she really wanted to forget the whole incident, she should go. The memorial was being held in the backyard of Molly's big old rambling Victorian on a side street in Newton. The block was filled with cars so they had to walk a ways after parking.

"So this is Molly's garden," Lucy said as they approached the picket fence surrounding the house. There were bushes of pink and red rhododendron spilling over the top.

"Yes, it's always been her passion," Cat said, opening the front gate. "Wait till you see the backyard. It's even more spectacular."

"And he was trying to take it in the divorce?"

"Yes, wasn't that mean?" Norah said. "I know we're here to remember him, but I'm not sure he deserves it. I hope that Lorna Lisbon doesn't have the gall to show up."

They followed the path around back, where the garden was indeed more extensive. There were a couple of crab apple trees with pink blossoms shedding petals, graceful pink and white peonies, and beds of light green shoots of more plants and some large terra-cotta pots of brightly colored petunias. The spring air was heavy with the scent of blossoms on some of the flowering trees.

"There's Suzie," Norah said. "I never got a chance to congratulate her. I suppose it might be embarrassing considering Jake was up for that award, too, but she deserved it. I'm going to go talk to her."

Lucy lingered with Cat on the soft grass. She noticed Molly mixing with the many people who had turned out. Molly looked appropriately mournful but relaxed.

"They pronounced it a heart attack?" Lucy asked.

"Oh yes. Jake had a condition, and he was terrible about taking his medicine, getting exercise. You saw how he ate and drank," Cat told her. "Molly said his doctor wasn't surprised."

"Lucky for her it happened when it did," Lucy commented. "Otherwise she might not have her garden."

"He was a nasty man," Cat said. "Nasty. But nasty is as nasty does." She stared at Lucy, straight into her eyes. "But they don't last, those nasty men. Like Rita over there, her husband was terrible to her. She put up with it for years. She used to fantasize about getting rid of him, you could see it in her books. Then he was killed in a car accident. It was such a relief. She was away at a conference in Chicago when it happened."

"You mentioned aconite, that day at our conference," Lucy said.

"Why, yes. Molly needed a poison for her next book." Cat looked away across the green yard.

"Seems like aconite poisoning might be mistaken for a heart

attack," Lucy said.

"Well, yes, that's exactly why I suggested it. That way, in the book it could seem like the victim died of natural causes."

Lucy shook her head. "Cat, I had the cupcake analyzed. How could you do it? You could have killed me or Norah. Or somebody else at that table. How could you know someone else wouldn't eat it?"

"I don't know what you're talking about." Cat's eyes blazed. "I would never do anything of the sort." She paused and sighed. "Of course, if I were to do something like that, I'd make sure to use a flavor my intended victim loved, like chocolate, so I could be sure he'd eat it. And I'd only put the drug in the cupcake made especially for him, one with a special appearance so I'd know which one to give him. And I'd only do it to someone who really deserved it."

Lucy thought about Jake's cupcake—the only cupcake Cat made that was chocolate. Was Jake's sweet tooth something that could be counted on?

"Oh, excuse me, Lucy, I really must go over and see Eleanor." Cat waved at a gray-haired woman. "She has finally been able to travel since her husband passed away. So I hardly ever get a chance to talk with her anymore." She gave Lucy a peaceful smile and slid away toward the pleasant-looking woman.

They were all pleasant-looking women, Lucy thought as she scanned the garden. Mostly middle-aged or older. Apparently they all wrote mysteries or tried to. Perhaps like Molly Keane they escaped unhappy marriages by indulging their pent-up frustrations in their stories of murder. Fictional murder.

In Lucy's mind there was no question about what Cat had done, despite her protestations. Yet Lucy couldn't do anything about it. She was stymied by her own action. She'd stolen the evidence, said nothing to the police about her suspicions, and now Jake had already been buried. Lucy thought about all the women who suffered at the hands of men like Jake, men who usually got away with their cruelty. Maybe it was okay that the tables had finally been turned and Cat had helped her friend. Besides, the medical and legal experts whose responsibility it was to certify the cause of Jake's death had had no suspicions. They hadn't questioned what he had eaten. They were satisfied that his own bad choices had led to his death. Who was she to question that? No one.

Lucy got herself a glass of wine and stood gazing around at the lovely flowers and the women all gathered to comfort Molly. She found herself wondering. She was not a fanciful person, but she remembered an old Alfred Hitchcock movie about strangers on a train who met by chance and arranged to do murder for each other. She shook herself. It couldn't be.

She managed to have a couple of conversations and nibble on some goodies away from Norah's watchful eye until they all finally decided to leave. As she turned for a last look at the peaceful gathering, she heard a humming noise. "What's that?"

Cat turned and smiled serenely at her. "Bees," she said. Norah had already tramped away toward the car. "Molly keeps bees."

# COVERTURE

## by KB Inglee

*July 18-20, 1848*
*Seneca Falls, New York*

Had I heard right? Was someone going to propose letting women vote?

I understood that women were far from equal to men in our world, but the vote?

Clutching the notebook and pencils my husband had thrust into my hands, I found a seat close to an open window. It was hot in the chapel. I was uncomfortable in both mind and body as I took on a task I had no idea how to accomplish, in an unfamiliar situation. The room was filled, and I made a quick count, number of pews times the number each held. Perhaps three hundred people. I wrote my name, Ruth Hill, at the top of the page followed by the approximate attendance.

My husband, Thomas Hill, was a journalist for the *Albany Gazette*. His editor had sent him to Seneca Falls to cover this Women's Convention. He was disheartened to learn upon arrival that only women would be allowed into the meeting. He was as adamant about getting in as the organizers were in keeping him out, but it looked like a losing battle.

He took my hands, and said, "They won't let me in. You will have to take notes for me. I can use the time to interview the other men, who, like myself, are excluded. I know you will see things differently than I would because I am a man and a journalist. Do your best for me."

\*\*\*

We had arrived in Waterloo, a few miles west of Seneca Falls, midmorning of the day before the convention. Tom's old school chum Paul Anderson and his wife, Lucy, had opened their home to us. Staying there with us were another old college friend and his wife, Ned and Martha Longwood.

The two wives could not have been more different. Mrs. Anderson was beautiful of form and dull of mind. Her house was fashionable and comfortable. Mrs. Longwood was horse-faced and intelligent.

Martha Longwood seemed to know everyone who was involved with the convention. She believed fervently that the next two days would herald a change for women. She was not shy about telling anyone within earshot.

After a drink with his friends, Tom left to interview two of the organizers, Mrs. Wright and her sister, Mrs. Mott, who with Mrs. Stanton had organized the meeting. In the evening he planned to find Frederick Douglass, who had offered them his support.

While Tom plied his trade, I joined the wives in the parlor for what I hoped would be a pleasant afternoon. Mrs. Anderson was a gracious hostess, but when Mrs. Longwood talked of the meeting we were to attend the next day, Mrs. Anderson's eyes glazed over and she began fingering the fringe on her elegant shawl.

"I understand your husbands are in business together. But one lives here and one lives in Albany. How can that be?" I asked Mrs. Anderson, more to be kind than of any interest.

"They broker food from the local farms and ship it to Albany and New York. You would not eat if it weren't for him." The reply seemed a bit sharp for ordinary conversation. I wondered if she had been unhappy with her husband's decision to let us stay.

Mrs. Longwood softened it some by adding, "My own dear Ned is the man in Albany who receives the shipments and makes sure they get where they are supposed to. They laid plans for the business while they were still at Union. I believe that your husband was involved at the beginning, Mrs. Hill."

I knew that both men had asked Tom to go into business with them after college, but Tom had already taken the job with the *Gazette*.

"Yes," I replied, "that was before we were married." Then Mrs. Longwood turned the conversation back to the convention, while Mrs. Anderson reached under her chair and slid her knitting basket out. Why had I not thought to bring my own knitting?

"What are you working on?" I asked.

She withdrew yards of lacy pink fluff. It was beautifully done but far too frivolous for my taste. As she pulled out the material, an array of implements spilled out onto the floor. There were fancy stitch holders, a rather oversized knife with a green onyx handle, cable needles, several wooden rulers and tape measures, and at least five things I couldn't identify.

Mrs. Anderson glanced at the pile at her feet. "This will be a baby blanket for our neighbor." She picked up one of the things I couldn't identify. "See how much Paul cares for me? He finds these things everywhere so I can be a better knitter. Why, I don't even know how to use most of them."

"Your work is beautiful," I offered, running the pink stuff between my fingers. The yarn was an expensive merino.

"Yes," said Mrs. Longwood dryly. "They do shower us with things. Does that prove they love us or only that they can afford to indulge us?"

Once more, Mrs. Longwood was off and running with the theme we were to face for the next few days. As I listened to her lecture, I began to sort through my own feelings. I remembered that on the death of my grandfather, his house became the property of his sons, who let their mother live there out of kindness. My mother always turned all her egg money over to my father, but only now was I beginning to realize that was his money, not hers. Now, thinking about it, neither of those things seemed right.

Finally, the dinner chime interrupted my thoughts and Mrs. Longwood's tirade.

I realized that Mrs. Anderson was the flower and Mrs. Longwood the thorn of the rose. I was surprised to find that I liked both of them very much.

Conversation around the dinner table was polite and subdued. That is, until Mrs. Longwood dropped the word *coverture* into the discussion of tomorrow's events.

Never averse to showing my ignorance if it promises to teach me something, I asked, "What is coverture?"

My husband began, "It is the legal premise tha—"

Mrs. Longwood cut in. "It is the notion that a husband and wife are one, and that one is the husband."

Mr. Anderson bristled with pride as he said, "It means that her," he tipped his fork toward his wife, "choice of elected officials is covered by my vote. She lives in the housing I provide. In return she keeps my home as I wish it to be kept."

Mrs. Anderson glanced at her husband, sighed, and looked away.

"And if you should die?" I asked, knowing full well her options were limited, "where is your wife to go?"

"It becomes the duty of my brother to take care of her until she marries again."

The look Mrs. Longwood gave Mr. Anderson could have set the tablecloth afire. "You must realize—" she began.

"How is the business working out, gentlemen?" I was grateful that Tom had shifted the conversation with such ease.

"Just fine," Mr. Anderson said.

"It was underfunded from the start," Mr. Longwood said. "We needed to have our own transportation instead of relying on what we could hire. Tom, you should have gone in with us. We would have had a more stable base. If you had, there would have been a tie breaker."

From what I could see, Mr. Anderson was the tie breaker simply by force of his will.

By the time we finished dinner, I was feeling the effects of the two-hundred-mile journey from Albany to Waterloo. I went up to my room as soon as I could politely do so. I changed out of my dinner dress into my wrapper and was enjoying the cool breezes that the evening called in off the lake when there was a tap on my door. Thinking it was either of the other two wives, I opened the door without enquiring. I was shocked to see Mr. Anderson, standing there leering at me.

"It can be quite cool at night, even in the summer. I could warm your bed for you until your husband returns to take over the job."

I was so astonished, I simply slammed the door in his face. My hands were shaking as I turned the key in the lock and slipped it into my pocket.

The room had a little balcony that overlooked the rose garden. I drew up a chair to listen to the night sounds and calm down. What would I tell Tom?

As I sat there, staring out into the night, trying to control my feelings, I heard the french doors below me open. The voices of Mr. Longwood and Mr. Anderson floated up to me along with the smoke from their vile cigars. I considered closing my window and going to bed. I changed my mind when Mr. Anderson began talking about their wives. I sat still and listened.

"How do you handle that hothead wife of yours?" he asked.

"Martha may be wrapped up in this women's thing, but she is kind and intelligent. I think I can allow her this one foible." The tone of Mr. Longwood's voice said he really cared for her, and his friend would do well to change the subject. Mr. Anderson didn't take the hint. "What is it these women want? We earn good livings, we care for our wives well. What more could they ask for?"

Mr. Longwood chuckled, "You had better ask Martha."

Mr. Anderson made an ugly sound. "What are we going to do about the freight wagons for next week? I have only two. We need six. Anything from your end?"

"The cost of wagons from Albany would be prohibitive, since they would have to come here first."

"It's the same distance either way, you fool."

Not interested in business matters, but glad my husband was not part of this, I shut the window and turned down the light.

Tom called out to me and rattled the bedroom door as the clocks were striking eleven. I let him in and began to tell him what had happened. He was so engrossed in his own activities from earlier this evening that he heard not a word of my explanation.

"You know that they have asked men not to attend the meeting tomorrow," Tom said. I nodded. "I tried my utmost to be allowed in, but Mrs. Stanton herself has asked me not to come. The women would be timid enough in front of men, she said, and more so if they knew there was a journalist in the room. I agreed on the condition that you be allowed to take notes for me. Will you do that?"

My mind was in such turmoil that I agreed without wondering if I were up to the task.

***

Early in the morning, the six of us climbed into a farm wagon and headed east for the opening day of the convention. Mr. Anderson and Mr. Longwood would attend to their business while we women would attend the sessions. Tom would interview any of the men who might be waiting outside for the women to join them for the midday meal.

It was a short and pleasant ride. I chose a seat as far from Mr. Anderson as I could.

When we arrived, we found that the door to the chapel was locked. A crowd of both sexes milled about on the grounds. Someone had the idea to put a lad through an open window to unbar the door from the inside.

As we found our seats, Martha Longwood continued to enlighten me. Perhaps I should hand her the paper and pencils.

After the call to order and a few greetings, the women got down to business. Mrs. Stanton read a document called the Declaration of Sentiments. It sounded much like the Declaration of Independence to me. I listened to both the words and the tone of each speaker and noted the things I thought were important. Martha whispered the speakers' names to me and helped me spell them correctly. I couldn't write fast enough to get down everything that was said, but I was sure there would be printed copies that Tom could use to write his article. I had filled about half a page when my mind was swept up in what I was hearing.

There were phrases that stood out, and I jotted them down. "Civilly dead" was one. Was I dead, simply because I chose to marry? If Tom died, I would have to pay taxes, but I would have nothing to say about the government I paid them to.

A whole world was opening before me, one I had lived in but never seen. Then, there it was: "The first right of a citizen, the elective franchise."

These people, not just the women here, but the men gathered

outside, were indeed asking that the right to vote be extended to women.

As I listened I realized two things: these women were right in their condemnation of the status quo, and I had led a very sheltered life, ending up, by some twist of fate, in good hands. It might easily have been otherwise. I was so engrossed in what I was hearing that I hardly noticed when Lucy excused herself and left the building, telling us she would walk home.

The morning advanced, and what cool air there was turned warm, then hot. Beside me, Martha seemed quite content and comfortable, but the large woman who had slid into Lucy's spot squirmed and fidgeted.

***

Tom joined me as we filed out of the first session sometime after two in the afternoon. I expected him to ask about the session, but he took my arm and led me away from the others and said quietly, "Two hours ago Paul Anderson was found stabbed to death in a ditch on the Waterloo road near the outskirts of town. A teamster found him."

My mind was so muddled from the morning's activity that I found it hard to take in his words. When I did I was too upset to reply. At last I gathered my wits and I stammered, "Why would anyone kill him?"

"I could give you a few reasons and the names of those who might have done it," Tom said.

I knew at once there were more candidates than Tom suspected. Any wife whose door he knocked on, any husband of a wife accosted. The underpaid drivers, perhaps even his business associates.

"Can they tell what kind of knife it was?" I asked.

I had learned a few things being the wife of a newspaper man, but why had I not asked after Lucy first?

"Yes. The police have it. Apparently it is unique, has a green handle, but the sheriff is keeping that information very close to his vest. It took all my training to get that much information out of them."

I was shocked at my own response. "That will not reflect well on the convention."

Then I asked what I should have asked first, "Does Lucy know? Is she all right?"

"The Seneca Falls police found her wandering along the road. She had blood on her clothing and hands. She seemed too dazed to talk about what happened. She has been driven home and is with friends now."

"The knife you describe sounds like the one from her knitting basket. I have never seen another like it." I couldn't picture Lucy picking up a knife and driving it into anyone, least of all her husband. Nevertheless, I felt compelled to tell him that Lucy had left the convention early.

"She left about an hour after the convention started. She might have caught up with him or they may have planned to meet. Even walking she could have been home before noon. You think she might have overtaken him on the road and killed him? Why?"

"I don't know," he said. "We don't know much about their life together. We may never know who did it or why."

"What will become of the business with one partner dead?" I asked. "Do you think Anderson's family really will take care of her?"

"It is too soon to know," he said. "The police have put a guard on their home and have asked us to seek other lodgings."

"I must find Martha and let her know. As bad as this is for Lucy, it leaves us with nowhere to stay."

He patted my hand and said, "You stay and take notes. I will try to find a place for the four of us to stay. Then I will borrow a horse and call on Lucy and make sure she is cared for." He glanced around to make sure we were alone, then gave me a peck on the cheek and headed for the livery stable.

Just then we were called back into session. I found Martha by the door and drew her aside to let her know about poor Lucy.

"Poor woman. She may be a dolt, but she deserved better."

I had no response as we took the same seats next to the window. I read through my morning notes, then I put a big question mark at the top of the next page. What would the outcome of our meeting here be, and how did I really feel about it? And the murder of Mr. Anderson, why here and now?

As the afternoon wore on, I began to weigh everything I heard against the situation in which Lucy Anderson now found herself.

*** 

I was torn between attending the evening session and going to call on Lucy to see what I could do. Tom made the decision for me when he handed me back the notebook and pencils. Mr. Longwood refilled the picnic basket he had supplied for us and carried it to the gig he had rented.

"Martha, what do you think Lucy will do now?" I asked. The four of us were enjoying a picnic of cold meat and pickled vegetables on a patch of grass outside the chapel.

She seemed eager enough to tell me. "Not to speak ill of the dead, but she is well rid of that husband. I couldn't stand him, and I didn't have to live with him. Pompous. Reckless. Money hungry. He runs—ran—roughshod over Ned." She touched her husband's hand. "Any business problems they are now having are his fault. Ned thinks he stole pay from the drivers. Told them it was some kind of fee or tax. That is why they are unable to hire good drivers."

"Do you think one of the drivers could have killed him?" Tom asked.

"It's unlikely," Mr. Longwood said. "There is plenty of work for teamsters, even with the canal."

"What about you? Has he ever given you problems?" I asked Martha.

"You mean pounding on my door in the evening? I bet he pounded on yours as well. Ruth, I am not an attractive woman, and I must admit to being flattered by his attention, but I was never going to put what I had in jeopardy to bed such a serpent."

***

Tom managed to find the only two beds in Seneca Falls that were still unoccupied. We would have to share the room with the Longwoods. While it was uncomfortable, it was not unusual to find oneself forced to make such arrangements while traveling. The room was built onto the back of a house with no access to the main building. The only door opened onto a lane that passed behind the house so we could come and go as we pleased. I thought it must have been built to house workers who were not welcome in the house itself. The place smelled musty, but the tiny fire on the hearth held the damp at bay. There were two windows and we joked that we could each have possession of one.

The complicated manners around sharing a room with strangers drove me to distraction. I liked both Martha and her husband, but I wasn't sure I cared to use the *pot-de-chambre* with them in the room.

I slept poorly. My mind would not stop grinding the grist of the day. The murder of Mr. Anderson unsettled me. But the things that had been said by the women who spoke today weighed heavily, as well. It was clear to me that women should be able to own property and to have custody of their children. But vote? I wasn't so sure about that. The notion of voting had never crossed my mind before I came here. Now I was thinking it might not be such a bad thing. Should we wait around to have our rights handed to us or should we be in a positon to take what we needed?

Nor was I alone in my thoughts. I could hear Mr. Longwood tossing and turning, though his concerns were probably different from mine.

As quietly as I could, I picked up my wrapper and slipped out the door for some fresh air. The night was alive with sound. Water lapped at the shore of the lake where the canal poured into it. Some insects buzzed in the trees overhead. The breeze rustled the leaves. The door behind me creaked opened.

"I didn't mean to disturb you, Mrs. Hill." I could see Mr. Longwood outlined by the light of the waning moon. As he approached, I noticed that he carried a tin cup with glowing coals in it and a small paper packet.

"Mr. Longwood, everything is topsy-turvy, so I don't imagine anyone will mind this small breach of etiquette."

"Couldn't sleep?" he asked.

"No, there has been too much turmoil, both with the convention and with the murder of poor Mr. Anderson."

"Poor Mr. Anderson? Yes, of course, but pity the others, too."

"The others?" I asked. Would he think of the same people I did?

"Shall I list them for you?" He lifted a finger. "First there are the wagon drivers who carry our goods. We have been having trouble recruiting new ones, and we ended up paying the exorbitant fees to ship on the canal. You don't know how lucky you are that Tom didn't go into the business."

He lifted a second finger. "Then there is Samuel Anderson." When I looked questioningly at him, he added, "Paul's brother. Who, by the way, now owns Lucy's house, in payment for the money he poured into the business so Paul could spend it willy-nilly. I can't imagine he will let her stay. Poor Lucy. Her parents will have to take her back."

He held up two more fingers. "Then there's me and Martha." Though he didn't explain, I knew that the business was in deep trouble because of Mr. Anderson's reckless management.

He picked up the tin cup and lit one of those new French cigarettes that he pulled from the paper packet. He sucked the smoke deep into his lungs. "In the end, you're right. Lucy is the hardest hit. She didn't care much for the rooster she married, but he did give her a good life."

Rooster? Had he knocked at more doors than mine and Martha's? "Lucy is a suspect, you know," I said.

"I can't see Lucy wielding a knife against her husband," he said. "She is too frail, too dependent."

Had I heard affection in his voice?

"She was found with blood on her dress and no explanation," I told him.

"Perhaps she found him, saw that it was her knife, and tried to pull it out."

"Her knife? The green onyx one?" I asked. He nodded.

How did he know? Wasn't the sheriff keeping that fact to himself? Perhaps Ned had found out the same way Tom had. Or perhaps he knew which knife it was because he had used it himself. Had he loved Lucy? Had he killed to protect her? Or the business? Or both?

"How did you get the knife?" I asked.

He looked at me sharply, but for some reason I felt no fear. Tom would come if I called to him. I don't know how long it was that we stared at each other in the moonlight.

At length he sighed and said, "She had her knitting bag with her when she met us. She was walking home. We had been trying to convince a teamster to work for us again, with little success. Paul grabbed her and was about to hit her. He had such a nasty temper. She dropped the bag. I knew the knife was there."

\*\*\*

Now both Lucy and Martha were at the mercy of whatever man was responsible for them.

Since this was a matter for the sheriff, and had nothing to do with the convention, Tom spoke to the police in my stead. Coverture had its advantages. Still . . .

The second day of the convention was far different with neither Martha nor Lucy beside me. I filled pages with words. I even managed to write a full article, which I believe Tom submitted without revision.

When the next issue of the *Gazette* came out I was astonished to find the article I had written unchanged and published under my own name, *Mrs. Thomas Hill.*

\*\*\*

*Author's note: My apologies to Elizabeth Cady Stanton, Lucretia Mott, Martha Wright, and the other great women who had the courage to arrange the first women's rights convention. I do not mean to sully your hard work with a murder.*

# DARK SECRETS

## by Kathryn Leigh Scott

On an oppressively hot July evening, when I truly regretted not being able to abandon the city to join my wife at our summer place, an old childhood friend happened to ring up asking if he could come around for a drink. I greeted him heartily and told him I'd be delighted to see him. Although we hadn't spoken in some years, I detected a note of strain in his usually buoyant voice. Fearing he had bad news to impart, I tentatively asked after his family.

"Fine, fine," he said, almost absently. "Jean and the kids are good. She's visiting her mother in Boston while I'm in New York. We're all fine. You?"

"Yes, fine. Fiona is in Amagansett for the summer with my daughter and some of the grandchildren. My sister is doing well in Connecticut. Lives with her cat and happily runs a bed-and-breakfast. Nothing much new."

With divorce and catastrophic illness off the table, I ventured, "So, thinking about moving back here, are you?"

"What? No, we're off to Sao Paulo the end of the week. I'll be joining Jean tomorrow."

"Well, then—"

"Actually, the thing is I got roped into attending this odd sort of convention here, and now I wish I hadn't because . . ."

"Yes?"

"Well, I think I witnessed a murder."

"What! Where?"

"At this convention. It seems so, anyway."

"What do the police say?"

"I don't know. I guess they've been called, but as soon as I saw the body, I left."

"You left? But shouldn't you—?"

"I had to get out of there. You see, I think whoever might have murdered this person thought he was killing me."

"Hang on, you're saying you were the intended victim?"

"I'm certain of it, but I didn't want to give whoever it is a second chance. So I left. "

"Then, have you any idea who was actually murdered?"

"No, but . . . I'm telling you, he looked like me."

I chuckled and relaxed my grip on the phone. Daniel was up to his old tricks, winding me up. He'd always had a flair for the dramatic and once again I'd fallen for it. "Cheating death is reason enough for a cold martini. Come over and we'll drink to your narrow escape."

"Thanks, Paul, I knew I could count on you."

"Right, then. See you shortly." I was about to add that I would meet him somewhere, if that was more convenient, but he'd abruptly hung up. I tucked the phone in my pocket and went to the kitchen to see if there was any cheese left to set out.

Of course, Dan was having me on, but still—what a thing to say. I couldn't shake off my uneasiness. I opened the fridge and peered into the cheese drawer, relieved to see a good-sized piece of English cheddar and an unopened cello-wrapped wedge of Brie. As if by rote, I placed them on a wooden tray with a bowl of Kalamata olives, some biscuits, two knives, plates, and some napkins. If he were to stay longer, I'd take him over to my club for a meal. The thought of having a companion for dinner cheered me, and I was intrigued by this talk of murder.

But who in the world would want to kill Daniel?

Certainly much had happened in the intervening years since I last saw him, but I'd be surprised to learn he was involved in anything criminal, or even the least bit unsavory. He'd always been a happy-go-lucky chap, warm and outgoing. He was a prankster, of course, but not the sort who would get himself into a real jam.

One could say we had little in common, yet we'd connected on a certain level as twelve-year-olds, and the friendship stuck, despite living continents apart for quite some time. In my sixteenth year, my family returned to England, much to my disappointment. But Dan and I kept in touch with robust letter writing and later e-mail, which cemented our longstanding friendship.

It had taken me more than twenty years to make my way back to New York under my own steam, landing a position in publishing with the same firm I'd started with in London. Meanwhile, Dan changed courses entirely, going into the restaurant business and then departing to South America, where he managed a chain of luxury resort hotels.

Daniel Harrison had grown up in New York City on Riverside Drive in the sort of sprawling prewar apartment New Yorkers call a "classic six" overlooking the park. Our own family lived on the same floor in a similar flat, which is how we came to meet.

At twelve years of age, Dan earned a sizable income as a child actor employed on a soap opera—and not just any run of the mill sudsy melodrama, but the show every kid in school raced home to watch in the 1960s. *Dark Secrets*, featuring a craggy-faced vampire named Sebastian Craven, scared the bejesus out of my sister, Emma, which was reason enough to lure her into watching it.

A good number of parents refused to let their children see the show at all, but due to our sitter, Thelma, our living room became a magnet for the disenfranchised adolescents in the building denied the privilege of watching the spooky series. Thelma, an elderly woman who lived in a one bedroom on the building's third floor, had been hired to mind us when we got home from school. Thanks to her vague presence, we were technically not latchkey kids and parents would therefore allow their own children to play in our flat after school.

But Thelma did little more than set out milk and biscuits before retiring to an armchair in the study to knit. It helped that she was practically deaf and unable to hear us in the living room whooping and shrieking around our twenty-four-inch Sylvania, with its rabbit ears antenna. Emma generally watched lying under the coffee table, her fingers squeezed over her eyes.

What was most remarkable about our after-school viewing party is that Daniel, himself, on days when he wasn't working, watched the show with us. He pointed out bloopers, such as mic shadows and missed cues that we'd otherwise have missed. On one memorable occasion, a supposedly dead body was seen to sneeze and rub his nose on camera. We were also privy to the behind-the-scenes stories Daniel told about the other actors on the show, gossip that included an illicit romance between an older married actor and a young ingénue. Daniel would often get up to mischief on the set, one time short-sheeting a burly character actor who had to play a scene with his legs doubled up in bed. Watching that episode, we screamed with laughter knowing what was going on with that actor under the bed linens.

We all envied Daniel. It wasn't just his star turn on *Dark Secrets*, however. It was his complete independence. While he lived with his mother and two older sisters, he came and went as he pleased with pocket money he'd earned himself. He attended a special school for children in performing arts and had a tutor on set, but it was clear he was in charge of his life to an extent none of the rest of us could begin to imagine.

He was, therefore, precocious in every regard—alarmingly so, in the view of my parents. Although it did not precipitate our move back to England, my parents were somewhat relieved to have an excuse to disengage my thirteen-year-old sister from her love-struck infatuation with Dan. At sixteen, he'd become a heartthrob sensation, gracing the covers of teen fan magazines. That he had kissed Emma (actually made out with her, only to be discovered by my mother) gave her bragging rights she boasted about for years. If I was unhappy to return to England, Emma was utterly distraught to leave "hunky" Dan behind. Still a spinster on the cusp of her sixtieth birthday, I'm not convinced she ever quite got over her schoolgirl crush on Dan.

But Dan wasn't at all unhappy to turn his back on teenage fame and fortune. At age eighteen, he abruptly gave up acting, went to university, and seldom again referred to his years in front of the camera. "It would've been the death of me," he once confided. "That much adulation can't be good for the soul."

As soon as the doorman announced his arrival, I poured martinis and presented one to Dan as he arrived at my flat. We greeted each other warmly, and I invited him in. He was wearing a tan linen suit and a cream-colored shirt opened at the neck. He may have turned his back on a promising Hollywood career, but he looked every inch the trim, tanned movie star. At age sixty-two, his light brown hair hadn't thinned and there was no sign of a paunch.

"I should never have agreed to attend this convention," Dan said, his voice rising. "I knew it would come to no good." He took a large sip, then sighed. "Thanks. I needed that."

"I figured you might," I said, saluting him with my own martini. "But surely murders don't happen at all these conventions or attendance would drop off."

My jocular comment was met with a grim stare. "A man was murdered, Paul. That's not to be taken lightly."

"No, of course not," I said hastily. "Please, sit down and tell me all about it."

We settled ourselves in club chairs on either side of the coffee table. Dan distractedly rearranged my offerings of snacks—force of habit, I imagined, for a man steeped in high-end food and beverage catering.

"If I hadn't attended, this probably wouldn't have happened. I've always declined these invitations, but this time, the woman who runs the event insisted I come because they were celebrating the fiftieth anniversary of the series. It would be their last big convention. She's very persistent and signs herself, 'Your Lady in Waiting'."

"Of course, a reference to your longing for the ghostly apparition of the girl in the attic. Very clever," I said, recalling the steamy plotline.

"It's really quite something to see so many of yourself just wandering around," he mumbled, shifting the Brie on the platter before cutting into it. "Doppelgangers everywhere."

"Come again?" Hoping to look as practiced as Dan, I gave the martini shaker a sharp swirl or two before pouring refills, then wiped up the spill with a soggy napkin. "Doppelgangers? As in doubles?"

"Everywhere, lurking throughout the hotel. All ages. Short, thin, fat, tall—bald, even. But all meant to be me, or some semblance of Chuckie, the role I played on *Dark Secrets*. You remember, of course."

"The world remembers," I said drily. "Has that series ever been off the air?"

"Not that I know of. I still get residual payments wired directly to my account several times a year. All the episodes were available in boxed sets of VHS, then DVD. Now I'm sure it's streamed, decanted, and poured into every other new device available. It's *Star Trek* for Goths."

"Your kids watched it?"

"Oh yes, in reruns. In Portuguese, of course. It's quite a novelty to see yourself talking in a foreign tongue about werewolves and witches. The children found it hysterically funny to see old Dad cavorting with vampire types. Then I began to get recognized in the hotel by people on package tours, so I grew a beard for a few years until the craze slacked off."

"But what about these Chuckies at the convention?"

"Cosplay is what it is. They call these annual events Dark Secrets Festivals, and fans come dressed up as characters from the show. This year, because I'd never attended before, everyone seemed to want to come as Chuckie."

"With bare chest and rippling muscles?" I couldn't help but smirk.

"No! The brown leather jacket and newsboy cap version, circa thirteen years old. My voice was cracking. It was essentially live television in those days, so I figured no one would ever see those dreadful shows but one time." Dan swilled down the last of his martini and set the glass rather too firmly on the glass-topped coffee table. "I mean, Chuckie, for God's sake. Falsetto!"

"Is nothing sacred," I murmured, recalling those particular episodes. Indeed, most of the surviving production images one still saw of Danny showed a dreamy-eyed kid looking wistfully into camera, a tweed newsboy cap cocked fetchingly low over one ear. As I remember, Emma had a signed copy of this photograph that migrated with her to college.

"The other actors, who regularly attend these shindigs, are used to it, but it's unnerving to be surrounded by people looking like a former you. They love the cracking voice bit. Some of them have got the falsetto down pat."

"But how dreadful that one of them was murdered—"

"Before my eyes." Danny winced, his hands white-knuckled as they gripped his knees. "Horrible."

"You couldn't stop it?"

"Yes, yes, I think I could have, had I known what was in store. You see, there was a scene in which I played a prank on my governess—don't ask why I had a governess at age thirteen, unless that's what was referred to as 'home-schooled' back then—but she found me hanging in the closet, one of my uncle's neckties artfully slung around my throat and tied to the clothes railing. Well, we did that show live, but when it came time for reruns and all the VHS and DVD copies, that scene was excised. I mean, for obvious reasons. After the fact, programmers realized kids at home were reenacting scenes. I believe there was one incident where a young boy actually hurt himself. Dreadful!"

"So someone actually got *hanged* at the convention? Someone pretending to be you?"

"Yes, that's what I've been trying to tell you."

"But are you sure it was murder? Could it have been an accident?"

"Not as it was staged. You see, they'd asked me to participate in this skit in which, of course, this woman dressed up as my governess was supposed to open a closet door and find me. You won't believe how perfectly they recreated this set. I was shown the closet with this clear Plexiglas cube on which I was supposed to stand. I was presented with a brown leather jacket and newsboy cap—they even had a replica of the necktie to sling around my neck. The curtains were drawn, so the fifteen hundred or so fans sitting out front couldn't see the preparation, and it was set to go once I was costumed. All I had to do was step in . . . And, of course, I refused."

"Of course. But then—"

"I agreed to stand in the wings and wave to the crowd when it was over. But I certainly made my objections to this reenactment clear. I think the only reason I consented to witness the proceedings at all is because they'd gone to so much trouble. Honestly, you can't imagine how devoted these people are. Scary."

"So, I'm guessing someone else stepped in."

"Yes, some middle-aged guy put on the leather jacket and cap meant for me. By this time I just wanted to get the hell out of there and figured I'd be able to hit the hotel bar in ten minutes, tops."

"They played out the whole scene? The governess, I recall, was played by a leggy brunette wearing a miniskirt—"

"Right, and she comes in calling, 'Chuckie, Chuckie, where are you? You haven't finished your maths,' or something—"

"Whatever happened to that actress?"

"Oh, Margot Ramsay? She was already ensconced in the bar running an open tab, looking very jolly at two hundred pounds with orange hair graying at the roots. I think they hoped she'd don a miniskirt for the reenactment, too, but she absolutely refused. Someone else wearing a miniskirt put on the wig and geeky glasses. Good call on Margot's part."

"So she didn't even watch?"

"Margot's a regular at these things, apparently with a reputation for downing buckets of chardonnay in the hotel bar. But there I was hovering behind the curtain as this surrogate governess opens the closet door and lets out an almighty scream. I nearly jumped out of my skin. She clutches her heart, backs away—and that's when I see Chuckie hanging there. His face blue, feet dangling. Someone had kicked the clear plastic cube over. My God! Horrifying!"

"So you rushed in to get him down?"

"Before I could budge, the organizer and two crew people were untying him—"

"Someone kicked the cube?" I shook my head. "This calls for another martini, Danny. Good show! You almost had me."

Danny stared at me, his face white. "I'll have another martini, but as God is my witness, that man was dead. I stepped up. I saw him as they laid him out on the floor. I saw the bruising on his neck, his blackening tongue—awful. There was complete panic as someone called for an ambulance. I'm telling you, Chuckie was dead. And it was meant to be me."

"Nonsense. It was a prank gone wrong, not murder. Didn't you stick around for the EMTs to arrive? That would have told the story right there."

"The ambulance arrived as I left. I slipped out through the back doors to the kitchen and let them deal with it. For God's sake, I'm a businessman. I haven't been around that craziness for decades, and I can't afford to be associated with it now. I should never have gone. I'm lucky to be alive. I'm telling you, it was meant to be me hanging there."

I looked hard at my friend and, good actor though I knew him to be, I sensed his horror at what had happened was genuine. "So let me get this straight, Dan. You think someone meant to do you harm?"

"Without question." He handed me his glass, a sheepish look flushing his handsome face. "I hate to admit it, but up until the murder I was kind of enjoying myself. Those were good times back then, my friend. It made me wonder why I'd given up work I loved so much."

I looked at him incredulously. "You miss acting?"

"Sorta," he said wistfully. For a moment I saw the dreamy-eyed kid in the newsboy cap that Emma mooned over and the rest of us all wanted to be. "Maybe I've left it too long to come back now, but I used to be pretty good."

"The best," I said, with some feeling.

He leaned forward, looking me square in the eye. "I could go for that martini, if you don't mind. Maybe a touch less vermouth—and stir, don't shake."

Dan got his martini. I got my suit jacket. If, indeed, murder had taken place at the convention, my friend was required, by decency alone, to return to the scene of the crime. I'm not an attorney, nor do I have any relationship to law enforcement, but I've edited enough crime fiction in my capacity as a book editor to know what's expected when murder is involved. I rang down and had the doorman secure us a taxi.

Dan protested, but three martinis in, was relatively compliant. The hotel he directed us to was in Midtown Manhattan, part of a large chain of the sort where most of the clientele haul their own luggage to their rooms. The lobby was a sea of roller bags and humanity outfitted appropriately for a day, say . . . cleaning out the Winnebago? We saw no Chuckies on our way to the mezzanine-level ballroom, where the Dark Secrets Festival was taking place. The double doors were shut when we arrived.

"Odd that there's no police presence," I mumbled. "Perhaps the body has been removed and they've secured the room to question everyone. It's what I believe they do in these cases."

"Fifteen hundred fans?" Dan sucked in breath. "Could take a while."

"Well, we may as well have a look." I made a move to open the door, but Dan caught my arm.

"Down this way. There's a service door that opens on to the stage area up front," he said with the authority of a man who knows his way around hotel service doors.

I followed Dan down the corridor, my heart banging with trepidation. With a quick glance at me, he pulled the door open a crack and peered inside. "What the . . .?"

I looked over his shoulder as a tidal wave of laughter rumbled through the darkened room. A video was playing, casting an eerie light that illuminated the faces of hundreds of people rollicking with glee at the scene unfolding on the big screen. Many of the fans were holding up cell phones and video cameras to record the proceedings.

Dan, larger than life, appeared in close-up on the screen, gasping and looking horror-stricken as the camera pulled back to show several people grappling with the body of a man wearing a Chuckie jacket and cap hanging inside a makeshift closet. As they dragged him out, the face of the ragdoll-limp corpse was neon blue, the blackened tongue lolling at a ludicrous angle. Meanwhile, using a bit of trick camera work, a clip of Dan gasping, gaping, and stepping forward, then back, was replayed over and over to comical effect, his horror-stricken face contorted in some cross between the tormented visage in Edvard Munch's *The Scream* and Macauley Culkin's in *Home Alone*. Then, as the audience roared with laughter, Dan was seen turning on his heels and fleeing the stage.

I glanced at Dan standing next to me, his face in his hands. "I've been had," he mumbled. "This is why I don't do conventions."

Just then, the bulky figure of Margot Ramsay, the erstwhile ingénue and Queen of Screams, strode onstage, drink in hand, moving at a speed remarkable for someone of her age and girth. "Stop!" she bellowed, halting center stage, her well-upholstered silhouette blocking the image of the "corpse" and its handlers. "This ain't funny! Not one bit! Shut that damn thing off!"

A groan swelled from the audience as the lights came up, obliterating the video. Margot took a swig of chardonnay and glared at the audience.

"My God, what's that all about?" I whispered to Dan.

"Remember that sequence when her character jumped off a cliff with the vampire? Apparently some gal fell off a roof emulating her. Didn't come to a good end."

Somebody handed Margot a mic, which I suspected wouldn't come to a good end, either. The woman was clearly angry, her voice shaking.

"You numbskulls can't seem to understand what this sort of thing can lead to. You can dress up however you like, but you can't just play around with death like this. You don't know what can happen. We did because we had scripts, you idiots. Get a life!"

Another figure, just as angry, strode on stage, mic in hand. I recognized her immediately, despite geeky spectacles and an odd wig with ringlets cascading down her back. Her '60s-era miniskirt revealed the stick-thin legs that could only be the ones Emma inherited from our mother.

"It's Emma," I hissed. "What's she doing here?"

"Emma? That's our Emma? She was playing the governess, and I didn't even recognize her."

"I had no idea she was mixed up in this fandom scene. How

awkward."

Emma boldly stepped up to Margot and shouted, "You're not pulling a Shatner on us! We don't need you to tell us fans to get a life. This is what we do . . . and it's for fun! Maybe you forgot that what was so great about *Dark Secrets* is that nobody stayed dead. You all came back from the dead again and again, maybe in different roles, but . . ."

"We played supernatural characters, you fool! Vampires and witches can do that. But don't do it at home. Kids play around and bad things happen."

"Really? Well, look at Brian, then." She flung her skinny arm toward the corpse, who was busily wiping blue powder off his face. "Seems fine to me."

"Well, it's not so fine when a sweet young girl in Des Moines jumps from the garage roof and breaks a leg trying to be me. As Clarissa, the governess, I leaped two feet off a parapet onto a mattress. It's called acting when we make you believe it was a fall from a cliff onto a rocky shore. You're setting a bad example with these asinine reenactments and it's got to stop. Why do you think poor Dan beat it out of here when he did?"

"He's back, in case you didn't know it. Right there!" Emma waved in our direction and fifteen hundred pairs of eyes turned to see us standing in a shaft of light at the doors to the ballroom. As if on cue, Dan stepped forward and waved. At once, a sea of cell phones and video cameras focused on Dan turning this way and that, screen royalty acknowledging the genuflecting masses.

"Hey there, Dan! Welcome back!" Emma shouted. "C'mon up here, my darling. Your Lady in Waiting is waiting for you."

"That was you, Emma?" Dan called out, blowing her a kiss. Then he waved to the crowd as he trotted up the steps leading to the stage, cell phones and video cameras recording it all. I shrank back, watching my old friend flinging himself headfirst back into the limelight.

He wrapped his arms around Margot's bulk, kissing her on both cheeks. She slapped his behind and said, "Naughty boy, you should be doing your homework!" The crowd lapped it up, laughing uproariously.

Emma was bouncing up and down in her vintage saddle shoes, arms outstretched, ringlets bobbing, no doubt recalling those make-out sessions of yesteryear. Dan obliged, kissing her on both cheeks, then planting a smacker on her lips, possibly recalling those long ago make-out sessions himself. The audience swooned, recording it all for uploads to Facebook and Instagram.

"Hey, Danny, how about a photo op as Chuckie," Emma cooed

into her mic. "Everyone would love it—wouldn't we?"

The applause and cheers were tumultuous. Dan brushed his foot on the stage in an *aw, shucks* kind of way and grinned.

"Sure, what the heck. I'm here and glad to see you all." He waved again, to foot stomping approval.

"Photo op! Photo op!" The fans clamored in unison, cheering and clapping. "Photo op now!"

"Hey, hey, guys, okay!" Dan grinned. "I think I know what you want, okay?"

To thunderous applause, Dan turned to Brian, the corpse, and accepted the Chuckie jacket and cap he proffered. I watched in dismay as my friend donned both. Margot, too, seemed to overlook her previous revulsion to reenactments and accepted the geeky glasses Emma handed her. Thankfully, Margot would not be wearing the ringlet wig, nor the plaid miniskirt.

Dan stepped up on the Plexiglass cube as Brian wound the necktie around the closet rail. The flimsy door was then closed. Margot, with winks to the audience, cleared her throat and called out, "Chuckie? Chuckie, where are you?" The audience roared with laughter. Margot slowly circled the stage, milking the scene, calling, "Chuckie, you haven't finished your maths."

Margot made a show of looking around again before finally flinging open the closet door, and I caught my breath in unison with the vast communal gasp heard throughout the ballroom.

"Danny!" Margot screamed, stepping back. "No!"

"No!" screamed the audience, jockeying for position, cameras focused on Danny hanging, legs twitching, the Plexiglass cube kicked over.

Unencumbered by any recording device, I raced to the stage and mounted the steps, reaching Danny split seconds before shock wore off and other hands grabbed at the taut necktie tethering him to the closet rail.

"Call an ambulance!" I shouted, grabbing Danny by the hips and lifting upward. "And the police! Now!"

We untied Dan and shifted him onto the floor. I fell to my knees, pushing Emma out of the way, and began resuscitation efforts. "You fools!" I spat out between breaths. "Whose macabre idea was this?"

"Mine!" a voice pitched in fury screamed. "Mine, and I'd do it again!"

I looked up to see Brian, the corpse, smears of blue powder still streaking his face, shaking his fist at Danny. "I hope he's dead!" he shrieked, his eyes crazed. "He made my life a living hell."

"You kicked the cube!" Emma cried. "You set him up to be

killed!"

"Damn right! When I was nine years old I almost hung myself trying to be Chuckie. I could have died, but post-traumatic stress syndrome is almost as bad. The nightmares. Day-mares. I can't look at a necktie without passing out. He deserves to die!"

Kicking and screaming, Brian was wrestled into a chair and secured by two hefty fans until police arrived. EMTs showed up, and I let them take over while I comforted my sobbing sister.

"I had no idea, none. Brian's one of our most stalwart fans. I guess Dan showing up set him off. It was just too much for him. I'll never forgive myself."

Dan did not survive. In real life, bodies stay dead. I knew it was already too late when I lifted his lifeless body down from the railing. His death was hard on everyone, not least Emma, who suffered a nervous breakdown. As his "Lady in Waiting," Emma admitted she'd made it her mission to lure him back to the fold. But Dan had been right after all. That much adulation couldn't be good for the soul. It turned out to be the death of him.

# TARNISHED HOPE

## by KM Rockwood

"Don't forget the meeting," Cora said as she maneuvered her housekeeping cart next to mine and reached for a towering stack of towels.

"What meeting?" I put a supply of coffee packets on my cart. Nothing sends tips in the wrong direction faster than not replacing coffee packets in the rooms.

As I straightened up, a stab of pain snaked from the small of my back down my right leg all the way to my toes. I had one pain pill left, unless I could score a few more from Rico, who usually had a supply.

"Mandatory meeting at the end of the shift today. Didn't you see the notice on the bulletin board?"

"Guess not."

"It's been up for two days."

Why today? I rubbed my aching back. My head throbbed. The quarter hour of overtime pay for the meeting would be welcome—a single mom working as a hotel housekeeper couldn't afford to turn money down—but I had things to do.

Cora and I finished stocking our carts for the next morning and hurried into the starkly furnished staff lounge that doubled as a meeting room. We slid onto a bench next to one of the new girls. They'd taken to hiring recent immigrants. Most of them wore hijabs. They didn't talk much, but their English was good enough when they did. Everybody said they worked harder and complained less than the rest of us.

Geraldine, the housekeeping supervisor, came in, a clipboard in her hand. Her starched uniform was a little too small. Love handles bulged at her waist and the buttons over her bosom strained.

If my uniform looked like that, she'd have been on me in a minute. I always wore the optional apron—it covered a multitude of sins.

She cleared her throat and swept her eyes over the staff. "Good afternoon. I have some good news for us."

We could use some good news. Business had been slow lately.

"You've all heard about the fire at the Crystal Dome hotel out by the airport?"

I'd heard about it on the news. I hadn't thought much about it.

"I'm sorry for their misfortune." She smirked. She wasn't sorry at all. "But their loss is our gain. We've acquired a last minute convention. It starts Monday morning and runs five days. People will start arriving throughout the day tomorrow."

She checked her clipboard. "I know this is short notice, but we can handle it. There will be schedule changes for most of us. All leave is canceled. If that's a problem for you, see me privately and we'll see what we can arrange."

Cora dug her elbow into my side. "That might mean an overtime shift or two for us. I could use the money."

I nodded. I could, too. Between putting money aside for my handicapped son and for pills from Rico, things were always tight.

"It's an education convention," Geraldine continued.

A sigh rose from the assembled crowd. Teachers were notorious low tippers. And even the bigwigs on expense accounts weren't free spenders.

"But not teachers. This is a for-profit business. A group called Charter Schools America. I believe they have some schools right here in the city."

Tears pricked my eyelids.

Indeed, they had schools here in the city.

When they first opened, I signed up my son, Peter, for high school. Peter was bright, but he always struggled in school. He qualified for special education. Emotional disturbance. Maybe autism, I now thought, but at the time it wasn't diagnosed. The intake counselor assured me that they had a psychiatrist on the staff. Not just a psychologist, but a medical doctor who could prescribe meds. Peter would receive individual attention and close monitoring. It sounded good.

It was the worst decision I ever made.

Cora nudged me.

Geraldine was droning on. "No vacancies . . . banquets . . . breakfast buffets . . . a lot of work, but good for business."

"And," she said with a flourish, "the Presidential Suite is rented out."

Wasn't that often the Presidential Suite was rented out. It was ridiculously expensive, with three bedrooms, four baths, a formal dining room, a reception room, a sauna, its own exercise room.

"The occupant is one Harrison Detwilder, the renowned child development expert. You may have seen his television show."

I hadn't.

After learning I'd scored an extra shift on Monday, I changed out of my uniform, took my coat from the locker, and wrapped my white scarf around my neck. Sometimes I'd find myself crying unexpectedly, and I'd discovered I could pull up the scarf to hide the tears on my cheeks. I didn't used to cry like that. But now, I found that the pain in my back, combined with everything else, could overwhelm me.

The employee exit went through the garage. I looked around for Rico, a valet parker and my supplier. I didn't like to think of him as a drug dealer. That sounded so sleazy. But that's what he was.

He came walking from the valet parking area, whistling and tossing a set of keys in the air and catching them in his hand. His dark hair was slicked back and his skin was pale. He'd always been thin, but now he looked emaciated. And he had an open sore on his neck. I wondered if he was sampling his own wares a bit too freely.

When he saw me, he stopped, grinning. "End of the month, huh? What d'you need?"

Rico knew I took oxycodone for my back pain, but he always asked. The doctor at the clinic said she couldn't prescribe any more than she already had. And no matter how I tried to ration the pills, I always ran out at the end of the month. Monday, I could stop by the clinic and they would give me a renewal. But the pain wouldn't wait until Monday.

I squinted at him in the harsh overhead light. "You got oxies?"

"You're in luck. I just got a supply. How many you want?"

"How much are they?"

"Thirty-five, just like last month. I try to keep the price down. 'Specially for you." He tilted his head and winked.

Outrageously expensive, but I had no other choice.

I closed my hand on the pharmacy bottle in my pocket. It contained the one remaining capsule and the hundred dollar bill I'd taken from the small stash under a loose floorboard in the closet of my one-room apartment. "At least two." That might get me through. But I'd be on my feet for that extra shift on Monday. And I wouldn't get to the clinic until after work. "How many have you got?"

He shook his head. "Enough. What did you have in mind?"

An idea was forming in my head. "How about ten?"

"Ten? That's a lot. You want to be careful."

"Some extra to have, just in case."

Rico sighed. "Don't usually work that way. People tend to take all they got."

"I know. But I'm pretty good about making my prescription last for most of the month."

"That you are," he agreed. "You got three hundred and fifty dollars?"

"Not with me."

"What've you got on you?"

"A hundred."

"I'll give you three. You can pay me the five when you bring the other two fifty."

"I'm good for it."

"I know. But I'm not letting them go until I get the money. Business is business, you know."

"You'll hold onto them for me?"

"Yeah. Until tomorrow night."

"Make that Monday night. I don't work tomorrow."

"Okay. Monday night. Usually, it's first come, first served. But just for you, I'll keep them back. After Monday night, though, they're gone."

I handed him the hundred. He gave me back three little capsules, which I slipped into the pharmacy bottle and snapped the lid shut.

The bus ride home took forever. I skipped my usual shower, ate quickly, and hurried off to the nursing home my son had called home for the last three years. Well, *called* wasn't the right word. Peter hadn't spoken since he jumped off the roof of our apartment building in a failed suicide attempt at age sixteen. The doctors at the hospital told me Peter had severe head trauma. He might get a little better, but it had become increasingly obvious that he'd never walk or talk again.

I spent all my spare time at the nursing home, trying to take care of him. By scrimping and saving, I managed to bring him whatever he needed that the home didn't cover. Lotion for his dry skin, a soft warm shawl to wrap around him when he was in his wheelchair, a radio so he had something to listen to for the hour after hour he spent staring into space. And since he'd need money after I was gone, I'd have to set up some kind of special needs trust. I was saving for that, too.

When I reached Peter's room tonight, the only sound in the room was the whirr of the heat/ventilation system. He sat in a wheelchair. His supper tray lay on a table beside him, barely touched. A pool of greasy gravy was congealing around the ground meat patty. The scoop of dingy mashed potatoes was the same color as dirty snow a week after it had been plowed off a parking lot. The applesauce was undisturbed in its little bowl.

The nursing assistant, carrying some bed linens, stuck her head in the room. "Glad you're here. He wouldn't eat anything at all when I tried to feed him."

*And how hard did you try?* I wanted to ask. But I didn't say anything. If I made her mad, she might take it out on Peter.

I picked up a napkin and gently wiped drool from Peter's chin. He didn't look at me, and his expression didn't change. Sometimes I thought Peter recognized me when I talked to him. But it was probably wistful thinking on my part.

"Mama's here." I rested my hand on his.

His skin was ice cold. His shawl was on the foot of his bed. I sniffed it to make sure he hadn't thrown up on it or something, then wrapped it around his shoulders, giving him a kiss on the cheek.

Peter showed no response. I picked up the spoon on his tray and put a little applesauce on the tip of it. When I touched it to his lip, his mouth opened and I could slip it in. His teeth closed on the spoon and he swallowed.

Forty minutes later, I had managed to get most of the supper into him.

I was so tired. My whole body ached. I couldn't think of anything to say to him. I turned on the radio and sat beside him, holding his hand.

The nursing assistant came in to get Peter ready for bed. I couldn't stand to see the diaper-changing routine, so I slipped out to the lobby. Opening my pharmacy bottle, I popped a capsule in my mouth and washed it down with water from the drinking fountain.

Maybe Rico was right. Have extra pills, and you tended to take them.

When I got back to his room, Peter was lying in bed, his blank eyes staring at the ceiling. The radio was off.

I turned it on, softly, and pulled the chair up next to his bed. I stroked his forehead until his eyes closed and his breathing was slow and regular.

Gathering my coat and scarf, I left.

Since tomorrow was my day off, I would spend all day sitting with Peter. Maybe I would splurge and bring him a milkshake. Sometimes he seemed to like them.

***

By Monday morning, I'd made up my mind about the oxies. I retrieved three hundred dollars from the hidey-hole in my closet and went to work.

I was surprised to see Cora in the staff lounge, changing into her uniform. "I thought you were working the evening shift yesterday," I said.

She rolled her eyes. "I did. But Geraldine said I could work today, too, if I wanted. It'll be time and a half."

"Was it busy yesterday?"

"Horrible." She eyed the foot of her white pantyhose critically.

A small hole showed in the heel. "I spent half the shift cleaning up the Presidential Suite."

That was where Harrison Detwilder was staying.

"Why?" I asked.

"He had some kind of party in there, and somebody blew lunch all over. Didn't make it to the pot in time, of course. But whoever it was couldn't just stay in one place, either. Had to puke all over the carpet in the reception room, the dining room, one of the bedrooms. The stink was something awful. So they called the front desk to have somebody come clean it up. Lucky me."

"Did you get it cleaned up all right?"

"I guess I did. I used lots of deodorizer. It didn't seem to bother them all that much. They just kept on partying while I was down on my hands and knees scrubbing the carpet." Cora yanked the pantyhose on.

"Really?"

"Yeah. Spilling drinks all over. There was some white powder and razor blades on one of the tables. I just left that."

"Did you get the smell out of the carpet?"

"I think so. By the time I got done, all I could smell was the disinfectant, anyhow. But the guy who rented the suite, that TV guy Detwilder, he sat right down on the couch next to the worst spot, and he seemed okay with it."

"Then what did he do?" I asked.

Cora reached into her locker and pulled out a bottle of clear nail polish. She dabbed some on the hole in the pantyhose. "He poured himself a glass of Irish cream whiskey—one of those big water glasses. Then he turned on the TV. And pulled out his cellphone."

\*\*\*

We were shorthanded, and I hurried from one room to another, skipping lunch break in favor of a quick granola bar from the vending machine in the staff lounge.

I could only hope the tips would be decent.

As I pushed my cart through the hallways near the end of my shift, the public areas of the hotel were surprisingly empty.

All the guests were gathered in the banquet room. First hors d'oeuvres and an open bar, followed by filet mignon and Yorkshire pudding. Cases of wine were stacked in the service hallway. Harrison Detwilder was the keynote speaker, scheduled to give his presentation during the dessert and coffee.

When the end of the shift rolled around, I went to the staff lounge and tried to stretch my shoulders. My knees were stiff and my back was locking up. I debated taking another capsule.

We'd all worked extra, and most people were in a hurry to get home. Cora was so tired, she stumbled trying to put on her blue jeans. She yawned and said, "I'm gonna go home and get some sleep."

Instead of changing, I put my coat on over my uniform and went into the garage to find Rico.

I handed him the three hundred dollars. He gave me my change and seven capsules, which I put into my bottle.

"Now, you be careful," he warned. "It's easy to OD on them things."

I nodded and thanked him.

When I got back to the staff lounge, it was deserted. I put my coat back in the locker and straightened my uniform, taking off my apron and hanging it up next to the coat. I put my white scarf around my neck and over my head, like a hijab. Then I went to the linen storage closet, where I took a stack of bath towels.

Using my housekeeping key card, I called the service elevator. When it came, I got on and punched the "penthouse" button. The trip took about a minute, and as the elevator doors opened, I realized I hadn't been up here since my introductory tour when I was first hired.

Two doors opened off the small lobby. One said Utilities. The other said Service Entrance.

Two security cameras winked in the corners. I kept my head down.

When I swiped my key card on the service entrance, the little green light came on. I turned the handle, pushed the door open, and stepped into a dark hallway with a tiled floor. I felt my way along the wall and shoved open the unlocked door at the end of the hall.

It opened into a kitchenette. Beyond that was the reception room of the Presidential Suite. Through the tall windows, I could see the lowering sun outlining the skyline of the city.

I stepped out into the suite.

Fresh flower arrangements perfumed the air. Delicate white figurines touched with gold accents graced the tables. Plush cushions lay scattered over sofas and easy chairs.

I closed my eyes for a moment. Peter's barren room would fit in a corner of the dining room.

The bar stood against the far wall. I went over and scanned the bottles. Most were on shelves on the wall, but a few sat on the bar.

One was a bottle of Irish cream whiskey, about a third full.

A marble board held several kinds of cheese.

I moved the cheese onto the wooden bar surface. Then I got out my pharmacy bottle and emptied the contents onto the hard marble.

Using a sturdy spoon from the kitchenette and the cheese knife,

I crushed all but one of the capsules. I swept the now-powdery contents into the spoon and emptied it into the whiskey bottle, screwed the top on tight, and shook it, hard.

I returned the remaining capsule to my pharmacy bottle, put the cheese back on the board, and scanned the bar. As far as I could tell, it looked just like it had when I'd first seen it.

Picking up the towels, I carried them to one of the bathrooms and arranged them on the sink counter. The marble floor gleamed underfoot. I stepped back into the reception room. No luxury or comfort had been overlooked.

What had Harrison Detwilder ever done to deserve living like this?

Three years ago, he'd been Peter's psychiatrist.

A month into the school year, on a slew of new meds, Peter started acting weird. Weird even for Peter. I talked to the counselor at school, who assured me that the psychiatrist would look into it and give me a call. The meds could take a while to work, and I needed to be patient.

By the time I got in touch with Dr. Detwilder, it was too late.

Peter had left me a suicide note and jumped from the top of our apartment building.

He didn't die, but he might have been better off if he had.

I certainly would have been better off. Then I could have made a decision on whether I wanted to go on with my sorry life or join him in death.

But now he needed me.

When I called from the hospital, Dr. Detwilder didn't return my calls. When I finally managed to get him on the phone, he made some sympathetic sounds, but he didn't seem very upset.

"Peter almost killed himself," I said, trying to choke back the tears.

"But he didn't, did he?"

"No. He's in the hospital. There's permanent brain damage. They can't tell me exactly how much."

"I'm afraid this can be an uncommon side effect of the medication," Dr. Detwilder said. "Suicide ideation in the first few weeks after beginning to take it. It's rare for someone to follow through with suicide attempts, though."

"Peter did."

"Yes. Well, I'm sorry. But at least he wasn't successful at it."

Dr. Detwilder made a few more vapid statements and hung up.

He just didn't care.

I took one last glance to make sure everything in the suite looked all right.

They'd throw out the opened bottle if Dr. Detwilder didn't finish it or take it with him. So I could be pretty sure no one else would drink any of it.

I left through the service entrance and used my key card to call the elevator. Once again, I kept my head down.

The white scarf would have to go. I'd throw it in a dumpster on my way to the nursing home. And buy a new scarf. Not a flamboyant one, maybe beige. With some kind of pattern on it, so it would look different from the one on the surveillance video.

The elevator came and I got on it.

Dr. Detwilder hadn't cared what happened to Peter. I couldn't pretend I didn't care what happened to Dr. Detwilder. But this was the closest I could come to replicating what he'd done to Peter.

Would Dr. Detwilder drink the Irish whiskey tonight? I had no way of knowing.

If he did drink it, maybe the overdose would make him sick. Or maybe it would kill him.

Or maybe, just maybe, he'd end up sitting in a wheelchair in a nursing home, staring vacantly at nothing while someone deposited tiny spoonfuls of applesauce into his slack mouth.

I could always hope.

# NOT FORGOTTEN

## by L.C. Tyler

So, what's it to be? Comedy or tragedy? I can write both—comedy or tragedy as you please, my lords and ladies—but mainly I write historical crime novels. So does Jeremy Stone, with whom I am now talking, in a casual way, him leaning against a door frame, me drinking coffee from a paper cup, while the crowd mills round us, as one does and as they do at conventions.

"You don't remember me, do you?" I ask.

"Dear lady," Jeremy says, because that is how he clearly believes women like to be addressed and it saves him the considerable effort of remembering our names. "Dear lady, how could I not know who you are? You are one of this year's highlighted authors. It was in the publicity materials: the organizers were delighted to inform us that Emma Littlewood will be present and that she will be interviewed by Barry Forshaw, no less. How could I not know you?"

Jeremy does not mention, because I cannot be unaware of the fact, that he is the Guest of Honor at this year's convention. He has been a guest of honor at almost every crime writing conference in Britain and America, and even India, though for some reason not France. I have no idea why not France. Now he is the Guest of Honor here. Conference organizers all over the English-speaking world, when searching for a guest of honor, must ask each other, "Have we ever invited Jeremy to do it?" And the reply comes back, "Of course. He was Guest of Honor ten years ago." Or "God, no. We really must invite him this year. Does anyone have his e-mail?" Nobody ever asks, "Who is Jeremy?" or "What's Jeremy's last name?" Jeremy has reached the stage where a second name is superfluous. He is Jeremy.

I, by the way, have never been Guest of Honor anywhere. "Highlighted Guest Author" is actually punching above my weight. I'm a bit midlist, if you see what I mean. I've written quite a few books and the dedicated mystery fans know me, but I don't trouble the best-seller charts. Maybe one day. And in the meantime . . .

"But do you *remember* me?" I ask.

Jeremy looks at me oddly. Hasn't he just answered that question?

I take pity on him. "What are you writing now?" I say.

"Ah," he says with a smile. "That, dear lady, is a very good question. A very good question indeed."

So, he does not remember me. But I remember Jeremy.

\*\*\*

I was twenty-seven? Twenty-eight? Some years ago, anyway. Many gallons of literary water have passed under the bridge in the meantime. I had just published my first novel. Jeremy was then in the first flush of his fame, being midway through his original and, to be brutally honest, only really successful crime series. He was a Featured Guest Author (only one down from Guest of Honor) at this very convention. I had never attended a convention of any sort before. I was excited and nervous in equal measure when contemplating my first public appearance as a published author. And I was pleased to discover that Jeremy Stone (he still needed a surname then) was to chair the panel I was on. Having no idea what to expect, I e-mailed him, enquiring what questions he would ask. He replied that he never revealed such things in advance—it was better, he thought, to keep authors on their toes—but we would have a chance to discuss topics in the Green Room beforehand. I really shouldn't fret too much—it was just a matter of him asking questions and us recounting our usual anecdotes.

I had no anecdotes, usual or otherwise. Nobody had ever assumed I might have anecdotes. In the months leading up to the convention, I tried to come up with a few—things that were illustrative of the theme of our panel: Plackets and Periwigs—Getting the Historical Detail Right. I thought maybe I had produced some good ones. Jeremy was a known raconteur. The standard would be high.

In the Green Room, just before the panel, Jeremy chatted with the other three panelists, who were old mates and had appeared with him before. Two had been at Cambridge with him—he'd rowed in the same boat at something they referred to as the May Bumps. I never found out exactly what the May Bumps were. My requests for more information about what the panel was to be about were met with gracious promises that he would come to that in a bit. He never did. Jeremy carried on with a story about how Fitzwilliam had bumped Lady Margaret in the Long Reach, whoever she was and whatever they were all doing there in the first place. It all sounded a bit sordid, and I honestly didn't like to ask.

Later, with my heart pounding, he led us to the panel room, up onto the platform, and sat us down, me at the far end of the table, farthest from him. I sometimes write about people who are about to be guillotined or burned at the stake—it happened a lot during the periods that I specialize in. You pretty much can't avoid pain of one sort or another if you do Early Modern. I try to convey how the characters must have *felt* in the run-up to that sort of event. Did they hope they would die bravely? Or did they just hope it would be quick? It's not always easy to get into their sixteenth- or eighteenth-century minds, but after that panel I knew much better what they had been through, tied to the stake with the flames licking round them. After that panel, I knew first hand that there was a point at which death comes as a blessed relief.

Jeremy started by announcing that this was the least distinguished panel he'd ever chaired. That drew both laughter and applause. Everyone knew Jeremy, even then; whatever would he say next? Never a dull moment with Jeremy Stone in the chair. He proceeded to introduce the panelists one by one, inviting them to say a few words about their work. I say "them" because he never quite got to me. I'd prepared carefully for this question, but my heart rate still increased noticeably as he worked his way along the table. He finished with my right-hand neighbor and I took a deep breath, my first carefully crafted anecdote on my lips, but Jeremy had become fascinated with a story of his own that he was telling, and then with something that the story reminded him of. In the end I went wholly unintroduced.

When he asked the next question, the audience still had no idea who I was, and one or two of them looked at me curiously, as if I were some witless interloper who had strayed into the wrong room and whom Jeremy was too polite, too damned charming, to eject. As I sat there, I wasn't sure that the audience wasn't absolutely right. The invitation had been issued in error. My preparation had been utterly in vain. Then, halfway through somebody else's response, Jeremy looked at me, held up his hand and said, "This is Emma, by the way. She hasn't said a lot yet. Come on, Emma, these people have paid good money to listen to us. Say hello at least."

The audience laughed, as they did at most things Jeremy said.

"Hi," I said nervously, to nobody in particular. I may have waved. I prefer not to remember.

"Hi?" Jeremy said. "You'll have to do a bit better than that. Is there anything else you'd like to say, dear lady?"

"Which question am I answering?" I mumbled. "The first or the second?"

"Whichever you prefer," Jeremy said. "We're very informal here."

More laughter from the audience. I was suddenly the focus of attention. I must have looked like a startled deer.

"So, what was the second question?" I asked hoarsely. I made a grab for my water bottle and sent it flying. I was relieved to see it land harmlessly just short of the front row. But I could have used some of that water.

The audience was now ecstatic. Good old Jeremy. Never ever a dull moment.

"We'll come back to Emma when she's a little more on the ball," he said. "I don't know about you, but I'm greatly looking forward to that moment."

I think he did—ask me further questions, I mean. After that start, I never was on the ball. Every answer I gave seemed slow and trite. I stuttered, forgot where I was; my answers tailed off into a vast amorphous void that only I had access to. I seriously contemplated sliding under the table and out of view. I'm not sure why I didn't. It would have got a laugh at least. Comedy and tragedy often go hand in hand.

That night, in an obscure corner of the convention hotel bar, my agent said, "Jeremy Stone was totally out of order. Since you were a debut panelist, he should have gone out of his way to make you feel at ease—not used you as a butt for his cheap jokes. Wait until your next panel, Emma—not all chairs are like that. Fortunately."

"I'm never doing a panel again," I said, draining my fourth gin and tonic. "Never, ever. I would rather slit my own throat with this swizzle stick. I'm useless. I've probably just lost any fans I ever had in the audience. Just bury me over there under that stained bit of carpet."

"You're not useless, Emma," my agent said. "You're actually very funny and have lots of interesting things to say. It's simply that Jeremy Stone is a bastard. Thinking about it rationally, he deserves to die."

Thus it was we swore a solemn oath on one or two things that we held sacred that, at the first convenient opportunity, we would murder Jeremy Stone and then dance on his grave. After that we went off to our respective beds. I went to sleep, woke up, had a shower, had breakfast, and, in the months and years to come, I completely forgot that that was what we had agreed to do.

*** 

"So," I say to Jeremy, "what is the plot of this new novel of yours?"

Jeremy smiles. "That, dear lady, is a very well-kept secret. It is, you might say, the novel that I shall be remembered for. It is innovative and springs such a surprise on the reader in the last chapter that they will never forget it. Think, if you will, of *The Murder of Roger Ackroyd*. Or perhaps of *The Spy Who Came in from the Cold*. The reader is persuaded that certain things are so, then, at the last moment, their little world is turned upside down. They gasp with amazement because it is not just that the denouement is possible—it is *the only possible outcome*. It is the simplicity of the twist that I am most pleased with—it is as though the reader had been looking at the plot in the mirror. Suddenly the image is reversed and things that make no sense before come sharply into focus."

"Looking at things in a mirror doesn't make them come into focus," I say. "It just turns them 'round."

Jeremy smiles. "I spoke metaphorically, dear lady. It was simply a picturesque turn of phrase using a suitable analogy."

"No shit?" I say.

"Quite," he says.

"But you can't tell me the plot?"

"No. You, like the rest of the world, will have to await the publication of *Mirror Image* by Jeremy Stone."

"You think I'd stoop so low as to steal your plot?"

"How can I tell? You might promise not to now, but later . . . Ladies are such fickle and changeable creatures. As you know."

"We ladies say that to each other all the time," I say, "though later we change our minds and say we aren't."

"I rather wish I'd said that," he observes archly.

You will, Jeremy, you will, I think. But what I actually say is, "But can you at least reveal whether it has poison in it. Death by poison is rather your trademark."

"So it is," he says. "I must say I do poison better than anyone since Agatha."

"Dear Agatha," I say. Somebody else who needs no surname. "Yes, she was good. She knew her stuff all right. She had first-hand knowledge of many poisons, of course, having worked in a dispensary. But I've learned a great deal about poisons from your own books, Jeremy. If I ever wanted to kill somebody, all I would have to do is to open the appropriate volume and check the dosage. I must admit that I have occasionally stolen *that* from you—how to administer cyanide, for example—how somebody who has ingested cyanide dies. It's not as quick as people think, is it?"

"The victim experiences a certain amount of discomfort," Jeremy concedes. "But if I say that two hundred milligrams of cyanide is enough to kill a man, then that's the amount you should use—it would be wasteful to buy more. And if I say that death follows after a couple of minutes, then that's how long it takes. Of course, if your readers believe that cyanide causes almost instantaneous death, and most people do, then you can run into difficulties telling them the truth. P. D. James got into terrible trouble when she had a motorbike reverse down a street. She was inundated with letters telling her that motorcycles have no reverse gear. It became a famous gaffe. Then a gentleman wrote to her and said, 'about that motorbike—it can if it's a Harley Davidson'." Jeremy looks at me and chuckles. It is one of his anecdotes. That is the third or fourth time I've heard him tell it. He's never told it quite as well as P. D. James originally told it herself.

"Well, as a female, P. D. James could scarcely be expected to understand machinery," I say.

"Other than a vacuum cleaner," he says.

"Your wife must love your sense of humor," I say. "She must be in stitches. Is she here, by the way?"

"She never comes to conventions," he says. "She says she's heard all my stories before."

"Me, I can't get enough of them," I say.

"You're too kind," he says.

"So," I say, "if you were to be poisoned tonight, which one would you choose?"

"I'd rather not. I have a novel to write. I could not deprive the world of such a masterpiece. That would be too cruel."

"Have you actually started it yet?"

"I tell my publisher I have," he says with a smile. "And I've taken the advance."

"Okay, let's say that you could write it by midnight and that the book is no longer an impediment. There's nothing else, contractual or otherwise, to stop you dying if you wish to. You are free to be killed by the poison of your choice. What's it to be?"

Jeremy considers this carefully. "I've always thought," he says, "that an overdose of heroin would be a perfectly good way to go."

*Really*? I think. Heroin?

"Well, no problem about getting some of that in this city," I say. "If you know the right people."

"I'm sure that there isn't," he says. "I probably passed half a dozen dealers on my way in from the station."

"At a minimum. I bet it's as easy to buy as whisky. Do you fancy a drink later?"

"I'm having dinner with my agent," he says.

"Oh, I don't mean early evening," I say.

"In the bar?"

"I thought we might go back to my room," I say.

He raises an eyebrow. "You seem to forget, Emma, that I'm a married man," he says.

"I forget nothing," I say. "Nothing at all."

One of the many things that Jeremy clearly fancies himself to be is what once was called a ladies' man—the sort of person who wore a silk cravat and lit your cigarette for you, one hand brushing your tit as he did it. He'd open the bedroom door for you as you both slid in, checking the corridor for possible witnesses. I suspect that Jeremy normally opens the bedroom door for slightly younger women. Well, I may be over forty now, but I've kept myself in good shape. Hell, I could pass for thirty-eight any day of the week. Jeremy is over sixty and has not checked his waist measurement for some time.

"What's your room number?" he asks.

I tell him. He commits it to memory.

"What time?" he asks.

"Why don't we say eleven?" I suggest. "Most people will have cleared off to bed by then. You won't be missed in the bar. I won't be missed in the bar or anywhere else."

He winks at me and sidles away to talk to one of his mates. One of his many mates. Jeremy, this year's Guest of Honor.

***

So what is this to be? Comedy or tragedy? Well, it's crime, obviously. I have until eleven. I think I'll take a stroll round the city. Maybe stock up on one or two things.

***

At eleven on the dot, I hear a gentle tap at my door. I get up and open it. Jeremy is there, leering at me, slightly the worse for wear.

I look theatrically to the right and left, then usher him in. He flops onto the bed, semirecumbent as if unsure whether the action will begin straight away or whether he will have to pay me a compliment or two first. Maybe I don't sleep with guys who don't praise my use of tragic irony. Lots of girls don't.

I take a glass and a bottle of whisky—a proper bottle of malt, not some minibar miniature of God knows what.

"You remembered my little weakness," he mumbles.

"I shouldn't have taken it for granted," I say. "Perhaps I should have asked: what's your poison, eh?"

"Ha!" he says. "Very good!"

I mix a drink for him carefully, my body shielding the precise proportions of the various ingredients from his sight.

"I've added a little water," I say. "Let me know if that's strong enough for you. I bet you like it stronger than I do. As a man."

"And you?"

"Water with a dash of whisky."

"What a waste of good malt."

"I have some work to do later. I'm chairing a panel."

"Last-minute nerves? Why don't I do something to settle them?

I'm good at that. You've never been on a panel with me, have you?"

I have a moment of doubt. Is it right to do this if he has forgotten the original offense? Should I remind him what happened? So that, when *this* happens, he will understand. He will see why he deserves it. Is there any point in revenge if the victim of it has no idea why they are being punished? These are questions that might, in themselves, occupy a panel for the allotted forty minutes. But I really don't have that sort of time to spare.

"Drink up, Jeremy," I say. "I'll fix you another one."

"I'd like one exactly the same as the first," he says.

"Don't worry," I say. "It will be precisely the same."

***

So, I repeat, neither comedy nor tragedy but just crime. I make him another drink, good and strong. I sit down on the bed beside him and watch him drink it.

But . . . hold on one moment . . . you don't think I am about to murder him, surely? I'm sorry, but you really have got hold of the wrong end of the stick if you believe I'd do that. It is true that, fifteen years before, he gave me an uncomfortable thirty minutes (plus questions from the audience). But I've done dozens of panels since then. Maybe hundreds if I counted carefully. What doesn't kill you makes you stronger, as my agent had insisted just before they closed the bar and threw us out. By my third panel I was well into my stride. I was soon being asked to chair them, and I knew how new panelists felt and how to get the very best out of them. You might say Jeremy made me the panel chair I am today. Anyway, it was scarcely as if he had mugged my grandmother or set fire to a bookshop or groomed somebody's pet cat on the Internet for immoral purposes. Death by heroin would have been wrong on so many levels. Even if I knew what heroin looked like or where you found a dealer.

And there are crimes other than murder. There's theft, for example. That's good, too.

***

It must have been about three o'clock in the morning when I got the last of the plot of *Mirror Image* out of him. It was every bit as original as he had claimed. By then the whisky bottle was empty and he'd forgotten pretty much what had first drawn him to my room. I kissed him on the cheek and ejected him, politely but firmly, into the corridor. Then I sat down and spent an hour and a half making notes.

I assume Jeremy made it back to his own room. He was at breakfast the following morning in a clean shirt. He looked at me cautiously, as if he half-remembered his indiscretions of the night before, but not much more than that. I waved back in a cheerful manner.

"What time's your panel?" he called across the room.

"Sunday," I said. And sailed on toward the man who made the nice omelettes.

***

So, there you have it. Jeremy had the idea first, but he's already admitted he hasn't started writing the book. I reckon I can get my version out first—*Mirror Image* by Emma Littlewood. No, I'll have to come up with a new title. I shall leave him that at least. It really will be my finest book to date. My breakthrough novel at last. Sales will be phenomenal. No more Little Miss Midlist. I'll be invited to be Guest of Honor all over the English-speaking world.

And if Jeremy wants to complain, let him first explain to his wife how I got the information out of him.

Emma Littlewood. Remember the name. Shortly coming to a convention near you.

# BOSTON BOUILLABAISSE

## by Nancy Brewka-Clark

"I detest manga." Deidre poked at the little book in its bright jacket like a small child shoving a bowl of pureed peas away. "Mash-ups, too."

"My dear woman, what on earth are you talking about?" Charles didn't bother to stifle a sigh. "What in heaven's name is *mawngah*? And why would one apply a kitchen utensil to it? And, above all, what does any of it have to do with poetry?"

With a trembling finger Deidre pointed at the sticker on the little book's cover. "If Yvonne Narbonne can win a prestigious prize writing nonsense like this, all of us are doomed."

"It depends on what you consider to be prestigious." Charles smiled complacently. "I personally find it quite appropriate that her little tome has garnered a gold star. After all, it is a children's book, is it not, written in some form of Japanese meter?"

"No, it is not." Deidre had agreed to represent the North American Guild of Published Poets at the Boston Booksellers' Convention because she expected to see that star glittering on the cover of her latest book of sonnets. But *Pistils of Death* hadn't even made the short list. "Manga is Japanese in origin, but let me assure you that's the only thing it shares with *haiku*, *tanka*, *waka*, or *kanshi*." Deidre dropped her voice even though no one had ventured within ten yards of their booth all morning. "This dreadful little book's merely written in words of one and two syllables. It's about cats and pirates and robots from outer space. Can you imagine?"

"Must I?" Charles mumbled, caught in a yawn.

"And the illustrations." Deidre slid the book back toward her and flipped it open. "Simply ghastly." She tapped the glossy page. "Look at this. Just look at it. It's supposed to be a cat. Not exactly Sir John Tenniel's Cheshire cat, is it, Charles?"

"One must move with the times," Charles said. "Shakespeare had the sonnet market covered almost half a millennium ago, or didn't you know?"

"That's rich, coming from you," Deidre snapped, only to regret it instantly. Charles Bitterwyn Blakely was a near-mythical figure in the poetry world. He'd won a Pulitzer in 1973 for a small book written exclusively in the Welsh *Cyhydedd Hir* style, sixteen lines composed of two sets of eight-line stanzas with two quatrains each of complex internal rhythms. The fact that he'd never published a line since had merely added to his cachet. "What I mean, Charles, is that Yvonne's nonsense hardly requires the skill of your *koor-heer-ded hee-hah.*"

"My dear lady, do forgive me, but may I remind you it is pronounced *cuh-hee-ded heer*," he said, plucking at his snowy mustache.

"Why, Charles, that's what I said." Deirdre blinked at him through her massive red and gold plastic Iris-Apfel-inspired glasses. "I distinctly said *koor-heer-ded hee-hah.*"

"Why, yes, you did. Twice. But it's incorrect. The Welsh language, my good woman, demands precisely . . . displacement of the glottal . . . in which the lips . . ."

The longer the pompous windbag lectured, the more Deidre wished she'd brought along a little something to shut him up. Her sonnets about belladonna, blue passion flower, lily of the valley, rosary pea, jack-in-the-pulpit, moonseed, mandrake, bleeding heart, autumn crocus, and angel's trumpet were the most haunting she'd ever written. To inspire her, she'd filled the bay window of her apartment with great green swaths of dieffenbachia, a common houseplant otherwise known as—ta-da!—dumb cane. Lethal in larger doses, just a bit of leaf rendered one speechless. Mute. Dumb.

"So I shall say it once more. *Cuh-hee-ded-heer.* Not *koor-heer-ded hee-hah.*" Charles waggled a fat finger at her outraged face. "Not that you do it on purpose. You merely have a *Bahstan* accent."

"I don't speak with an accent," Deidre snapped.

"Indeed." Charles was staring at a stunning young blonde making her way toward them over the vast sea of black and red paisley all-weather carpet while towing a medium-sized black suitcase on wheels. "Who's that?"

"Don't you recognize her?" With a sniff, Deidre flipped the little book over to display the colored photo. "Thar she blows."

"Hardly an apt cliché." Charles stroked his mustache the way another man might pet his cat, although not if the creature looked like the illustration in the book beneath his nose. "I had no idea she was so young."

"She's late," Deidre spat. "She was supposed to relieve us an hour ago."

"She's obviously just gotten off the plane," Charles said. "A bit tousled but it becomes her."

"Jeans." Deidre's frown turned into an outright scowl. "And a

T-shirt. Who does she think she is, a female Thom Gunn? Why doesn't she just stick a cigarette behind her ear and call it a day?"

"I doubt the girl's ever heard of Thom Gunn," Charles said with a touch of sadness, "nor read *The Man with Night Sweats.*"

The two of them watched as Yvonne Narbonne stopped at first one booth and then another to exchange pleasantries, which often included hugs. "Friendly sort, isn't she?" Charles observed.

"People are such suck-ups," Deirdre muttered. "Take away that award and see—"

Deidre broke off as the younger poet loomed up before them. "Howdy, pardners! Yvonne Narbonne at y'all's service. You must be Ms. Dunhall. I love your work."

Deidre's gaze fell on the star. "That's quite a compliment coming from the winner of the Longfellow Award."

"And I've learned so dang much from yours, Professor Blakely." Yvonne widened her blue eyes. "I can't tell you how many nights I just lie awake thinking of your masterpiece, 'Being, Breath, Death,' and wondering how you ever managed to pack so much meaning into those itty-bitty lines."

"It's a matter of the scheme itself," Charles said. "When one thoroughly immerses oneself in the process, *i.e.*, first line consisting of syllable, syllable, syllable, syllable, and rhyming syllable, second line consisting of syllable, syllable, syllable, syllable, and second rhyming syllable, then third line the same, followed by syllable, syllable, syllable—"

"I know," Yvonne cooed. "It's just, like, very, very cool. And that brings me to the next thang. Do y'all think I should change?"

"Change what, exactly, my dear?" Charles asked.

"My clothes." Yvonne looked down at herself and then at their twin tweedy presences.

"See, my little book has inspired a bunch of costumes. You can get 'em on Amazon. My agent got in touch with Johnny Depp's agent and, wow, they got him to pose for Kyrol the Pirate King."

"Really?" Charles said. "Who posed for the cat?"

When Yvonne was done hooting with laughter, drawing more attention to the poets' booth than they'd achieved all weekend, she said, "Well, tomorrow's the big day, anyway."

"For what?" Charles and Deirdre asked in sync.

"A bunch of us, I mean writers who have in-print and e-books out right now in Amazon's top one hundred, are doing readin's around the world. Each live event'll be digitally recorded and uploaded so everybody can get literate in, like, sixty seconds."

"How marvelous." Deidre's fingers clenched painfully into fists beneath the table. "Why, you'll sell thousands of books. Hundreds of thousands."

"Well, the thang is," Yvonne said, "we're not readin' from our own works. This is really a benefit kind of thang to bring culture to kids in a way that doesn't scare the little rug rats to death." She drew a deep breath. "Li'l ole me was asked to read the works of Anne Bradstreet, Lucy Larcom, Sylvia Plath, and Anne Sexton."

In the silence Deidre could have sworn she heard Charles's heart banging, although it might have been her own. When she didn't keel over, she managed to say, "Those are all New England writers, dear. Bahstan writers. Were you aware of that before you accepted the assignment?"

"Well, sure." Yvonne slapped her forehead as if one of the region's infamous deer ticks might have dropped on her from the exposed heating ducts. "OMG, it's the way I talk, 'n' it? Don't y'all worry, I can sound real snooty when I have to." She gave the suitcase a little kick. "I was supposed to be here earlier, but things got all messed up. My crew was supposed to all fly in together from New York and stay the night at the Cooper Plaza, I think it's called?"

"Copley," Charles said gently.

"Uh-huh. Excuse me. I should call them—Copley, right? About my room." Whipping out her cell, she did exactly that. After a short but heated exchange, she disconnected. "Dang. They don't have me listed. Whoever was supposed to handle the plane reservations must have messed up the hotel reservations, too. Publishers, huh? I'll have to find someplace else."

Deidre said, "This time of year everything's booked. But you know, dear, I live right here in town. Well, Dorchester, actually, not that that means anything to a Texas gal. But I'd love to have you if you don't mind sleeping on my sofa bed." Feeling Charles's eyes boring into the side of her head like a brain surgeon's drill, she added sweetly, "Charles, would you care to join us for dinner? I'll cook."

"Why, yes," Charles gabbled. "I'd love to. How nice."

If—no, when—they started to show the symptoms of a mild dose of dumb cane—hoarseness, swelling throat, inability to speak—she'd tell them they must be coming down with a virus. Nobody could ever blame her for that.

Looking from one wrinkled face to the other, Yvonne sighed. "And they say New Englanders are cold."

\*\*\*

"Why didn't you let me call a cab?" Charles shouted as the Boston Red Line subway car rattled around a curve in the tracks. "This is positively—"

"Amazing." Yvonne gazed around the jam-packed car as if she'd just landed on Planet Earth from a far-off galaxy.

"I think so, too, dear." Deidre managed to stand, thrusting her way between a young black man in a robe and strings of beads and a rabbi, both of whom were dangling from straps like UNICEF Christmas ornaments. "Ashmont. This is our stop. Let's go."

Twisting her head from side to side as they walked down the narrow street, Yvonne said, "Say, there's no trees here. Just like home. I'd just love to live on the top floor of one of these big, ole skinny houses. And I adore the porches. Imagine sitting way up high there and looking down at all that traffic pouring by. Why, you'd be way above the fumes, wouldn't you? Oh, look, what-all's goin' on?"

Deidre peered down the street into the brick square seething with life. "It's a street fair." She'd grown so used to ethnic festivals that she'd barely noticed the rattles, drums, electric guitars, and trumpets making lively music that came flooding from speakers the size of small cars. All around the square, booths and tables were offering foods that smelled divine but packed a digestive wallop. "Let's see if there's something special you'd like for dinner."

Deidre knew from experience that most of the dishes were so heavily spiced they simply had to be disguising the main ingredient, as had been done in medieval Europe. Cat? Snake? Squirrel? Old inner tube? Any of them could be in the giant stew pots. And all of it would disguise a leaf or two or six of dumb cane.

The three of them walked around the tables, circling and sniffing like wolves on the fold. "Um, that looks divine." Yvonne pointed to a giant cauldron from which steam rose like fog from a swamp. "What is that?"

The cook flashed white teeth beneath a black top hat, waving his ladle like a scepter. "Boston bouillabaisse."

"We surely don't have that down Texas way," Yvonne drawled, swaying back and forth coquettishly like a little girl asking for ice cream. "What-all's in it?"

Charles started to supply the classic French recipe, but the cook cut him off. "Fish. Fresh fish. Fresh shellfish, too, lovely shellfish." He pointed in the general direction of the ocean with the handle of the ladle. "Caught this very day." He made a yanking motion with his free hand, laughing. "Me, I pull the mussels from the rocks myself, pull them like I am pulling an old man's beard."

"Perfect." Deidre pulled out the balled-up mesh bag every conscientious go-green shopper carried these days. "Three bowls, please."

"Bread, we must have bread," Charles said, and loped off to the next stall where a matronly woman in a long white apron sold him a long loaf he brandished like a sword. "And cheese."

"I'll buy that," Yvonne caroled, and before Deidre could say Velveeta, the award-winning poet had returned to her side with a great chunk of something wrapped in waxed paper and tied with brown string. "This is going to be some party."

A few minutes later, Deidre scurried up her building's four flights as if she had wings on her heels. Two flights behind her, Yvonne was prattling to Charles. Deidre could hear his labored wheezing. Unlocking the apartment door, she rushed to the small table in the parlor and banged down the bouillabaisse bag with its collection of white plastic spoons. "Soup's on," she shouted.

"We're gettin' there," Yvonne called back, "slow but sure."

Her heart beating wildly, Deidre bent over her thriving window garden. Pinching off a dumb cane leaf, she paused to listen. They were just reaching the third landing. Pinching off another six, just to be on the safe side, she rushed into her tiny kitchen—little more than a broom closet, really. Thrusting the handful of greenery into her old stainless steel Revere Ware coffeepot, she held the pot under the sink until it was full. She was just reaching up for an old-fashioned tin of loose tea and her mesh tea ball when Yvonne called, "Here we are."

"Soup's on the table in the parlor." Deidre plopped the full tea ball into the coffeepot. "I'll just be a minute. I'm making tea." She banged the coffeepot down on the burner and turned on the gas flame. "Feel free to start without me."

"We can't do that," Yvonne began.

But Charles cut her short. "We must obey our gracious hostess." Even from the kitchen Deidre could hear him inhaling the steam from his open bowl. "How can you resist that magnificent perfume, Neptune's own elixir from the briny deep?"

Deidre kept her eyes on the corona of blue flame. Why wasn't the water boiling?

"OMG," Yvonne called, "Ms. Dunhall, you've got to get in here right this minute. This is just super!"

"Coming," Deidre sang, fishing in the cabinet for two extra mugs.

"This delicious concoction," Charles boomed, "reminds me of the time . . ." And off he went on a windy discourse about a Greek isle he'd visited in the 1980s.

Tiny bubbles were just beginning to break the surface when her guests started to cough, first Yvonne, then Charles. "Everything okay?" Deidre called as the tea ball began to jitter. Giving it a dunk, she shoved a spoon into the water to stir the leaves as the coughs grew louder, then walked toward the parlor to investigate. "Yvonne? Charles?"

"Call—" Charles choked, his eyes bulging out of a face as red as one of the lobster shells floating like wreckage in his bowl. "Nine—"

"One," Yvonne rasped through swollen lips an old-fashioned poet might once have described as bee-stung. "One."

Two ambulances and one police car later, Deidre looked out in stunned satisfaction at the empty square. Boston Bouillabaisse Man had been arrested for harvesting seafood illegally during the last toxic algae bloom known as Red Tide, scourge of the New England shellfish industry, and freezing it to use in his stew. Ingesting shellfish infected with the toxin caused instant tingling of the lips and tongue, and then muscular paralysis. Oh, it wasn't fatal, not usually, although Charles would have a harder time recovering because he was old and out of shape.

As for Yvonne, the amount she'd eaten was quite unlikely to kill a healthy young woman but enough to render her speechless for quite some time to come. Time enough for another woman with the proper Bahstan accent to read her way to worldwide fame because, along with a great big nasty helping of *Alexandrium fundyense,* poetic justice had at long last been served.

# KILLING KIPPERS

## by Eleanor Cawood Jones

Snow in the Midwest in January is hardly news. So it didn't make headlines on that Thursday afternoon when the temperature and dewpoint combined to dump nineteen treacherous inches of snow and ice on Green Bay, Wisconsin. Salt trucks and snowplows drove in circles, but the rest of us stayed put. *Put*, for me, was the Running Stick Resort and Casino. I was in town on business. The clowns, including the one on the barstool next to me, were at the end of a four-day clown convention. News to me, that clowns convened.

"Two days," Kippers the Klown moaned into her Jim Beam and ginger ale, and downed the dregs. She made a sucking noise to get every last drop and plinked the glass on the bar. "They say we'll be snowed in for at least two more days before the planes run. I'm going to miss two gigs, and I really need the money."

I made a noncommittal noise. Kippers had already told me at least six times how she would miss a Shriners' breakfast and a cat's birthday party. That's why I planned to spend the next two days hiding—hiding in the casino, in my room, in the lobby, in the parking garage, and in a bottle. (Mostly the bottle.) In short, hiding any place where Kippers wasn't. I'd been barnacled by this wanna-be entertainer since last night, and she was shaping up to be not only seriously not funny, and in fact whiny, but an alcoholic to boot.

Kippers the (Depressing) Klown was, in fact, pickled, and had been since I'd made the mistake of asking to borrow her phone charger the night before, seated at this same bar. I'd forgotten mine and the hotel gift shop was sold out. Apparently the charger came with a price of everlasting friendship. She'd been following me around since then, showing up at breakfast and turning my time in the casino afterward into a disaster.

I calculated. If I only used my phone for essential calls, like to my therapist who understood how I felt about being trapped in general and with clowns in particular, I could surely drag it out for another twenty-four hours before I had to borrow her charger again. Maybe in the meantime I could find a way to ditch her and her constant moaning and carrying on about how the other clowns didn't like her, the lack of work at parties, and how, if clowning was her calling, why was it all so hard?

I took a swig of my manhattan and glanced at Kippers out of the corner (korner) of my eye. All five-foot-nothing of her. What kind of clown dresses in all-black sequins—who knew they even made sequined pantaloons?—topped by a colorful dunce cap with her short, scraggly, bleached blond hair poking out the bottom of it? The effect was black and shiny and round with a burst of color on top. Audrey Hepburn, Kippers was not. More like Tweedledee.

Or Dum. Whichever.

"My boyfriend will miss me. Who knows what he'll get into? And my poor, sick kitty needs me."

Kippers had a boyfriend? Boggled the mind. The cat I could understand. Twenty-seven cats would be even more understandable. This Klown had all the makings of a Krazy Kat Lady.

"I'm sorry about Kibbles, Kippers," I said for the seventy-second time. Kibbles the cat has gout and needs a special diet and exercise routine, according to Kippers.

Kippers turned to me as if seeing me for the first time. "You got a boyfriend back home?"

"No," I said shortly. No boyfriend, no husband. Not anymore, anyway. No cat, either. But a manhattan? A manhattan I did have. I took another, heftier swig and signaled Peet the bartender for a refill. (Earlier I made the mistake of asking Peet about the unusual spelling of his name on his employee badge. He told me his mom had spelled it that way so he wouldn't get confused with his twin brother, Pete. Yep, I was in Crazyland for sure.)

Soon I'd be just drunk enough to take another trip down the long hall that led to the casino. I could hear the Wheel of Riches slot machines calling my name, taunting me. This morning I'd been one pull away from a jackpot. I'd gone to find an ATM and asked Kippers, who was following me around and talking to me while I tried to play slots (not casino-savvy behavior at the best of times), to watch my machine and make sure no one touched it until I returned. She'd seen no harm in letting some guy take a turn while I was gone. He'd won the thirty grand progressive jackpot on the very next pull.

I could have used that money as a down payment for a new car and taken that trip to Hawaii I'd been promising myself for years. Maybe even paid off a credit card or two. Even after taxes.

When I came back to find the bells flashing and the guy who won cackling maniacally with glee—and cackle he well might, with all my money in his grip—Kippers was too drunk to even understand what she'd done. There was no point in explaining it to her, or beating her with the stick I could easily have snatched from the dealer at the craps table, or murdering her with my bare hands. To add insult to injury, she'd chosen that moment to lurch into me and spill her rum and coke all down the front of my one remaining clean blouse and suit jacket. At that point I simply descended into a black spiral of despair and resigned myself to starting over on another machine, staying drunk and sticky-suited, and hating all clowns everywhere forever. Especially Kippers.

And to getting out of town as soon as possible. Which brought me back to reality, which informed me in no uncertain terms that I'd be here another two days at least. I watched Peet mix my refill and then my cell phone rang.

Blessed mercy, it was my good friend Bambi. An anti-clown antidote if there ever was one.

I'd met Bambi three years before, when I'd first arrived in Green Bay to supervise the printing of an important client's direct mail fundraising campaign, consisting of billions of pieces of paper that would be inserted into millions of envelopes on a gigantic, larger-than-a-football-field printing press available only here in the Midwest. Like the casino, the press ran twenty-four hours a day.

Compared to the compact D.C. suburbs, everything here seemed sprawling and giant to me, including the gorgeous young woman who met me at the airport.

She had to be at least six-foot-two, with a killer body, wide blue eyes, and stick-straight, whiter-than-white hair cascading down her broad, parka-clad back. Everything about her screamed healthy outdoor activity and Scandinavian descent.

She had smiled a blinding Crest 3D White smile. "Welcome to Green Bay! I'm Bambi, and I'm with Packer Worldwide Printing." Her deep, booming voice echoed in the practically deserted airport.

Since then, I've made this same trip every three months, and Bambi and I have grown to be close work friends and then some. She's seen me through some tough times, and I've listened to her talk about her mother-in-law, Hilda, whom we call Hitler. (And not in a nice way.) I grinned tipsily at her name on my cell phone.

I found the right button to push, held the phone up to my ear, and heard her voice rumbling out of it. "Girl, where are you right now?"

Peet plumped my drink in front of me, and I grinned at it, too. "Bar." No point in not mincing words. I was preserving my energy for the slot machines.

"Well, have Peet mix me up a gin and tonic. I'm on the way over."

"Impossible. Snow. Ice." I may have given out a little hiccup at this point. "Weather."

"No problem. I'm cross-country skiing over to see you." Of course she was. Bambi lived no more than what, five miles away? I rolled my eyes. Bad move, as Kippers came into view. I focused back on my drink.

"I was getting cabin fever," Bambi continued, gracefully ignoring the hiccup. "Figured I could use some exercise and then a drink and maybe a little round or two in the casino."

I could use some exercise, too. I pictured the long hallway between the hotel and casino, which turned in on itself twice before you arrived at that glorious, open room filled with the unique combination of buzzing and binging slot machines, shouts of eager customers, and ice-filled, clinking glasses found only in gambling establishments the world over. It was a really, really long walk to get there.

"Walking the mile, walking the mile," I mumbled into the phone.

Bambi understood. "Kippers there?" She had spent last evening with Kippers and me in the bar.

"Yeppers." I giggled.

"Well, stop drinking, and when I get there we'll get her so drunk she won't be able to follow us down to the slots. Okay?"

"'S a plan." I found the right button and hung up on her. Things were looking up.

"Cheese curds." Peet plunked a bowl of the fried, steaming Wisconsin specialty on the bar in front of me and winked. He knew I wasn't normally much of a drinker. He probably wanted to feed me before I slid onto the floor. I sniffed the bowl. Heavenly. I reached for a curd but Kippers's mitt beat me to it. She dug out a handful and scattered most of the rest onto the bar.

I went back to my drink, waited for Bambi, and listened to Kippers smack her loathsome lips while she ate my curds.

Kippers was talking nonstop and I had half a drink left when I sensed Bambi sliding onto the barstool on the other side of Kippers. Good. We had the clown surrounded.

"Kippers, my clown friend. What's shaking?" Bambi's voice boomed, and I heard Kippers mumble something in return.

"Gin and tonic for me, Peet, and I think some hot green tea for these two clowns." I resented being included as a clown, but before I could protest, Bambi snatched something out of Kippers's gigantic purse, which was open on the bar. "Kippers, what's this?"

I peered around Kippers, who was frantically trying to retrieve something out of Bambi's man-hand.

"Diazepam?" Bambi read the label of the prescription bottle in what was, for her, a whisper. "Girl, what are you doing with this?"

Kippers gave up the fight. "The clown's life is a depressing life," she intoned dramatically. "Besides, it's just a weensy dose. You know, to take the edge off."

"Two milligrams twice a day," Bambi read aloud. She upended the bottle and shook a few into her hand. "This prescription is from last week. Why's the bottle nearly empty?"

"I've been stressed, all right? Don't know what business it is of yours anyway." Kippers took a swallow of her drink and popped another curd.

Bambi dropped the bottle back into the purse and shrugged. "Used to be a nurse."

Wow. I could imagine Bambi as a nurse. Efficient and capable, large and in charge. I bet no patient had the nerve to die on one of her shifts, either.

"Still." She moved the drinks away from Kippers and me as Peet delivered two mugs of hot tea. "Best watch the alcohol intake. You know those pills will make you sleepy on their own."

Kippers gave me a *do something* look born of alcoholic desperation, and out of the corner of my eye I could have sworn Bambi dropped one of the pills she'd palmed into the mug in front of Kippers. She moved the mug closer to the clown, and nudged her. "Tea will make you feel better. Promise."

Bambi and I made eye contact, and she read my tacit, drunken approval of her spiking Kippers's drink. The sooner this clown was out of our hair, the better.

Kippers grumbled, picked up a spoon and stirred, and took a couple of swallows of tea, then a few more until her mug was empty. I sipped mine, too. After all, I had a long walk in front of me. The heat felt good, though it was no manhattan.

"What's dramazipipam, anyway?" Was I slurring? Surely not.

"Light tranquilizer," Bambi answered carelessly. She signaled Peet for another gin and tonic.

Kippers made some sort of noise, shoved her mug away, and put her head down on the bar with a little more force than I thought was necessary.

Peet ambled over. "Damn. That'll leave a mark."

"We'd better get her to bed," I said reluctantly. We all looked at her.

"Maybe I'd better get security to take her," Peet said. "You don't seem all that steady." He eyed Bambi. "Though I suppose Bambi could handle her solo."

I nudged Kippers. "Wake up. Bambi's going to put you to bed."

Peet leaned over. "Kippers?" He stared at Bambi. "Seriously,

Bambi, is she breathing?"

And that's when all hell broke loose. Peet vaulted over the bar, knocking Kippers's purse onto the floor, and Bambi dragged me off the stool and away from Kippers. She parked me at a table, simultaneously dialing 911, and with her phone under her chin started grabbing Kippers's belongings off the floor and stuffing them into the purse, taking a moment to wipe the pill bottle on her shirt, I noticed. She requested an ambulance, tossed the purse on the table with me, and went to help Peet who had started CPR. Others, solemn-faced, gathered around to watch and worry.

By the time emergency services arrived in the form of two EMTs hauling several cases of equipment, we were all openly speculating that it might be too late for Kippers. I wanted to weep, but the alcohol had numbed me. What if it *was* too late for her? Who would take care of her gouty cat now?

The EMTs took over, and Bambi came to sit with me. I turned to her, and she answered my unspoken question, speaking directly into my ear. "No way a dose that small would have hurt her like this. Especially that fast. It was just one pill. It may have helped her go to sleep sooner is all. But it appears to me she had a massive heart attack. Peet told me he has EMT training, and even he couldn't help her. They'll do an autopsy if she doesn't make it, you know."

I believed her. I had to. I'd seen her put the meds in Kippers's mug and hadn't done a thing to stop her. The alternative to not believing her was too painful to contemplate. Besides, she'd been a nurse. She knew about these things.

I hoped.

The EMTs were asking aloud if anyone knew whether Kippers was ill or took any medicine. Peet told them she had been drinking heavily for days, and Bambi dutifully reported that the clown had a low-dose diazepam prescription.

But it was all to no avail, and a few minutes later the EMTs stopped their efforts, covered Kippers with a thin blanket, and began to pack up their equipment. Peet, now back behind the bar, began weeping.

"Uh-oh." Bambi had given the EMTs Kippers's oversized purse once they had given up working on her. Now one of them, a tall, blond man who could have easily passed for Bambi's brother, was holding the pill bottle that had been tucked inside. He talked quietly with his partner as they stood beside Kippers's body.

"What's he saying, Bambi?"

The EMT holding the pills had opened the bottle and tipped a few pills into his hand. I thought I heard him say something along the lines of "wrong dose." What did *that* mean?

Bambi and I sat still.

His partner, a slim, dark-haired woman, answered him in a low voice. "The bottle says two milligrams."

"Well, take a gander at these pills. These are ten milligrams. Much stronger."

There was a pause. Then the female EMT whipped her phone off her belt and, dialing, left the room.

Bambi looked sick. "The pills are wrong. I bet she's gone to call the cops. Oh my God. Ten to one Kippers poisoned herself. And all that booze on top of it."

Poisoned herself? Maybe. Unless someone switched out her pills. But I kept that thought to myself. I closed my eyes for a moment, willing myself to unsee that one extra pill slipping into the clown's drink. And unwilling to catch Bambi's eye.

Everyone in the bar was still speculating about Kippers in hushed voices when a handsome man in a suit appeared in front of our table, asking us all to go into the next room, a mini-ballroom normally reserved for special events. I supposed this qualified.

He was met with stunned silence followed by a buzz of panicked conversation. "What was it, a heart attack?" "Something must be wrong. Otherwise why would they ask us to stay?" "Foul play. It's got to be foul play." "No way! She just had too much to drink and her heart couldn't handle it."

As the handsome guy turned away from me, I could see he'd taken a tumble in the weather. The back of his coat and pants were covered in slush and mud. I resisted an urge to brush him off. It might have been misinterpreted.

Twenty or so of us followed him next door to a room filled with comfortable seating, couches, and overstuffed chairs, even a fireplace. We were all choosing seats when he beckoned for Bambi and me to follow him into a small office adjoining the main area. A uniformed police officer sat at a table with four chairs, and he asked us to join him.

The slushy (but still handsome) guy remained standing. "I'm Detective Dave DuPrey," he told us. Detective DuPrey. I filed the name away, changed it to Detective Damp Pants and shortened it to DDP in my head. (Memorization technique.) "I am told by the bartender that you two were with the deceased when she passed out."

I winced at the idea of Kippers being called "the deceased." Not that Kippers the Klown was any great shakes as a name, but it sure beat "the deceased."

He was staring directly at me.

"It's true!" Perhaps I was a little overenthusiastic. He really was incredibly good-looking. If you like that tall, dark-haired, blue-eyed type. I reminded myself he was covered in slush all over his backside.

"And who are you?"

I spread my arms in front of me. "Well, DDP, I can explain."

He raised his eyebrows.

"She's not much of drinker," Bambi offered.

"I can see that."

"Hey!" I waved my arms in case they'd forgotten I was sitting right there. "I'm just here on business. Kippers decided she'd rather hang out with me than the rest of the clowns. She had five or six drinks. Then, wham! She keeled over and her head hit the bar. We tried to wake her up to get her back to her room, and nothing. I mean, no breathing."

My voice broke and I swallowed hard. I hadn't liked Kippers. But nobody deserves to die stone drunk at a clown convention. Surrounded by, you know, clowns.

"That's when Peet hopped the bar and went to work. He told Bambi he's a trained EMT. And the EMTs got here, and then they called you."

"Okay." He flipped open his notebook. "Your name?"

"Princess."

"Your given name."

"Princess."

He waited.

"Princess Jenkins."

"Princess Jenkins?" He eyed me up and down, taking in my pinstriped suit and dress heels, highlighted hair, big brown eyes, and skinny frame. I pretended he also checked to make sure I wasn't wearing a wedding ring. His gaze lingered on the now slightly crusty rum and coke stain on my chest. "What? You a working girl?"

I sighed and gave the short version. "It was the '80s. My parents liked Prince. They wanted a boy."

He raised an eyebrow.

"I think they drank a lot."

He returned the eyebrow and turned to assess Bambi. "And you are?"

Bambi grinned at him. I was temporarily blinded by the flash of white so I didn't quite catch his expression when she offered up her name. "Bambi."

Silence.

"Bambi Swenson."

I could swear he turned pale, but he wrote Bambi's name in his notebook.

"And the deceased, what do you know about her?"

"Kippers," I confirmed.

He grimaced.

"Oh, wait." I fished in my purse for one of the dozen or so business cards Kippers had pressed on me during our brief acquaintanceship.

The card was simple, black and white, and plain, with just the words "Kippers the Klown" and a phone number on it, plus a small graphic of a circus clown in a dunce hat holding a balloon bouquet in one hand. It made the marketer in me cringe. What were her specialties? In what geographical area did she ply her trade? I knew she could do balloon animals. She gave me those, too.

"Do you think she overdosed?" I blurted out. "Or maybe someone offed her?" Hey, I watch a lot of cop TV. Maybe too much.

DDP stared. "What makes you say that?"

Oops. Maybe I shouldn't have. "We were sitting by the EMTs. We heard what they said about Kippers's pills."

"Ah. Well, anything's possible. I'm going to take everyone's statement and contact information. We'll know more in a few days. There's always an autopsy in cases like this."

"Told you so," Bambi mouthed at me.

I sighed. "Statement? I have a statement." I ignored Bambi shaking her head at me. "You know what, detective? I think Kippers was a fish out of water. Frankly, she was one of the most annoying people I've ever met and I can imagine any number of people had a boatload of reasons to kill her if it turns out that's what happened. And on top of that, she was an awful clown. I think maybe clowning wasn't her cup of tea."

Apparently I was just getting warmed up. "This was her first big convention. She said hardly any of the other clowns showed up for her ballooning class, and she didn't feel welcome at the juggling seminar, powder-base makeup session, or the keynote speech either. She didn't even fit in at the clown ministry class. She wasn't having a good time. I felt sorry for her. She felt shunned by the other clowns."

He shook his head. "Shunned by clowns. Imagine."

Bambi shook her head, too. Not to be left out, I nodded, which somehow seemed right.

"She just wanted to go home to her cat, which has gout. And her boyfriend."

"Her cat has a boyfriend?"

"No." What was with this guy? "She wanted to go home to her cat *and* her boyfriend."

"She had a boyfriend?" DDP sounded incredulous.

"I know. Hard to believe, right?" Bambi sounded sad. "Big, tall guy. She showed us a bunch of pictures on her phone. Weird-looking couple, but someone for everyone, I guess."

"Was he depressed, too?" I wanted to know.

"What do you mean, 'Was he depressed, too?'" The detective snapped to attention. "How well did you two actually know this clown?"

I shrugged. "Except for a couple hours I was sleeping, she's been talking nonstop to me since yesterday."

"I just met her last night," Bambi said. "But tonight I saw she had that prescription you already know about for diazepam in her purse. It was for a tiny dose, according to the label on the bottle, but still, not what you'd find in a purse every day."

"A clown's life is a hard life," I intoned dramatically. Perhaps wisely, they both ignored me.

"And you'd know this because?" The detective looked at Bambi.

She shrugged. "I used to be a nurse a long time ago. So I know a bit about meds. But the shift work and patients got to me after a while. I do PR for Packer Worldwide Printing now."

Detective DuPrey eyed her again. "I bet you were a good nurse. Okay, I'll call the number on the card and see if I can get hold of the boyfriend." He sighed. "So I'm finishing with Princess and Bambi and next up I have"—he consulted his notebook—"Bobbles and Wobbles, with their twin clown act." He glanced around. "When are Dopey, Grumpy, Doc, and Sweepy going to show up?"

"Sleepy," I said.

He gave me a strange look. "Well, yeah, it's late. I'm sure you are."

"No. Sleepy. The dwarf. Not Sweepy."

"Hunh. You sure?"

"Sure as shootin'," I told him. At this point I absolutely did *not* hiccup.

"Hunh," he said again. He opened the door and stuck his head out. "Okay, I'm through interviewing these two. Now send in the clowns." He turned and cut his eyes to me, waiting.

Was that a cue for me to sing? I sat up and took a breath, but Bambi poked me in the back. Hard.

"Funny," I heard Bambi rumble behind me. Good old Bambi.

He gave me a little nod and I swear that eyebrow quirked again, then we were out the door. There were a dozen or so clowns draped about the party room waiting to be interviewed. I grabbed Bambi's hand and bolted before one of them could offer to make me a balloon giraffe or juggle scarves at me.

We wound up—where else?—back at the bar.

We were a glum bunch. I worried the detective would find out that Kippers had cost me a jackpot in the casino that very morning. Bambi worried someone else besides me may have seen her put that tiny pill in the clown's tea. Even Peet was worried. It turns out Kippers hadn't tipped him as much as one red cent, and he'd told several people at the bar that people like her were so miserable they were better off dead. Ouch. But I figured the way Peet had leaped over the bar to perform CPR on Kippers sort of took him out of the running as a suspect.

And was it my imagination or did the clowns who came back to the bar after giving their statements to DDP all seem highly nervous? (Well, I mean, more nervous than clowns usually seem.) Rumors were already spreading about the pill bottle in Kippers's purse. Was it Kippers herself who had switched her pills? Or did someone do it without her knowledge? Did one of these clowns dislike her to that extent? And why?

Like DDP had said in all his damp-panted wisdom, anything was possible.

Anything at all. Especially with this bunch of clowns who, along with us, closed down the bar before we all eventually straggled off to get some sleep, Bambi taking the spare bed in my double room.

And speaking (again) of clowns, I had to revise my opinion of clowns in general before I left Green Bay. The conference clowns, spearheaded by the ones who had been in the bar with us, held a short memorial for Kippers the next night in the long hall between the hotel and the casino. It was a touching service, with a moving speech by the convention president and a demonstration of balloon animal crafting by the few clowns who had been in Kippers's class.

The clowns I met were quite serious about their profession. Most had gone through years of training, not only for professional gigs but for volunteer work at children's hospitals and charity events. Many were third- and fourth-generation clowns. Some had even been planning to mentor Kippers on her techniques. They were well aware she was feeling left out. Great people. And, as I said, a very touching, very professional memorial service.

All the clowns and several hotel employees came, plus Bambi and me, and I'd like to think it wasn't because we were all still snowed in and had nothing better to do. DDP came, too, in a clean suit this time.

And two days later, without learning anything new, we all finally flew home. Well, all of us except Kippers.

***

Bambi called a week later with the news that we were all red herrings in the demise of Kippers. We were, in fact, saved by the autopsy.

"So, guess what, Princess? Turns out Kippers was loaded up with so much diazepam that it's amazing she didn't keel over before we had that last drinking session in the bar."

"Oh wow. You sure?" I was relieved and sad at the same time.

"I'm e-mailing you the link to the story in the paper this morning," Bambi said. She paused and I could hear her fingernails clicking on her keyboard. "According to this, there's no way she should have had that much tranquilizer in her system, even if she'd swallowed the entire bottle of pills she had with her. She must have been high as a kite before she even arrived at the convention."

I opened my e-mail and scanned the story while she was talking. The reporter had interviewed Detective DuPrey, who had retrieved the meds from Kippers's purse and confirmed that indeed the pills labeled two milligrams on the bottle were actually ten milligrams.

"According to the prescription bottle you saw, Kippers should have been taking only four milligrams a day," I said. "But she must have been taking at least twenty and probably a lot more. I wonder if we'll ever know exactly how many pills she was taking to cope with her stress at the convention. And you saw how she liked to drink." I shuddered. In spite of my best intentions, I still didn't like to remember being surrounded by clowns.

"No kidding," Bambi said. "Well, I think you're the one who accidentally sent Detective DuPrey in the right direction when you asked if Kippers's boyfriend had been depressed, too."

"Maybe so," I agreed. Turns out the boyfriend Wallace (not a clown, but in fact a casino employee in Las Vegas where he and Kippers lived) had been taking large doses of diazepam and he had switched his own pills with Kippers's. The two-milligram-sized pills were found in Wallace's medicine cabinet, in his own prescription bottle.

I read on. The reporter quoted Wallace during his confession as saying, "I didn't mean to kill her. I just wanted her to relax so she would shut up. Is that a crime?" There was a picture of a distraught-looking man waving his hands about. He was a big, tall guy, like I remembered from Kippers's photos. I could see why he'd need a giant dose of tranqs. Especially living with Kippers and Gouty.

"I never would have confessed if I was Wallace," Bambi said, bringing me back to the present moment. "I'd have said Kippers switched the pills herself."

I agreed with Bambi. I would have accused Kippers of making the pill switch and then I would have lawyered up. (As I mentioned, I watch a lot of crime television since the divorce and I'm a bit of an expert at police lingo. And I know my rights.) Still, it was a crime and the charge would be involuntary manslaughter.

To tell you the truth, my sympathies were with Wallace.

Meanwhile, I knew one marketing director, one publicity employee, one bartender, and a whole bunch of (nervous) clowns who were all no doubt secretly breathing sighs of relief that they wouldn't be labeled as murder suspects in the death of Kippers the Klown. Because, let's face it, there's nothing funny about that. And as for one extra pill in a mug of tea playing a role in the clown's demise, I am almost one hundred percent certain it made not a whit of difference.

"Has Detective DuPrey called you?" I could hear the smile in Bambi's voice. "I mean, in an unofficial capacity, now that none of us are on his suspect list anymore."

She couldn't see me blushing. "What would make you think that?"

***

Shortly after charges were filed against Wallace, DDP attended a forensics conference in my neck of the woods in the Virginia suburbs of our nation's capital. He came down for four days at the end of February and ended up staying an extra four days. Seems there were some sights he wanted to see. And I know D.C. very, very well.

I've been up to Green Bay twice since then, once for business and once to stay with Bambi and her husband, Lars, so she could teach me how to cross-country ski on what she calls my matchstick legs. Next time, she says, we're going to the firing range so I can learn to handle a gun properly before she takes me hunting. (And don't think the twenty-five-ways-to-Sunday irony of going hunting with someone named Bambi escapes me, either.) Bambi has formed an impression I might move to Wisconsin permanently, and she's appointed herself my self-sufficiency and survival coach.

During both recent visits I spent a lot more time with DDP. He has two kids he's raising by himself. Seems his ex didn't like being married, much less to a detective. Shelley is four and Matthew is eight.

Shelley demanded to know why I was named Princess, and I may or may not have allowed her to believe that if I was not, in fact, a Disney princess, I was at least related to them. (The word *cousin* may have been used.)

And I may or may not have memorized the performance statistics of the entire Green Bay Packers starting lineup to impress a certain precocious eight-year-old with eyes just like his daddy's. (That part was easy. I'm in marketing, and we eat statistics for breakfast.)

I never imagined myself as a potential stepmother. Then again, I never imagined myself missing a casino jackpot by a buck, aiding and abetting in accidentally offing a clown, or bagging a deer with a woman named Bambi. So I'm keeping an open mind.

Stranger things have happened.

Heck, maybe someday I'll even tell him why I call him DDP. Then again, maybe Detective Damp Pants never needs to know.

# ELEMENTAL CHAOS

## by M Evonne Dobson

A single firework shoots out of the clay volcano on the table next to ours, exploding above student heads. The loud boom echoes around the courtyard between Iowa College's towering buildings and overhead walkways. Before the sound fades, a second firework rips skyward. Smoke fills the air as bits of volcano glob rain down. The judges and nearby high school exhibitors scatter, tables overturn. The volcano's owner stands in the fiery maelstrom, stunned. Another round goes off near his face.

I tackle him, and his skinny body folds under me. Shoulder to shoulder, my schoolmate Kyle and I drag the frozen kid under his display table. A fourth, fifth, then sixth explosion rocks.

Small white cubes ping the tabletop, doing a hail bounce onto the ground. I reach out for one. Rock salt fired from the volcano. If it rifle-bullets into your skin? It'll hurt. Take a direct hit into the eye? You could lose it.

Volcano Kid shakes underneath me, screaming, "I didn't do that! I didn't do that!"

***

An hour later, I'm sitting in a private conference room with Luis. He and I share history. He is Iowa College's head of campus security, and this January he'd agreed to mentor my high school team of crime solvers. We'd helped in a suicide/murder case. It was a one-off, but then cases kept happening. Today, I'm Luis's ace in the hole, an on-the-spot witness.

"I believe him," I say about the Volcano Kid. "He was terrified."

"I agree, Kami. Sam posted video that caught the explosions."

Sam is a charter member of my crime-solvers group, but he's also a blogger/journalist. "Let me guess, he posted on the Internet first?"

"The *Chicago Times Online* picked it up, and then bumped it to television." Luis growled. "And it's probably the best evidence we'll get because there are no courtyard security cameras. We'll collect selfies and social media videos, but it'll take time."

Sam's been ecstatic since the *Chicago Times* arranged for a reporter to cover today's statewide science convention and to mentor him for the day. Sam gained their attention after our first case report went viral.

"You were ground zero," Luis says. "Who spiked the volcano?"

Rubbing my hair, I touch a small bump on my head. When did that happen? *Ouch.* "Could be anyone—anyone with science knowledge. If the chemicals were powder and simply mixed in, there'd have been one *vaaabooom.* That didn't happen, so I figure the volcano was stuffed with chemical-paste doughballs that went off one by one. Volcano Kid isn't capable of pulling that off."

"That takes planning," Luis says. "Who knew a volcano would be here? I mean that's baby stuff for a competition at this level, right?"

I nod. "But each student's project is posted on the convention website after their school registers them. And you're right, a volcano is elementary, but every year one new school enters their no-way-ready students. Non-geek judges who are mayors or other celebrities vote for them at the school level, but when the kids get here with actual scientists doing the judging, volcanoes can't cut it."

"Start at the beginning. Tell me the sequence—who, what, where."

And I relive the past. . . .

***

The college lets the state high school science con use its coliseum and the area adjoining it. Once a year, the courtyard is crammed with frantic students setting up projects before the judging begins. Overhead, small blimps soar, tethered by lines to wranglers below them. There'll be a blimp race later. It's state fair-type fun—but torture for the competitors.

On my knees, I unwrap my science project to display it on Kyle's and my table. For the umpteenth time, he lets out a juvenile and irritating *muahaahaa.* I cringe and wish I were anywhere else on the planet. He's unpacking his cardboard boxes containing his handwrought machines. They come out one by one like shiny brass Christmas gifts, designed to professional standards. The steam engine and the companion devices scream out *Touch me! I'm cool!* I shove my twitchy fingers into my jeans' pocket.

Someone shouts, "Kam!"

My name is not Kam, and only one person calls me that—an irritating creep from Fort Daryl named Ferd. My project squeaked by his last year to win the whole competition. His voice is nasal gross. "So Geek Girl screwed up! Second place, huh?"

*He's right, second-place projects never take home the big prize.* Last year as a sophomore, I placed first at my school's fair, then went on to win here, too—highest honor in the whole state of Iowa.

This year, I'm an also-ran. Kyle took first place at our school. Nothing bites more.

Kyle and Ferd have a lot in common, both being brilliant and goal-oriented, but dorky, out-of-place socially, and generally disliked by all. I can say that because I'm a geek, too, but I have friends.

Kyle says hi to the guy, but OCD Ferd taunts me, "So, your project is a locker filled with junk, right?" He's got a bulky backpack slung over his shoulder.

"Her chaos locker is more than that!" Kyle says. "The math she put together! And that 'junk' represents her data sets. But mine . . ."

Then he bores me, vomiting out endless details on his project. Still, Kyle had defended my chaos theory exhibit to the Ferd. Who would have thought? He's been a pain all year, hiding his steam-engine project, taunting me about my chaos locker, and then grinding salt into the wound by winning at home.

Ferd ignores Kyle and powers his way around the table, closing in with his baconator breath. "My year, Kam."

*I so want to land a power kick to his belly, but I don't.*

Our school's newest student teacher, Call-Me-Matt, joins us. He showed up last week out of nowhere and has been way too excited to meet everyone. "And who is this, Kami?" he asks with his typical overeagerness. His enthusiasm is annoying as hell.

Before I can answer, Ferd switches to Ivy League recruit, introducing himself and sticking his paw out to shake hands. Call-Me-Matt is friendly but his eyes keep roving the jammed bodies of students and projects. Matt bothers me because he doesn't fit. He's ripped, not string-beany like the typical student science teacher. Ferd glances over his shoulder, maybe to find out what Call-Me-Matt is looking at, and his eyes stop at Kyle's professional engineering goodies.

Ferd gasps, bites his lip, and hugs his backpack. In a second, he's flipped from arrogant prick to vulnerable and scared kid, going weird as he cradles the pack like a teddy bear. Before I can ask questions, Ferd peels off into the crowd.

A voice over the loudspeaker says, "Ten minute warning. Ten minutes. This is your last notice." Around us, student excitement rockets up, paired with fear. Kyle drops one of his posters, and then drops it again.

"You'll do fine, Kyle." I unload my trifold poster board and duct tape it to the table.

He flashes me a serious look. It could mean *shut the hell up* or a milder *give me a break*. I ignore him.

Sam wanders past, trailing his reporter, a guy named Johnston, who stops at run-of-the-mill exhibits, ignoring the more complex ones. Johnston fiddles with everything as the awkward duffel slung over his shoulder bangs against the tables. He stops for a few minutes, admiring the unfreaking-believable how-did-it-make-it-to-state-finals volcano project beside me. The Volcano Kid's holding his poster board, not sure how to secure it.

Call-Me-Matt drops to his knees with his silver toolbox open, revealing glass bottles of powders and liquids, plastic tubing, and other stuff. He says to the terrified kid, "Don't worry. I've got duct tape. We'll get you set up in no time." Then Call-Me-Matt takes off to help other students.

On the other side of our table, three red-haired girls are unloading trays of legumes. Their poster board shows a detailed drawing of root systems with small white bubbles latched onto them. One tray is tight with seedlings; the other has a teen-sparse beard look.

I nod my head toward the trio and take a stab at my tablemate. "Your competition, Kyle. Ag projects in the Midwest have an innate edge."

He blanches and polishes harder on his mini-steam engine—no comic book laugh now. I grin, positioning a tiny replica of a school locker in front of my tri-fold. Next to it, I set out some of the *junk* I'd collected this past year—everyday items either tossed away or saved as high school mementos. For me, they are data sets, but the meat of my chaos-theory project is the pages and pages of mathematical projections bound into three separate reports. Each pinpoints a single bit of data that had a huge mathematical consequence later, like the butterfly wing flapping in Brazil that creates a tornado a year later in Texas.

Then the real buzz starts.

Kyle gasps, "Oh my God. The judges came out."

"Yep."

The judges spread out with score sheets on clipboards to grill each competitor on the decisions they made, challenge their science basics, and attack the projects. The students will defend like doctoral candidates.

When the judges approach the Legume Sisters on our left, Kyle drags his sweaty palms on his khaki pants. I take pity, because if it's between Kyle or Ferd, I want Kyle to win. I pull out a hand-sized baby powder pack, the kind gymnasts use.

"Here," I say as I hand it to him. "Remember to shake every judge's hand." A confident attitude can seal a win.

I notice Volcano Kid dumping baking soda into his volcano.

Then he pulls out a vinegar bottle and lifts it to the top.

"Wait! Don't pour it in yet!" I say. But it's too late. He's added the vinegar. His volcano spews foam. The rotten smell drifts toward us. The poor kid's chemical reaction will be over before the judges make it to his station. On our other side, the Legume Sisters and judges are beaming.

*Deep breath.* Kyle and I will be next.

\*\*\*

Back in the conference room with Luis, I say, "And then the feces hit the fan. . . . After the fireworks stopped, we came out from under the table like tornado survivors. Tables were upset and projects ruined.

"My poster was riddled with ashes, smoking. As I watched, it ignited. I stomped it out, but it's smudged and barely legible. Two other student projects were on fire. Call-Me-Matt put them out, using a tiny freaking fire extinguisher from his Boy Scout science case."

Luis says, "And that's when . . ." He points to some red and green slips of paper on the table between us, near a bag of doughnuts.

"Yeah. In the confusion afterward, there was this ear-splitting *kapow*. Everyone dove for cover again. Little squares of paper crinkle-rustled as they trickled into the courtyard." The green ones read, $\gamma \tilde{\eta}$ *ge;* the red ones, $\pi \tilde{\upsilon} \rho$ *pur*. I'd Googled the words in the explosion aftermath. "They're Greek symbols for the elements earth and fire—two of four elements the ancients believed made up the world. Between the fireworks, rock salt, and flying slips of paper, it was chaos."

"Kami, we're lucky the injury count is low: a couple twisted ankles, a few abrasions from diving under tables, and one student is at the hospital for rock salt shrapnel in her arms."

I shake my head in disbelief. "And then a voice on the loudspeaker said, 'Just a prank gone wrong. The judging will continue.' But things weren't normal. Local police and your security team swarmed the courtyard. Anyone near ground zero was asked to a private interview." Once I'd finished mine, Luis asked to speak to me.

Luis leans forward. "It may not be a prank. There was a recent Homeland Security warning, very soft, about science fairs like this one. There have been threats made against the winners."

He pauses while I take that in. *Homeland Security?*

"No one wants to believe this was terrorism," he continues, "but we're keeping an eye on the finalists, just to be safe. Kami, do me a favor? Stay next to them. You're our inside source. We're on it for protection, but we want you sitting with the finalists, watching."

That sends my eyebrows up. "I won't make it to the finals. My display is trashed."

Luis crams a doughnut in his mouth and talks around it. "Got you covered. Just do your thing. Sell your chaos exhibit to the judges."

And I've got a free pass to the finals.

***

Half an hour after our talk, I'm back in the courtyard. Local news services are everywhere. In the media crunch, Sam, Kyle, and I stand by our table, waiting for the judges. Everything is behind schedule.

"Good job on the explosion video," I tell Sam.

"Not everyone thinks so. I sent it direct to the producers before Johnston filed his story. They put it on the net, and I got the credit." He frowns.

"That's bad?" I ask.

"Johnston is pissed. And get this: he named the prankster," he air quotes, "'the Elemental Terrorist.' It's stupid and cheesy, but with the terrorism angle, his online webcast—that I recorded for him—got bumped live with breaking news. And guess what I found out? He's supposed to be at the Helsinki terrorism conference, but he got in trouble. Ended up here instead, having to hang out with me."

Sam backs away as the judges walk up with their clipboards and pens. They talk to Kyle, then to me. My display is trashed, but I have the data reports to show how chaos theory works in large data systems. Luis asked me to sell it, and I do.

When the judges retreat to the coliseum and Sam leaves to find Johnston, I decide to give Kyle the credit he deserves. "No matter what happens, your steam engine is awesome." He breaks into a wide smile. "And the little companion machines you made, like the fan, those are cool."

Before a sheepish Kyle can let rip with his *muahaahaa*, I say, "If you do your villain laugh, I'll take it back."

He closes his mouth and sticks out his hand. I shake it. Then I hear my name called from the overhead walkway where Sam is training his smartphone lens on us. I elbow Kyle, and we wave for school blog history.

The loudspeaker crackles, and Kyle jumps as the happy announcer lists the top ten names: Kyle, the Legume Sisters, Ferd, six others, and ringer me. Kyle collapses over his project in happiness.

"You made it, too, Kami! We both made it!"

Sam texts: *Way to go!*

Last year as a finalist, I'd danced around the courtyard, but this time I'm worried about exploding volcanoes and a girl in the hospital ER.

Blimp wranglers lead us with their floating charges from the courtyard into the coliseum for the final judging. For most people, the volcano prank is a passing exclamation point. The Legume Sisters are on full beam. I can't see Call-Me-Matt anywhere. Ferd is on a bipolar high, blustering how he'll win. The news crews, including Johnston and Sam, are relocating, too. I slip my vital data reports into my backpack and help Kyle carry his project. No way will we leave them behind and unattended.

Our feet rustle the little green and red slips of paper with the symbols for earth and fire. The volcano represents earth, I think; the explosions and burned displays, fire. That leaves two unclaimed elements of the ancient world—air and water. Those blimps on leashes draw my attention. *Air . . .*

"Kyle?"

I fill him in on my thoughts, and when I'm done, Kyle nervously agrees to help. He heads over to a blimp pilot, taking his little steam engine and the eight-inch fan that works with it. After they converse, Kyle gives me the thumbs up. My plan is set to go—if it turns out we need it.

***

Inside the coliseum, *Star Wars* theme music is playing on repeat. "Da, DAAA, Da da da DAAA da." A teacher is directing traffic from the stage, using the loudspeaker. "Blimp crews, line up to my left of the stage. Finalists, please sit right of the stage. The front rows in front of me are reserved for science teachers. Other contestants and their families can fill in behind the teachers."

While I take a seat with the beaming Legume Sisters, I see Kyle working on a blimp. And Luis is standing by the stage, checking lanyard IDs before the judges and dignitaries can find their seats on the stage.

I twist around, scanning the crowd for terrorists. But in reality, I'm looking for one guy—Call-Me-Matt—who's been carrying a hefty case of convenient chemicals. I'm feeling guilty I didn't mention my suspicion to Luis. I don't see Matt anywhere in the crowded coliseum.

Thanks to Johnston's webcast and subsequent live posting, the Elemental Terrorist has generated interest. Curious townspeople are packing the seats. Up in the media section, Sam is shooting smartphone vid. Luis asked him to act as another set of eyes, too.

I text Sam: *Anything new?*

Sam stops videotaping long enough to read my text and responds: *Johnston's reading my tweet feed like he wrote them. And he's live—Internet and television. He's gloating. Kami, I don't like this guy.*

Call-Me-Matt passes Sam, mixing with the crowd drawn to the media booths.

Sam: *Good luck, Kami. Hope you win.*

Not a chance, but I'm okay with it. I'm distracted watching Call-Me-Matt, who is as twitchy as a cat seeking a mouse. *Who is this guy? Terrorist? Prankster? Or something else?*

I text: *Did you interview the Legume Sisters?*

Sam: *Who?* Then he texts: *Ha! Got ya. Ag exhibit. Yep, why?*

Me: *It's good, Sam. Groundbreaking-Borlaug-Food-Prize good. Uses moisture-collecting bacteria for 35% faster germination. It will shorten growing seasons. It could feed millions.*

There's a pause, and then he texts: *Thanks for the lead. I'm on my way.*

Sam begins heading from the upper deck to the Legume Sisters sitting beside me. Call-Me-Matt looks right at me and flicks a finger wave. *And what does that mean? Does he know I'm on to him?*

The assembly—that's how it feels—starts when a science teacher, I kid you not, dressed in a short black skirt and a 1960s *Star Trek* red shirt takes the podium.

She taps her fake communicator brass emblem. "Scotty, going to fix this?"

The iconic space opera music mix changes to the four soft chimes that build to the original *Star Trek's* theme song. The audience splits by preference: half cheer, half jeer. *It's a science thing.*

Red Shirt says, "Are you ready for the blimp races?"

Everyone stamps their feet, whistles, and screams.

"Scotty?" A trumpet heralds the race, and Red Shirt shouts, "And they're off!"

Sort of. There's a reason that blimp races aren't well known. They are *slow.* Like nasty slow. An obstacle course of round rings hang overhead. One by one, the blimps pick up sand-filled, whisper-thin baggies as cargo from a suspended platform, weave through the rings, and then deposit them at the finish line—if the baggies don't break first. Rough sandpaper lines each ring's interior surface. If a blimp bumps the edge, the baggie can tear, dumping sand on the audience. To avoid that, the dirigibles fly slowly through the rings. Emphasis on slow.

At the end of the line, Kyle screws his small steam engine and a fan to a blimp's power platform. Then he knuckle-bumps each crew member.

The dirigibles fade to background entertainment as Red Shirt says, "Here are the top three finalists selected from the original ten. When your name is called, please join us on stage for your interview."

She explains, "Judges will quiz each finalist on his or her project. Based on earlier scores and the answers here, the final winner will be chosen."

With Oscar-worthy suspense, she opens an envelope. "Our first finalist: from our host city, Kami 'Chaos Theory' McCloskey—last year's winner!"

I don't move. The Legume Sisters poke my side. *But I'm the ringer, not a final three contender!* I stumble to the stage steps where Luis waits. "I'm not supposed to be here," I whisper.

Not looking at me, his eyes rake the stadium for threats instead. "Yes, you are."

"But you set it up—"

"I said, 'it was covered.' I knew you'd step up your game. Believe in your project, Kami. You got here yourself."

Overhead a blimp knocks a gate and sand bursts free. People laugh. I think of exploding volcanoes as I head to the podium.

One of the math judges pulls an Alex Trebek: "Kami's chaos theory exhibit explains how an infinitesimal data bit in the right place can create huge changes years later in complex systems. Kami, the judges were impressed with the time and effort you took working your data to show chaos results using three separate sources. Could you explain one of them?"

"My first data set was a life insurance-policy projection with assumed interest rates, expense charges, and premium payments." I go into detail about my statistical research while I scan the upper balcony. Call-Me-Matt has left his spot, shoving his way to the railing.

The judge prompts me. "And then?"

"After weeks of fiddling the projection cell by cell, it happened. The end product collapsed."

"Impressive work, Kami, but why should chaos theory concern us?"

Shocked, I say, "Because if we can figure out how to identify that miniscule point that changes everything and creates chaos, if we can identify that point before it happens, we've changed the future. Alexander Fleming found mold in a petri dish and did something with it. That tiny moment of discovery saved millions of lives. And that's just one example. That's what the items I collected in my locker signify—possible chaos trigger moments: a musical program that leads to a future opera singer, a note scribbled on a napkin that creates a famous journalist later. They are little things representing moments of time that can change people's lives forever!"

I whisper into the mic and it carries around the coliseum, "Chaos theory maps life, and we need a road map. That's why we should care."

"Thank you, Kami." The judge guides me to a chair on stage. Red Shirt calls up the Legume Sisters. The blimps continue to fly one by one overhead.

At the podium, the redheaded girls babble about growing food in shorter growing seasons. Meanwhile Call-Me-Matt is leaning over the balcony railing, searching the audience. And Sam's reporter guy is no longer in front of a camera. I remember his bulky duffel bag.

I text Sam: *Where's Johnston?*

Sam, who is now beside Luis, posts back: *Camera break. Top row in the upper balcony Section 14.*

Johnston is up there working on something in his hands. Something small, maybe a phone. No . . . it's bigger than that. Then I notice a nearby blimp pilot waving his control box as if it isn't working anymore.

And overhead? A blimp is off course, rising with slow but steady speed, past the obstacle course rings, toward the ceiling.

*OMG. Earth. Fire. Air. Air vents?* The ceiling has massive air vents and the dirigible is heading straight for them. Did Johnston hack the remote control on the runaway blimp, sending it toward the ceiling vents? He'd fiddled with exhibits earlier, including the volcano. What could he do with an air vent? . . . A toxin release? I'd thought something might happen with the air ships, but I hadn't considered how the ceiling vents could be used.

I punch in Luis's number and whisper, "Sam's press guy! Section 14!"

As the Legume Sisters head toward their chairs, I slip out of mine, jump from the stage, and race for Kyle's team.

Red Shirt announces, "And our last finalist is from our host city as well—Kyle 'Steam Punk Engineer' Oberwitz!"

But Kyle's noticed the runaway dirigible, too, and has begun priming the engine he attached to his team's blimp. It kicks into high gear with a mechanical whir, its fan spinning with rapid *click, click, clicks*. It should be the fastest airship here. I yank its tether line free and let it go while Kyle grabs the remote and banks the blimp at a sharp angle to intercept the errant one. As Kyle promised, his engine adds superior speed. I'd never seen one fly that fast.

Apparently unaware of what's happening overhead, Red Shirt repeats, "Kyle Oberwitz?"

The audience members don't seem to care that Kyle isn't running up on stage. They're riveted by the upcoming blimp collision—every neck in the audience is craned upward. Everyone's but mine and Call-Me-Matt's, who is flying up the upper balcony stairs, off by one section. Johnston doesn't seem to notice.

Kyle's larger blimp bumps the smaller one, and they career off course. Both dirigibles stabilize, the smaller one rising again.

I shout, "The cargo arms. Hook the cargo arms together! Bring it down!"

Kyle nods, and his air ship surges again.

In the balcony, more linebacker than teacher, Call-Me-Matt races through the seat rows toward Johnston.

Kyle's blimp hooks the smaller one, dragging it downward. In the balcony, Johnston must have triggered something, because purple smoke is now trailing from the errant blimp. Wraith tendrils are spreading out and rising. And rising. And rising.

*Earth—volcano eruption. Fire—resulting fires. Air—the blimp's smoke . . .*

*Water!* The overhead sprinklers kick into gear as the fire alarms go off with a deafening *clang, clang, clang.* With water spraying everywhere, people begin charging toward the exits. Then a potato cannon boom echoes, putting the fire alarms to shame. Slips of blue and white paper spin out from Johnston's position, drifting through the water spray. It's a good guess the slips read *air* and *water* in ancient Greek. I see Johnston through the falling water shoving a cannon back into his duffel.

With the boom, everyone screams and pushes toward the exits faster. People stumble and fall into each other, striking metal railings.

Across the way, Johnston charges down the stairs toward the panicked crowd. From behind, Call-Me-Matt takes him with a tackle. Johnston's face pile drives into the concrete walkway. He-Who-Is-Obviously-Not-A-Student-Teacher shoves a knee in the guy's back, cuffing Johnston's hands.

Stinky water that smells like it's been stored for years in the fire-suppression system sprays nonstop. Sopping wet, I look around. The stage is empty. The coliseum is an anthill, and the ants are streaming for the exits.

All except . . . In the middle of the disappearing main floor crowd, Ferd is standing motionless, ignoring the cascading water, with the lumpy backpack he'd teddy-bear-hugged this morning at his feet. Then he starts to rock side to side, eyes closed. He tips his head back with a gaping open mouth. Something is very wrong.

I race to him but pull up short. His fingers are tenderly wrapped around a cell phone, holding it like a small bird in his hand. His thumb hovers over the keypad.

"I'll show you what I can do!" he screams. "I'll blow this place up!"

No one but me seems to hear him over the fire alarm. It doesn't take a genius to know that if he presses the button, things will go boom—including me. I consider running for an exit, but they're jammed. I pray his phone has shorted out from the water gushing down, but I can't take any chances.

"Ferd?"

He opens his eyes.

I nod at his right hand. "If you hit the phone's send button, it goes *kaboom*?" I don't define *it*, hoping against hope it's a smoke or stink bomb.

He nods back. "I got the design plans on a Darknet site. Take a look." He gestures at his backpack. "It won't hurt you unless . . ."

He wipes water off his face, using his phone hand. I sweat bullets. I kneel and unzip the pack, peeling the bag from around the pressure cooker inside. A bomb made famous by the Boston Marathon bombers. Ferd plans to die in the blast. My hands shake as I stand. I want to throw up.

*Keep him talking. The longer we talk, the more people get out.*

"Are you a terrorist?"

"Nah, but I posted threats on the Internet. Bounced my IP address. Hid my location."

*Delay. Give people a chance.*

He sighs. "It's my senior year. I told the whole school I'd win. They said I wouldn't, and I told them that if I didn't I'd bomb the place." Tears escape his eyes, visible despite the falling water. "They laughed at me. Kami, I've been bullied my whole life, but I thought this would finally be my chance to show everyone what I could do. But I'm not going to win. I'm not even in the top three. That damn steam engine, the ag bacteria exhibit. If I go back to school a loser, they'll . . . I can't go back there."

I consider kicking that damn phone out of his hand, but no matter how fast I am, he will be faster. "So don't go back."

He spins in a circle with water cascading onto us, holding the cell as if he's forgotten it. "Popular kids don't get us, Kami. They'll never understand scientists or what we can do!"

I step toward him. "They don't matter. We do. Don't you have more science to explore? More to discover?" I hold out my hand. "Give me the phone. Besides, you know who wins today, right? No one beats out the Legume Sisters."

He gives a shaky half grin and hands over the cell. It feels like a stick of dynamite.

## EPILOGUE

Call-Me-Matt? He's with Homeland Security. Ferd got the transfer he wanted, but it was to a *special* school where they helped him with his social issues—it was better than juvenile detention. Angry reporter Johnston? He's been fired and is awaiting trial. Sam's first byline tops his *Chicago Times* news story about it. And the Legume Sisters? Yeah, they won the state science fair. It's like I told Kyle—you can't beat an ag project in the Midwest.

***

*Author's note: See this link for information on the real global-winning Legume Sisters' experiment and its potential to feed the world.*

www.irishtimes.com/news/technology/three-irish-students-win-global-science-competition-1.1938595

# OUTSIDE THE BOX

## by Ruth Moose

On the table lay a handful of white plastic drinking straws, a roll of silver straight pins, and six blank sheets of paper. We, this team of four, have to construct a house. This is leadership school at the Smarty Pants Librarians conference. (There is an official name, but this is what I've been calling it since I got the flyer and signed up, drove four hours, and checked into this hotel. I would go to a conference called How to be a Hot Shit to get out of my library for a day, two days, any time, anywhere, any day, go to any place where students don't have to be catered to, pampered, instructed, fetched for, or handed to, or can't spell or read or find things. Stupid students. And some adults.) Here we are adults. We are lovely, carefree, day-out-of-school strangers.

This is the leadership class Part I of the conference. At the front of the room, two workshop leaders hold a timer. He in black suit, white shirt, red checked tie. She in black pantsuit, white blouse, and red-ringed scarf. They look like a married couple minus the bride on a wedding cake. He sets a timer. It dings. She says, "Begin."

The woman across the table picks up a straw, deepens the frown lines across her forehead. She blinks. Her eye shadow is deep purple, dark as bruises.

The bald man to my left pokes me with his elbow, runs his fingers along the row of straight pins, and hums a little off-key tune that makes me clinch my teeth.

"You can talk," Mrs. Workshop Leader says.

"So," Baldy says, "a house, huh?"

I try to imagine him in whatever job he has at some rinky-dink university or small private-college library. Something in a back office shuffling papers. A finance/book cataloging/ordering type job. Lower rung for thirty years, waiting for retirement. Won't get a rocking chair or gold watch. Just a plaque with his name misspelled.

I fold four sheets of the paper into a wobbly box.

"Won't stand," the woman to my right says. She pushes her heavy eyeglasses farther up on her nose. "I think it's got to be freestanding."

Baldy puts his chin on the table, stares eye level into the straws, pins, paper.

"No way." He sits back, folds his hands across his chest.

Oh Lord, I've ended up in a group full of idiots. What does that make me? How were we chosen? Names in a soup bowl?

Last night at the so-called reception/cocktail party, I tried to read the lower line on the name tags: university of something, college of something, school of something else. I felt very small. My two hundred-year-old university (ha!) of seven hundred students had miraculously just added a graduate program. One. So now we're Podunk U. When we somehow got university status, all of the college's monogrammed merchandise had to be changed to PU. Some of us snickered behind our hands. Why couldn't our name be University of Podunk and our acronym be UP? But what did I know? I wasn't a leader back at PU. And I certainly wasn't here for brownie points from my cement-faced director. I was here for the excursion, two nights in a nice hotel, meals, travel. I could play at leadership. Anything for a day away from the mold and academic mire.

Was everyone else on the same path that brought me here? Willing to do anything to get away from our weary, dreary, mind-numbing jobs, bowing to professors who never say thank you or please and who give you the stainless-steel eye if you dare address them as other than Dr. So and So? Even the adjuncts have to be called Professor with a capital P.

In the morning light, my team looks half abed, brain dead. I hear the other two teams chattering away, laughing, giggling, heads together over their "houses." The sounds sound like progress, like cohesion. Leadership. Teamwork.

"Okay," I say, being a bit serious. "We've got straws for corner posts. Pin the sheets of paper to them. Pin on the last two sheets for a roof. It's not like we're going to live in it. Voila. House."

Purple Eye Shadow raises one eyebrow.

Baldy snorts.

Miss Thick Glasses snickers.

I try to pin a sheet of paper to a straw. A very resistant plastic straw. My thumb hurts. I push, push, push. The straw holds firm.

"Wait," Baldy says, taking the pin, the straw, and the paper and putting them together with seeming ease.

"Wall one." He leans back. I hate him.

He pins a second sheet of paper. Purple Eye Shadow sneezes. The thing topples, lies flat on the table.

"Oops," she says. "Did I knock it over?" She half covers her mouth, suppressing half a schoolgirl giggle.

Do we have a subversive in our leadership-building team?

"Here." Miss Thick Glasses picks up another sheet of paper, props up the other two. We now have a triangle, not a square. Could we lift it partway, call it a teepee, and get by? People once lived in teepees. Traveled with teepees, houses on their backs like turtles.

"Gotta use all six sheets of paper," Baldy says. He picks up the sheets of paper, pulls out a few pins from the roll, and puts together the fourth wall.

Purple Eye Shadow silently taps her left palm with her right index finger. Typical libarian gesture of reluctant approval.

I, alone, send up a small cheer.

We have a house. Albeit a flimsy paper one, but it's square and it stands. Who knew he could do it? Genius with a piece of paper in his hands. A roll of pins at the ready.

Miss Thick Glasses blinks. "Two sheets of paper are left over." She twists around to look at our captors who hold up a timer. They point. "Five minutes."

Purple Eye Shadow looks back, then picks up the last two sheets of paper, pins them together like a pup tent, lays them atop our "house."

"Voila," Baldy says and raises both arms in the air as if he had done the whole deed himself, by himself.

"Are we supposed to have a door?" I try to see across and over the backs of the other two teams. Do they have a door? Was that in the instructions? To door or not to door?

"And windows," Miss Thick Glasses says, suddenly perky. "But we need scissors."

"Aha!" I reach for my purse and my Swiss Army knife, which has a miniature pair of scissors. I carefully, artfully, creatively, cut a door in our pale, delicate, four-sheets-of-paper-and-a-roof house.

"Windows," Miss Thick Glasses repeats. She really sounds excited now. There is some life left in the old girl yet. Or is it that we are nearing the end of this stupid trial by paper and pins exercise?

I cut windows. My teammates smile. We high five. TEAM.

The timer dings. We are told to take our hands off the table and select a spokesman. Spokesperson, I correct her in my mind. Miss Thick Glasses and Purple Eye Shadow look at Baldy and nod. He puffs up. Mr. Superman. I don't say anything. Of course these wimpy women would bow to the only rooster in the bunch. Well, let him crow. Hens lay eggs, but the rooster gets to crow.

The team that goes first has used all its straws and pins. Overachievers. Their creation is a foot-tall swirl of a bird's nest structure. They tore their sheets of paper into strips to line their bird's nest. Well, bully. It wasn't a house. It was a nest for God's sake. Very mod. And it stood. Three dimensional. Workshop leaders can't say enough about this team. Quite creative. What imagination! What teamwork! Why wasn't I with this team? How had I gotten the dullards of the world straight from the academic dungeons?

Team two presents their creation, which is much like ours. Had they peeked as we worked? Had they copied? They have a traditional box, roof, and windows, and a double door. All with ragged edges.

The workshop leaders smile, nod. Ask how they made those *darling* doors and windows. "By hand," one of them says. "We very carefully tore them."

"Nicely done," Mr. Workshop Leader says. "Next."

Baldy points to our creation, which now looks like a copy except our door and windows have neatly cut edges. Ours is a much better-looking construction. I feel a shiver of pride. Maybe the workshop leaders will hold our construction up as an example. Precision teamwork, they'll say.

Instead they put their heads together, whisper.

No one had mentioned a prize, but maybe there is to be one. A blue ribbon certificate of accomplishment. Something tangible to take back to our respective institutions. Maybe hang on some board somewhere to show that even the little people, the lowlies, have a brain or two and are more than simply their rinky-dink jobs. I'd take a blue ribbon with gold lettering or some other leadership award home to show my supervisor that my day had been productive, even rewarding—they weren't employing some small gray mouse of a peon.

"How did you make the door and windows?" one of the leaders asks.

My team looks at me. "I did them," I say with pride.

"And did you use a tool?"

"Yes." I pull out my Swiss Army knife.

The leaders gasp. The other two teams gasp. It's suddenly like grade school. I am a criminal. A delinquent. I'd carried a weapon, *a knife*, into the classroom. My team only looks puzzled.

"You're not allowed to use tools," the female workshop leader says. "Disqualified."

I slink down in my seat, suddenly alone at the table. My team members had just risen in unison and slunk silently from the room. No tools? If that instruction had been given earlier, my teammates hadn't remembered. Or if they did, they hadn't said so. Miss Thick Glasses even said we needed scissors, which is what prompted me to pull out my knife. Yes, we'd been told to use the materials on the table, but I don't think they specified we couldn't use our initiative. I mean, isn't leadership thinking outside the box? Fearless? Going where others haven't thought to go?

For a long moment I sit there as the other teams and the workshop leaders file out of the room. There is a big as an auditorium, stunned silence after everyone leaves. I, the brown sheep, the outcast, the unloved little peon of peons, sit alone.

The room is so silent I could hear a pin drop if they all weren't already pinned to leftover rolls and pages. Ha, I say to myself. You are a cliché among clichés. The last sheep in the academic librarians flock.

On each table lay the discarded, unused rolls of pins, and on a table beside me, a stack of fresh paper, a whole unused ream, five hundred white sheets. Back at Podunk U library we write notes on the blank side of used paper. No budget for "stickies." Fresh, clean paper, a whole ream, is trophy. I gather all these materials, go back to my room, sit on my bed feeling slumpy and dejected. I lie back and start to count the little dots on the ceiling row by row. I multiply the rows, then I pace until I am worn and weary, then I sleep.

When I wake it is dark, a deep gray bruised night sky of dark. Outside the window and two stories down, various groups from the conference have converged around the pool, drinks in hand. Bitches. Baldy's in a red Hawaiian shirt holding some electric blue drink. Purple Eye Shadow has changed to a long dress that matches her eyes. Miss Thick Glasses is still wearing a brown denim pantsuit. She sits at a patio table alone, head down like the loser I feel. I would be with her, but nobody asked me. I am a double loser.

I reread the conference schedule, and no get-together is listed. On-your-own time, it says. Free time. I get just plain mad. Nobody had said you couldn't use tools. Nobody had said don't be inventive. They had said be creative. I *was* creative.

I pick up one of the rolls of straight pins, begin to pull pins out one by one. I poke them back into the paper, saying *take that, take that, take that* as I prick the sheet full of a million pinholes. Each hole is a person. A pinhead in my life, in this conference, in this whole leadership seminar. Baldy, Miss Thick Glasses, Purple Eye Shadow, workshop leader male, workshop leader female. Poke, poke, poke. Stab, stab, stab. If this paper had blood, it would gush red.

After a while I get more creative. What I had been doing was just making holes with pins. Now I pick up sheets of paper and begin to make origami people, fold and turn, fold and turn, male and female. I laugh. I giggle. I pick up a paper creature and dance it around on my extra bed. I make a whole conference of paper people. My leadership group is just a pin's worth in the whole conference. I put my paper people in rows, I march them up and down and around the bed.

Who says I'm not creative? I draw features on all the paper people. I draw hair and mustaches and beards, zits and freckles. I draw tits and penises . . . little dangles, squiggles on the front of some of my male paper people. I name them after everybody who had ever said or done a mean thing to me in my life, starting with today's workshop leaders, then going *back, back, back*: my second-grade teacher who kept me after school, the uncoordinated girl who got to be cheerleader instead of me because she was sleeping with the football coach, the neighbor next door when I was a child who wouldn't let me climb his apple tree, the rich woman I cleaned for when I was seventeen who made me iron things over three times, the music teacher who kicked me out of piano after whacking my hands with her metal ruler, the Girl Scout leader who stole my cookie money, the college professor who gave me a C minus, the meter maid who gave me a ticket, the banker guy who never smiles at me, my first husband, my second husband, the bitch who stole my last boyfriend, the bitch who cut my hair wrong, the bitch who held up the line in front of me at the food store, the bitch who got my parking place. I jumble them all on my bed and say, "Fuck, fuck, fuck you all."

I get giddy and take the rest of the paper from the packet, fold pieces into houses and stores. I make supermarkets and big box stores, little shops and schools, churches with steeples and apartments, condos. My extra bed becomes a city.

I people my paper city. With ink and markers from my purse I draw roads and rivers all over the hotel's white coverlet. I draw streets and trees. A park. A playground. When I have used up all the paper and my room is crowded with paper people, I have another idea.

Only the rolls of pins are left. Lots of rolls of lots of shiny silver pins with very straight tips. Sharp shiny silver straight pins that can prick a person. Or a paper person.

I grab a glass of water and several of my paper people and step out on my balcony. After taking a refreshing sip of water, I hold pins aloft and begin to poke them one by one into paper Baldy's head, neck, shoulders, legs. Lots of pins, lots of poking pins in the paper person.

Down below Baldy touches his head, rubs his arm, lifts his leg, then grabs his chest and falls over on the concrete.

Miss Thick Glasses screams, runs over to where he's face down by the pool.

I jab pin after pin into paper Baldy's legs. Then I stop. Down below, real Baldy is very still. The paper Baldy in my hand is as full of pins as a porcupine has quills.

A crowd gathers around the real Baldy. Cell phones light up and numbers are pressed. Oh, this is all so touching.

Music from some boom-boom band has stopped. Miss Thick Glasses runs toward the office area, trips, and falls into a second pool where she floats like brown debris, no one noticing. Her glasses float beside her. Can she see where she's going? Will she be able to see when she gets there? If she goes to the bottom of the pool, there is only dark.

Only moments before, my paper Miss Thick Glasses somehow managed to fall into my glass of water, float a bit, then get waterlogged and sink. Will the real Miss Thick Glasses keep floating or sink? Or will somebody pull her out?

I pick up Purple Eye Shadow and dance her around the balcony. She was the only one who believed in me, my little paper house with the perfect door and windows. She did not scoff, nor laugh, only a little girlish giggle of support.

I lean over the balcony and drop Purple Eye Shadow and watch her float down, down, down. She is rather lovely. I had colored her whole paper body purple.

A gust of wind picks her up and lifts her over the tall pool wall, then she is gone. Out of sight. Same as the real Purple Eye Shadow, who I notice is no longer at the pool. She left. Did anyone notice? Librarians are supposed to be the quiet ones. We are known for speaking in whispers, shushing with our finger to our lips. Oh, the clichés.

Now Baldy's body lies on the pool deck, with a few unknown people beside him. Mrs. Workshop Leader, still in her black pantsuit, has come over and put a rolled beach towel under his head. "Is he dead?" some ask, their voices floating up on the breeze.

Most of the gawkers don't care. They've gone back to the bar. Baldy is not their concern. They are not my concern either, but I have made paper people to represent them anyway. All the convention goers are represented in paper, each attendee. I must be fair. Not single out only my own group. My group of dolts. So many dolts. Is there a single person at this conference who has an administrative job? I think not. We are the peons of peons. We are the librarians who are never seen in the libraries. We are the walls, the floors, the ceilings, the spines of the books, the computer cords, the mice. So many working mice.

The boom-boom band starts to play again. So much for respect. How many seconds did Baldy get? Fifteen minutes. How much respect does any librarian ever get? "Oh Baldy," I say out loud, "maybe you got more than most of us will ever get."

I make another paper Baldy, blow some warm breath on him. The real Baldy begins to shake, pulls himself up to a standing position, holds his hand to his head, and looks around as if asking, *What the hell happened?* People applaud as he walks back over to the bar. They're probably saying to each other, "Too much to drink" and "It happens." I go back inside.

I have pins, paper rolls of pins unrolled in shiny rows. I pick up an unnamed, unknown paper person, a conference goer, an attendee. I stick a pin in the head and put it back on the bed. I only imagine I hear it groan. I pick up another paper person, and another, another. Stick pins in their heads until I get bored, then I stick a pin or two in their backs, their chests, a leg here and there. I have a jumble of wounded paper people on my bed. Every one of the paper people gets a pin or two. Too bad they are not badges or awards to show what they learned at the leadership conference.

Leadership. Ha. I show them what leadership is when I toss the whole batch, minus Baldy, Miss Thick Glasses, and Purple Eye Shadow, in the wastebasket. At my library we recycle. We must recycle as much as we can in these days of waste and worry and worship.

Worship for facts and figures, for the bright and beautiful. None for the worker bees.

I go downstairs to join the party that has grown so very much smaller. Odd coincidence. My group, my losing team, including Purple Eye Shadow, waves me over. Baldy holds another blue drink. Miss Thick Glasses pats her dripping wet hair with a bar towel. We laugh, we commiserate, laugh about the whole exercise of house building. The very idea. The stupidness of it all. We, who are the crushed croutons in the loaves of life. We who are nothings from Nothing U. Back we go to the ivy-covered boxes of academia to molder, molder, molder for all time to come.

We know not only did we not get blue ribbons, award certificates, or even applause, but soon we will return to our dungeons to lick our wounds and hope we never, ever run into each other again. At some regional or state meeting, we escapees for the day will not smile and wave across the room, saying in jubilant greeting, "Hey, don't I know you from such and such?" Not us. Not the disqualified. Not the D minus Disqualified Leadership Team.

# THE PERFECT PITCH

## by Marie Hannan-Mandel

This town, with its Victorian lampposts, chichi shops lit up as if to guide in planes, and restaurants with lines outside the door, is just as disappointing as the airport. I'd waited in line for my rental car hoping to see something quirky, unusual, typical of Maine, and instead I'd met nothing but strangers all visiting from somewhere else. Now I'm approaching my destination, and I could be driving down the main street of almost any shopping mecca. I see no quaint small-town businesses, crusty locals disparaging "blow-ins," or seafaring folks fighting and smelling of fish. Everything's way too modern and expensive—nothing like what I've seen on TV. This town is as much Maine as Disney World is Florida.

Worse, I'm not dressed for it. I'm a New Yorker. Not one of those people who populate the farms upstate, but a New York City girl, born and raised in Middle Village, Queens. I thought it was cold when I left home, but it's much worse here.

Before you begin to feel sorry for me, don't. I'm here for an inventors' convention with my lint-collecting dryer sheet prototype, the Lint-Locker—the guaranteed way to ensure your laundry doesn't get covered in lint—so I can meet James Maguire O'Reilly, megastar inventor. As soon as I'd found out he was going to be running workshops and hearing inventor pitches—something he never does—I'd registered, even though it meant coming to Maine in January. I signed up for every one of his morning workshops, and I'm going to make sure he notices me. He's going to love my product and help me get financial backing for it. All he needs is to hear my pitch.

Soon enough I've found my destination, a chain hotel on the edge of town. It has cookies in the lobby, racks of brochures, and a fake fire.

"I'm here for the inventors' convention," I say when I catch the front desk clerk's eye.

She takes my name and completes all the formalities quickly. "The event takes place at Bayview House." She hands me my card key.

"Where is that?"

"It's out of town about seven miles away. It's a beautiful old house overlooking the bay." She smiles an awful lot but doesn't have what I recognize as a Maine accent.

"It didn't say that in the literature. I assumed the convention would be here, at the hotel." I bend down to root through my bag to convince her that she must be wrong. I can't find the literature and suspect that if I did, there wouldn't be anything about where the actual sessions were going to be held. I straightened up.

"It's all in here." She hands me a folder with the convention logo on the cover.

What did it matter where the sessions were as long as I had a chance to get to know James Maguire O'Reilly? *I had to get to know James Maguire O'Reilly.*

"Are all the convention people staying here?" I ask in a psycho-calm voice.

"Yes," she says. "Everyone except the speakers, or I mean, experts. They're staying someplace else."

"Oh. Where are they staying?" The desperation in my voice is so obvious it covers me in a cloud of crazy.

"I'm not sure," she says in a tone that clearly shows it's me, rather than their location, that she's unsure of.

"Oh well," I say, smiling as if I'm fine about this, which I'm not.

"There's a swimming pool with a hot tub," she says, as if any hotel amenity could make up for these disappointments.

"What a shame. I'd definitely have brought a suit if I'd known," I lie. I know whale hunting is illegal, but given my age and physique, I wasn't taking any chances.

"You could go get one at the sportswear store?" Her tone is questioning, as if she already knows the answer is no. "It's open twenty-four/seven for the post-Christmas sales. You could get a swimsuit there." She motions to a brochure on the counter advertising said store.

"Isn't that great," I say. Twenty-four/seven? Really? Up here?

"It's world famous," she adds.

Like I'm going to drop my bags at eight o'clock at night and rush over there. I enjoy shopping, don't get me wrong, but this place is just not what I thought it would be, you know?

I go to my room and stay there.

***

The next day, the first day of the convention, I don't bother with breakfast and am on the road before I see anyone else. I have my heat cranked up high, and I'm still freezing. I'll have to break down and get myself to the world-famous store and buy outdoor gear that doesn't make me resemble some sort of half-woman/half-animal, all-blubber creature.

The directions to the wonderful and awe-inspiring location where the actual event is taking place—the organizers' words, not mine—send me through the town. In the dawn light, with snow flurries drifting down, the place looks even more plastic than it did the evening before.

Have you noticed how anything that's described in glowing terms is always a pain to get to? The main road goes on a bit, and then, when I turn off, whammy. Within minutes, I'm in the middle of the forest. Well, not really, but it's countryside, pretty countryside, and I can see there's a lot of trees up ahead.

I can't study the landscape, though, because the road is getting narrower all the time and the uneven surface makes me anxious for my car's suspension. This little Korean rental, wincing and grinding its wheels in protest, doesn't seem up to the task. What was the guy at the rental desk thinking giving me such a flimsy vehicle? I told him I'd be driving around, and he should have known what was needed in his own state.

The evergreen trees are becoming denser. The snow on the ground is getting deeper, and, of course, there aren't snow tires affixed to this car. All I need now is to run into a moose. Apparently, one contact with a moose and you and the car are history. It's not like hitting a deer. Nope. Slamming into a moose is roadkill apocalypse.

Just when I'm absolutely sure I'm lost, someone pulls out of a side road a little ahead with a sign for the Swallow Motel. I have no idea where they've come from, but I'm glad not to be alone. I'd deliberately left early because I wanted to be at the convention when James Maguire O'Reilly arrived so I could be sure to get a seat right near him in the first workshop. I don't care how pushy that sounds. I didn't spend all this money not to get as close as possible.

The car ahead slows down, and I see Bayview House, large and old and elegant. It's gorgeous. And not just because I'm relieved to see it. Even better, the parking lot in front is almost empty. We care a lot about parking where I come from. The person in front of me gets out. She's young and blond. I watch this gorgeous creature step daintily over the recently ploughed snow in low-heeled leather riding boots. I hope she's not in my workshop. I can't afford anyone distracting James's attention from me.

I walk into Bayview House and can see it's just the right place for the muse to sit and whisper in one's ear. I'll bet I come up with a new product idea every day I'm here. The huge hallway has many doors, and a carved wooden staircase rises with a full-length, wisteria vine stained-glass window at the bend. James Maguire

O'Reilly is going to fit right in here.

I won't bore you with the checking in and the chitchat, but let me say this: I avoid everyone else. I have no interest in talking with inventors who will either have too high an opinion of their product and make me want to laugh, or have no confidence in it at all and make me want to cry.

***

Standing by the fireplace in the library where we are to have the first session, I take a quick look around before training my eyes on the door across the room. The walls are lined with books with only a surprisingly small fireplace and two windows to break them up. The space is cavernous, with a long table sitting in the middle of the floor. There are eleven other people waiting, but I haven't spoken to any of them because it would be just my luck to get distracted and find myself sitting far away from James.

"Hi, everyone," James Maguire O'Reilly says from the doorway.

"Hi, Mr. Maguire O'Reilly," all twelve of us say in a raggedy way that makes it sound like his name is even more elaborate than it is.

"Call me James," he says looking around from one to the other of us. He is even more attractive in person than on television and in magazines. Who'd have thought it? I suspect, and my own observations have backed me up, that people use pictures taken years before, on a particularly good day, for their promotional material. He looks just as if he'd walked off the back of his books with his blond wavy hair and perfectly symmetrical face.

We all scramble to sit near James at one end of the table. I barrel my way to the seat on his left. When we are ready to start, the beautiful girl from the parking lot comes in. Unlucky thirteen, but I don't think she will be the unlucky one. She's rushing and breathless, as unwelcome as the last-minute plane passenger arriving just when you think you have a row of seats all to yourself. How could she be late when she'd arrive more than an hour before? James hurries to push an extra chair up to the table directly across from where I'm sitting, edging out an older woman who looks as sick as I would have felt had he done that to me.

"It's so nice to meet you. I'm Brandi," she says, holding out her hand to James. Her voice is so whispery it makes my throat itch. Close up, I see she's older than she appears, at least thirty underneath all that like-you-have-nothing-on makeup.

James cocks his head to the side like a questioning dog and takes her hand without saying a word.

Like being drawn to like, James and the girl chat for a couple of minutes as if they've known each other forever, almost ignoring the rest of us. I don't know what the others are thinking, but I'm pissed.

Finally, the workshop gets underway. I'm the first to present. We're allowed five minutes to pitch, after which we'll be critiqued. I'd practiced and practiced until I was sure of every nuance and emphasis of my voice, with every movement designed to show off my product to its best advantage. Now I lean forward in my chair and flash my best smile. I'm going to sell the hell out of my Lint-Locker. I'm not so sure about the name but say it with pride, hoping James will help me come up with a better one, if needed.

Brandi taps her pen on her notebook, a metronomic sound, and it throws me off. I don't need accompaniment. I pause from time to time, hoping my glare will stop her, hoping James will stop her, but the tapping continues. I fumble and my yellow and blue rectangular plastic prototype flies across the table, landing in James's lap. He picks it up, handing it across to me as if I were a dog who'd dropped her battered chew toy at his feet in the park. I flop back in my seat when I'm done, feeling so disappointed that my moment to shine has been wrecked. I hate Brandi.

"Interesting product, but you need to change the shape, color, size, and name." James says.

I write all this down. He looks at me, and I want to tell him I'd cut off my own legs if it would lead him to champion me to his investors, or better, invest in me himself.

"I thought the color worked," says a rotund man with a pronounced grayish mustache that appears to be sprouting directly from his nose and not his upper lip. He smiles at me, and I smile back. Well, grimace really.

"Do you think so? Why do you say that?" James asks him and they're off. I wish I could concentrate more on the discussion and less on Brandi, who stares blankly at the rather haphazard fire in the cast-iron grate.

Did I mention I'm still freezing? Yeah, turns out this old place is all beauty and no warmth, the fireplace be damned. Just like Brandi. I smile at my metaphor and mustache man clearly thinks I'm smiling at him because he winks.

Most of the presentations are tedious. The older woman next to Brandi, who is even more besotted with James than I am, feels it necessary to tell us her own very traumatic life story and barely mentions the weird multicolored shoe-warmer inserts that are supposed to keep you "toasty" (her word, not mine) no matter how cold it gets or what else you wear. She clasps these ugly things to her flat chest as if they are sacred relics. She cries as she reaches the end. James is kind to her, and she cries some more.

Then we get to Brandi. She is last, of course, and she glances around from one to the other of us before beginning.

She holds up a box and starts reading from a sheet of paper in front of her. She stumbles and pauses over the description of a mousetrap that lures the vermin in with music—apparently Brahms is most effective. It's clear to me she hasn't invented this thing. You know your own work. She repeats the word *extraordinary* over and over as if it's the only adjective she knows. You might stumble over the errors you didn't catch in your presentation (even though you'd read it aloud to yourself over and over), but you know what is coming next, for goodness sake. Not only does she mispronounce *annihilation*, but she sounds it out first, as if she doesn't have any idea at all of what the word is, like she'd never had it in her head. When she holds up the gadget, dangling it from two fingers like a dead mouse, the name—Killing Them with Kindness—is upside down.

Brandi is stealing someone else's work, it's as clear as the exquisite nose on her oh-so-regular face. I wait for the trap to snap, for the cat to pounce, for the girl to be called out on her perfidy.

"That was a great presentation of what will be a very successful product, Brandi," James says.

"Do you really think so?" she asks, her eyes ablaze.

"Yes. The use of music is a unique selling point."

Selling point? Was he kidding? What about practicality? What about usefulness? What about the fact that this chick isn't even pitching her own idea?

I gaze around the table to see what the others think. They are all staring down except for mustache man who winks at me again.

"We'll finish things there and break for lunch. Afterward, we have a talk on the importance of having a good marketing strategy. And we'll meet here tomorrow for our next workshop," James announces. "I know a great spot to sit and eat lunch," he says to Brandi, who walks away with him. It is of slight satisfaction to me that James is quite a bit shorter than her.

"I do, too," mustache man, whose name is Benjamin, says to me, and close up I see that he isn't winking at all but has some kind of a twitch. He's tall though, and that's something. Not much, but something.

"Where are you from?" Benjamin asks when we are seated with a few dozen other people in the dining room. The bowl of vegan salad, our only choice, looks as appetizing as the insides of a lawnmower bag.

"New York City. You?"

"I live in South Carolina."

"You must be even colder than I am," I say.

"Yes, yes, it's extraordinarily cold here for someone from where I come from."

"James seems to like Brandi an awful lot," I say.

"Of course he does," Benjamin says.

"I liked your pitch. It reminds me of something, but I can't think what," I say. He frowns and I add, "Very good, it was very good. I'd buy it." Though there wasn't a single chance that I would buy an adjustable shoe horn.

"Thanks. I liked your product, too. Don't change it just because O'Reilly says so," he says, twitching up a storm.

The rest of the day is agony. I don't need to tell you much except to say that James and Brandi spend the entire time together as we sit through two boring lectures. I'm so cold by the time the day ends I think I could have packed up and gone home, if it weren't for the slight, faint hope that James would come to his senses and drool over my Lint-Locker. I consider the possibility as I run out to my car before Benjamin can catch me and offer yet again to take me to dinner at some place named the Hacienda Grill. Hacienda? In Maine?

***

I can't sleep. It's cold. I turn the thermostat to the highest setting and wait. Not even a puff of air. I wonder what the symptoms of frostbite are and whether the fact I can't feel my feet is cause for concern. The clock, which is bright enough to read by, says 3:10 a.m. I call down to the front desk, and after several rings, someone answers. I'm surprised but relieved that there is a person on duty to deal with emergencies—like my imminent death from cold.

"It's cold in my room," I say.

"Yes. I'm sorry. There'll be someone coming to fix the boiler tomorrow morning. Until then, you'll find extra blankets in the closet," the young man says.

Extra blankets? Is he kidding? We'd passed the extra blankets phase a long time before.

"The heating is on in the lobby area," he says.

"The lobby?"

"Well, yes. The ground floor is heated by a different boiler. You could come down here."

I mean, really? Not that it would have been a bad idea if James had been staying with us. Then I'd be down there hoping to score time with him. But as it was . . .

"No, thanks," I say and hang up.

There's nothing for it but to go to that all-night place and get myself a coat. A cheap coat that would, in all likelihood, make me a dead ringer for a yeti. But do I care? I could walk into the session with James tomorrow wearing a combat uniform and no one but mustache man, I mean Benjamin, would notice.

I layer on as many clothes as I can and head down toward the parking lot.

As I near the lobby, I hear someone splashing in the indoor pool. At three a.m. Don't they lock that baby up at night? Unlike most pools I've seen, this one doesn't have windows all along the sides. I see Brandi through the door, standing in what I assume is the hot tub section of the pool wearing a white bikini that fits her perfectly. Trust her to find a warm spot in this place. Her head is bent back and she's laughing, putting on a show, and peeking up at someone I can't see. I come closer, but when Brandi glances my way, I leave. I don't want her to think I'm interested. But what if it's James with her? Luckily, the thought of him cavorting with Brandi makes me sick. Missing that sight takes no willpower at all. I walk out of the lobby, get into my car, and after a little coughing and groaning, it starts and I drive away.

There's a line at the outdoor clothing place's checkout counter. A line at three thirty in the morning. This certainly isn't anything at all like the Maine of my imagination. But within twenty minutes I've paid for a deeply discounted cerise-colored thermal jacket. It fits over all my layers and is guaranteed to keep me warm even without layers, which is good, because with the layers I resemble a poorly stuffed sausage.

As I pull into the hotel parking lot, I see an ambulance, a police car, and a lot of commotion in the lobby. I rush in and am met by a policewoman, who blocks my way.

"What's happened?" I ask, craning over her shoulder to see.

"There's been an incident in the swimming pool." She stares at me as if I were the kind of woman who goes out in the middle of the night wearing all her clothes to buy even more, which, of course, I am.

"An incident?" I hate that word. It can mean anything from people cursing at each other to murder. *Murder?*

"Someone's killed Brandi?" I ask. Surely I couldn't be the only person who despises her.

The policewoman straightens up, and I see at once I have made a big mistake.

"What makes you say that?" she asks. Again, not a trace of the Maine accent I'd expected when I came here.

"I saw her when I was leaving. In the swimming pool. Well, I wasn't in the swimming pool. She was." I'm a little nervous now; I'm not going to lie.

"Was she alone?"

"I'm not sure. She seemed to be with someone else, but I didn't see who it was." I hope I don't look suspicious, though I'm sure I do.

"She knows. Ask her," a shrill voice calls.

I turn to see Brandi, still in her white bikini, with a large dark green towel over her shoulders. She is wet from head to foot. I'm pleased she's not dead. Truly, I am.

"She saw us, and she can tell you who did this to me," Brandi says to the uniformed cop who is talking to her. Her voice carries across the lobby, and it's not whispery now. She points at me.

How embarrassing. Now I'm a woman who goes out shopping in the middle of the night and stops along the way to spy on other people.

"I didn't see anyone else. I told you that," I insist to the officer I am talking to.

"It was James. I swear." Brandi darts across the lobby with surprising speed. "I'd never met him before the workshop today, and I didn't invite him to come here. But he did, and when I wouldn't do what he wanted . . ." She pauses here, clearly for effect, her eyes cast down, her face tinged with pink. "He tried to drown me. He held me under the water, and I could have died."

"Well, why didn't you?" I ask. It seems a perfectly reasonable question to me, and one the police have probably already asked, but they won't tell me what she'd said.

"I was saved. By Benjamin." She says this like a Shakespearean actress, booming and with perfect timing.

"Benjamin? What was he doing down here at this time of night?" I ask.

The policewoman who'd been talking to me clears her throat. "That's enough. I'll ask the questions that need to be asked. You'll have to wait and talk to Sergeant Warkovsky," she tells me, tossing her head in the direction of a tall young man standing by the gas fireplace with uniformed officers. I hasten over to him because, well, I'm drawn to the artificial flames.

The heat is getting to me, and I take off my coat, then my cardigan with the reindeer on it, a present from my aunt who clearly doesn't like me very much. The sergeant's eyes widen.

"So, what did you see?" he asks, clearing his throat, his eyes following my every movement as if he's never seen a woman take off her clothes before. Of course, he's probably wondering why the uniformed cops get the pretty, barely clad beauty while he gets the chubby beast. I remove my plaid shirt. I'm down to the regulation one shirt, one pair of pants, and still he's staring, but I don't care.

I tell him everything I can think of, keeping my voice low. He tells me nothing. By the time we are done and he hands me his card, Brandi is long gone, and I wonder where Benjamin is. And James. What's happening with James?

I try to walk by the pool to have a peek, but I'm directed the long way around to the elevators. I don't get much sleep when I finally climb under the covers with all but my shoes on.

***

I enter the workshop the next morning right before it's scheduled to begin and look around. As I'd suspected, James isn't there and neither is Brandi, nor Benjamin. The other ten members of the workshop are talking about what's happened. They know very little, but eye me in a way that shows me they've heard about my part in the drama.

"James tried to, you know, attack her. Benjamin stopped him, and they're both in the hospital," says the woman who's invented a new way to bake squash.

"James isn't that kind of man," the woman with the shoe warmers and sad personal story says. She isn't crying now.

"I can't imagine Benjamin attacking anyone. He's a Buddhist, after all," the man with the electronic pickle dispenser says.

"He is? How do you know?" I ask, walking toward them, which is no hardship as they are standing around the fire, and that's where I always want to be.

"He told me," he says.

We have a substitute leader for the workshop, and we all sit down, feeling as much appreciation toward him as anyone ever does for a sub.

At the lunch break I go back to the hotel. There's no point being at the convention unless James is there. Besides, I want to find out what Brandi is up to. I'm sure she's up to something.

I meet Benjamin in the hotel lobby, and he beams at me. "I suppose you heard what happened?"

"A little bit," I say, allowing him to draw me over to the fire. One thing about the Maine cold, there is always a fire to huddle around.

"So, you didn't see who was in the pool with Brandi?" he asks.

"No. I didn't know she'd seen me, and I didn't want to pry," I say. A total lie.

"It was lucky I was downstairs. I was so extraordinarily uncomfortable in my room that I had to leave. The noise from the heater was so loud I couldn't sleep," Benjamin says.

"Me, too." I shiver at the memory.

"I left my room in just my shirt and pants and a pair of slip-ons, so I was able to dive right in and save her," Benjamin says, his chest puffing out.

"Wow. That was lucky." I try to hide my confusion by asking, "Where's James?"

"He's at the police station. You never know with people, do you? Who'd have thought he was crazy?" Benjamin is clearly thrilled.

"Has he confessed?" I ask.

"No. By the time they caught up with him in his room, he was dry and pretending to be asleep."

"Where's his room?"

"He and all the other leaders are staying in a guest house, the Swallow, not far from Bayview House. They didn't think it was a good idea to have them stay over here with us. Now I know why," Benjamin says with a dramatic flair reminiscent of Brandi's performance the night before. Was it catching? Would I be declaiming by the end of the weekend?

"Well, they could hardly have known James would do something like this." I wonder why Brandi had said she'd never met James before the workshop. Where else could she have been coming from but the Swallow Motel early yesterday morning? James's confusion at her introducing herself was because he already knew her.

"Anyone seeing those products he designs could have guessed it. All but the first one of his inventions is useless crap," Benjamin says. "Sorry, but I have to go."

He's gone before I can even say good-bye.

I make my own haste to the front desk. The clerk is the same young woman I'd met when I'd first arrived.

"Is the boiler fixed?" I ask without preamble.

"Yes, it is. All the rooms should be warm enough now. We're so sorry."

"None of the rooms had heat?" I ask.

"No, the boiler was turned off. But it's all fixed," she assures me.

I think about asking for a refund—freezing rooms, a discredited workshop leader, and not one sign of the Maine I'd wanted to see. Instead, I go to my room, take out Sergeant Warkovsky's card, and call him. Investigating is even easier than on television. Perhaps if James and the Lint-Locker don't work out, I have a real shot at being a sleuth.

\*\*\*

Warkovsky allows me, after much persuasion on my part, to go with him to Brandi's room.

"Don't say anything," he says before he knocks on the door.

"I won't," I lie.

"Oh, hello," Brandi says, opening the door slightly. Then she sees me. Her eyes flash with the fear of a trapped animal.

"May I come in?" Warkovsky asks.

I *accidentally* push the door all the way open. "I told you," I say, pointing to the bed.

"What? What did you tell him?" Brandi demands.

"What the—what the hell is going on?" Benjamin blusters as we stand in the tiny hall and stare. He's jumping up, grabbing his boxers, but we all saw him lying on the bed in what might be called a compromising position. His fake mustache is lying on the side table like a wounded centipede. He's not as fat as he appeared with his clothes on.

"Why did you set James up?" I ask.

"What do you mean?" she asks, trying her helpless routine on Warkovsky.

Warkovsky glares at me and scowls a shut-up look, which I plan to ignore. I'm the one who figured it out, after all.

"So, you did see everything last night," Brandi pouts.

"You were alone when I passed."

"I wasn't," Brandi says, but her heart's not in it anymore.

"You repeated the same movements and noises over and over hoping someone would walk by who you could use to back up your story—an old acting trick," I say.

"How did you—what do you mean?" Brandi asks. Her pretty face is all contorted and not so pretty anymore.

"What's more, you were looking up. James isn't taller than you, but Benjamin is. I'll bet Benjamin was hiding in the shadows waiting for someone to see you before 'saving' you." I glance at Benjamin, who doesn't look happy with me. "You knew that unless someone came right up to the door, they wouldn't be able to see who you were supposedly talking to. You've been setting James up from the very beginning—going to his room before the workshop, pretending not to know him, so it would look like he was the one chasing you."

"It's not true. I don't understand why you are saying all this." Brandi darts a glance at Benjamin, who does understand. And can you believe this? He doesn't actually have a twitch.

"So it's all about you?" I yell. "I came here to meet James, and you ruined it for me with your stunt." I'm really irritated, but maybe, if James finds out I helped save him, he'll help me develop my product? Hey, it's a possibility.

"You're just making things up," Benjamin says.

"Benjamin said his heater was noisy when the boiler was off. Then he implied that his room was too hot, and that's why he didn't have to remove a lot of clothes to get into the pool. Of course, if he was downstairs with you, where the heat was on, he wouldn't need extra clothes. And when I remembered what Benjamin's pitch reminded me of—the pitch you, Brandi, read, or mangled—then I knew. You both used the word *extraordinary* much too often." I was on a roll and loving it. Even better, James would have to be grateful after this. He'd have to recommend my Lint-Locker now.

"You don't believe her, do you?" Brandi demands of Warkovsky.

"Yes, I do. You are both coming down to the station to answer some more questions."

"James Maguire O'Reilly deserves it. He stole Benjamin's idea—a cordless rocking chair seat warmer. He took it, and it made him famous. We've been waiting for years for a way to get back at him," Brandi howls.

The nerve of this woman is not to be believed.

"Don't say any more," Benjamin orders Brandi, though his voice is gentle. He really cares for this stupid creature. Men are so predictable.

I'm feeling extremely proud of myself.

"Turns out, Mr. Maguire O'Reilly couldn't have done what you say because he never left his room. Mrs. Sharp was watching the whole time," Warkovsky says.

"Mrs. Sharp?" Brandi and I say in unison.

"Yes, she's a member of your workshop, or whatever you call it. She stood outside his window watching him all night," Warkovsky says. "Lucky for him, he was on the ground floor where she could see him. She said he was so kind about her pitch that she wants to spend more time with him."

Lucky and creepy. And here I thought it was a good idea to *close* the curtains in my room at night.

"She was the one with the shoe warmers, I suppose. I'm amazed they work," I say, rather pleased I hadn't gone *that* far in my obsession.

"She's lying," Benjamin says.

"Nope, a member of staff saw her there a few times during the night." Warkovsky seems to be enjoying himself.

"So, you didn't need my information after all." I see my one last chance with James slip away.

"We did. All we knew is that Mr. Maguire O'Reilly couldn't have done it. You showed us why they set him up." Warkovsky smiles at me. Could he be persuaded to leave Mrs. Sharp's surveillance out so I am still James's savior? I'll try talking him into it later.

"What's going to happen to us?" Brandi asks in that whispery voice she saves for special occasions.

"You'll both have to come down to the station, and my boss will decide."

"I don't suppose you could tell James, I mean Mr. Maguire O'Reilly, that I solved this all on my own, could you?" I whisper to Warkovsky on our way out to the police station.

"Nope. And don't you to tell him that, either," Warkovsky says.

"I won't," I lie.

# TWO BIRDS WITH ONE STONE

## by Rhys Bowen

*Castle Rannoch, Perthshire, Scotland*
*September 1934*

I have a confession to make. I'm actually not too fond of bagpipes, especially when played outside my window at dawn. Oh, I know that I'm the sister of the Duke of Rannoch and that those pipes were playing outside our ancestral home. I realize that my Scottish blood should stir with pride at the skirl of the pipes, but I am only one quarter Scottish and the other three quarters would rather not be awoken rudely at six fifteen.

\*\*\*

The ritual of the piper doing the rounds of the castle at dawn only happens these days on special occasions, such as visits from royalty, births, deaths, and marriages. Today was none of the above but was special enough to make our retired gamekeeper, old MacTavish, put on his kilt and full Highland dress to parade around Castle Rannoch playing "Scotland the Brave." I don't know whether the hundred or so people camped on our grounds greeted it more favorably than I did. My Cockney maid, Queenie, certainly wasn't thrilled.

"What the bleedin' heck was that God-forsaken row?" she demanded when she finally appeared with my morning cup of tea. "It sounded like someone slaughtering a pig."

I tried to greet this with a frosty stare. "A good lady's maid would greet her mistress with 'Good morning, Lady Georgiana, I trust you slept well?'"

Sarcasm doesn't seem to have much effect on Queenie.

"I don't know how anyone can sleep well in this godforsaken place," she said. "It gives me the willies. And now that awful noise . . ."

"It was the bagpiper," I said. "In Scotland it is traditional to greet the dawn with the pipes."

"Thank God we only come here once a year," she said, plonking down my cup on the bedside table. "Give me good old London any day. You're all stark, staring mad."

"The pipes are playing to celebrate the Gathering of the Clans,"

I said. "Binky felt we should do the right thing with visitors from all over Scotland coming together here. It's a great honor, you know, to be chosen to host the annual Gathering of the Clans. It only comes to us about every twenty years. I was a toddler last time it happened in 1913, but I vaguely remember all the fuss and that I was terrified of those huge men in kilts and ran back to Nanny."

"Huge men in kilts?" Queenie perked up at this.

"They'll all be wearing traditional Highland dress for the games."

"What sort of games?" She was looking quite interested now.

"The Highland Games are the main part of the gathering," I explained. "You know, they toss the caber and throw the hammer. All sorts of feats of strength."

"They have strong feet?" she asked, puzzled.

I tried not to laugh. "No, I meant contests to demonstrate how strong they are. You can go down and watch them practicing later, if you like. My brother has set aside the meadow beyond the stables as a practice field. Oh, and speaking of my brother, I have to go and inspect the facilities after breakfast to make sure all is in order. You know how—" I broke off. I had been going to say "You know how hopeless he is about organizing things," but one does not criticize the Duke of Rannoch to a family servant. It simply isn't done.

"How he worries about everything being just right," I finished. "So you'd better lay out my tartan skirt for me. I should be properly attired to appear in front of the clans. And I hope my best brogues are well-polished?"

I could tell by her face that they weren't. "You'll only go and get them muddy again," she said defiantly. Truly if the word *hopeless* applied to anyone, it was Queenie. I only kept her on because I knew nobody else would take her. Also because I couldn't afford a more efficient maid.

I dressed in my best Highland garb, breakfasted well on kedgeree and poached eggs, and met my brother, Binky, the current Duke of Rannoch, in the front hall.

"Oh, there you are, old bean." His face lit up when he saw me. "Good of you to come to do this, since Fig's still feeling under the weather and you know how hopeless I am."

My awful sister-in-law, Hilda, usually known as Fig, had just had a second baby and had been furious that Binky agreed to host the Gathering of the Clans.

"What were you thinking, Binky?" she had demanded in that sharp voice that could cut glass if it tried. "You know I'm too weak to host any sort of gathering, let alone a gathering of hairy

Highland men." She had kept firmly to her chamber and had had meals sent up on a tray since the participants began arriving three days ago. That was fine with me as she loathed me as much as I loathed her.

Binky and I set off. It was a beautiful, crisp autumn morning, the rare sort of day that makes one glad to be in Scotland. Before us was a hive of activity. On the lawns that stretched down to the loch two marquees had been erected—one for the Scottish dance and other competitions that might be ruined by rain, the other for refreshments. A host of smaller tents and booths were springing up around the perimeter of the grounds. Some proclaimed themselves to be headquarters for different clans, some were selling various items of Scottish regalia. One smart person had even set up a stall selling rain gear.

Binky and I were greeted with suitable deference as we walked around. "Good to see you, your Grace. And you, Lady Georgiana. We're honored to be at your home. As good as Balmoral any day."

"Don't relay that to Queen Mary when you meet her again," Binky muttered to me. I grinned.

"We should go and see how the practice for the games is getting along," he said. Actually I wasn't averse to watching big muscular men myself. We left the show grounds and crossed the parking area where vans were unloading supplies, and some keen early spectators had parked caravans. A van advertising Glenduig, Queen of Scotch Whiskys, was off to one side at the edge of the trees, its back open.

"They're allowed to sell whisky here, are they?"

Binky laughed. "It's the top seller in the refreshment tent. The organizers reckon the sales of whisky alone fund the whole event."

"Knowing the Scots I wouldn't leave that van open and unattended, would you?" I asked with a grin. I peered in as we walked past. The interior was empty. "I don't know why he parked so far from the refreshment tent," I said.

"I expect he'd finished unloading and wanted to take a peek at the competitors practicing," Binky replied. "I think that quite a bit of betting goes on at these events. In secret, of course."

We entered the stand of pine trees that separated the practice field from the main area. Amid the trees the hubbub fell away and we walked together in companionable silence.

"I'm awfully glad you're here, Georgiana," Binky said at last. "I couldn't have faced this on my own."

"Glad to help," I said.

"I hope you'll also help me present the prizes," he said. "You know what a duffer I am. I'm sure to say the wrong thing."

"Golly." An image of me dropping trophies swam into my head.

"Fig would do it normally," he said. "But in current circumstances . . ."

"Of course." Rannochs put duty above all things, didn't they?

At that moment there was a shout from the other side of the trees. Closer by there was a *thud*, a sound between a groan and a whimper, then something large falling.

"What the devil?" Binky asked. I came out of the trees to see one of the competitors running in our direction. In his hand he held a chain that dangled beside him.

"I don't know what went wrong," he was babbling. "I can't understand it." He held up the chain as we approached. "The damned thing just few off. I've never seen anything like it."

"What flew off?" Binky asked.

"The weight. A damned great stone at the end of this chain. You know, the weight-throwing event? You hurl it around your head and then let go. I was getting up to full speed when suddenly the stone came flying off and went sailing into the woods. My God, it weighs twenty-six pounds. I hope it didn't hit anybody. It would have killed them outright." He was still shaking his head. "I can't understand how it could have come loose. I've never seen such a thing in my life before, and I've been doing this for twenty years now."

Suddenly we were conscious of a commotion some way off to our left, among the trees, and a terrified man came running up to us. "There's been an accident," he said. "Some poor fellow has been hit with a rock. He's lying there dead."

A sob escaped from the weight-thrower. He staggered forward like a drunken man. We followed him. At the edge of the trees a man was sprawled face down among the bracken. His skull had been dented in and a great stone lay beside him, spattered with blood and hair. I swallowed hard and turned away.

More people were now gathering. "That's Archie Campbell," someone whispered in disbelief. "What was he doing here? Spying on Ross MacDonald?"

"He was saying that Ross MacDonald's new method of hurling was illegal in the bar last night," someone else claimed. "No doubt he wanted to see for himself."

"So he could copy Ross's action and beat his biggest rival," another voice added.

"This man was also a contestant in the weight throwing?" Binky asked.

They looked at him as if he'd just arrived from the moon. "Aye, he was. Archie Campbell—he and Ross MacDonald here are two of the best in Scotland. Always been rivals."

"Until now," a somber voice added, and they turned to look at the weight-thrower. There was an uneasy pause.

"You're not suggesting I did that deliberately," the man said.

"You are a MacDonald, are you not?" one man demanded. "And he was a Campbell, poor man."

"What's that got to do with it?" Binky asked.

Again the group looked shocked at his ignorance. "The Campbells and the MacDonalds? Did the Campbells not come down in the night and slaughter the MacDonalds, men, women, and children?" a thin, little man with bright red hair said.

"Did they? I never heard about it," Binky said. "Was it in the papers? When was this?"

"You know, the massacre of Glencoe, in the seventeen hundreds," I whispered to him.

"Oh, *that* massacre," he said, looking relieved. "It was a frightfully long time ago, wasn't it?"

"Old grudges die hard," one of the men muttered.

Ross MacDonald shook his head. "Not with me. Archie was a good friend. A rival, to be sure, but we got along just fine. And as for me killing him, I might be good at throwing the weight but even I could never have arranged for a weight to come free at the precise moment to hurl itself three hundred yards toward the woods and kill an unseen man. That's just plain daft."

"Someone should go for Constable Herries," one of the men suggested.

"His Grace is here," another man corrected. "He's a justice of the peace, isn't he? That's better than a village bobby."

All eyes turned to Binky. "Oh, I don't think we can possibly have a crime here," Binky stammered. "An awful accident, but as Mr. MacDonald said, it's just not possible to aim a dashed great stone so precisely that it kills someone so far away in a wood."

While they had been talking I had been taking a good look at the body. Not because I was ghoulish but I had happened to stumble upon a few dead bodies in my life and had picked up a thing or two from detectives. And if my brother were to be put in charge of the investigation, I hadn't much hope that we'd arrive at the truth.

The first thing I noticed was that Campbell had been struck on the back of the head and sprawled forward. That in itself was strange. If the stone had hurtled straight at him, wouldn't he have been hit on the forehead or, more likely, tried to get out of the way? I checked around the body. The ground was still soft from recent rains, and not too far away was a large, deep footprint. It might have been there for a while, but then again it might not. And on a bramble bush, not far from the body, I spotted a fragment of light brown fabric. I removed it and examined it. Not a tartan. So not from a kilt then. And most of the men around here were wearing their kilts.

At that moment I heard a strange sound. "Psst!"

I looked in the direction it came from and saw Queenie beckoning me from among the trees. "Over here, miss," she whispered. "I know I shouldn't have sneaked out of the house without permission, but I wanted to get a look at the big blokes for myself. And I saw it happen. Just like he said. He was whirling the bloody thing around his head when suddenly there's a snap and it goes flying off at the woods. But I'd swear it wasn't in this direction. It was more down that way." And she pointed farther off to where the battlements of the castle rose above the trees.

"Thank you, Queenie," I said. "That's most helpful." I went over to Binky. "I think we should summon the police after all. This could be a case of murder."

"But we've already agreed it was impossible . . ."

"Not Mr. MacDonald," I said. "Someone else. Someone who staged this whole thing."

The small crowd that had assembled around us stared at me in disbelief.

"Take a look at where he was struck on the head," I said. "If he'd been watching Mr. MacDonald, as you all suggest, then how could he have been hit on the back of the head?"

"He saw the stone coming at him and had turned to run away," one of the men suggested.

"No time," I said. "By the time he realized it was heading straight for him he would only have had a second at the most."

"Then what are you saying?" Binky asked.

"That someone else set this up to frame Mr. MacDonald or to get rid of Mr. Campbell by making it look as if it was an accident."

There was a muttering among the crowd. I realized, too late, that this was now a crime scene, but a dozen men had tramped all over it. I checked their feet to see if one of them could have made the footprint, but none of them seemed to be wearing boots or have a foot that giant-sized.

"Did Archie Campbell have a falling out with anybody that you know?" Binky asked, trying bravely to act like a justice of the peace.

This produced laughter. "Archie fell out with just about everybody when he'd had a drop too much," someone said. "And that was every Saturday night. And he had an eye for the ladies."

"So plenty of people with a motive for wanting him dead?" I asked.

They looked perplexed at this. "You don't go killing a man just because you've had an argument in a pub or because he's flirted with your wife," one of the men said.

It looked as if we had an impossible situation. A deserted woodland and plenty of people in the vicinity with a possible motive for murder. The only thing I could think of to narrow it down was that it had to be someone who knew when Ross MacDonald was practicing and the mechanics of the weight throwing. But again, that could apply to half the men here.

"Look at this, would you?" Ross MacDonald demanded, holding out the chain to us. "Does that not look to you as if the metal has been cut through, just where the chain joined the band around the weight?"

We were all peering at it when we heard shouts from through the trees, and two men came running toward us.

"Come quickly," they called, beckoning furiously. "There has been a terrible accident."

"Not another one? Where now?" Binky asked.

"Up this way, in the trees at the edge of the meadow."

We followed them, and it was a case of deja vu. Yet another man was sprawled among the bracken, his head smashed and a big stone lying beside him, spattered with blood and hair.

The rest of the men had come with us, including Ross MacDonald. He gave a hysterical laugh.

"Well, surely nobody could claim that I killed two men with one throw," he said. "I might be the best hurler in all of Scotland, but I surely can't pull off a feat like that."

"We should maybe stand back and treat this as a crime scene," I said. The men hastily stepped away, glancing at one another nervously. I stood looking down at this new body. Another big man but he was not wearing the Highland dress. Instead he was wearing some kind of tradesman's brown coat. His tradesman's cap had fallen from his head, and he was slumped to one side. I noticed his hand was also bloody as if he had put it up to ward off a blow.

Before I could take in any more someone exclaimed, "This poor man was surely killed with the weight from Ross MacDonald. Look at the stone—it has the groove on it where the metal band usually goes around."

Then someone yelled, "Look who it is. It's Fergus Finlay!"

"Fergus Finlay? What's he doing here?" a deep voice demanded.

"Who is Fergus Finlay?" I asked. I should have said who *was* Fergus Finlay because the poor man was very dead.

"He was the third athlete who vied for the overall champion at Highland Games," someone muttered to me. "Ross and Archie and Fergus. They were always the best of the bunch."

"I heard he wasn't up to competing this year," one of the men said. "Wasn't he struck by a car and in the hospital?"

"Aye, he was," another agreed. "And was that car not driven by Ross MacDonald himself?"

Eyes turned again to focus on Ross. He was glaring now. "I did knock him down with my car. That's correct. But the fool stepped out in front of me blind drunk. He lurched out of the pub. I was only doing ten miles an hour, but he literally fell under my wheels. There were plenty of witnesses, and they all agreed with me. I was *nae* charged with anything. And I've *nae* a grudge against Fergus Finlay."

I was watching the blood still flowing down Fergus's skull and dripping onto the ground. And I realized that Archie Campbell had been dead quite a while longer. The blood on his head had already congealed. I also noticed something else . . . There was a jagged tear in the deliveryman's coat that Fergus was wearing. The light brown coat. And I knew that the scrap of fabric I had seen on that bramble bush would match. And he was wearing massive boots . . .

"Tell me," I said, addressing all of them now, "did Fergus Finlay have a grudge against Archie Campbell?"

There was a pause and then someone said, "Wasn't there that scandal with Fergus's wife and Archie Campbell a while back? Didn't he catch Archie sneaking out of his house in the early morning when he came back early from that fishing trip?"

"It sounds as if he had a grudge against both MacDonald and Campbell," Binky said, unusually quick on the uptake for once.

My brain was racing now. I was putting together the brown deliveryman's coat with the tear in it, the big boots, and the scrap of fabric caught on the bramble, and the pieces of the puzzle were beginning to fall into place. "I think we should examine that whisky van parked nearby," I said.

"The whisky van? But what's that got to do with it?" one of the men asked, but the others were already heading toward it. They were all ready to examine whisky, even this early in the morning.

"They are only allowing competitors and deliveries onto the grounds at the moment," I said. "Since he wasn't scheduled to compete, I think Mr. Finlay must have gained access driving that van."

They all followed me like obedient dogs through the trees. The back of the van was still open. Inside there was no sign of any whisky bottles but only a small bag of tools. I heard a definite sigh of disappointment.

"Could this be used to cut through a chain or the metal band?" I asked, pointing to a pair of what looked like big pliers.

"Aye, it could that," several voices replied. "Those would cut through metal. No problem."

"So what are you suggesting, lassie?" one of the men demanded, frowning at me. "If someone killed Archie Campbell and Fergus Finlay and it wasn't Ross MacDonald, are we looking for yet another person? An unidentified murderer?"

I shook my head, willing for once to ignore the fact that he'd called the sister of a duke *lassie*. "Fergus Finlay was not murdered," I said. "His death was an accident."

They were all staring at me now. "This is how I think it happened," I said. "I believe that Mr. Finlay plotted this whole thing to get rid of his biggest rivals—both of whom he had a grudge against. He wanted it to look as if Mr. MacDonald killed Mr. Campbell either deliberately or accidentally. Either way he'd be eliminating his two biggest rivals from future Highland Games. He knew that Archie Campbell would be trying to spy on Ross MacDonald's practice session to see how his new throwing method worked. So he sneaked up behind him and killed him with a stone similar to the weight on MacDonald's chain. He had managed to cut through the chain earlier so that during the windup for the throw, the weight would come loose and go flying into the trees.

"Everyone would then think that Archie Campbell had been killed by Ross MacDonald's weight. Everything went as planned. The weight flew off perfectly when the chain broke. There was only one thing he hadn't counted on—MacDonald's new method really did make the weight fly farther! He was watching from the trees, and suddenly he sees the weight come hurtling in his direction. He tries to get out of the way, to defend himself, but he's too late. He is struck by the flying stone. Poetic justice, wouldn't you say?"

They were all looking at me as if I was a magician or a witch. "I say, Georgie," Binky said. "How on earth did you figure that out? Dashed clever of you."

"Well, we saw the whisky van parked far away from the refreshment tent with the back open. I found the footprint made by a big boot near Campbell's body and a scrap of fabric caught on a bramble near the body that matches the tear in the coat Mr. Finlay is wearing. And he certainly had the inside knowledge of the sport and a strong enough motive."

"Aye, she's a bright lass all right," someone nattered. "She'll make some laddie a grand wife."

"Hush now, she'll no be marrying a laddie. She'll be marrying a prince or a lord," a voice replied in shocked tones.

"As long as they let her choose for herself."

I said nothing but allowed myself a secret smile. I did have someone in mind.

*** 

Queenie had been waiting and watching some distance away. She joined me as I walked back to the house.

"I've decided I don't like this sort of sport after all," she said. "Too bloody dangerous, if you ask me. Hurling ruddy great rocks around? I always said the Scots were mad."

"It's all right when they are hurled in the correct direction," I said.

"And what are these great tree trunks doing all over the place?" she demanded. "Look at this one, lying across the path. Anyone could trip over that in the dark."

She bent down, lifted up one end, and tossed it clear. I stared at her in amazement. "Queenie, you just tossed the caber."

"Is that good or bad?" she asked. "Because I don't want to find myself in trouble again."

"Actually if you were a male, you could enter tomorrow's competition," I said, laughing.

"After seeing what can happen to people who compete in the Highland Games? Not bloody likely." And she stalked ahead of me back to the safety of Castle Rannoch.

# A GATHERING OF GREAT DETECTIVES

## by Shawn Reilly Simmons

"He sure did take a header, didn't he?" Detective Murphy crouched next to the man lying at the bottom of the stairs. The man's arms and legs were twisted at odd angles beneath him, and his head was jerked violently to the side, his fleshy right cheek lying heavily on the floor. Murphy's eye traced the steep wooden staircase and the worn brocade runner striping its middle.

"Yep, it had to hurt on the way down," Detective Sullivan agreed. She stood behind him and gazed at the man on the floor.

"I don't know, Sully," he said. "If he was dead before he came down, he wouldn't have felt a thing. I'm thinking this didn't happen on the stairs." He pointed to a perfectly round goose egg on the man's forehead that rose red and shiny between his eyes. "Or these," he said, indicating the angry red fingerprints encircling the man's throat.

"Detective Murphy." A uniformed officer approached from the back of the Nob Hill Inn through the main hall, leading a handsome older couple into the foyer. "This is Richard and Doreen Adams. They own the place." The stained glass panes surrounding the front door tinted his face in shades of blue and green.

Detective Murphy eased up from his crouching position, his knees popping quietly under his brown dress pants. He rested his hands on his belt and nodded at the couple. "Mr. and Mrs. Adams, what happened here?"

They gazed down at the man lying in the hall, his face frozen in a surprised grimace.

Mrs. Adams stepped forward, her hands twisting nervously at her waist. "I'm sorry, we're not really sure. We were all outside touring the Poison Garden when we heard shouting coming from upstairs. Rick came in and found him here, just like this, right dear?"

Her husband cleared his throat before saying, "Yes, Dora's right. I checked for a pulse and when I didn't find one, and when I saw the state of him, I called the police."

The uniformed officer stepped forward and said, "It looked suspicious, sir, so I radioed in for a detective."

Detective Murphy nodded and walked around the man on the floor to observe him from a different angle.

"Did you move the body at all, sir?" Detective Sullivan asked. She pulled a small notebook and a pen from her blazer pocket.

Mr. Adams drew in a sharp breath. "No, of course I didn't. I know better than that."

"And you didn't see anyone else come down the stairs after you found him here like this?" Detective Sullivan asked.

"No, no one. We were out back with our guests, and Bill told us he'd forgotten his notepad upstairs so we assumed he went to his room to get it. Then I heard a commotion inside, and found him like this."

"Bill?" Detective Sullivan asked.

"Oh yes, that's Bill Hartman from Cleveland," Mr. Adams said, crossing his arms over his chest and continuing to stare at the man on the floor.

"Is there any other way off of the second floor? A back stairway?"

"No," Mrs. Adams said. "There's just the main staircase."

"Has anyone else been through the foyer, gone in or out?" Detective Murphy asked the uniformed officer.

"No one, sir. I waited with him until you got here."

"What's going on here today?" Detective Murphy asked, making eye contact with his partner briefly before turning his gaze back to the couple. "Are you having some kind of event or something?" He glanced at their vintage clothes and Mrs. Adams's hair, which was curled and sprayed into place. They looked like they'd stepped out of one of those old black-and-white movies his mother was always watching. Mr. Adams wore a tux with a white bow tie and Mrs. Adams was in a shimmery black evening gown with a string of pearls around her neck. They were pretty decked out, especially for noon on a Saturday.

Mrs. Adams placed a hand lightly on her chest and said, "It's our annual convention, A Gathering of Great Detectives." She waved at a wooden table along the far wall of the foyer near the reception desk. A few leather badge holders with names written on yellowing paper tucked inside were lined up on the table. "We gather every year, about sixty of us, and solve a mystery."

"Murder," Mr. Adams boomed from behind her, causing his wife to jump slightly.

"Yes, murder, that's right, dear," she said. "We're different from the average murder mystery weekend though. Attendees must appear as their favorite detective and stay in character all weekend, or until the mystery is solved."

"I see," Detective Sullivan said. "So, where is everyone?" She walked over to the table and glanced at the scattering of unclaimed name badges.

"They're outside with the poison expert, taking a tour of the garden," Mr. Adams said. He waved down the hallway behind them toward the back of the house.

"The poisoned garden, right?" Detective Murphy asked. "What is that exactly?"

"It's the *Poison* Garden, Detective," Mrs. Adams corrected. "It's a collection of poisonous plants. You know, nightshade, foxglove, larkspur, oleander . . ." She ticked off on her fingers as she spoke.

"Okay, I get it," Detective Murphy said, "and you have this garden because . . ."

"We visited one on our last trip to the U.K.," Mr. Adams said, "and decided it would be an interesting attraction for our guests."

Detective Murphy sighed and looked back down at the man on the floor. "So, you said his name was Bill? I'm assuming he's one of your convention attendees?"

"Yes, Bill Hartman. He's a regular GGD attendee. Actually he's been coming since we began the convention, eleven years ago now."

The late Bill Hartman was dressed in a gray wool three-piece suit, the coat tails long enough to brush the backs of his knees. A black stovepipe hat had rolled toward the wall near him.

Detective Sullivan walked back over to the body and felt his jacket pockets with a latex-gloved hand. She stood and shook her head. "No wallet. He's only got one of those name badge things on him." She pointed to his lapel, and the badge pinned over his chest.

"Oh, that's Bill, all right," Mrs. Adams said. "We've known him for years."

Voices filled the hall behind them and Detective Murphy said to the uniformed officer, "Keep them out of here, will ya?"

The officer nodded sharply and headed toward the crowd, directing the attendees through the doorway on the left in the main hall.

"They're supposed to go in the library now anyway," Mrs. Adams said, her eyes flicking to a large chalkboard behind the main reception desk. It had the convention itinerary listed, each day a different color. "After the garden tour, they have their tea, and that's when the murder will be presented."

Detective Murphy watched the attendees file into the library. He picked out a few dressed like Sherlock Holmes, a group of older ladies in housecoats chatting with each other, a few men in trench coats, and a couple of portly gentlemen in three-piece suits, poking the red carpet with walking sticks.

"Who are you supposed to be?" Detective Murphy asked.

"We're Nick and Nora Charles. We always are this weekend," Mrs. Adams said.

Detective Murphy took another look at their outfits, then went back to watching the last of the attendees file into the room.

"Mr. Adams, did Mr. Hartman have problems with anyone? Can you think of any reason someone would want to kill him?" Detective Sullivan jotted down a few notes.

Mr. and Mrs. Adams shared a glance, and after a moment he said, "Bill started a blog about the GGD. It's called *Yet Another Stupid Theory*. He's been posting about the different members of the convention and their ideas that haven't, well, that haven't been the best."

Mrs. Adams squeezed her gloved hands together tightly and narrowed her eyes. "Also, Bill has won the weekend for the past four years in a row. He's solved the crime, received the cash prize, and the Falcon, too."

"The what?" Detective Murphy asked.

"The Falcon. The Maltese Falcon," Mr. Adams said a bit impatiently. "The Falcon is awarded to the attendee who gets the fewest demerits during the convention."

"Demerits?" Detective Murphy asked.

"Yes, they're given when the attendees break character, or do or say anything the detective he or she is portraying wouldn't say or do."

"And how do you determine that?"

"We have bells all around the inn. When you see or hear someone acting out of character, you ring the bell and assign them a demerit. It has to be witnessed by two or more other attendees to count against you, or we'd have nonstop bell ringing for everyone. All of our attendees are after that Falcon."

"Is it worth anything?" Detective Murphy asked.

"It's worth everything to those of us in the GGD," Mrs. Adams said. "It's prestige, bragging rights. It's very valuable."

"And how much is the cash prize you mentioned?" Detective Murphy asked.

"Five thousand dollars," Mr. Adams said quickly. He nodded at Bill Hartman, lying twisted on the floor. "Bill wins every year. If he'd taken the weekend again, he'd be up to twenty-five thousand dollars by Sunday."

"They're all settled in there," the uniformed officer said when he returned to the foyer. "They're having tea and sandwiches."

"You stay with the body," Detective Murphy said to him. "Mrs. Adams, please keep your guests in the library." She nodded and headed down the hall, followed by Detective Sullivan. "Mr.

Adams, would you please show me Mr. Hartman's room?"

The two men headed upstairs after Mr. Adams plucked an antique key from a drawer in the front desk. They eased up the stairs slowly, stepping purposefully so as to not disturb any evidence that might have been left during Mr. Hartman's fall. When they reached the landing at the top, Mr. Adams said, "He's staying in the Poe Suite at the end of the hall."

The door to the Poe Suite was slightly ajar, and Mr. Adams pushed it open gently, the key still held in his fist. "Hello?" he called into the room.

"Step aside, please," Detective Murphy said. Mr. Adams let him pass and then followed him into the room.

"Wow, nice digs," Detective Murphy said. The suite was large with a king-size four-poster bed made from heavy dark wood, an olive-green canopy draped over the top of it and twisted down the posts. A rolltop desk sat in one corner with an ink pot and fountain pen on top. A large portrait of Edgar Allan Poe hung on the wall next to the door to the adjoining bathroom.

"It does appear that something happened in here," Detective Murphy said, noticing that the bedside table was overturned and the papers on the desk looked rifled through.

Mr. Adams crossed his arms and put a finger to his lips, considering the scene. "What's that?" he asked, pointing to something shiny poking out from under one corner of the desk.

Detective Murphy slipped on a latex glove from his coat pocket and walked over to pick it up. "That's an iPhone," he said, holding it up for Mr. Adams to see.

"Oh dear," Mr. Adams said. "How did it get under there?"

Detective Murphy shrugged. "Must have been dropped during the struggle. Maybe whoever killed Mr. Hartman left it behind. It doesn't look familiar to you?"

"Oh no," Mr. Adams said, shaking his head quickly. "There are to be no cell phones, laptops, or any other electronic devices in use during the weekend. We strongly encourage our guests to leave those items at home. It makes the weekend that much more authentic, and fairer to all the players, too, if the attendees aren't sneaking upstairs to look up theories of our crimes on Google."

"I see," Detective Murphy said. "Looks like someone might have been cheating, huh?" He pushed the home button on the phone with a latex-covered finger and the screen lit up—Bill Hartman in a top hat grinned past the cracked glass. Detective Murphy swiped the glass and saw that the phone was passcode protected. Pulling a plastic evidence bag from his coat pocket, he slipped the phone inside, sealed it up, and put it back in his pocket.

The window on the far wall offered a view of the garden and the roof of the inn's garage down below. Detective Murphy pushed the window open and leaned out, judging how far one would have to climb, or possibly fall, to get there.

He turned back and noticed a suitcase sitting on the floor at the foot of the bed. Flipping open the lid, Detective Murphy glanced inside. "More costumes like the one he has on," he murmured. He shifted toward Mr. Adams and said, "Who's he supposed to be anyway, Sherlock Holmes?"

Mr. Adams laughed quickly and then said, "No, Bill always comes as Inspector Bucket."

Detective Murphy stared at him blankly.

"You know, Inspector Bucket from *Bleak House*? Charles Dickens?" Mr. Adams said in a slightly condescending tone.

"Oh, Dickens, yeah, I think I read that in high school. Something of his anyway. I don't remember Inspector Bucket, though."

"Well," Mr. Adams said, taking on a more instructional tone of voice, "*Bleak House* was published in 1853, and many people consider Inspector Bucket the first notable detective in English Literature. Of course, Bill Hartman couldn't be just any run of the mill Sherlock Holmes. He had to be an originator, 'the beginning of the genre,' he always said."

"Does anyone else come dressed up as this Bucket guy?" Detective Murphy asked distractedly as he leafed through a few papers on the desk.

"No," Mr. Adams said. "And I wouldn't say we're *dressing up* as our favorite detectives. We're emulating them, studying them, and using the lessons from their cases to solve new crimes."

"Fake new crimes, though, right?" Detective Murphy asked, stopping on his way to the bathroom and eyeing Mr. Adams.

"Yes, of course," Mr. Adams stammered.

"You didn't decide to spice up your mystery weekend by providing your guests with an actual homicide, did you?"

Mr. Adams's cheeks burned bright red. "I should say not, and I'm offended you would think that of me, if you want to know the truth."

"The truth is what I'm after, Mr. Adams," Detective Murphy said. He continued into the bathroom and fingered through the shaving kit on the counter. He then turned and swept aside the white shower curtain, glancing into the footed tub, the shower rings chiming against the circular rung suspended above it. He took a quick look at the bags under his dark brown eyes in the mirror and made his way back out into the suite.

"So where's this Falcon?" he asked.

"It must be up here somewhere. Bill brings it with him wherever he goes, especially during the convention," Mr. Adams said, glancing quickly around the room.

"I don't see it. Are you sure no one else was inside the inn when you came in and found Mr. Hartman at the bottom of the stairs?"

"No, I told you that earlier, it was just me. The staff was in the kitchen but that's at the other end of the house." Mr. Adams straightened his jacket and ran a hand over his slicked-back sandy hair. "Why do you ask?"

"Because someone was up here with him. It looks to me like he got into a fight in this room and someone clobbered him on the forehead. Then they choked him, and he either fell or was thrown down the stairs. Which one of you hated Bill Hartman enough to do all of that?"

***

"CSU will be here in five, sir," the uniformed officer said as they passed back through the foyer, pulling his phone away from his ear. Detective Murphy cut his eyes at him and nodded curtly. He and Mr. Adams stepped carefully through the foyer and joined the crowd in the library.

"Hey, how'd it go upstairs?" Detective Sullivan asked.

Detective Murphy leaned close to her and spoke quietly. "I think that's where the altercation happened. Someone was looking for something in his room, too."

"You think it's that trophy they were talking about him always winning? What was it?" Detective Sullivan asked.

"The Maltese Falcon trophy," Detective Murphy said, rolling his eyes.

"Yeah, that's it. Hey you know what's funny?" she asked quietly.

"What's that?" he asked, scanning the room for any suspiciously acting attendees.

"They think we're part of the weekend, keep referring to me as a red herring. What's that?"

Detective Murphy shrugged. "How should I know, Sully?"

"Maybe we better find out, if we want to solve this guy's murder," Detective Sullivan said grimly.

"Excuse me," a woman with gray hair and a purple housecoat said from one of the far tables. "Is there something we can help you with, Detectives?"

Detective Murphy glanced at his partner and said, "What's your name, ma'am?"

"I'm Miss Marple," the woman said, slightly affronted. "I'm a consulting detective."

"Amateur," a man dressed as Sherlock Holmes coughed into his hand. The woman ignored the comment, keeping her eyes on Detective Murphy.

"Okay, Miss Marple," Detective Murphy said, "there's been a suspicious death of one of your group, and we're here to ask you a few questions."

A wave of expectant murmurs rippled through the room, and all eyes turned to him.

"Have you determined the cause of death?" the woman asked.

"The coroner is on his way, but it appears Bill Hartman was involved in some kind of struggle and ended up dead at the bottom of the stairs."

A loud pinging sound rang through the room as several attendees began tapping anxiously on the round desk bells on the tables in front of them.

"They ring the bells when you break character," Mr. Adams murmured from behind him. "You just got a demerit for using Bill's real name."

Detective Murphy sighed. "Look, we're not part of your convention. We're real detectives, and we're investigating the death of Bill Hartman."

The bells began ringing before he could finish talking.

Detective Sullivan hid a smile behind her hand and shrugged at her partner.

"Stop with the bells, okay?" Detective Murphy said. "Now, who here knew Bill?"

More bells rang in response to his question.

"Wow, if you were playing the game with them you might as well go home," Detective Sullivan said quietly.

A man in a trench coat stood up from one of the tables. "I know Bucket. Guy's a real jerk."

"And you are?" Detective Murphy asked, relieved at last someone was talking.

"Sam Spade," the man replied.

"Wait, Sam Spade?"

"That's right. Like I said, Bucket was a real piece of work," the man said, tipping his fedora back farther on his head and squinting at the detectives.

"What do you mean, sir?" Detective Sullivan asked.

"You know the type," the man said, "always has to be the smartest guy in the room."

"Sounds like you didn't like Mr. Hartman," Detective Murphy

said. "Did he blog about your stupid theories on his website?" Bells pinged back at him from around the room. "It's enough already with the bells," he said, failing to hide his exasperation.

"Yeah, that's right. It didn't make him a popular guy. So what?"

"So maybe you hated him enough to knock him over the head and grab the Maltese trophy," Detective Murphy said, taking a step closer to the man.

"What do you mean, the Maltese Falcon is missing?" another man in a Sam Spade outfit stood up and asked loudly. The room erupted with excited conversation.

"It's not in his room, and it's not with the body," Detective Murphy said. "Maybe one of you wanted it so badly you decided to kill him for it."

Several of the attendees were jotting notes down in little spiral notebooks, flipping the pages back and forth to review them.

"Maybe one of you couldn't stand losing to him again this weekend, and decided to take matters into your own hands," Detective Sullivan said, moving to stand next to her partner.

"Pfft," the second Sam Spade said. "Mulder and Scully here have a theory." Bells pinged in response. He gave an irritated wave and huffily sat back down in his chair.

"What's his problem?" Detective Murphy asked Mrs. Adams.

"Mulder and Scully?" she whispered. "Sam Spade doesn't know who they are. He just got a demerit."

Just then the door to the library swung open and a young woman dressed in a maid's uniform rushed in. "Help! There's been a murder!" she yelled.

Detective Murphy turned toward her and put his hand on his gun. "Another one?"

Mrs. Adams patted his forearm and whispered, "This one is our crime, the staged one."

Detective Murphy's shoulders relaxed slightly, but the irritated expression remained on his face. A few of the attendees got to their feet.

"Now wait a minute," Detective Murphy said. "Nobody is going anywhere."

"You will step aside at once and let us investigate this matter." A short man with dark black hair and waxed mustache stepped to the front of the room. He limped between the tables holding an ornate walking stick in his clenched fist.

"Sir, we're going to have to ask you to stay in your seat," Detective Murphy said, moving to block the man from the doorway. A few of the attendees sat back down, unsure how to respond.

"Step away from the door. I, Hercule Poirot, am not amused." The short man squared his shoulders and walked determinedly toward the maid who was waiting in the doorway with a worried look on her face.

"Will you tell them that the game is over? That we're solving a real crime here?" Detective Murphy asked Mr. Adams. Bells rang around the room.

Mr. Adams shrugged his shoulders. "Those are the rules, Detective."

Poirot paused to question the maid in the doorway, hitching his pant leg up. "Tell me what has happened," he demanded.

"It's the chef! He's been poisoned!" the maid yelled loud enough for all of the guests to hear.

"Take me to him at once!" the man dressed as Poirot said. Several other attendees got to their feet and began to follow him.

"Hold on a minute," Detective Murphy said, yelling over the excited murmurs of the crowd. "Everyone stop right now."

They began to file past him, walking out into the hall to observe the crime scene.

"Hang on, Murphy," Detective Sullivan said to him, putting a hand on his arm to quiet him. "Maybe they can help us."

"You think this bunch can help us solve a murder? I hope you're not going shopping for a Miss Marple outfit and signing up next year," Murphy huffed at her. He stormed through the door, following the herd of detectives.

The group entered the kitchen and stood over a man in a white chef coat, lying on his back on the floor between the stove and the ovens. One of the Sherlock Holmes attendees went over to the large pot and smelled the simmering tomato soup.

"Nightshade," he said, nodding. "It's in the tomato family but has a bitter odor. Now why would the killer use an easily detectable poison like that? It must be to throw us off the real motive."

"I can see his chest going up and down," Detective Murphy said. "He's still breathing." Angry bells pinged behind him. "Fine, you guys go ahead and solve this fake crime. I'm going to find out which one of you killed Bill Hartman, and I'm going to nail you for it."

He stormed out of the kitchen, bells ringing behind him.

The uniformed officer stood in the foyer, rocking back and forth on his boots, a bored look on his face.

"No CSU yet?" Detective Murphy said, blowing out a sigh.

"No, sir."

Detective Sullivan came through the hallway and joined them.

"The current theory is the chef killed himself while trying to disguise the poison in the soup. He tasted it too many times."

"So he poisons the soup and then he wants to be sure it tastes okay? And what, he was going to kill all of them at once? What kind of theory is that?" Detective Murphy asked.

"I think they're thinking he had one or two targets in mind and poisoning everyone at the same time would disguise his motive. But then he accidentally killed himself."

"Yeah, well, if we went to the boss with something as half-baked as that he'd ask us to turn in our badges," Detective Murphy said.

Detective Sullivan eyed the man on the floor. "What are you thinking with this one?"

"I think it was greed, pure and simple, and whoever has that Falcon trophy is our killer. Now we just have to find it."

"What about his blog?" Detective Sullivan asked. "Maybe it was a crime of passion on the part of someone he publicly shamed, called stupid."

Detective Murphy considered it. "Yeah, I can see that. But I still think finding the missing statue is the key."

"Did you find anything interesting in his room?" Detective Sullivan asked.

"As a matter of fact, I found this." He reached into his pocket and retrieved the plastic bag containing the iPhone. "It's got a password on it, though."

"Here, let me see," she asked, taking the phone from him. She began typing numbers on the screen through the plastic bag.

"Don't try too many times or you'll get locked out," Detective Murphy warned. "Wait, try one, eight, five, three."

Detective Sullivan typed the numbers on the glass screen. "That worked. How did you know?"

"That's the year *Bleak House* was published. He's Inspector Bucket."

"Hey, Murphy," she said, holding the phone up for him to see, "look at this. The posting date on this blog entry is this morning."

Detective Murphy took the phone from her and held it at arm's length. "'Witless Wonder Wows Again With Worthless Speculation At The GGD.' Some headline."

"Who is he calling out for being stupid this time?"

"It's some guy named Parrot," he said, squinting at the screen and scrolling down through the article.

"Parrot? Let me see," Detective Sullivan said. He turned the screen toward her and she said, "*Poirot*. It's French, I think. He only uses the detective name?"

"Yeah, no real names. He's assigned his targets code names, I think," Detective Murphy said, sighing again. "Do me a favor and Google this Poirot guy so we know what we're dealing with. Maybe we can beat them at their own game."

***

Everyone had gathered back in the library, after much protest from the guests and urging from Mr. and Mrs. Adams. Detectives Murphy and Sullivan stood in the front of the room, eyeing the group of attendees.

"We'd like to question the Poirot who . . ." Detective Murphy said, and paused. He turned to Detective Sullivan and whispered, "Which one was it?"

"The one with the limp," she murmured.

"All the Poirots were limping, weren't they?" Detective Murphy asked under his breath.

"No, I only noticed two of them," Detective Sullivan said, scanning the room. "One of them was the guy in the brownish suit over there."

"Okay, you," Detective Murphy said impatiently, waving the man forward. "Come here, please."

The Poirot attendee made his way to the front of the room, limping quickly past several tables.

"How did you get that limp?" Detective Murphy asked.

"During the war," the man answered in a forced accent.

Bells pinged around the room.

"Why the bells this time?" Detective Murphy asked.

Another man dressed as the detective stood up and offered, "Poirot was not in the war, and his limp is only mentioned early on, never in the later books. Demerit." Several people nodded in agreement around him.

"Fine. Whatever," Detective Murphy said. "Can I take a look at your walking stick, please?"

The man obliged, handing over his cane. Detective Murphy squinted at the silver ball at the top of the stick, looking for signs that it had been used to clock Bill Hartman on the forehead. A chair toppled over on the right side of the room with a loud bang and another Poirot limped quickly toward the door, grasping his walking stick tightly in his fist.

"Hold on a minute," Detective Sullivan said, moving to block his way. "No one is leaving. Please go back to your seat."

"No, I won't," the man spat. "You can't keep me here unless I'm under arrest."

Detective Murphy pulled the iPhone from his pocket, entered the passcode and held it up for the man to see, eyeing him up and down. The man fidgeted nervously and threw longing looks toward the exit. "I have a feeling you'll be under arrest shortly. You're the Poirot Bill Hartman called a dimwit, aren't you?"

Bells pinged behind him, but he ignored them, focusing on the man's response.

Poirot's forehead was slick with sweat. "Sure, fine, he's blogged about me lots of times. And I'm not sorry he's dead, but I'm far from the only one. I'm not feeling well, so I'll be going now if you don't mind."

"We do mind," Detective Murphy said, squaring his shoulders. "You fell from the trellis after you attacked him, trying to rejoin the other guests in the garden without being noticed. That's how you tore the cuff of your pants. Poirot would never walk around in torn trousers, it's totally out of character," Detective Murphy scoffed knowingly.

"You have no idea what I would do," Poirot said arrogantly.

"That's where you're wrong. We looked it up. You decided to confront Bill Hartman upstairs, tell him what you really thought of him, right?" Detective Murphy urged.

Poirot wiped sweat from his thin black mustache. "I didn't believe for a minute he forgot his notebook. I knew I'd catch him cheating up there. And I did. He was up there on his phone, taking notes."

"So you attacked him because he was cheating?" Detective Murphy asked.

"No," Poirot said, straightening his jacket. "I told him he was disqualified, that I was going to tell everyone he cheated. I told him he should pay back all of his winnings and surrender the Falcon. He was a fraud, finally exposed. He went berserk, started pushing me, threatening me. I hit him in self-defense."

Detective Murphy nodded and said, "I think you went up there intending to hurt the man. This wasn't about you exposing him for cheating. You were furious that he called you an idiot on his blog this morning, and you were looking for a little payback."

Poirot's face turned red, then purple. "I'm not an idiot!" he yelled. "Everyone knows that." The room was deadly silent around them. "Hartman was the stupid one, as I proved."

Detective Murphy eyed his walking stick. "That's what you hit him with?"

Poirot scoffed. "No, I hit him with the thing he loved the most, the damn Falcon. It was right there on the desk, and I whacked him. That shut him up."

Detective Sullivan pulled her handcuffs out. Poirot continued talking as she linked his hands behind his back. "And then he started yelling, saying he was going to sue me for hitting him. So I choked him. I choked the life out of that miserable jerk."

A few muffled gasps escaped from the crowd.

"Come on, let's go," Detective Sullivan said, ushering him toward the door.

The detectives walked with him onto the front porch of the inn just as the coroner's van was pulling into the driveway.

"One more thing. What did you do with the Falcon?" Detective Sullivan asked.

"I slipped it into the soup on the way back in from the garden. I figured out what the crime was going to be the minute they brought out that big pan, by the way. Poisoned soup, so obvious. I'm a good detective."

Detective Murphy shook his head as he led him down the steps. "A good detective, maybe, but you're a terrible criminal."

# AFTERWORD

# "HELLO, MY NAME IS PLOT"

## by Max M. Houck, Ph.D., FRSC

Vice President, Forensic & Intelligence Services, LLC
St. Petersburg, FL

---

**plot** /plät/ *noun*
    1. A plan made in secret by a person or a group of people to do something illegal or harmful.
    2. The main events of a play, novel, movie, or similar work, devised and presented by the writer as an interrelated sequence.

---

### Time "Runs" Forward

Take an egg from the refrigerator. Hold it over the floor. Now drop it. See those pieces of shell and the viscous splatter? All you need to know about detection and solving crimes is right there in one messy example.

Let me explain.

Physics, time, evidence, and history—all the information required to solve *The Case of the Broken Egg* is evident and irrefutable to anyone who did not witness the event. The crime is easy to solve because of the way the universe runs behind the scenes, so consistently and reliably that the rules are rarely considered. Yet every detective, every writer, every reader, every person uses these rules to answer questions all the time; some of those questions involve crimes and murder, most do not.

For writers, these factors are embodied in plot. Plot is the sequencing of motivation, actions, and resolution in a story. In crime fiction, it involves the transgression of personal and social norms (motivation and actions) and the return to some form of normal life (resolution) by the solving of the crime. Someone is wronged/jilted/jealous and decides to take revenge in the form of humiliation/theft/assault/murder, thinking this will put the axis of life back on a normal (if selfish) tilt. The actions of the "criminal"[1] are central to plot and the factors running the universe make them

---

[1] I put criminal in quotes this one time to suggest that not all crimes are such; going back in time (violating physical laws) to kill Hitler (violating human laws) should not result in any punishment a reasonable person could think of. All criminals feel justified in their actions, however; otherwise, why do it?

so because of one irreducible feature: the actions are committed forward in time. Once committed, they are history and exist only in the past. The actions of the criminal are revealed out of order, however, to those in the present by the process of detection. Finally, the story of their revelation and reconstruction is told in forward time from a certain perspective using much, if not most, of the available information.[2]

Look at the egg. *Look* at it. It hit the floor (forward in time). How is that known? The pieces and the mess are there on the floor. In the commission of the crime, the breaking of the egg came *last* in that particular chain of events, but for the detectives it was seen *first* in their investigation. The shells, yolk, and albumin splashed everywhere are *evidence* of the crime, the historical indicators of past activities. Shell fragments and eggy goop on the floor are *de facto* proof that an egg fell and hit the floor.

Those indicators are an example of Locard's Exchange Principle, which states that when two objects come into contact, information is exchanged. Formulated by the French forensic pioneer Edmund Locard in the early 1900s, the Exchange Principle is a central philosophical concept in forensic science. All evidence consists of stuff left behind or picked up while committing a crime. Whether DNA, fingerprints, wounds, fibers, or instant message files, they are all the "leftovers" of past criminal actions discovered in the present.[3] The remnants may be very small or obscure but it is the viewer's responsibility to see the traces for what they are: flags, clues, evidence.

As Edward Heinrich, another pioneer of forensic science, said, "Rarely are other than ordinary phenomena involved in the commission of a crime. One is confronted with scrambled effects, all parts of which separately are attributed to causes." Detectives and forensic scientists must understand "ordinary phenomena" in order to unravel the clues left behind at crimes.

Saying that the egg "fell" may seem a bit passive, both temperamentally and grammatically, but that kind of distance is necessary until an agent—in police parlance, a suspect—is suggested. This is where many real investigations go wrong, by not considering all of the reasonable hypotheses open to the circumstances under inquiry. Biases creep in, potential avenues of

---

[2] "Narrative is a sequencing of something for somebody." R. Scholes, *Language, Narrative, and Anti-Narrative.*

[3] Elsewhere, I call this *proxy data*, a term borrowed for forensic science from paleoclimatologists when they talk about ancient weather. The rainfall in the Mesozoic Era cannot be seen today but it can be estimated by its proxies, the plants, animals, and geological materials left behind and fossilized. A detective or a forensic scientist would call the proxy data of a crime "evidence."

questioning get closed off, and mistakes are made.

Confirmation bias is a good example. Looking for, collecting, and using only those bits of information that support or confirm a particular pet theory is confirmation bias. "The husband was out and has no alibi for the time period when we think the wife was killed," says the detective. "That's funny. Let's focus on him." The husband was out with an old female friend ("Must be an affair"), had a couple of beers ("He didn't get the promotion; his wife must have been nagging him"), and won't hand over his cellphone without a warrant ("He's hiding something"). Fixated on the 'husband theory', the detectives ignore other possible reasons for the evidence they find. This is one of the big reasons that wrongful convictions happen. Interestingly, a host of analytical thinking methods to avoid this kind of mental error is openly available and is used by professional intelligence analysts.[4] Why this kind of training is not required at police academies and in forensic science programs is a different kind of mystery that should be solved, and soon.

## Detection Works Backwards

How do these indicators, these clues mean something? Because time only works in one direction. Time does not flow, *per se*, but rather is a series of events that form an irreversible sequence that is cumulative in only one direction. Broken eggs do not spontaneously reassemble.[5] Thus, the world is asymmetrical *in time* and that provides detectives, historians, and the like with the ability to sort out what actions have taken place—to reconstruct the egg, so to speak—if given enough evidence (shells, mess, etc.).

If a video was taken of the egg dropping and breaking, running the video backwards would look ridiculous and be obvious for what it is. Again, broken eggs do not suddenly become whole. If the video were cut up into individual images and scrambled (much

---

[4] A great start is Heuer's book, *Psychology of Intelligence Analysis*, available for free at the CIA website: https://www.cia.gov/library/center-for-the-study-of-intelligence/csi-publications/books-and-monographs/psychology-of-intelligence-analysis/PsychofIntelNew.pdf .

[5] For those so inclined, this is an example of the Second Law of Thermodynamics. The Second Law states that the disorder (or entropy, in technical terms) of a system will increase over time. Things break, stuff rots, time always wins. An egg that is intact has a lower entropy than a broken one; the entropy will inevitably increase whether the egg is dropped or is allowed to spoil and decay. Nature is filled with—run by—irreversible physical processes and the Second Law is central to a universal infrastructure with an obvious asymmetry between past and future events.

like the egg), they could be re-ordered into a sensible sequence because the asymmetry of time is intuitively understood. What is revealed, in real life by the crook and in fiction by the author's plot, is the logic of the criminal actions, the logic that the real or fictional criminal has imposed on the world through plotting and committing the crime.

That detectives are historians is a short leap in logic (or faith). Many professions are historical in nature, including astronomy (you think that starlight just left the Crab Nebula on Monday?), geology, paleontology, archaeology, forensic science, and investigations of many sorts.

The three things these professions all share are the manipulation of space, time, and scale.

First, space is manipulated by the choice of where to look, what to pay attention to, and how much to use. For example, not everything at a crime scene relates to the crime and not all evidence at a crime scene can be collected. Evidence may degrade or decay, be lost or damaged, or be obscured. Working a crime scene involves hundreds of decisions about what is relevant (Do you collect a kitchen knife in a shooting case?) based on the various hypothesized scenarios (plural) of the crime. Not every scrap of evidence can be collected at a scene and not every bit that is collected can be used to solve a case or reconstruct a crime. Some of it just will not make sense or be relevant.

Second, historical professionals play with time by being in more than one place or time at once. The detective is here *now* but is thinking about the scene *yesterday* and when the crime occurred *last week*. Authors do this routinely, if more abstractly. This mental time travel helps to sort through the individual images (like from the egg video) and put them in the correct order.

Finally, historical professionals play with scale by looking at the "big picture" and then a tiny scrap of incriminating or misleading evidence, and then stepping back to the larger view to see how it compares. Macro, micro, macro. Similarly, detectives jump scales by looking at evidence (like egg shells), interviewing suspects and witnesses, talking with informants, comparing activities to larger patterns across a jurisdiction, and so on.

Why space, time, and scale? Because a literal interpretation of reality is too cumbersome and impractical. A distillation of relevant information (editing, in other words) is required to present a coherent story or narrative. Again, plot is bound within these elements and makes use of the author's abilities to manipulate space, time, and scale to best effect in storytelling.

We have an expectation of how things are going to work, time being asymmetrical and all, and when they do not behave as expected, we are surprised. Plot twists do just that; they bend our expectations of space (The killer is in the back seat of the car!), time (The killer knew the victim in high school?), or scale (The postage stamps *are* the fortune!), and violate our previous assumptions about the story or characters. A proper plot twist is enormously satisfying ("I am your father"), but a clunky or wholly unbelievable one can ruin the entire narrative. Just as bad are twists that the reader has not been properly prepared for; too-clever-by-half authors also make assumptions about what they have told the reader and the groundwork they have laid. Caution and craft are therefore recommended when twisting plots.

The main reason a literal interpretation of reality is impractical is because of the asymmetry of time. Ironically, because time is asymmetrical, far more evidence of a past action is produced than is actually needed to conclude it happened.[6]

Consider this: A baseball is thrown through the window of a living room. Not every piece of glass would be needed to conclude that the window was broken. Notwithstanding the baseball on the floor, many other types of evidence also could lead to that conclusion, such as sounds (the birds are now louder), moisture (rain on the floor), a breeze, and then there are all those glass fragments on the floor.

Time's asymmetry highlights why the perfect crime is nearly impossible to commit. *ALL* the evidence, every last speck, each skin cell, all the tiny traces would have to be eliminated to cover up the crime. Miss one piece of evidence and a modern-day Sherlock Holmes will discover it. And each clue is not independent: removing a fingerprint does not erase the footprint or the other fingerprints. As Raymond Chandler said, "The boys with their feet on the desks know that the easiest murder case in the world to break is the one somebody tried to get very cute with; the one that really bothers them is the murder somebody only thought of two minutes before he pulled it off." The spontaneous crime will have fewer moving parts, less complexity, fewer anomalies and patterns to leave evidence. As a final proof that time is asymmetrical, consider that there is a very easy way of erasing all traces of a crime and eliminating any potential evidence: Don't do it. But that would make for a very boring plot.

★ ★ ★

---

[6] This is referred to as the past being overdetermined; the future, by contrast, is underdetermined, which is why it can be difficult to predict things.

The stories in this collected volume range from poisonings and defenestration to digital death by social media, as well as more tried-and-true methods. The motivations are the usual sack of baser primate emotions that led us from the savannas to the cities, dooming us in the process, like revenge, greed, and love.

The one thing these stories all share is that the crimes involve that most human of activities, a social gathering. The gatherings in this book are all of a particularly bittersweet flavor, called a convention. Conventions are where people who are ostensibly interested in the same topic come together to learn about and discuss it with the other people at the meeting. Ideally, they are intellectually stimulating events filled with insights that improve the attendees' pursuit of the topic and that swell with bonhomie between colleagues and friends.

A few stories into *Murder Most Conventional*, however, and the true nature of conventions is seen: they are cauldrons of steaming schemes, huddles of hatred, and bursts of bad behavior sufficient to make any Machiavellian devotee cheer with pride. Frankly, I'm surprised more people aren't offed at conventions, given the close quarters and large bar tabs. Kudos to the authors in *Murder Most Conventional* for exorcising their demons in the socially acceptable and publicly enjoyable mode of fiction.

# AUTHOR
# BIOGRAPHIES

# AUTHORS

**JOHN GREGORY BETANCOURT** is a best-selling science fiction writer who saw the light and began writing mysteries about a decade ago. Since then, he's published about a dozen mystery short stories in *Alfred Hitchcock's Mystery Magazine* and other places, one of which ("Horse Pit") won a Black Orchid Novella Award. He doesn't write much these days; his day job running Wildside Press keeps him busy.

**RHYS BOWEN** is *The New York Times* best-selling author of two historical mystery series: the Molly Murphy mysteries, set in early 1900s New York, and the lighter Royal Spyness novels, featuring an impoverished minor royal in 1930s England. Rhys's books have been nominated for every major mystery award, and she has won thirteen to date, including three Agathas. Rhys was born and raised in England but now divides her time between California and Arizona. rhysbowen.com

**NANCY BREWKA-CLARK** began her writing career as features editor for a daily newspaper chain on Boston's North Shore. Her poems, short stories, and nonfiction have been published by Adams Media, Three Rivers Press, the University of Iowa Press, Level Best Books, Conari/Red Wheel, the International Thomas Merton Society's *Poetry of the Sacred*, and *The Boston Globe*, among others. Her plays and monologues have been published by Smith and Kraus and produced by YouthPLAYS of Los Angeles and NYC Playwrights. She's a member of the Short Mystery Fiction Society and Sisters in Crime. www.nancybrewkaclark.com

**M EVONNE DOBSON**'s young-adult crime fiction, *Chaos Theory,* was published by Poisoned Pencil, an imprint of Poisoned Pen Press, in 2015. Her flash fiction has placed twice at Writers' Police Academy, and a short story entitled "Politics of Chaos" was included in the Sisters in Crime–Desert Sleuths Chapter's 2015 anthology. That short story and companion teacher guides are available for free download from Amazon.com. Meg is a professional member of Society of Children's Book Writers and Illustrators, Mystery Writers of America, Sisters in Crime, and International Thriller Writers. www.MEvonneDobson.com

**KATE FLORA**'s fascination with people's criminal tendencies began in the Maine attorney general's office. Deadbeat dads, child abusers, and employers' acts of discrimination aroused her curiosity about human behavior. Her books include seven "strong woman" Thea Kozak mysteries. Her true crime book, *Finding Amy,* was an Edgar® finalist. *Death Dealer* was an Anthony and Agatha award finalist and won the Public Safety Writers Association 2015 nonfiction award. The gritty police procedurals in her Joe Burgess series have twice won the Maine Literary Award for Crime Fiction. Kate has published sixteen crime stories. Her latest book is *A Good Man with a Dog,* co-written with a Maine game warden. www.kateflora.com

**BARB GOFFMAN** is an award-winning short story author. Her *Don't Get Mad, Get Even* won the Silver Falchion Award for best collection of 2013. She won the 2013 Macavity Award for best short story, and she's been nominated seventeen times for national crime-writing awards, including the Agatha (nine times—the most ever in the short story category), the Derringer, and the Anthony and Macavity awards (three times each). Her new story "Stepmonster" appears in *Chesapeake Crimes: Storm Warning* (Wildside Press, April 2016). Barb runs a freelance editing and proofreading service focusing on crime and general fiction. www.barbgoffman.com

Raised in Ireland, **MARIE HANNAN-MANDEL** now lives in Elmira Heights, NY. She is an assistant professor and chair of the Communications department at Corning Community College. She was shortlisted for the Debut Dagger award in 2013, longlisted for the RTE Guide/Penguin Ireland short story award in 2014, and received an honorable mention in the *Writer's Digest* Popular Fiction award competition in 2014. Her short story "Sisters, Sisters" will appear in *Adirondack Mysteries 3* in 2016. For more information, follow Marie on Facebook.

**MAX M. HOUCK, PH.D., FRSC,** is Vice President, Forensic & Intelligence Services, LLC. St. Petersburg, FL. Dr. Max Houck is an internationally known expert in forensic science and management. For over 25 years, Dr. Houck's career has spanned government, academia, and the private sector. He is an expert in anthropology, trace evidence, and management. Dr. Houck has worked hundreds of cases, including the September 11, 2001, attack on the Pentagon, the D. B. Cooper case, the Scott Peterson case, and the West Memphis Three. He is one of the most published forensic experts in the world. Among other awards and honors, Dr. Houck is a Fellow of the Royal Society of Chemistry.

**KB INGLEE**'s stories are informed by her work as an historical interpreter at a 1705 water-powered grist mill. To better understand the life of her characters, she has tended heritage sheep, hand sewn her own period clothing, and driven oxen. She lives in Delaware with far too many pets. kbinglee.weebly.com

**ELEANOR CAWOOD JONES** began writing in elementary school, using a Number Two pencil to craft short stories about the imaginary lives of her stuffed animals. While attending Virginia Tech, she got her first writing job as a reporter with the *Kingsport Tennessee Times-News*, and has never looked back. Eleanor lives in Northern Virginia and is a marketing director, freelance copywriter, avid reader, traveler, and remodeling-show addict who spends her spare time telling people how to pronounce Cawood (Kay'-wood). Her short story compilations include *A Baker's Dozen: 13 Tales of Murder and More* and *Death is Coming to Town: Four Murderous Holiday Tales*.

**SU KOPIL's** short stories have appeared in numerous publications including *Flash and Bang*, a Short Mystery Fiction Society anthology (Untreed Reads Publishing), *Destination: Mystery!* (Darkhouse Books), *Fish or Cut Bait: A Guppy Anthology* (Wildside Press), and *Woman's World* magazine. A book cover designer obsessed with books, dogs, and creepy old houses, Su invites you to visit her website, www.sukopil.com, or follow her on Twitter @INKspillers.

**FRANCES MCNAMARA** is author of the Emily Cabot Mysteries, set mostly in Chicago in the 1890s. *Death at the Paris Exposition* (2016) is the sixth in that series. Her story in this anthology, "Wicked Writers," introduces Lucy O'Donnell, who will be featured in a new series set in contemporary Boston, MA. Frances grew up in Boston, where her father was police commissioner in the 1960s, and she is a librarian who formerly worked at The University of Chicago Library. When not writing, Frances can be found sailing one-design boats on the Charles River or Boston Harbor. fmcnamara.wordpress.com

**RUTH MOOSE** has published three collections of short stories, including some stories that originally appeared in *Atlantic*, *Redbook*, and other places. She's also published six collections of poetry. Ruth was on the creative writing faculty at the University of North Carolina at Chapel Hill for fifteen years. Her first novel, *Doing It at the Dixie Dew*, won the Minotaur/Malice Domestic Competition for Best First Traditional Mystery Novel in 2013. The sequel, *Wedding Bell Blues*, is due out in the summer of 2016. She lives in Pittsboro, NC. www.Ruthmoose.com

To date, Malice Domestic 28's Lifetime Achievement Award recipient **KATHERINE HALL PAGE** has published thirty books: twenty-three in the Faith Fairchild series with *The Body in the Wardrobe* released in April 2016; five juvenile/young adults; a cookbook, *Have Faith in Your Kitchen*; and *Small Plates—Short Fiction*, a collection. She was the first author who received or was nominated for Agathas in Best Novel, Best First, Best Short Story and Best Nonfiction. Katherine and her husband live in Maine and Massachusetts.

*USA Today* best-selling author **GIGI PANDIAN** is the child of cultural anthropologists from New Mexico and the southern tip of India. She spent her childhood being dragged around the world, and now lives in the San Francisco Bay area. She writes the Jaya Jones Treasure Hunt mystery series (*Artifact*, *Pirate Vishnu*, and *Quicksand*) and the Accidental Alchemist mysteries (*The Accidental Alchemist* and *The Masquerading Magician*). Gigi's debut mystery novel was awarded a Malice Domestic Grant, the follow-up won the Left Coast Crime Rose Award, and her locked-room mystery short fiction has been nominated for Agatha and Macavity awards. www.gigipandian.com

**NEIL PLAKCY** lives in South Florida where "Djinn and Tonic" is set, but regrets that he has yet to encounter any genies, though he regularly comes in contact with squirrels and Russian immigrants. He is the author of the Golden Retriever mysteries, inspired by his own dogs Sam, Brody, and Griffin. www.mahubooks.com

**KM ROCKWOOD** draws on a varied background for stories, including working as a laborer in a steel-fabrication plant, operating glass melters and related equipment in a fiberglass-manufacturing facility, and supervising an inmate work crew in a large medium-security state prison. These jobs, as well as work as a special-education teacher in an alternative high school and as a GED teacher in county detention facilities, provide most of the background for short stories and novels, including the Jesse Damon Crime Novel series. kmrockwood.com

**HANK PHILLIPPI RYAN** is the on-air investigative reporter for Boston's *NBC* affiliate, winning thirty-three Emmys and dozens more journalism honors. The best-selling author of eight mysteries, Ryan's also an award-winner in her second profession—now with five Agathas, two Anthonys, two Macavitys, the Daphne, and the Mary Higgins Clark Award. Her *Truth Be Told* won the 2015 Agatha, and she edited the 2015 Agatha-winning nonfiction *Writes of Passage*. Critics call her "a superb and gifted storyteller." Her *What You See* is a *Library Journal* Best of 2015. A founder of MWA University, Hank was 2013 president of national Sisters in Crime. www.HankPhillippiRyan.com

Author/actress **KATHRYN LEIGH SCOTT**'s *Jinxed* (2015) and *Down and Out in Beverly Heels* (2013) are the first two mystery novels about amateur sleuth Jinx Fogarty. She's also written the memoir, *Last Dance at the Savoy: Life, Love & Caring for Someone with Progressive Supranuclear Palsy* (2016), and has completed the novel *September Girl*. Kathryn wrote the memoir, *Dark Shadows: Return to Collinwood,* and the paranormal mystery, *Dark Passages,* with an affectionate nod to her stint on the television cult classic, *Dark Shadows,* which is celebrating its fiftieth anniversary this year. She continues to work as an actress. www.kathrynleighscott.com

**SHAWN REILLY SIMMONS** is the author of the Red Carpet Catering mysteries published by Henery Press. The third book in the series, *Murder on a Designer Diet*, will be released in June 2016. Shawn is a member of the Malice Domestic board, a coeditor at Level Best Books, and a member of both Sisters in Crime and Mystery Writers of America. www.ShawnReillySimmons.com @ShawnRSimmons

**B.K. (BONNIE) STEVENS**'s first novel, *Interpretation of Murder*, is a whodunit that offers insights into deaf culture and sign language interpreting. Her young adult novel, Agatha-nominated *Fighting Chance*, is a martial arts mystery set in Virginia. Wildside Press is publishing *Her Infinite Variety: Tales of Women and Crime*, which collects some of the over fifty short stories B.K. has published. Most originally appeared in *Alfred Hitchcock's Mystery Magazine*. B.K. has won a Derringer and has been nominated for Agatha and Macavity awards. This year, "A Joy Forever" is an Agatha nominee. She and her husband, Dennis, live in Virginia. www.bkstevensmysteries.com

**MARCIA TALLEY** is the author of *Daughter of Ashes* and thirteen previous novels featuring Maryland sleuth Hannah Ives. A winner of the Malice Domestic grant and an Agatha Award nominee for Best First Novel, Marcia won an Agatha Award and an Anthony Award for her short story "Too Many Cooks" and an Agatha Award for her short story "Driven to Distraction." She is the editor of two mystery collaborations, and her short stories have been published in more than a dozen magazines and anthologies. She divides her time between Annapolis, MD, and a quaint cottage in the Bahamas. www.marciatalley.com

Malice Domestic 28 Guest of Honor and Agatha and Edgar® awards-nominated author **VICTORIA THOMPSON** writes the Gaslight Mystery Series, set in turn-of-the-century New York City and featuring midwife Sarah Brandt and detective Frank Malloy. Her latest is *Murder in Morningside Heights,* May 2016. She also contributed to the award-winning writing textbook *Many Genres/One Craft.* Victoria has taught at Penn State University and currently teaches in the Seton Hill University master's program in creative writing. www.victoriathompson.com

**CHARLES AND CAROLINE TODD** are the authors of the best-selling Inspector Ian Rutledge Mysteries and the Bess Crawford Mysteries. They were the guests of honor at Malice Domestic 27 and won an Agatha Award for *A Question of Honor* in 2013. They also had a short story published in *Malice Domestic 9. No Shred of Evidence,* the eighteenth Rutledge (William Morrow), was published in February 2016, and the eighth Bess Crawford, *The Shattered Tree,* will be published in the summer of 2016. www.charlestodd.com

**L.C. TYLER**'s comic crime series featuring author-and-agent duo Ethelred Tressider and Elsie Thirkettle has been twice nominated for the Edgar® (Allan Poe) Award in the U.S. and has won the Goldsboro Last Laugh Award (best comic crime novel of the year) with *Herring in the Library* and *Crooked Herring* in the U.K. His new historical crime series (the latest of which is *A Masterpiece of Corruption*) features seventeenth-century lawyer John Grey. L.C. has lived all over the world but is now based in London. www.lctyler.com

Lightning Source UK Ltd.
Milton Keynes UK
UKOW01f1938230916

283690UK00001BA/127/P